HAWK

No amount
overtook him
some reason, just as they got airborne, it hit him like a punch in the stomach: There was a real possibility that Hawk Hunter and the rest of the B-2000 crew *were* dead. Zoltan was convinced of it, and Crabb was too.

Now sitting alone at a dark corner table inside the aircraft's entertainment room, nursing an ice water, Y found the same somber thoughts kept going through his mind.

Hawk Hunter. *Dead.*

Y knew from his experience with the fighter pilot that his being in this universe was not at all typical. Hunter's very presence affected the world in odd, subtle, and sometimes not so subtle ways. He also knew that over the years people who had claimed to see "angels" had just assumed they were messengers from God. Most people believed this was rubbish, but Y was privy to a secret study the OSS had undertaken after Hunter's sudden appearance. Combining information from his experience with reported "angel sightings" over the years, they concluded that somehow, some way, certain individuals had been able—maybe without their knowledge or through no fault of their own—to pass from one universe to any other. But while these people looked and acted like anyone else on Earth, they were just *different* and could have an affect on everything from raising the dead to winning global conflicts single-handedly. The study concluded that these people were the "angels."

And Hunter was probably one of them.

Trouble now, this particular angel was, at the very least, missing in action and it was up to Y to find out whether or not angels could actually die.

And if they could, where did they go?

BOOK YOUR PLACE ON OUR WEBSITE AND MAKE THE READING CONNECTION!

WINGMAN:
THE TOMORROW WAR

Mack Maloney

Pinnacle Books
Kensington Publishing Corp.

http://www.pinnaclebooks.com

PINNACLE BOOKS are published by

Kensington Publishing Corp.
850 Third Avenue
New York, NY 10022

First Printing: October, 1999
10 9 8 7 6 5 4 3 2 1

Printed in the United States of America

PART ONE

CHAPTER 1

The Sea of Japan

The *Kumo-Do Maru* had been at sea for almost four days.

It was a small fishing barge, thirty-four feet long, with a very shallow draft, a cranky diesel engine, and a crew of five. Four scientists were also on board. Two were marine geologists, the other two, triatomic physicists. They were all from the University of Seoul.

They had been plying the waters around 35 degrees latitude and 140 degrees longitude for nearly one hundred hours, through rough seas and very heavy downpours. This typhoonlike weather had been the norm in this area for the past week.

But now it was close to dawn and the weather was settling down. The skies were clearing, the rain had stopped, and the wind was dying to a breeze.

For the first time in a long time, the sea was peaceful.

The senior scientist on board was Dr. Chin Lo Ho, a triatomic physicist with nearly thirty years of experience studying quantum fusion. He'd been at his daughter's wedding when the Great Blast occurred. He would never forget the feeling of the earth moving beneath his feet and seeing all his wedding guests stagger in unison as they danced the bride's tribute. The whole reception building shook—the *entire* city of Seoul shook—for more than two hours.

When Ho called his colleagues in the seismic department at the university on the last working phone in Seoul, he learned two were unconscious and two were busy trying to fix their earthquake-monitoring station. The two-hour rumble had been the largest earth disturbance ever recorded, by a factor of *ten*.

But Ho knew even then that this titanic disturbance had not been an earthquake. Not a natural one anyway. And though it might have seemed perverse, the first thing he wanted to do once the ground stopped shaking was hurry to the east coast of Korea and see what the oceans were doing.

He was finally able to secure transport to the city of Kangnŭng two hours later, arriving on the coast just before dawn. He and two students set up a small control station on a ridge that rose about seven hundred feet above the sea. At the time Ho believed what he was doing amounted to little more than an experiment in suicide. He was convinced that if his estimates were right, he and his students would be washed away by a tsunami he was sure was going to come sometime later that day.

But it never did.

That was six days ago.

Now, standing on the bow of the fishing barge looking out at the ever-calming sea, Ho's brain was stuffed with more questions than before. The whole of Northeast Asia was still in chaos because of the Great Blast. Communications were out everywhere, power grids thrown off-line, water main breaks, thousands of scattered fires. But amazingly, no tidal waves, and very little earthquake-related damages. That's why Ho knew that whatever event shook the Earth six days before, it had not been "natural."

The biggest question in Ho's mind was: Had it been "*super*natural?"

Ho studied the water before him now, and then turned back to the captain of the skiff.

"Are you certain your coordinates are correct?" he asked Tuk-Pak, the grizzled old skipper.

"They are the coordinates you gave me, Professor," Pak replied. "Because I've never had the opportunity to *actually* sail in waters at these particular coordinates, I cannot tell you if we are at the right place or not. I can only tell you that we sailed to where you told us. Nothing more. . . ."

Ho looked in all directions—all he saw was water.

He checked his map again. Did he have the coordinates right? One hundred forty degrees longitude, 35 degrees latitude. Yes, they were correct.

Then there was only one explanation. . . .

He turned to the skipper and said crisply: "Bring us to a stop."

Pak motioned to his second in command to kill the barge's engine. Soon the vessel slowed to a stop.

To the amazement of all on board, Professor Ho then did a very strange thing: He stepped over the railing, and lowered himself down the side of the vessel into the water below.

The crew rushed to throw him a life preserver—but none was needed. Ho simply stepped from the skiff's bottom rail into the water—and stood up.

Those aboard the barge stared in amazement. For a moment it seemed like Ho was walking on top of the water!

But then the reality of the situation began to sink in—and this was even more startling.

They had entered a part of the sea that, though vast, was at best, just a couple of feet deep.

Ho looked up at them and spread his arms wide.

"My friends," he said. "*This* is where the city of Tokyo used to be. . . ."

CHAPTER 2

Off the coast of South America

The huge B-201 "Supersea" Navy bomber was approximately 250 miles off the coast of Peru when it finally detected the withdrawing Japanese fleet.

The aircraft had taken off from Panama two days before. An enormous aircraft with a crew of forty-two and a dozen double-reaction engines, which allowed it to stay airborne for weeks at a time, it had been flying recon up and down the west coast of South America since arriving in the area.

Its mission was to locate what remained of the once mighty Japanese fleet. At exactly 1234 hours on this day, it had done just that.

The war with Japan had lasted not quite nine months.

It had begun with a massive Japanese bombing raid on the American naval shipyard at Pearl Harbor on December 7, 1998. Soon after that, Japanese forces attacked and occupied the Panama Canal. A few days later, huge troop-carrying submarines began landing Japanese forces, first in Peru and then throughout South America.

This initial invasion was not opposed by the Peruvians.

To the contrary, they celebrated the Japanese occupation—at first anyway. The Japanese Imperial troops rapidly took over every country on the South American continent except Brazil. With its new territory consolidated, the Japanese occupation quickly turned brutal as the conquerors forced the native citizens to become slaves and servants, while new colonists from Nippon exploited South America's untapped resources, mostly cattle and oil.

It took awhile for the United States to gear up for war with Japan. America had just won a fifty-year struggle against Germany, and the country's resources and its citizenry were exhausted. But after Japan attacked Pearl Harbor and Panama, there was never any question as to the United States' reaction. It was just a little bit long in coming.

The element for winning this war, and making it last just a few months instead of fifty-plus years, turned out to be a weapon that had fallen into the hands of America's staunchest ally, the United Kingdom, through very serendipitous means. A joint team of American and British scientists working in an ultrasecret laboratory inside a hill on the isolated West Falkland Island created a "saturated warhead" nuclear bomb whose power potential was so intense, even they didn't know just how much destruction it would cause.

Coordinating several feints as attacks on Japanese forces in Panama and in South America—including a land invasion from Brazil—the U.S. sent a lone airplane carrying the "superbomb" on an odd transpolar mission. Its goal was to drop the superbomb at precisely the right moment on the city of Tokyo.

Flying under complete radio silence, this bombing mission was accomplished. And Honshu, the main island of Japan, was utterly devastated, and literally sunk, as a result.

What happened during that bombing run and the fate of the crew were not known.

In fact, many people in the U.S. were still unaware of the superbombing, thinking instead that the Japanese simply gave up after the lightning-quick invasions of Panama and occupied South America.

However, the reality of the situation was different—and still top secret, as were the names of the crew that had piloted the enormous B-2000 superbomber that had dropped the incredible weapon.

The most secret element of all was the identity of the superbomber's flight commander.

Only a handful of people in the U.S. military knew that his name was Hawk Hunter.

Now flying over the recently spotted Japanese fleet, a man known only as "Y" had his nose pressed up against one of the many observation bubbles located along the fuselage of the huge B-201 Navy bomber.

Y was an agent for the Office of Strategic Services (OSS). What he saw below was a fleet of thirty-six ships. Most of them were mammoth troop-carrying submarines, with a few equally large aircraft-carrying submarines mixed in. They were all riding on the surface; apparently none of them had enough power or ambition to submerge.

They were a ragged group. Once mighty and fierce, most of these vessels now looked rusty and in an advanced state of disrepair. Each was flying an enormous white flag just above its bridge. Many had coffins lined up on their decks.

Looking down at them, Y could not help but feel a pang of sadness in his chest, albeit just a small one. This was a navy in retreat, a disgraced and defeated force, returning to a homeland that simply did not exist anymore.

What could be sadder than that?

He arranged to have a few miles of long-range TV insta-film shot of the retreating fleet and prepared to send a detailed report back to OSS headquarters in Washington. But just as he was heading for the communications room, he met the radio officer coming out. He was holding a folded sheet of yellow paper held together with a piece of bright red tape.

"This just came in for you from Washington," the comm officer told him. "Level Six priority."

Y just stared at the piece of paper. Level Six was the security level used only in times of war—or a similar crisis. The war with Japan was over. Why, then, would a message for him be rated so high?

"Did you read it?" he asked the comm officer.

The man nodded sheepishly. "Couldn't help it, sir," he replied.

Y just shook his head. "Don't worry about it," he said. "Just give me a heads-up. How heavy is it?"

The comm officer just stared back at him.

"The heaviest," he said.

Y reluctantly took the message from him. He'd been planning to take two months of R and R after this flight was completed. Now he knew that idea was probably in serious jeopardy.

"It doesn't say anything about a promotion in there, does it?" Y asked the comm man jokingly.

The officer just shook his head. "No, sir," he replied. "But it does say you should prepare for the biggest assignment of your career."

Y's face fell a mile.

"Damn," he said, turning the secret message over in his hands. "I don't like the sound of that."

CHAPTER 3

Chicago, South Side

It was a sweaty night inside the King Krabb Klub.

The place was packed as usual. A line of limos and taxicabs was stalled outside. Passengers were climbing out; a longer line formed at the door. Greasy blues were flowing out of the place. The streets were still littered with red, white, and blue confetti, the remains of the huge celebration ending the Great Pacific War, as the recently completed conflict against Japan was now called.

Details were few on exactly how the war ended—but people in this place weren't as inquisitive about such things as in other universes. The war was over, ended by some secret military operations, and that was good enough for them. For the first time in nearly six decades, the United States was not in the midst of a global conflict. To them, peace was a very unusual state of affairs.

So the celebrating had been going on for nearly a week, and the King Krabb Klub, like the dozens of other blues bars along McKinney Street, had been packed around the clock since the announcement of Japan's surrender.

There was no sign that the revelry would slow down anytime soon.

It was about midnight when a military vehicle known as a Jeepster pulled up in front of the King Krabb Klub.

Three men got out. Two were soldiers of the OSS's military wing; the other was Agent Y.

One look from the doorman and the crowd parted for the three men like the Red Sea. Y left the two OSS soldiers at the door with orders to stay cool and not bother anybody. Then he stepped inside the foyer of the small but very hip South Side club.

As always, the man known as Colonel Crabb was sitting in a huge chair right near the front door. As always, he had a young beauty on each knee—short skirts, long curly hair, one was a blonde, the other a redhead. Like his knowledge of the blues, Crabb's taste in females was always impeccable.

Crabb looked up and recognized Y right away. Their paths had crossed more than a few times in this universe—as well as in others.

Crabb was a big man, but he lightly lifted the two females from his lap and gave Y a hearty handshake. "Here to celebrate, I hope?"

Y just shook his head. "Have you ever known me to celebrate anything?" he asked.

Crabb took stock of the man. Y was small, wiry, tough-looking, perpetually twenty-seven years old. Crabb knew Y's reputation inside the OSS was exemplary. And it was true, he'd never seen the man in anything other than an all-business mode.

Still that was a mold Crabb might break.

"Take a look around," he told the OSS man. He swept his hand to indicate the bustling club. Beautiful women were everywhere. The blues band on stage was superb, the smell of Creole food and the aroma of fine liquor was thick in the air. "It's criminal not to enjoy yourself here. At least have a drink. . . ."

Y shook his head again.

"I don't drink," he said. "Besides, I'm here on official business."

Crabb's shoulders fell a bit. It hurt him that anyone would not be seduced by his establishment.

"How official?" he asked Y.

The OSS man looked him straight in the eye.

"Hawk is missing," he said. "And I need some help in finding him."

Crabb just stared back at Y. Suddenly he knew exactly why the OSS man had come.

"Our friend is playing cards in the back room," Crabb said. "I'll bring you to him."

Zoltan the Magnificent was in the process of pulling an inside straight when Y and Crabb walked in.

If possible, the small room at the rear of the club was smokier and smelled more of alcohol than the main room. Five men were seated around the table, ten young girls, in various stages of undress, lingered around the periphery. The walls were adorned with photos of old blues greats and long-ago sports heroes. A single bare bulb provided the only illumination. It cast odd shadows everywhere.

There was more than one thousand dollars on the table. The atmosphere was friendly but tense.

That all changed when Y and Crabb appeared.

The players saw Y's uniform and gasped. Gambling was against the law, and no one wanted to have the OSS anywhere near such illegality. Some players went to hide their cards—but Y just raised his hand.

"Everyone freeze," he said.

Then he looked at Zoltan's cards and shook his head.

"This man is clairvoyant. He was once an officer in the U.S. Psychic Corps. You are foolish to play with him. . . ."

The other four men just stared at Y and then over at Zoltan. It was true of course—Zoltan *did* hold a reserve officer's commission in military psychic ability. He couldn't read minds very well, but he did have success at correctly guessing which cards were going to be drawn at any given time from a deck. And he had just drawn an inside straight.

But now the thousand-dollar pot was vaporizing before his eyes. On a nod from Y, the other players began quickly pulling their money out and slinking from the table.

Crabb nodded to them. "Drink free for the rest of the night, guys," he said. "Just keep your mouths shut, OK?"

The four men left the small room quietly, taking the girls with them.

Y sat down next to Zoltan as Crabb stood watch by the door.

The psychic was crestfallen, but not that surprised to see the OSS man. He'd had a quick flash of Y's face about thirty minutes earlier.

"I could have used that grand," Zoltan told Y as he rustled through the few dollars he still had on the table.

Y just shrugged. "Something more important has come up," he said. "I have an assignment for you."

Zoltan's spirits should have soared at this. In civilian life he was a professional psychic/nightclub hypnotist. But his bookings had been very sparse lately. With the war over and everyone seemingly certain about the near future, there was no need for the services of a psychic. Oddly enough, that had been the attitude while the war was on, as well.

Now Y was offering him a job—maybe. But it would be for the Government and worse yet, the OSS. Not only did the intelligence service pay notoriously low wages, their assignments were usually fraught with danger.

"What if I'm not interested?" he asked Y.

Both Y and Crabb laughed. All three of them had spent time during the war against Germany in a place called Dreamland, up in Iceland. They all knew each other pretty well. And they knew if the gig was a paying one, Zoltan would be interested.

"Here's the dilly-oh," Y began, looking across the smoky table at the middle-aged, goateed psychic. "Hawk Hunter is missing. I've been ordered to find him. I can pick anyone

I want to help me. My own psychic instincts are telling me I should pick you."

Zoltan just stared back at him. He knew Hunter of course. They were friends—sort of.

"Missing?" he asked. "Missing where?"

"That's top secret . . . ," Y replied.

Zoltan looked deeply into the OSS man's eyes. Then his face turned a bit pale.

"Aw, shit . . . that huge bombing?" he gasped. "The bomb that sunk Japan? Hunter was in on that?"

"He sank Japan for Christ's sake, who else could have done that?" Crabb said from the door.

Zoltan closed his eyes and felt a shiver go through him.

"Man, he wasted the place . . . ," he said slowly, conjuring up a mental image of the newly expanded Sea of Japan. "I can't tell you how many dead. But the vibes I'm getting tell me they were mostly military. Could that be so?"

Y nodded. "Most of the main island is gone. That's the reports we get. And that it was totally under military control. Most civilians had been deported about six months before."

Zoltan nodded. "Yes, somehow I knew that."

Y looked up at Crabb, who opened the door and magically reached out and retrieved a tray carrying a bottle of scotch, a pot of coffee, and three huge mugs. He set it on the table, poured out three cups of thick joe, then added a gigantic splash of scotch to a pair of the steaming brews. He pushed one of the booze-laden mugs in front of Zoltan, taking the other laced coffee for himself.

All three men took a huge swig. Zoltan more than the others.

Then Y reached inside his uniform pocket and came out with a photo of the huge B-2000 bomber that had dropped the superbomb on Japan.

Zoltan took one look at the airplane and felt another series of shivers go through him.

"Oh, man, them is some bad vibes," he said, nervously

pulling on his goatee. "Talk about the angel of death. And look at the size of that thing!"

"Are you saying it will be easy to find?" Y asked.

Zoltan studied the photo. The airplane looked like a battleship with wings.

"Even the moon is hard to find if you don't know where to look for it," he replied solemnly.

"OK," Y said finally. "Here's what I have to do: I've been ordered to assemble a small—a very small—expeditionary force. We transit to Asia and look for, and hopefully find, Hawk and the rest of his crew."

Zoltan looked up at him. "And . . . ?"

"And your government has requested that you come along," Y told him.

Zoltan's mind flashed through a series of images: bowls filled with rice, stagnant water, and snakes. Lots and lots of snakes. He shivered again.

"What would be my role exactly?" he asked.

Y thought a moment. "As an advisor," he replied. "Help me pick the rest of the unit. Help me get the right kind of transportation. Then come along and use your, well . . . *unique* abilities to aid in the search. Simple as that."

Zoltan just laughed. Nothing was simple in this universe.

"And if I refuse?" he asked Y.

Y just smiled. "Then I'll have to reactivate your military status—and *order* you to go. That way you'll not get paid a dime over minimum wage."

Zoltan looked up at Crabb for help, but the burly nightclub owner was deep into his booze-laced coffee cup.

Zoltan turned back to the OSS agent.

"Well, I guess I have no choice," he said.

Y shook his hand. "Welcome aboard," he said quietly. "Let's set up a time tomorrow so I can brief you."

Zoltan wiped the sweat from his lip. He had a very bad feeling about all this.

"Are you talking about a search party or a body-recovery team?" he asked Y.

The OSS man just swigged his coffee.

"Well, that's the first question I want to ask you," he said.

Y moved a bit closer to him. Crabb made sure the door was locked.

"Can you tell . . . ?" Y asked, his words trailing off.

Zoltan just looked at him. "What? If Hawk is still alive?"

Y nodded solemnly. "Are any of them still with us?"

Zoltan felt a sweat break out on his forehead. "I'm not so good at that particular aspect of thought transfer."

Y's face became grim. "Take a guess."

Zoltan wiped his brow, closed his eyes, and put his hand to his right temple. He stayed like that for a very long time.

"If I had to guess," he finally replied slowly, "I'd say 'no.' "

A cold chill suddenly swept the room.

Zoltan was shaking his head.

"Nope," he said quietly. "I'm afraid none of them are still alive. . . ."

Y stared down at his hands for a moment. "Will that make our job harder or easier?"

Zoltan laughed grimly.

"You should know by now, my friend, that looking for the dead is much more difficult than finding the living," he said.

He paused a moment, then saw quick visions of an empty ocean, a jungle on fire, and a very long railroad track.

"Yes," he added. "Dead men always leave a cold trail. And this one seems very cold. . . ."

CHAPTER 4

Edwards Air Corps Aerodrome
California

One week later

It was a blazing-hot day.

There were high clouds off to the west, gathering with a slightly ominous look to them.

Agent Y was standing out on an auxiliary flight line of the huge, bustling Air Corps base, sweating his ass off. All around him, gigantic Air Corps bombers were being decommissioned and put back into their hangar storage areas, possibly never to see combat again. He nervously checked his watch. Timing was everything in this world. And unlike the big bombers and their crews, so soon returning from war to the rest of their lives, Y's future was now being compressed into a very small window of time, one that would keep closing at a very rapid pace.

One week had passed since the meeting in Chicago at Crabb's club. It had been a hectic seven days for Y. He had spent the majority of it in Washington getting briefed for his impending search mission by a legion of military and OSS higher-ups. Listening patiently to their cautions and advice, he'd pretended to take copious notes at each session—only to throw them all away once he'd left the Beltway.

The main concern in D.C. was one of appearance—that was the bottom line. The greatest fear of everyone he talked to was that the story of the whole superbombing affair would reach the media before the B-2000 and its crew were found. Hawk Hunter was a high-profile, if somewhat mysterious, war hero, and the public would demand to know what happened to him when word of the superbombing eventually did leak out. The Government did not want to be put in the awkward position of having to say: "We don't know what happened to him." To do this would signal the country's rabid celebrity-driven press to look into security matters that no one in the military or the OSS wanted them to see. It would also revive the biggest question of all: Where did Hawk Hunter come from in the first place?

And that was a secret no one who knew the truth ever wanted to reveal—Y included.

So Hawk and the B-2000 crew had to be found—and found quickly. Dead or alive, it really didn't matter. The affair just needed closure, and it needed it now. Then it would be up to Y to write the last chapter in the history of the country's sixty years of war. Like the huge bombers being put into mothballs, maybe for forever, this story finally had to have an end.

However, with Y tied up in Washington, it had been left up to Zoltan to gather together the resources they would need for the mission to proceed. There were a few times when Y had wondered if he would come to regret his decision to include the psychic in his search plans. Like it had once been said about someone else, Zoltan certainly worked in mysterious ways.

Y's first assignment for Zoltan was to find a team to use

in searching for the missing B-2000 bomber and its crew. Zoltan had just about the entire U.S. military to choose from, and Y had really thought the psychic's ability would locate a team of tough, combat-hardened, special-forces types who would be just right for the job. Now, one week later, Y was, to say the least, skeptical about the group Zoltan had chosen.

They were standing nearby on the flight line, bags packed, ready to go. And indeed Zoltan had rustled up some special forces. But instead of arranging for an attachment from some famous Army teams such as the 882nd Airborne or the Air Corps Blue Berets, he'd somehow uncovered a fairly obscure unit of Sea Marines reservists called Unit 167.

There were twenty-six of them in all, and they were essentially shock troops. The odd thing was their specialty was not exactly combat search and rescue, rather it was taking over enemy ships on the high seas, and if need be, sailing them to friendlier ports. Why Zoltan felt the need to bring them, Y wasn't sure, and with time running out, there was nothing he could do about it anyhow. Like it or not, Unit 167 would have to do.

Standing in line with them now was another person Zoltan felt should go on the mission: Colonel Crabb himself. Crabb was not a military officer, his "colonel" rank was one of pure invention. And while Crabb was an outstanding guy and certainly had a perceptive and level head on his shoulders, Y wasn't really sure that the search mission would be something he'd find to his liking. After all, Crabb was in his late forties, and looked more at home with a drink in his hand and a blonde on his knee than a Fritz-style battle helmet and a double-barreled assault rifle. But when Y asked Zoltan why he'd selected Crabb to join them, the psychic had simply replied: "Two reasons: he's a friend of Hawk's, and my vibes tell me we'll need a morale officer."

Y chose not to argue the point.

* * *

Now they were all waiting for their air transport, and that would prove to be the oddest aspect of all.

When Y was first ordered to organize the search party, he was torn between going to Asia by air or sea. Flying would be quicker, of course, but there was always the pain of trying to find a place to land and refuel, especially in what might be a hostile environment. A surface ship would be slower, but their mobility options would definitely be increased.

When Y told this to Zoltan, the psychic did his fingers-to-the-temple routine and shouted, "Ah ha!" He then said he had just the dude they needed.

They were all waiting for this "dude" now.

He was late.

Y finally walked over to Zoltan. The sun was climbing higher, the air was blistering, and everyone was dressed in heavy jungle fatigues. It was getting very uncomfortable. And they were already one hour behind schedule.

"OK, swami," Y said to him. "Where's our ride?"

Zoltan was stung by his comment—it was a grave insult to call him "swami." But instead of getting angry, he just closed his eyes, put his fingers to his temple . . . and smiled.

Then he turned to the east, pointed, and said: "Here he comes now."

Y heard it a few seconds later.

It was a deep, growling noise, definitely an airplane but not like one he'd ever heard before. He keyed his radio phone and buzzed the Edwards tower.

"You have something coming in for us?" he asked.

" 'Something' is the operative word," the tower man responded wryly.

They saw it a few moments later. It was huge, it was airborne, and for a moment Y thought he'd at last been the beneficiary of Zoltan's peculiar genius.

While Y had been torn between needing a ship or an airplane, Zoltan had cooked up a combination. What was now approaching them was a seaplane. But a very strange one.

It looked like an airplane Y was familiar with called a UVF-100 Super Albatross. But in this universe of bigger-is-always-better, this flying beast was at least ten times the size of the substantial UVF-100.

It carried twelve double-reaction jet engines on its top-wing assembly, with four wing float-pylons below, and a fuselage curved into a distinctive amphibious bottom. The plane was studded with dozens of observation bubbles and blisters, and was painted in a garish tropical-style yellow-and-green color scheme. Y could feel the eyeballs popping out of his head. This airplane seemed much too large to fly. If the missing B-2000 bomber looked like a flying battleship, then this airplane looked like a flying cruise liner.

The massive aircraft circled the air base twice—eating up ten minutes—and then came in for a landing, taking all of Edwards's ten-mile landing strip to do so. Hundreds of wheels extended, its dozen jet engines screaming in reverse, it slowly rolled to a gentle stop right in front of them.

Five minutes passed, Y imagined it took that long for the plane's commander to unstrap and climb down to earth. The hatch did eventually open and the seaplane's commander dropped out. He was in his forties, a rugged individual, but with long nonregulation hair stuffed back into a ponytail, an ancient aviator's cap on his head, a desert camo flight suit, and black sneakers. He was drinking a beer.

Y looked at him in amazement.

Zoltan was beaming. He greeted the pilot like they were long-lost brothers. Then they walked over to Y.

"I'd like to introduce Bro," Zoltan said.

" 'Bro'? "

The pilot stuck his hand. "Yeah, Cowboy Bobby Baulis. But most people call me Bro, like in 'brother.' You dig, man?"

Y finally shook hands and found that the man's grip nearly crushed his fingers.

"You're the guy who wants to hop over the pool, right? You got your doodles packed?" he asked Y, sipping his beer.

Y turned to Zoltan for translation.

"He wants to know if we're ready to go, for a trip over the Pacific."

At this point Y pulled Zoltan aside.

"Are you certain about this guy?" he asked him sternly.

"Certain in what way?" Zoltan replied. "Is he a competent pilot? Will he stick with us? That sort of thing?"

Y just shook his head in frustration. "No, " he replied. "Are you certain that he is sane? That he has all his cards? You know?"

Zoltan just waved away Y's concerns. "Believe me, Bro is as good as gold. I did an intense psychic background search on him. Just like Unit One-sixty-seven and Crabb, this man will be a vital part of the team. You'll see."

"It's *essential* that he become a vital part," Y told Zoltan. "We've got an important job to do and the lives of many people are in his hands. If he fucks up, it will be your head."

Zoltan's hand unconsciously went to his neck. As a youth he'd had the words "Cut along dotted line" tattooed around the back of his neck. Since then, any mention of his head leaving his body in an unnatural manner sent chills through his spine.

Y studied the enormous seaplane and had to admit it appeared well-kept, sturdy, and rugged enough. And it certainly looked nonmilitary; in fact, there were no numbers or markings on it at all. But even if it was falling apart, he had no choice but to use the winged beast for transport. Time was running out. They had to leave right now.

"OK, " he said finally. "It will have to do."

He gave the nod to Unit 167's CO and soon the Sea Marines were trooping up the cargo ramp and climbing into the vast seaplane. Crabb climbed aboard with considerably less elan. This bothered Y. He knew that when the easygoing Crabb looked worried, it was usually time to be concerned.

And at that moment the colonel looked *very* worried.

CHAPTER 5

It took almost twenty-four hours for the "Bro-Bird" to make the Pacific crossing.

The airplane sailed through the sky like a huge clipper ship sailing across the sea, a slave to the shifting winds. At some points on the journey, its airspeed dipped to a perilously low eighty knots. Most times, though, it cruised at about 140 and change.

Still, the Bro-Bird was quite an aircraft. Besides having an enormous cargo hold, the huge amphibian held a crew of twenty-four, had room enough to accommodate the entire twenty-six-man Unit 167 with their own private berths, had a large galley the size of a midtown restaurant and a midlevel "function room" that was decked out like a nightclub. This place was called, appropriately enough, "Cloud Nine." Colonel Crabb took to Cloud Nine right away. Show biz was in Crabb's blood, and a few of Bro's crew doubled as passable jazz musicians. Once airborne, Crabb soon had them up and playing his favorite songs. Drinks were served, tables put together. It was like being in the famous Blue Note—just four miles up.

* * *

No amount of music, however, could drag Y out of the funk that overtook him shortly after takeoff from Edwards.

For some reason, just as they got airborne, it hit him like a punch in the stomach: There was a real possibility that Hawk Hunter and the rest of the B-2000 crew were dead. Zoltan was convinced of it, and Crabb was, too.

Now sitting alone at a dark corner table inside Cloud Nine, nursing an ice water, Y found the same somber thoughts going through his mind.

Hawk Hunter. *Dead.*

What did that mean exactly?

Y knew from his experience with the mysterious fighter pilot that his being in this universe was not at all typical. Hunter's very presence affected the world in odd, subtle, and sometimes not so subtle ways. And there was proof. Over the years those rare persons who had claimed to see "angels" just assumed they were messengers from God, beings from On High. Most people, though, believed this was rubbish. But Y was privy to a secret study the OSS had undertaken after Hunter's sudden appearance in this world about a year before. Combining information from his experience with reported "angel sightings" over the years, they concluded that somehow, some way, certain individuals had been able—maybe without their knowledge or through no fault of their own—to pass from one universe to any other. How or why was not known. But while these people looked and acted like anyone else on Earth, by their very presence they were just *different* and could have an effect on everything from raising the dead to winning global conflicts single-handedly. The study concluded that these people were what had been termed down through the ages as "angels."

And Hunter was probably one of them.

Trouble now, this particular angel was, at the very least, missing in action. So what was really up to Y and the odd collection of personnel he'd pulled together: Find out whether or not angels can actually die.

And if they could, where did they go?

And what did that mean for the rest of them?

And what if . . .

Y shook away these disturbing thoughts and had them replaced by a sudden, very unusual craving for a drink of alcohol.

That's when he saw Crabb approaching.

"Bro says we're over the G-spot," he told Y. "I suggest we get up to the flight compartment."

Y agreed and together they left Cloud Nine and made their way up through the gigantic airplane.

After a ten-minute climb, they reached the huge flight deck and found Bro hovering over the controls. No less than six of his men were at various stations around the cockpit, manning various instruments and monitoring gear, all of them necessary in keeping the mammoth plane airborne.

There was a massive tracking screen next to Bro's control suite. It had long-range insta-film TV-projection capability, and at the moment it was broadcasting a wide swath of ocean, four miles below them. Bro's navigator was at his side doing calculations on an immense laptop computer. The man looked slightly perplexed.

"The coordinates check out," he was saying, with a tone that indicated this was not the first time he uttered these words. "But the visual doesn't match. There's supposed to be a huge landmass down there."

Y looked at Crabb; Zoltan had now joined them.

"The rumors?" Crabb whispered. "They could be true?"

Bro just looked up at Y. Neither he nor his men had been briefed on this part of the mission. Indeed, it was still very top secret. But Y knew the time had come to let them in on it.

"Everyone on this airplane will have to sign a security agreement," Y told them.

Bro just nodded; his men did, too.

"Wouldn't be the first time for us," Bro said. "We're trustworthy."

Y just shrugged and looked at the TV screen again.

"Well, if you're not, my office will track you down and have you all killed," he said matter-of-factly, adding, "Though I don't know how they can keep such a thing secret very much longer."

Now all of the crewmen were staring at Y. They had no idea what he was talking about.

Y walked over to the huge TV-projection screen.

"Gentlemen," he said, pointing at the vast tract of ocean below them. "If our calculations are correct, that's where the island of Honshu used to be. And right here, is where the city of Tokyo used to be. . . ."

Their reaction was a laugh at first. How could that be? they all seemed to say at once.

Then Y gave them a very quick version of the events from earlier that month: The U.S. had dropped a superbomb on Japan, and this weapon had exhibited more destructive force than anyone ever imagined. *Much* more.

"We still don't know why," Y said. "But that bomb apparently leveled everything and . . . well, *sank* most of the main island of Japan. As crazy as that sounds."

Silence.

"And took several million military personnel with it," Y added solemnly.

He felt a crushing sensation inside his chest as these words tumbled out. Even though the U.S. had been at war with Japan at the time of the superbombing, and even though the Japanese troops occupying South America and the Panama Canal had displayed sadistic excess in their domination of the South American and Central American people, the thought that the U.S. had dropped one bomb that *sank* quite nearly an entire country and killed at least three million people—it was almost too much to bear.

Y looked up again.

The crew wasn't laughing anymore.

"I need a drink," Zoltan said, breaking the silence.

"I do, too," Y finally agreed.

CHAPTER 6

West Falkland Island
South Atlantic Ocean

The storm had been raging for three days and nights.

It had blown in, as all the fiercest storms did, from the south, from the bottom of the world, and battered West Falkland with winds up to ninety-five miles per hour, and snow and rain mixed together so thickly, the combination created a wall of solid white ice.

The twenty-eight civilian residents of West Falkland had endured these ferocious storms before. They knew the drill well. Most would all gather at the small administration building near the small town of Port Summer Point and ride out the gale with a hot meal, a large beer, and a game of cards.

But this very isolated place was also the site of the most top secret research facility on Earth. Though its very isolation was its best means of security, there were 150 military personnel scattered throughout the island. It was one of their posts located on the northernmost tip of the island that picked up the Mayday call just before midnight. A ship passing nearby was in trouble. Its captain reported it was breaking up in high seas about four miles off of West Falkland. There were many children on board. After that, the radio went dead.

The British soldiers left their post and made their way down to the nearest beach, a cove known as Tenean. A massive battle had been fought there about a month before, and the remains of that conflict—sunken landing craft, downed Japanese airplanes, and even some bones—were still in evidence everywhere.

The soldiers had no boat—no means of getting out to the stricken ship. Even if they had, it would have been suicidal to try to reach the luckless vessel. The winds on Tenean were now blowing at more than one hundred miles per hour. The snow and rain felt like millions of tiny nails hitting the soldiers. All they could do was set up a large light beacon on the beach and shine it out into the stormy sea. If there were any survivors from the ill-fated ship, there was a chance they would follow the beacon to the relative safety of the cove.

The soldiers waited for about an hour, huddled inside their overlarge armored personnel carrier (APC), taking turns braving the howling wind to move the beacon back and forth. They continued to try to contact the stricken ship by radio but with no luck. Finally at 0130 hours, the APC commander announced that it was no use. No one could have survived such a gale. The unit began preparations to leave, when one of the men saw something way out in the approaches to the cove.

At first it was just a single lifeboat. It was floundering, obviously taking on water, obviously in the process of falling apart. It was coming out of the thick wind, riding on waves that were topping twenty feet high, disappearing from view for several chilling seconds only to miraculously reappear again, a bit closer to the shore.

As the amazed soldiers watched, they came to realize that there was actually a group of lifeboats out there. They were all lashed to one another, somehow being held together by thick coils of rope. As the lifeboats came more into view, the soldiers were astonished. There were more than twenty riding the raging seas, heading for the beach at Tenean.

The soldiers finally knocked themselves out of their stupor and went into action. One radioed back to their main base and reported the rather astonishing events. The APC commander ordered his crew to take the huge vehicle down to the waterline itself. Though not adapted at all for amphibious action, the drivers nevertheless plunged the huge vehicle into the surf. Now the waves were crashing against its hull, their power moving the fifty-ton behemoth like it was a toy.

Once in place about fifteen feet out, the crew set up a line of its own—a metal strand, thin but strong enough to tow a vehicle the size of the APC. They attached it to a powered flare and fired it out of one of their mortar tubes. The line sailed through the howling winds—and landed about fifty yards short of the lead lifeboat. This was too far from the lifeboat to do any good. The line was hastily reeled in and shot back out again. This time it landed within thirty yards of the lifeboat. Close, but still too far away to be helpful. The APC commander was about to order the line be reeled in again for one last desperate try—the lifeboats were now just a few seconds away from being dashed on the jagged rocks that formed the outer reaches of the cove. That's when the soldiers saw another unbelievable sight. A man was standing on the bow of the lead lifeboat. He looked in at the beach and then at the rocks and then plunged into the hellish sea and began swimming for the line.

"He's daft!" one of the troopers yelled into the gale.

"You mean he's dead," another said. "No one can survive that surf."

But somehow the man did. They could see him swimming mightily against the tide, finally reaching the line with the help of an especially large wave. He wrapped the line around his waist and swam back to the lead boat. With admirable dexterity, he somehow tied the line to the front of the lifeboat and began yanking on it.

"Jeesuz! Start reeling!" the APC commander screamed. His men promptly obeyed.

The line began swaying with the raging winds. The APC drivers gunned their engine, which in turn supplied more power to the winch, and began yanking the metal strand with some authority.

It took ten terrifying minutes, but finally the first boat was pulled into the relatively calm waters of the Tenean Cove. The other nineteen followed behind.

The British soldiers just couldn't believe it. Even over the wind, they could hear the wails of children.

Three troopers plunged into the water and literally yanked the first lifeboat by hand toward the beach. Once the first boat was up, it took brute manpower to pull in the other nineteen. But the waves were rising in such a perverse manner, they actually helped this effort. Several of the boats ran up on some smaller, nearby rocks, but none of the children on board were hurt too badly.

Finally, after yanking and pulling and swimming to the point of exhaustion, all twenty lifeboats were within the somewhat calmer waters of the cove.

Reinforcements from the Royal Army unit had arrived by this time and soon all of the lifeboats were being emptied of their passengers. They were all children. One hundred and thirteen of them.

Many had been saved because they were able to cling to the wreckage left over from the fierce battle between these very same soldiers and an invading force of Japanese. The wreckage of the landing craft provided places for those kids thrown overboard to keep their heads above water until they were rescued.

It took nearly a half hour, but finally all were safe

onshore. Many of the children were in a state of shock, but most were in remarkably good shape.

But what had happened to the man who had so bravely jumped into the water to secure the APC line?

He was finally found on the beach on the other side of the rocks. He had somehow dragged himself up after pushing in the last lifeboat. The troopers surrounded him. He was spitting up water and looked like he was about to expire.

One of the troopers acted quickly and pulled out a flask of brandy. He opened the man's mouth and poured it in. The man miraculously came back to life. His eyes opened, his nose was cleared, and he started breathing more regularly.

The troopers picked him up and carried him to the shelter of the nearest APC. Once inside, the shivering man began coughing again, but at least it appeared that he would live.

The APC commanding officer hunched beside him, wrapping him in a heavy wool blanket. He just looked at the man. He was thin of face and body, with jet-black hair and a longish, thin beard. His eyes were slanted a bit, giving him a slightly demonic look.

"You saved more than one hundred children, mate," the British commander said.

The man just looked back at him numbly.

"And you almost got yourself drowned doing it," the officer went on.

Again the man couldn't respond.

Then the British commander looked deep into his eyes and saw something from another faraway world.

"Who *are* you?" the British officer finally asked him.

The man just shook his head. He was still confused, still disoriented. He could hardly speak.

But then some words came slowly.

"I'm not sure," he replied. "The ship is gone—but on board I was known as Rower Number One-four-four-six-seven-nine-eight."

The British officer pressed him. "But what is your name, man?" he asked. "Try to remember."

The man just shook his head.

"I don't know for sure," he said. "But I think, at one time, my name might have been Viktor."

CHAPTER 7

South Pacific

Y was drunk.

It was the first time for him, in a very long time. He never had the chance to drink to the end of the war against Japan. He'd had a small glass of champagne to mark the end of the war with Germany, but that was all. In fact, he couldn't recall the last time he'd had more than two drinks in a row, never mind being this drunk. In reality, though, he couldn't remember much of anything at the moment.

Y had been drinking since viewing what was now referred to as the Japan Sink, the hole in the sea where the island of Honshu and three million people used to be. It was Zoltan who poured that first drink for him as soon as they retreated from the cockpit to the Cloud Nine room. The psychic told the OSS agent that he was picking up some stress vibes from him. He convinced Y that he had to be in top shape for whatever lay ahead, so he suggested Y have a pop or two now and listen to Crabb's pickup jazz band.

Relax, Zoltan had told him. Settle down. Get calm.

Y had decided to take the psychic's advice.

That had been three hours and six drinks ago.

The Bro-Bird was now cruising at twenty thousand feet somewhere over the bright blue Pacific. It was on a due southerly course, moving slowly down the Pacific Rim, following as best it could the B-2000's projected flight path after dropping the superbomb. The huge seaplane's long-range, radar-imaging TV cameras were scanning every part of the ocean and the few scattered islands below, looking for any telltale signs of wreckage.

So far, they had found nothing.

Now Y was stoned and looking out at the blue-pearl Pacific Ocean himself, the not-unpleasant sounds of the makeshift jazz band running in one ear and going out the other. What if they did spot the carcass of the massive B-2000 somewhere on the ocean's floor? Then what? Take pictures of the wreck, he supposed. Then search the nearest islands for any survivors. And after that? Well, after that, they would have nothing but the long ride home to look forward to.

Y signaled for another drink, and one of Bro's crew delivered it to him promptly. Just one sip into it, Y spotted Zoltan making his way across the dance floor to him. The psychic had retired to his berth for a "cosmic nap," as he called it. Now he was wearing a slightly perplexed look that Y had come to interpret as a harbinger of not-so-good news.

Zoltan greeted him, produced a drink for himself, and set it down on the table in front of Y.

"Can we talk?" he asked the OSS agent.

"Sure," Y said, sliding over in the small corner booth.

Zoltan sat down, noticed Y's six empty glasses, and began yanking on his goatee.

"I just talked to Bro and he just received a rather odd report," he began.

Y just groaned. He was becoming a bit psychic himself. "Now what?"

Zoltan leaned in a bit closer.

"Well, it was sort of an SOS call," he told Y. "A distress signal from an island close by."

Y sat up a bit.

"What kind of SOS? Was it from Hawk?"

Zoltan shook his head no.

Y slumped back down in his seat. "Who was it from, then?"

Zoltan seemed to pick his words carefully.

"I know it's going to sound a bit crazy . . . ," he began.

Y laughed. "I'm very used to crazy by this point."

Zoltan swigged his own drink.

"Well, it seems that there is a type of hostage situation on this island," he continued. "Some, well . . . uh . . . civilians are being held against their will by some pirate types. These hostages managed to send out a Mayday, and Bro's long-range radio equipment picked it up."

Y just stared back at him for a moment. "Can we alert someone for them?"

Zoltan shrugged. "That's an option, I suppose," he said. "But . . ."

"Well, what are you suggesting?" Y pressed him. "Surely not that we stop ourselves?"

Zoltan's brow furrowed and he was positively yanking on his chin hairs now. Not good signs.

"Well, it might actually be the wise thing to do," Zoltan replied. "You see I'm getting a very strange feeling about all this, and—"

Y held up his hand.

"We are on a very secret, very important, very *classified* mission here," he told the psychic, slurring his words slightly. "It would compromise our goals if we stopped to help everyone who can type out SOS. I'm not being cruel here—but you know the score. This part of the world is in a major state of upheaval—especially after what has happened in Japan. I'm sure there's a million places we could stop and lend a hand if we wanted to. But our mission has to come first."

"I realize that," Zoltan replied. "But the vibes I'm getting from this. I don't know. They are usually not this strong. And Bro feels them, too."

Y just shook his head and drained his drink.

"So now Bro is a psychic, too?"

Zoltan bit his lip. "He has intuitions," he said slowly. "We all do."

Y raised his hand, and one of Bro's men came over with his eighth drink.

"Look, why make this any harder on us?" Y said, taking his first sip of bourbon and ginger juice. "We're probably going to run into a pile of shit as it is? Why make the pile any higher?"

Zoltan finished his drink and signaled for another. This wasn't going to be easy, what he had to tell Y. But he had to try.

"Can I ask you a very strange question?" he said to the OSS man after his glass of rye appeared.

Y laughed. "When have you *not* asked me anything but strange questions?"

Zoltan looked deep into his eyes—an embarrassing thing to do.

"Have you ever dreamed you were on an aircraft carrier . . . one that was being towed by tugboats?" he asked him.

Y dropped his drink onto the table, causing a small crash and splashing bourbon all over his lap.

He was astonished.

"What . . . why would you ever ask me that?"

"It's true, isn't it?

"*Why* would you ask me *that?*"

Zoltan just shook his head. "I can't tell you," he said. "Not because I don't want to, but because I don't know. I'm a psychic. Not the best in the world—but not the worst, either. And I just know things. And I know that at some time in your life you dreamed this thing . . . am I correct?"

Y stared back at him for the longest time. He'd had the dream since childhood. He was on an aircraft carrier. It was huge, with immense power plants in its belly—but for some reason, the power plants didn't work. So they had tugboats. Pulling it. Pushing it. *Push-pull.* Back and forth the ship rocks from bow to stern, not port to starboard. It was such a detailed dream . . . it was like a movie. They were going somewhere. On a crusade. There was a crazy guy named Peter. Then they saw the Pyramids. And birds with wings on fire falling out of the sky. It was all nonsense really, like a child's daydream. And it would not have been so compelling if he hadn't dreamed the damn thing so many times in his life.

But he had never told anyone about it—never spoke about it. Until now.

"Yes, I have dreamed this thing," Y finally replied. "But I don't see how—"

Zoltan just held up his hand, and Y stopped talking. The psychic pulled a sheet of blue photo paper from his coat pocket. Y recognized it as a still video capture taken from one of Bro's long-range insta-film TV cameras.

Zoltan unfolded the paper and presented it to Y. It showed an island, one that was indeed very isolated. It was tropical in nature, with a large connecting atoll and a massive lagoon on its eastern face.

And tucked inside that lagoon was an aircraft carrier. And surrounding it was a small fleet of tugboats.

Y's jaw dropped when he saw it. He tried to say something but couldn't. It was his dream come to life.

Zoltan ran his finger along the edge of the photo, past the carrier, up a steep hill to a prisonlike building located in the middle of a cleared section of jungle.

"This," he said, "is where the SOS is coming from. . . ."

CHAPTER 8

The place was called Kibini Atoll.

Located at the northernmost end of the Bonin Islands chain, it was just one of several hundred dots floating in the South Pacific Ocean.

Kibini was the home turf of a gang of pirates known as the Cherrybenders. They had been terrorizing this part of the Pacific for many years now. Under the auspices of the Imperial Japanese government in Tokyo, the Cherrybenders provided a kind of roving terror service, an instrument to keep the native peoples who populated these islands in line, freeing up Japanese imperial troops for their more ambitious adventures overseas.

But it had not been a good month for the Cherries. Usually their Japanese masters were in touch every day in some manner, whether it be by secure radio, back-channel video conferencing, or highly secret face-to-face meetings.

Twenty-nine days ago a delegation from the High Command was supposed to visit Kibini. Their flight was due in at nine in the morning. It never arrived. When the mucky-mucks atop the Cherries' food chain tried to send a radio message up to Tokyo to inquire about the delegation's flight, there was no reply.

Repeated attempts all that day to get ahold of any one connected with the Japanese High Command were fruitless. The next day brought the same result, as did the next. And the next. It was almost as if Tokyo had disappeared off the map.

Which, of course, is exactly what had happened.

Word about the massive bombing of the home island gradually made its way around the Pacific Rim, and suddenly the Cherrybenders were without their protection. Knowing the power balance in the Pacific would now change dramatically, the sea pirates became desperate. They'd made hundreds of enemies over the years, and now without their Japanese protectors they were extremely vulnerable for payback.

The Cherries did two things they thought would shore up their position: They raided the nearby island of Wiki-Wiki and took its entire population back to Kibini and were now holding them hostage. Then they pulled off one more high-seas pirate action. They boldly turned against their previous Japanese masters and planned a raid on the former High Command naval base on the island of Okinawa. It was here, the Cherries' cut-rate intelligence operatives had told them, that a massive aircraft carrier was being refurbished. It had no crew on board but was stacked with hundreds of airplanes and thousands of weapons. Even better, most of the ship's navigation, steering and internal systems were automatic and run by computers.

In other words, amateurs could sail the big carrier. Such a warship would be very helpful in the post-Japanese Pacific.

So the Cherries raided Okinawa, sailing up to the island in their small fleet of gunboats and assault ships and sneaking in under the cover of darkness. Two thousand troops landed secretly on the west end of the island and quickly overwhelmed the practically nonexistent contingent of home guard protecting the naval base.

But this was when the Cherries realized that they had not paid enough for their intelligence.

There *was* a naval vessel tied up at the Okinawa docks—but it was not the massive aircraft carrier the Cherries had wanted. Most of the Japanese High Command's carriers were actually superhuge aircraft-carrying submarines of the same type the imperial forces had used to invade South America nearly a year before. But this vessel at Okinawa was a surface ship. And while not small, it was only about one tenth the size of the massive Japanese submarine carriers. In fact, this ship was not Japanese-built at all. It was an escort carrier, built years before by an Italian firm not to carry massive jet bombers but to transport small jet aircraft and supplies only. There were no aircraft on board, save for a few small jet-powered helicopters, and practically no weapons to speak of.

Though disappointed, the Cherries knew it was wise to get away with whatever prize they could. They took over the small carrier and found that many of its mechanisms were indeed automatic. They sailed it out of Okinawa and back down to Kibini with little trouble, parking it inside their well-protected lagoon. The plan was to evacuate Kibini, take the hostages, and sail to another island farther south, away from the bad vibes of the newly created Japan Sink.

But then problems developed. Suddenly the automatic systems on the carrier no longer worked. The computer glitched up and only a minimum of power could be generated on the ship. It couldn't move on its own any faster than five knots, essentially a crawl.

The Cherries were forced to plan another raid—this one on the island of Ugo, just off the coast of Taiwan. Here they captured twelve tugboats and took their crews hostage. If their carrier couldn't sail under its own power from Kibini, then they would tow it to where they wanted to go.

These plans went full steam ahead for a while. But the Cherries, never accused of being very smart, spent so much time trying to get the carrier ready to sail, they became lax in the holding of the hostages snatched from Wiki-Wiki. These civilians, a plucky group, had somehow managed to get hold of a radio and turned its guts into a transmitter. For two weeks they had been sending out a rudimentary SOS signal.

And now that signal had been picked up.

And that was the beginning of the end for the Cherrybenders.

The lagoon on Kibini Atoll was nearly three miles around.

Even in the best of times, the Cherrybenders had had a tough time guarding its perimeters against threats from both the land and the sea.

Now with the pirate band planning to move on, men were being drained from the supply of lagoon guards to work on the stolen carrier. But morale was very low. The pirate band wanted to leave within forty-eight hours, but nasty rumors were swirling about the island that the Cherries had not stolen enough tugboats to move the carrier. They had twelve in their custody, at least eighteen were needed to get the carrier to budge. This problem had caused their concerns for perimeter security to grow even more lax. Many checkpoints were now manned by only two guards, where at least six had been stationed before. For the Cherries, this was not a good situation.

So it was strange, then, when two guards at a checkpoint located near the northernmost approach to the lagoon spotted two people walking down the path toward them.

These guards were both rookies. One was named Aki, the other Laki. They knew there weren't too many people on the island who weren't connected in some way to the Cherries. And they had certainly never encountered anyone just casually walking down the beach path that they were charged with guarding. Yet two individuals were definitely coming their way.

But there was something else slightly strange here. It was near dawn. The sun was just rising over the water to their right. But oddly, both Aki and Laki found a bright glare was hindering their vision to the point where they could not make out exactly who was approaching them.

Confused, both guards raised their rifles and clicked their safeties to off.

A few seconds passed and the glare still remained in their eyes. But then Aki, the elder of the two, squinted mightily and in doing so, thought he noticed two things. First, the people approaching them appeared to be two young girls. Secondly, both were apparently topless.

Both guards lowered their weapons.

Perhaps this was a present for them, they thought rather naively. A gift from the top pirates for their good work in previous campaigns. Though Aki and Laki were "newbies," they had been among the most bloodthirsty of the Cherrybenders. Their specialty was slitting throats. Men, women, children—it didn't matter to them. They had slaughtered more than two hundred innocents in that grisly manner in just the past six months.

And now they believed two young, beautiful girls were walking toward them, bare chested and laughing. With such pretty necks.

The two visions reached the small guardhouse and just stood there for a moment. Aki and Laki spoke only Japanese. But it made no difference—these girls could not speak at all. Instead, they began stroking the barrels of the guards' rifles. It seemed like they were speaking in a very universal language.

"You are gifts for us?" Aki asked in Japanese.

The girls just smiled.

"From our commanders?" Laki asked.

The girls smiled again.

"And we can do anything we want to you?" Aki asked.

More smiles.

Aki laid down his rifle and pulled out his razor-sharp

knife. His idea of "anything" went way beyond normal sex.

"Come here, sweet one," he said to the nearest girl, hiding the knife from view.

The girl took a step forward. Aki, bulging with anticipation, looked over at Laki to give him a wink. Laki was looking back at him—but he had the oddest expression on his face. His eyes appeared twice as big as normal, and his complexion had turned pale white. His mouth was open as if he was trying to scream, but couldn't.

That's when Aki noticed a silver shaft protruding from Laki's chest, just below his rib cage. It was the handle end of a long, razor-sharp bayonet. A gurgling sound came from Laki's mouth, and then, in a very strange way, he began laughing.

"If they . . . try to . . . rescue the princess," he said in halting Japanese. "They have to take . . . the train first. . . ."

And with that, Laki toppled over face first.

He was dead before he hit the ground.

Aki just stared down at him. When he looked up again, the two girls were still smiling at him. But then, in the space of a heartbeat, their images dissolved, only to be replaced by those of two paunchy, middle-aged men, one with an outrageous goatee. This man was swinging an old gold timepiece, back and forth at the end of a long gold chain. This accounted for the glare in Aki's eyes.

"What demon thing is this!" Aki cried out.

"It's called hypnotic suggestion," Zoltan told him. "Scary, isn't it?"

Aki did not understand what Zoltan was saying, but it didn't matter. Aki dropped his weapon and began running down the path, heading toward the interior of the island.

Zoltan spun his watch around once and returned it to his pocket with flare.

"Mission accomplished," he said.

"Hypnotism, I've heard of," Crabb said, taking the weapon from the dead guard. "But how can you project the suggestion that *we* are two young girls? I mean, that's a real stretch. . . ."

Zoltan tapped the side of Crabb's head.

"You would not believe what I can make you—or anyone else—see up there," he replied enigmatically. "Want another example?"

Crabb watched as the hysterical Aki scrambled over the next hill. He was screaming at the top of his lungs.

"I don't think so," Crabb replied.

The next Cherryblender outpost was a small launchpad located about a half mile from Aki and Laki's position.

This housed one of the few aircraft the Benders knew how to fly—the TRX jetcopter. In a world dominated by huge eight-rotor helicopters/airliners known as "Beaters," the jetcopter, or Bug as it was also known, was a fish out of water. Large enough to carry four people, and that rather uncomfortably, the Bug took off like a helicopter, its smallish rotors powered by movable jet thrusters located on each tip. Once airborne, the Bug could translate to the horizontal and move with the speed of a slow jet fighter. They could be incredibly maneuverable under control of the right pilot, and could pack a minor wallop in armaments, including a machine gun in the nose and up to five hundred pounds in bombs carried under two small winglets sprouting from its forward fuselage.

Its nickname was apt, as well. With a bubble cockpit and long, thin fuselage behind it, the TRX looked like a fifteen-foot-long metal-coated flying insect. Most were painted bright green, adding to the giant-fly appearance. Best of all, just about anybody could pilot one. The controls were simple and not much more complicated than driving an automobile. In this part of the world, TRX jetcopters were as numerous as real flies. The Cherrybenders had a small squadron of six at their disposal.

It was to this small air base that Aki stumbled about fifteen minutes after Laki's skewering.

The guards who saw Aki approach in full panic nearly shot him on sight. He looked so horrible they thought they were being attacked by some kind of evil spirit.

"Ghosts!" he was screaming in Japanese to the startled guards. "Ghosts . . . are everywhere!"

The guards grabbed Aki and held him down.

"What are you talking about!" one screamed at him. "What is happening?"

By this time, there was a strange green foam coming from Aki's mouth.

"If they try to rescue the princess," he stuttered through the foam, "they must take the train first!"

The guards were in no mood to play heroes. Things had been strange on Kibini for days and they did not want to see just how much stranger they could become. Aki had gone insane, that was the most obvious conclusion. So the lead guard simply shot him twice in the head—this stopped his bloodcurdling squeals. Then they all made for the jetcopters. If the atoll was indeed under some kind of ethereal attack, the air-base guards wanted to be anyplace other than this isolated hilltop, six miles away from the pirates' main base.

So they tried to flee. But by the time they reached the southern end of the base, where the jetcopters were kept, they made another grisly discovery. The small contingent of air mechanics, who were charged with keeping the Bugs in flying condition, were all dead, sliced through the heart with bayonetlike skewers. Each man had died with an astonished look on his face.

The air-base guards were desperate now. All six of them piled into one of the Bugs and hastily took off. The man who wound up behind the controls was somewhat experienced in driving a TRX jetcopter. He lifted off cleanly, but had some trouble maintaining a high enough speed to complete the translation over to horizontal flight. Built for four, the Bug was overloaded by a factor of two bodies. The pirates had a quick solution. The two last men who'd climbed aboard were summarily pushed back out the door; both fell several hundred feet to their deaths.

Lighter now, the pilot was able to get the jetcopter level and moving horizontal. He pointed the nose of the Bug due south, toward the main base of the Cherries.

The hasty flight proceeded well for the first minute or so. The guards were convinced that if they just got to the main base, the strength in numbers would protect them from whatever had spooked Aki and had killed the air mechanics. But just as the glow of the main lagoon came into view, the guards were astonished to find another Bug flying right beside them.

They looked over at this jetcopter and were further dismayed to see that it contained not sea pirates but four huge Caucasian men in black combat fatigues and battle helmets. Two were pointing large infantry weapons at the guards.

The pilot in control of the pirates' Bug was named Zushi. At first sight of the second jetcopter, he banked the Bug wildly to the left. But the second aircraft stayed right with him. He tried increasing speed, but like a banshee, the second Bug stayed right up with them. Zushi put the jetcopter into a steep climb; the second Bug remained on his tail. He tried to dive—but the second aircraft perfectly mimicked his maneuver. Finally he slammed on the air brakes, hoping the second Bug would shoot past him—but the pursuing pilot did not fall for this. He pulled up right alongside the pirates' aircraft. A second later, the men inside the second copter opened up with their heavy weapons.

Zushi's Bug was suddenly filled with tracer fire. Zushi felt two bullets enter his right arm and saw a piece of another guard's head flick off the control panel and land in his lap. Zushi immediately panicked and, in trying to sweep the piece of bloody skull away, hit the Bug's vertical-translation lever. The aircraft was now on fire and plunging rapidly toward the dense jungle below. Just beyond the next hill, Zushi could see the glowing green lights of the

Cherries' main base. He looked around the Bug cabin and saw his three companions were dead, their skulls perforated with still-glowing tracer bullets.

The Bug plunged into the jungle seconds later.

Just how Zushi managed to survive the jetcopter's crash, he would never really know.

One moment the aircraft was totally out of control, on fire with his dead companions' bloody bodies being thrown around the small cockpit like mannequins, and the next thing he knew, he was lying facedown in a jungle stream. The water was warm, gurgling up against his face—it felt too good to be true. He looked up and saw that a colleague's body was lying in the stream about ten feet away from him. It was spewing blood and other bodily fluids, and it was this warmth that was washing across Zushi's face.

Zushi leapt up in horror and began scrambling away from the corpse and the bloody stream.

He nearly ran right into the burning wreckage of the Bug—it was hanging from a tall tree, gas and oil leaking down on him just as his dead colleague's bodily fluids had done. Zushi bounced off the tree and threw himself into the jungle, running as fast as he could away from the crash site.

His body pumped with adrenaline and fear, he topped a hill and saw a bunch of lights over the next ridge. He heard voices—urgent, commanding tones, but not in Japanese. These people were speaking English.

Zushi immediately dove into a thick bush and hugged the ground. Fifty feet away he saw more of the black-uniformed soldiers running this way and that, carrying huge weapons, talking into radios and looking up into the early-morning sky as if a battalion of angels was about to descend down upon them.

Beyond these men was the red brick mansion, a house that had existed on the atoll for a hundred years before the Cherrybenders ever came to this place.

It took Zushi a few moments to realize what he'd stumbled onto. The mansion was where the Wiki-Wiki hostages were being held. The Cherries' ace in the hole. Now these soldiers in black were running through the building and bringing the hostages outside.

Out from the darkened sky, one Bug appeared over the treetops and went into a hover. It began a vertical translation, and no sooner had it done this, another Bug appeared above the tree line. Then another and another.

As Zushi watched, the hostages were taken out of the mansion, were loaded on the Bugs, and were lifted away. Zushi was amazed at the precision. Within two minutes the Bugs had landed, all twelve hostages taken out, loaded on board, and lifted away.

The thing that stayed on Zushi's rather rattled mind was the fact that the hostages, while being loaded onto the Bugs, never once lost their poise, their bearing, or even the slightest curl in their hair.

They *looked* like princesses, he thought. But Zushi knew better. These people were comfort women. The hostages the Cherries had taken from Wiki-Wiki were actually high-priced prostitutes who had once served the top echelon of the Japanese Armed Forces.

Each one was more beautiful than the next.

Zushi felt a foam start to dribble from his mouth. He began to lose consciousness. He felt his temple, and for the first time realized he had a bloody gash stretching down to his earlobe. Stars appeared before his eyes, yet he couldn't take his eyes off the lovely painted women.

They were so beautiful . . . .

Zushi passed out shortly afterward—and yet he dreamed.

He saw in his dream frightening air machines flying overhead. The huge soldiers in their black combat fatigues were running all over the island, stepping on him as they did so.

They were cutting down all the trees and burning the rocks and draining all the water out of the lagoon—and . . .

And taking the beautiful comfort women away with them.

What could be worse? Zushi's bleary unconsciousness was asking itself. The island without trees would be barren, hot, like a desert in the middle of the vast ocean. The island without rocks would be formless, a puddle of mud—not solid enough to stand upon. The island without water in the lagoon would mean no fish, no coolness in the heart of day.

But the island without the comfort women—that would be the worst of all.

It was deep into the night when Zushi woke up again. The air was filled with smoke. The smell went up into his nostrils, into his lungs, and it felt like it was leaking back out his ears. It was a combination of cordite, burned flesh, and perfume.

It was the perfume that had brought Zushi around in the first place. He began sniffing, and in his semi-delirious state he picked himself up, wiped the blood from his head wound, and began following the smell of perfume.

He stumbled over rocks and bush and down into the creeks and larger streams, and once he'd passed the waterfall, he knew he was approaching the lagoon.

He reached a tall cliff that looked out over the lagoon. And that's when all his fears came true. He realized that most of the trees on the island were either on fire or had already been destroyed. He saw that many of the huge rocks that had anchored the atoll had been blown to bits, and now the tide was rushing in on the lower parts of the island.

It was at this point that Zushi realized that while he was unconscious, a massive battle had taken place on the island, specifically around the lagoon. There were fires everywhere and bodies and shot-down Bugs and destroyed weaponry.

It was like this little bit of the world had come to an end.

Zushi then saw the most incredible sight of all. For the

lagoon was indeed empty—not of water, but of the aircraft carrier he and his colleagues had stolen earlier and had planned on using to escape this haunted part of the Pacific.

The carrier was now about five miles out to sea, covered in thick early-evening fog. There was a bunch of tugboats pushing it, and another group pulling it. But how could this be? The pirates had not been able to get enough tugboats to move the damn thing. How was it moving now?

Zushi had his answer as soon as a fateful wind blew away some of the fog surrounding the carrier. He saw an enormous seaplane riding in the water about a quarter mile in front of the carrier with a huge line attached to its rear end and tied to the bow of the carrier. Along with the tugboats, the seaplane was pulling the vessel, and their combined strength was enough to get the ship moving.

It was such a strange sight!

Tears streaming down his face now, Zushi collapsed to his rear end and just watched as the strange group of vessels faded over the horizon.

He realized that he was probably the only one left alive on the island. All the food and drinkable water was probably gone, and there were no more weapons left, so complete the destruction had been.

But that wasn't why Zushi was weeping. It was the absence of one more thing, neither food nor drink nor a means of protecting himself.

No—it was the absence of something else. There was no longer any scent of perfume in the air.

And *that* was why Zushi was crying.

CHAPTER 9

The Falkland Islands

The two jet fighter planes lifted off from McReady air base at the first light of dawn.

The huge storm had blown itself out by this time, and though the seas were still very rough, with very high swells, the sky was clear and the sun was peeking through the typically dense overcast.

The jet pilots were on a search mission. They had heard the story of what had happened over on West Falkland Island the day before. How the strange man had somehow shepherded ashore twenty boats filled with children he'd apparently saved from a ship that had been caught in the raging storm.

The pilots were now looking for the ship itself.

But this would prove to be a fruitless task. They flew in box patterns for three hours, covering hundreds of square miles of ocean north of the Falklands, but they could see nothing. No wreckage, no flotsam, no sign at all of the ship that had been carrying the children and the strange man.

The fighter planes were called back to base shortly before noon. The British Royal Army contingent on the island knew that if a ship was caught in a storm such as the one of the previous day, the South Atlantic was quite capable of swallowing it up whole. That no other survivors were found surprised no one.

The fact that the strange man had saved so many children was what everyone was baffled about.

Colonel Neal Asten was commander of all British Royal Forces on both East and West Falkland. His command consisted of 150 men and a squadron of SuperChieftain tanks. These behemoths held a crew of nearly two dozen, featured twin 188-mm guns and a myriad of antiaircraft, radar, and night-detection equipment.

Their mission was basically to protect the ultrasecret research facility located deep in the ground beneath West Falkland Island at a place known as Skyfire.

Just what went on below the farmhouse that sat atop the hill at Skyfire, Asten had little idea. He'd heard rumors of everything from superbombs to Life itself being created within the facility that stretched some sixteen stories into the earth.

The farmhouse had just been recently rebuilt. It had been destroyed a month earlier in the huge battle fought against Japanese forces on the island. The house had taken no less than the brunt of a massive bombing strike. The facility beneath, however, had survived intact.

Two people lived inside the house—a husband and wife, both were in their late fifties. Asten didn't know their real names. He rarely talked to them on anything but a professionally cordial level. But he did know the Man was an American who many believed knew all the secrets of the universe, and then some.

A person like this was very special. So after the battle had been won and the Japanese defeated, Asten and his men built a new farmhouse for the Man and his wife.

The new farmhouse looked exactly like the old one, right down to the slight lean to the east caused by the raging storms, which always blew in on the island from the southwest. Everything on the island leaned east—and less than a month after its completion, the farmhouse was no different.

Asten was inside the command SuperChieftain when he received the report from McReady air base across the sound on East Falkland. No sign of any ship had been spotted by the search planes. This was no surprise to Asten. He'd been on the Falklands long enough to know what the brutal storms could do. He'd seen some so fierce, he doubted even one of the Americans' huge megacarriers could make it through without some kind of damage. A smaller vessel would have no chance.

After confirming the radio report, Asten ran out the pilots' official report on his signal printer and then placed it into a white envelope, which he sealed with red tape. Then he left the command tank and began the long walk up the hill toward Skyfire.

It was up to him to inform the Man of the pilots' fruitless search.

He found him sitting in his new living room, his back stiff against the new chair Asten's troopers had provided as part of the refurnishing of the house.

Across the room sat the survivor named Viktor, the man who had somehow saved the children from the storm. The children themselves were down in Port Summer Point, the small civilian settlement located about a mile away from Skyfire. Viktor, however, had been kept at the farmhouse since the dramatic rescue. Asten had learned the night before that Viktor was suffering from shock, exhaustion, and partial amnesia.

Asten knocked once on the front door, and the Man motioned for him to come inside. Asten did so, snapped off a sharp salute, and removed his battle beret.

Asten had seen Viktor briefly the day before, but now he was able to get his first full measure of him. He looked very odd, slightly different than most people Asten had met. It was his eyes, his mannerisms, his very being that made him, well . . . *different.* In fact, Asten had met only one man before that had this same undeniable yet indefinable alienness about him.

"You have the search report, I take it?" the Man asked Asten.

"I do, sir," Asten replied crisply. He handed the envelope to the Man. "No surprises in there, sir," he added.

The Man quickly read the report, then resealed it and put it inside his suit-jacket pocket.

"I didn't expect any," he told Asten.

They both turned back to Viktor, who was slumped in another chair near the window, staring out at the cruel sea beyond.

The Man walked over to him, and for a moment Asten thought he was going to pat Viktor on the shoulder. But the Man kept his distance. He lowered his voice.

"I'm sorry to have to tell you this," he began.

But Viktor simply lifted his hand.

"I know already," he said, his voice dripping with sadness. "No one else survived."

The Man just nodded—and the room was suddenly filled with intense melancholy. Asten himself felt a mist come over his eyes. Why was this happening? He'd been in war before. He'd seen brutal combat, the most intense here on this very spot a month before, during the invasion by the Japanese. He'd not had any sense of weeping then. So why now? And why so intense?

It was a most eerie feeling.

"I didn't expect there'd be anyone else left," Viktor said slowly. "Not after seeing what I saw."

The Man stood hovering near him. Asten was sure that if it had been anyone else the Man surely would have touched him to comfort him. But the Man still kept his distance.

"Well, you should take heart in the fact you saved so many children," the Man said softly.

Viktor remained silent.

The very awkward moment continued. The Man looked over to Asten for help, but the British officer could only shrug weakly in return. The sadness in the room was now so thick, it seemed to be dimming the daylight.

"I, for one, would like to hear how you were able to save those kids," Asten suddenly heard himself say.

Viktor just shook his head.

"I don't really remember how I did it," he said. "I was in charge of the children on the ship. I used to be a rower but they put me in charge of the kids and I loved it. And we'd sailed these waters and others before—but never through a storm like that. And now—now, they are all gone. Now, it's just me . . . and the kids."

At this point Asten became aware of someone stirring in the kitchen. A moment later the Man's wife walked into the room. She was an attractive, middle-aged woman with a bright smile and large blue eyes. But as soon as she stepped into the room, something happened to her. She was carrying a tray of coffee and sandwiches—but she dropped it. A stunned look went across her face. She put her hand to her chest and grasped it. Then she collapsed to the floor.

Asten and the Man reached her at the same time. Her face was already turning blue. Her lips were trembling. Her eyes were open, but she could not speak.

"I'll get my corpsman!" Asten yelled, dashing off.

Asten ran down the hill, literally dragged his medic out of the command tank, and ran back up to the farmhouse.

But by the time they arrived, Asten knew it was too late. The woman was no longer breathing. Her eyes were closed. She had already turned cold. There was no pulse. There were no signs of life at all.

The Man just stared down at her. He couldn't believe what was happening.

"No," he murmured. "This cannot be."

Then something very strange happened. Asten looked up and saw Viktor was standing over the woman.

He was crying.

Then he knelt down and held her head in his hands and whispered in her ear.

"It is not your time to become a ghost," he said.

And with that, the woman's eyes opened. She began breathing again and the heavy sadness that had weighed down on the room was lifted.

Suddenly, the woman was alive.

Again.

CHAPTER 10

Y was drunk. Again.

He was sitting in Cloud Nine on the Bro-Bird, a bottle of rice wine in front of him.

Zoltan was sitting across the table from him. The band had just taken a break. They were both drinking rice wine, but Y was the only one who was drunk.

"This is ridiculous," he was saying. "This just isn't how this mission should be proceeding."

Zoltan didn't say a word.

Y took another gulp of wine.

"I mean, my orders were to get over here as fast as possible," he went on. "With minimum of exposure. We were to determine the last known position of the super-bomber and track the crew from there."

He took another gulp of wine. His head was beginning to spin. The attack on Kibini Atoll had been a success—with no loss of life on their side, thank God. If Y had lost any men to such a bizarre operation, he wasn't sure he could have lived with himself. But Unit 167 proved its worth, and the Cherrybenders had been ripe for the picking. The pirates had been caught off guard—demoralized, confused, and unprepared. Managing the operation from the Bro-Bird's combat room, he had taken Zoltan's advice and played upon the pirates' well-known superstitious nature. When it was over, most of the cutthroat pirates were gone and the Americans had . . . well, they had themselves an aircraft carrier.

"Now look at what we're doing," Y went on. "We're way behind schedule. We've attacked the largest pirate force in the region—and now . . ."

He looked out the large porthole window to see one of the towropes stretching from the Bro-Bird's port-side wing.

"And now we're towing a freaking aircraft carrier!"

Zoltan pulled his goatee in thought.

"I know it seems strange," the psychic said. "But you asked me to come along on this operation because you said you wanted a psychic option. That's what I've been providing for you."

Y nearly hit the roof. This was not like him. He was usually the coolest cat in the room.

"We are *towing* a freaking *aircraft carrier,*" he repeated slowly for effect. "We are probably sitting ducks out here. We are calling more attention to ourselves than the superbomber did when it sank Japan for Christ's sake."

"Well, I do admit we have raised our exposure a bit . . . ," Zoltan agreed quietly.

"A bit?" Y asked him back. "Have you seen the size of that thing?"

Zoltan looked out the window. From this angle—yes, indeed—the size of the carrier was in full view.

"Is it as large as the one in your dream?" he asked Y.

The question surprised the OSS man. In his dream the carrier was always enormous.

"Well, it's not as big," he began to say. But then he came back to reality—such as it was. "But that doesn't matter. We have put ourselves in a very vulnerable position. I don't know why I let you talk me into this."

"We were just following the psychic path," Zoltan said. "It might seem crazy now—but somewhere down the road we might need this vessel. That's what the vibrations are telling me."

Y just shook his head. He needed more wine.

"When my office gets wind of this," he said, slowly pouring them both another drink, "they'll have me tapping phones in Idaho."

The seaplane lurched forward a bit—this was a typical movement now and they were used to it. There were twelve tugboats in all. When it turned out that their operators had been held against their will, too, by the pirates, they agreed to sign on with the American force and help move the carrier farther south. The odd thing was, all of the operators were Irishmen.

Zoltan took a sip of his wine.

"I agree we do have a defensive problem now," he said. "That is, if there is anyone left in this area that can challenge us."

Y just shook his head. "You know how these things work. You have to assume the worst, and hope for the best."

They were silent for a few moments.

"And you're sure the damn carrier was empty?" Y asked him finally.

Zoltan nodded glumly.

"Just the few Bugs we were able to get from the atoll," Zoltan replied. "Six in all."

Y swigged his drink again.

"If there is anyone out here with any kind of air power, we'll be sunk with only a half-dozen jetcopters to defend us," he said darkly.

Zoltan stared at him and countered, "Well, we can always get us some air power of our own."

The OSS man looked up at him.

"Get some?" he asked. "Get some where?"

Zoltan suppressed a smile. His world was better if he was following his psychic vibrations. If he wasn't, it was like swimming against the tide.

He felt the tide turning a bit.

"We might have someone on board who can give us some information on that," he said.

Y just shook his head. "I know I don't want to hear this."

Zoltan just shrugged. "This person's presence has a very high psychic value to it," he said.

Y didn't comprehend this part, for he was too busy pouring another goblet of rice wine.

"Just explain it to me," he said to Zoltan.

"Well, the hostages we picked up," Zoltan began. "They were, as you know . . . ladies of the evening. 'Comfort women' was how the Japanese once described them. These girls were the top of the line, believe me. Anyway, they've been going through debriefing by the Unit One-sixty-seven guys and they've come up with some very interesting information."

"Such as?" Y asked, slurring his words mightily.

"Such as the location of a free-lance fighter-plane group nearby," Zoltan said. "Good guys who know how to fly jets and protect ships."

"Air mercs?" Y asked. "Trustworthy ones? Out here?"

Zoltan nodded slowly. "That's what they said," he replied. "But they have some even more interesting stuff for us. It's the real value of why we rescued them."

"And that is?"

Zoltan leaned forward a bit and lowered his voice; outside the seaplane shivered as the push and pull of the towing operation jerked them all forward.

"I should let one of them tell you herself," Zoltan said.

Y didn't say anything one way or the other, so Zoltan took the opportunity to leave the room briefly. Y swallowed his entire glass of saki and poured yet another. He let the gasolinelike fluid run over his tongue, down his throat, and felt it reignite the already raging inferno in his gut.

Why was he drinking so much?

He didn't know . . . .

The door opened again, and Zoltan stepped back inside. He was followed by a goddess . . .

Or at least that's what she looked like to Y.

She was wearing a long flowing silk gown, and her hair was piled on top of her head. She smelled of lilacs. Her nails were painted red, as were her lips. Blond hair. Slightly pouting lips. Small perky breasts. Deep-blue eyes . . .

Y nearly fell off his seat. She looked like an angel. One from his dream . . . .

He staggered to his feet. This girl looked very familiar to him. But he wasn't quite sure why.

She stood before Y—he could hardly take his eyes from her.

"Tell him what you told me," Zoltan prompted her.

The girl looked so sweet and demure, Y was having trouble believing the line of work she was in.

"I saw it," she said simply.

Y just stared back at her—for a moment he wondered drunkenly if his fly was open.

" 'You saw it?' " he asked, baffled. "Saw what exactly?"

She looked at Zoltan, who urged her on with a fatherly nod.

"We saw the Big Plane," she finally replied.

Y felt his heart start to pump mightily. His eyes grew wide.

"Are you sure?" he managed to blurt out.

She just nodded. "It was the biggest flying thing I've ever seen," she said. "It went right over our heads the same day the world turned dark at daytime."

Y took out a piece of paper and a pencil from his leg pocket and handed it to her.

"Draw it," he said.

The girl learned forward on the table and started to draw. Y couldn't help but look down her low-cut gown to see all but her entire breasts. They were small and erotic.

The girl drew a credible picture—she was artistic, too! And the drawing she produced looked exactly like the missing B-2000 superbomber. It was gigantic, all engines and wings and fuselage. Even more interesting, she added the tow plane the superbomber was towing when it left Bride Lake on its secret transpolar mission.

Y felt another surge of excitement go through him. This was their first solid lead of the journey. He looked up at Zoltan, who was smiling slyly.

"OK, OK," he said to the psychic. "One of your things finally panned out."

Zoltan just threw his shoulders back and shrugged with practiced nonchalance.

"Just doing my duty, sir," he said with a smile.

Y turned back to the young girl. She was so delicate and beautiful—and he could not get rid of the feeling that he knew her from someplace before.

"We will have to ask you a lot of questions about this," he said to her. "Exactly when you saw the big plane, which direction it was going, and so on. Do you mind? It will be a great help for us."

She nodded sweetly.

"Not at all," she replied. "You saved us from those pigs on the island. I owe you that at least."

Now Y felt another surge of energy go through him. This one started south of the border and made its way northward.

He finally stood back up and straightened himself out.

"And you are?" he asked, trying to be cool and not succeeding in the least.

She smiled, seeming a bit embarrassed, but took his outstretched hand and shook it lightly.

"My name," she said softly, "is Emma."

CHAPTER 11

In another world this place was once known as Bloody Iwo.

Its full name was Iwo Jima. It was a spit of land, about four hundred miles south of what was left of Japan. There was a huge airfield consisting of four massive runways and eight smaller ones. This place was a stopping-off point, a gas station for the behemoth cargo planes and passenger carriers that plied the skies above the South Pacific.

The island was now nicknamed the Hellhole. The airfield itself was known simply as the Pit.

It was, quite accurately, the worst place on the Pacific Rim. Homicide was an hourly occurrence. The sound of gunfire was heard as frequently as that of the wind blowing through the palms, or the patter of the rains that arrived like clockwork at one o'clock every afternoon.

The Pit was such a dangerous place that even at the height of its power, the Japanese Imperial Army never came here. Not in force anyway. As for pirate groups like the Cherrybenders—they never came within one hundred miles of this place.

It was here, though, that Zoltan, Crabb, and Y landed one of the captured Bug copters.

They were smart enough not to bring the jetcopter down right in the middle of the vast airfield. The people in the Pit would have shot them out of the sky just for target practice. No, landing a Bug at the Pit would have been like showing up at the Grand Prix in a golf cart. That's why they set down on the beach about a mile from the outskirts of the base itself. It would be easier, they felt, to bribe guards and whomever else they met along the way to get into the place. As it turned out, this was a wise decision.

The currency in these parts was gold: coins, bars, ingots, rings—anything. Just as long as there was gold in it, it passed for money on Iwo Jima.

Before leaving the U.S., Y had had the good sense to carry with him the equivalent of $10,000 in gold. This included four sets of earrings, several rings, a tiepin, a Relox twelve-jeweled twenty-four-carat watch, and a bag of gold coins.

These items were now locked in a small strongbox fitted into the leg pocket of Y's battle fatigues. He was dressed, in his opinion, as a bummy air merc. His fatigues, borrowed from one of the Unit 167 Sea Marines, were slightly frayed and torn in a few places. He was wearing a crappy beret and an ancient weapons belt that could barely hold his pistol holster.

Zoltan and Crabb were dressed similarly. Zoltan was carrying a huge twin-barrel Thompson machine gun; Crabb was lugging a 4.57 Magnum triple shot.

They left the Bug on the beach and began walking toward the lights of the Pit. The sun was just going down, and the sky was a beautiful crimson-red. The sounds that mixed together were the crash of waves, the wind in the palms, and the roar of jet engines warming up. All were shaking the early-evening air.

"I wonder what kind of booze they got around here?"

Y asked, still rather puzzled by his infatuation with demon alcohol lately.

"Probably that crappy Scottish stuff," Crabb replied knowingly. A standing rule at his Chicago club was that no Scottish liquor of any kind could pass through the doors. In this world, booze from Scotland was the worst.

"The ambient vibes tell me that the liquor here is actually very good," Zoltan said, touching his hand to his forehead. "And so is the food."

They topped a sand dune and came upon a roadblock. It was manned by two guards in a small armored personnel carrier commonly known as a Gnat.

One man was sitting next to the vehicle's top-mounted machine gun; the second was throwing a net into a small tidal pool nearby—no doubt fishing for his supper.

They barely raised their heads as Y, Zoltan, and Crabb made their way down the path toward them. The man fishing took a quick glance and went on about his business. The man at the machine gun actually yawned. Y decided already these two would get a gold ring from him, and not much else.

"Peace!" he greeted them with an upraised hand. "Friends here . . ."

Crabb and Zoltan looked at him like he was from outer space.

"What do you think, you're in a cowboy movie here?" Crabb asked him.

Crabb stepped up and looked at the man fishing.

"We want to get to the Pit," he said. "What is the quickest way?"

The guard shrugged. He was Fijian—far from home. But not that far.

"Many, *many* ways to get to town," he said, finally snagging a couple of sunfish.

Crabb looked back at Y and stretched out his palm. The OSS man stalled a moment.

"Is it too late to hypnotize these guys?" Y asked Zoltan.

The psychic just rolled his eyes. Y just shrugged, then

finally came out with two rings and the tiepin. Together they added up to a substantial amount of gold.

"I asked what's the quickest?" Crabb said, displaying the rings.

The two soldiers looked the bribe over and then smiled.

"Over the next two dunes, around the mine field, then a half mile north," one said.

Crabb was suddenly displaying the gold pin.

"OK, now," he said. "How much for a ride?"

Ten minutes later the Gnat was rumbling through the very muddy main street of the Pit.

The place was very aptly named. It featured what might have been the largest collection of Quonset huts on the planet. They were lined up for a mile along the main muddy drag, and some of them went at least a dozen blocks deep.

These plain tin houses were not used just for living areas. Many were converted into bar rooms, gambling halls, and brothels. The neon around these structures was so bright, Y noted that there was no need for streetlights. And indeed, there weren't any.

The red, orange, and yellow glow was nearly blinding. The muddy streets were thick with vehicles of all descriptions. A few air bikes fluttered high above. The land traffic included mercs of all shapes, sizes, uniform color, and ethnic persuasion. There were hookers everywhere, too.

"Jeesuz, look at all the fuckware!" Crabb said, looking at the talent parading up and down the streets. "No wonder Emma knew where we should look."

Y felt a sudden pang in his heart. Was Crabb insulting the beautifully delicate Emma?

And if he was, why would Y care?

The Gnat dropped them off at the largest Quonset hut in the vast airport city. This place was the combination saloon, black-market armory, and the unofficial headquarters for the fighter-plane mercenary group that Emma had told them about.

The trio thanked the Gnat crew and jumped off the APC to the muddy streets below.

True to form, the sound of gunfire soon punctuated the night air—not just pistol shots, but the loud reports of heavy-caliber machine-gun fire. Yet the crowds in the streets went about their business as if nothing more serious than a truck backfiring had happened.

Zoltan turned to Y and asked, "OK, now that we're in, how are we going to get back out again?"

Y motioned his head toward Crabb.

"Ask our tour guide," he said. "That is, if you don't know already . . ."

Just as a matter of course, all three men checked the weapon clips in their guns and then walked into the huge Quonset hut.

The place looked like a cross between a movie set—bright lights everywhere—and an Old West saloon. A long bar stretched around three quarters of the immense space. The place was packed with mercs and hookers, all of them drinking, fighting, arguing, or eating.

Y took one look around and felt a strange sensation well up in the back of his head.

"Damn, I've been here before," he said.

Zoltan looked at him. "That's my line, isn't it?"

Y wasn't listening, though. He was too busy studying the interior of this place. It was strange. It was as if he was seeing it for the first time, yet he still had intimate knowledge of the saloon. The long bar, the crowd of soldiers and hookers, the very bright movie lights.

It was a very strange sensation.

Like a dream within a dream . . .

They walked over to the bar, and the bartenders all ignored them.

Y pulled out the gold necklace and began waving it in full view of the nearest beer jockey—but again to no effect.

Zoltan looked around, took out his massive gun, and fired two shots into the ceiling. The report from his weapon was earsplitting, the smoke and cordite like a small storm.

Not one person turned a head.

"Wow . . . tough crowd," the psychic said.

"If Hawk was here, we'd have a drink by now," Y said, more to himself than to the others.

It was just dumb luck that a waitress was passing by with a huge pitcher of beer and three mugs. Zoltan lifted the brews from the tray. All three quickly quenched their thirst.

This done, they had to start looking for the people they'd come to find.

Y knew very little about the air merc group, other than their name: the AirCats. Emma had told them only that they flew odd-looking airplanes—the norm in this world—and that they were fearless, which could also mean they were simply crazy.

Y knew a bit about military aircraft, as did Zoltan. In this world there were literally dozens of current military aircraft models, not just a few top-of-the-line fighters, bombers, and so on.

And there was a fighter-bomber manufactured by Boeing-Grumman-Northrop-Bell called the AirCat. It was a big, powerful, quick, double-reaction-powered airplane, with straight wings, a central power plant, and a small compartment able to hold three crew members: a pilot, a copilot/bombardier, and a navigator/tail gunner for big jobs, a single pilot for small ones. AirCats could lug a lot of bombs, hold as many as eight cannon on its wings and, ironically, was able to operate off of an aircraft carrier.

But how to spot a certain gang of air mercs in a place that was full of them?

Y turned to Zoltan.

"Got your antenna up?" he asked the psychic.

Zoltan grimaced—he disliked any suggestion that his ability was anything less than genuine. But he closed his eyes, wrinkled his brow, and put his finger to his goateed-chin.

Then he simply spun around and pointed to a table in the nearest corner.

"There . . . ," he said, without opening his eyes.

Y and Crabb looked in the direction Zoltan was indicating—and found themselves staring at a table teeming with transvestite hookers.

"Please guess again," Y said, horrified.

Zoltan opened his eyes, saw his mistake, yanked his chin in thought, and then thrust his finger straight up in the air.

"There!" he yelled above the din.

Y and Crabb looked up and saw that indeed there was a table full of mercs sitting on the second level right above the girly-boys.

They all looked rugged, grizzled, and drunk. So at least they knew they were pilots.

"See? My location was right," Zoltan said by way of explanation.

Crabb patted him on the shoulder. "Yeah, you just gotta work on that altitude thing."

Y had already made his way through the crowd and was bounding up the stairs toward the merc table. Zoltan and Crabb were quickly behind him.

Arriving on the second floor, Y fought his way through another crowd of drunks, hookers, and soldiers, and finally arrived at the table of mercs. There were thirteen of them—each one had a girl on his lap, except the two men who seemed to be the leaders of the group. Each of them had two girls on his lap.

Both these characters appeared tough-looking, with identical gnarly beards, handsome if rugged faces, all-in-all two no-nonsense guys. Both were small and wiry. Both were older than the rest of the group. And though they were both wearing caps pulled down low and dark sunglasses, it was obvious after a while that these men were identical twins.

The whole table looked up at Y. His arrival seemed a bit sudden, putting the group on guard.

"Hey, waitress?" one of the twins said to him. "We need another round. . . ."

Y remained silent.

One of the mercs shooed the girl off his lap and was suddenly nose to nose with the OSS agent. He was a head over Y and had about fifty pounds on him, big for a fighter pilot.

"My boss told you to get us some drinks," the man snarled at Y.

Y reeled back and leveled the man with one massive punch. Zoltan and Crabb arrived at this very moment, and only Crabb's perfect basket catch prevented the man from hitting the floor.

The table full of mercs was stunned—except the twin pilots, who simply smiled a bit.

"He might kick your ass, when he wakes up," one of the twins said.

"I might not be here when he does," Y replied. "Unless you want to talk some business."

There was a long silence. Then Crabb let the man simply crash to the floor, knocking him further into unconsciousness.

The twins gave the eye to the six men sitting on their right. The pilots were soon pushing girls off their laps and making room for Y to sit down.

"What do you need?" one twin asked Y. "We do intercept stuff, close air support. Armed recon—"

"At the moment all I need is some information," Y said. He dramatically pulled the bag of gold coins from his leg pocket and slammed it on the table.

This was enough to impress the twin pilots.

"Ask away," one said.

Y drew his seat a bit closer to them. The rest of the mercs, the girls, Zoltan, and Crabb were all now leaning against the railing a respectable distance away, watching the meeting. Already Crabb had several girls buzzing around him. The guy Y hit was lying on the floor, an odd smile played on his face—even though his lips were bleeding a bit.

"You know what the Japan Sink is?" Y asked them.

Both men looked back at him; their bravado faded a bit.

"What if we do?" one asked.

"If you do, and you know exactly how it happened," Y said, nudging the bag of gold coins their way, "then this is yours . . . maybe."

The twins contemplated the bag of gold. It represented a lot of money in their world.

"OK," one said finally. "Here's what we know. . . ."

The tale the twins told soon had Y on the edge of his seat.

They were working a job up near Okinawa, raiding a Japanese fuel convoy at the behest of some Chinese warlords. It had been a risky operation because at the time the Japanese Imperial Forces were still extremely strong, and the AirCats were operating practically in their backyard. To be caught would have meant a very painful death for them.

The job went off without a hitch, though. There was no fighter escort for the Japanese fuel convoy, which was highly unusual. The twins said at the time they felt in their guts that something unusual was up.

Then after the raid was complete, the AirCats went back up to altitude for the trip back to Iwo Jima.

That's when they saw a most startling sight.

The sky was filled with fighters. Japanese aircraft of all shapes and sizes were flying in groups all over the sky above southern Japan. The twins estimated there must have been more than one thousand planes in these pre-intercept formations. The sky was so filled with them, they blotted out the midday sun.

Fascinated and a bit curious, the twins sent all but one of their group back. The third pilot who stayed with them was named Vogel. The three AirCat fighters—one man in each—began orbiting at fifty thousand feet, all the while keeping an eye on the multitude of Japanese aircraft.

They were trying to follow the cacophony of radio calls going back and forth between the Japanese fighters when suddenly the twins said everything just went silent. The radio airwaves were suddenly empty. Then they saw "the sun on Earth" as they described it. There was a huge bright yellow ball rising up from the horizon. It covered their entire field of view for hundreds of miles around.

Both twins were blinded for more than a minute, forcing them to feel their way around their controls until their vision returned.

When they were finally able to see again, their first sight looked like something out of a horror movie. It was a huge airplane almost totally engulfed in flames flying at more than Mach 3, a legion of Japanese fighters trailing it, attacking it, pouring cannon fire and rockets into it, as it went by them at three times the speed of sound.

It was gone as soon as it came, and the twins were left in a minor state of shock. When they heard later that this was the airplane that had dropped the bomb that actually sank the main island of Japan, they put two and two together.

That was the day the mighty Japanese Empire ceased to exist.

Y listened to the story, wide-eyed and silent. There was no doubt in his mind these men were telling the truth. Though gruff, they seemed trustworthy, were obviously American in origin, plus the tale sounded so outlandish, Y believed no one could just make it up.

But it didn't answer Y's main question: What happened to the airplane and its crew?

The twins had a less direct answer for that. It lay with the other pilot, the third man, they said. The guy named Vogel.

When the twins finally regained their bearings, they searched the sky for their comrade. But his aircraft was nowhere to be seen. Quickly turning on their long-range

TV monitors, they received only the faintest indication of his aircraft. It was heading due south, following the gigantic bomber and the last of the pursuing Japanese fighters.

They tried madly to radio Vogel, but he was long gone and never answered their repeated calls. They turned and pursued him, but he had switched on his double-reaction late-burners and shot so far ahead of them, catching him proved impossible.

The last they saw of him, he was passing over the island of Taiwan. He and the remaining Japanese fighters were still following the giant flaming airplane.

The twins returned to base and sent out a search and rescue squad. They found Vogel's body floating near the wreckage of his plane close to a jetty off the southern coast of Taiwan.

Both twins became slightly emotional at this point.

"Vogel was a good guy," one finally said. "And a fine pilot. When he died, our group lost more than just one pilot. . . ."

"Yeah, but the story he told after that," the other twin said. "It's really unbelievable."

At that point Y stopped them.

"But I thought you said he died. . . ."

Both men nodded solemnly.

"That's true," one finally said. "But that doesn't mean we haven't talked to him since. . . ."

CHAPTER 12

Y was staggering drunk as they started climbing the huge sand dune.

The night was brilliant with stars. To Y's bleary eyes they seemed to fill the sky from one horizon to another.

This little expedition was taking longer than he thought. He, Zoltan, and Crabb were bringing up the rear; the twins and two of their mercs were leading them up and over the huge dune with the promise that the ocean—and a small shack—would be found on the other side.

Y trusted the AirCats. No names had been exchanged yet—and no real business transacted. But there was something no-nonsense about them, and he admired that.

But what they were going to do now was not something Y looked forward to. Zoltan also looked particularly concerned. He was closest to the psychic realm that enveloped this world. He knew just how weird it could be.

Crabb was a bit more subdued. He was a world-weary veteran, someone who had seen it all—twice. Still, Y could sense a bit of tension coming from him.

They finally topped the dune and, as promised, saw a small shack at the edge of the water about two hundred yards beyond. There was no light inside this hut. No signs of life at all.

But that was the whole point.

They went down the other side of the dune. Y had gulped a few more drinks inside the bar and now their full effect was hitting him. He was beginning to love the feeling of juice running through his veins—even the scotch crap he'd consumed. The stars seemed so fucking bright. And so close! Was it real? Or was it the booze coursing its way through his bloodstream?

He didn't know, and at the moment he didn't care.

They trooped down to the beach. The AirCats were carrying side arms and rifles but didn't seem to be overly concerned about their security.

They made it down the beach to the small hut. One of the twins told two of the Cats to stand watch outside of the door. The pair did not seem unhappy with the assignment.

One of the twins pushed the door open with his foot. The hut was dark within. Y could see the outline of a table and several chairs. It was very cold inside.

"What is this place?" Zoltan asked, his voice stuttering a bit.

"You'll see," was the only reply from the Cats.

The twins walked in cautiously, though Y wasn't sure exactly what they were being so cautious about. Crabb stepped in next, then Zoltan. The psychic was positively shaking now.

Once the small group was inside, the twins kicked the chairs around the table and indicated they should all sit.

"You never know with the V-man," one said. "You never know when he'll show up."

The twins leaned back on rickety chairs at one end of the long bamboo table, while Y, Zoltan, and Crabb sat across from them. Only one chair was unoccupied, the one at the far end. Y was waiting for some guy to come in through the door or the pane-less window, sit down, and start jabbering.

Crabb had the good sense to bring a bottle of brandy

along with them; he took it from his fatigue-pants pocket and using plastic cups stolen from the bar, poured everyone a drink.

Y sipped his brandy like it was the nectar of the gods—it seemed important to him that he maintain his high, that he stay at this level of intoxication until . . . well, until he thought it was time to sober up again. It had been four days since he'd asked for that first drink after seeing the spot in the sea where Japan used to be. He'd been in some form of inebriation—awake or asleep—ever since.

The waves were crashing very loudly outside the hut now. The wind was picking up, too. The sound it made while blowing through the thatched hay-straw roof was almost melodic. Y sipped his drink again. In what key did Nature sing? he wondered drunkenly.

But then, quite suddenly, all noise stopped. The waves ceased crashing, the wind stopped blowing. The hay roof ceased singing.

Y looked up and saw that a man was now sitting in the previously unoccupied chair at the far end of the table. A large chunk of his skull was missing.

Zoltan fainted. He collapsed as soon as he saw this man, slumping first to the table and then off the chair and to the floor completely. No one moved to help him. No one could take their eyes off the man who so suddenly appeared at the end of the table.

"Jeesuz and Mary," Y heard Crabb whisper. "A ghost. . . ."

Y looked over at his friend for a second, saw his face had drained of all color, and then looked back at the man at the end of the table. No brandy could fog this vision. The man was there, but he wasn't. He was solid but Y could see clear through him. At least one quarter of his head was missing—blown away—and parts of a bloody brain mess were visible. Yet he was staring back at Y, with his eyes blinking, and his mouth was moving, though no words came out. His hands wrung themselves nervously on the table in front of him.

He looked . . . *uncomfortable.*

"How . . . how are you, V-man?" one of the twins asked finally. Talking to a ghost would humble just about anyone's words.

"How the hell do you think I am?" the ghost replied bitterly. *"I'm dead."*

The twins shifted uneasily in their seats. One glanced back at Y and made a face that said it all: Just because there were ghosts in this universe, and the living could see them and converse with them, that didn't mean it was necessarily enjoyable to do it. Yet here they were.

The second twin's expression was even more direct. Face hard, brow furrowed, mouth tight. Why are you putting us through this? his eyes asked.

"It's business," Y heard himself say out loud. "Don't you remember?"

The twins stared back at him for a long second and then turned again to the ghost.

"Can you see these guys, V-man?" one asked.

The ghost shrugged and stared at his dirty hands. "I can see everything," he replied simply, coldly.

"You know who these guys are?"

The ghost looked first at Y and then Crabb.

"The little guy is OSS," he said in a mumble that strangely reverberated as a slight echo. "The big guy runs a bar. With music played by black men."

The ghost unconsciously went to push back his hair, but wound up touching the gaping hole in his head.

"The guy on the floor . . . he's a psychic," the ghost murmured, adding, "He has his moments."

"Do you know why these guys are here?"

The ghost shrugged again. Y stared even more intently at him. No, he wasn't breathing.

"The big plane," the ghost replied. "The thing I chased. The thing that got me killed. They want to know about it."

"Why did you chase it?" Y heard himself ask.

The twins looked back harshly at him.

"If . . . if it's OK for me to ask," Y hastily added.

He took a deep gulp of his brandy and felt it burn his throat, his stomach, his intestines and travel as a stream of fire right through his toes and directly back into his brain.

"We'll ask the questions," one of the twins barked at him.

"I followed it," the ghost said, still staring and examining his dirty hands, "because I thought they needed help. I knew it was an American airplane. I'm an American. Or at least I was. I wanted to help out one of our Joes. That's all."

One of the twins leaned a bit closer to the ghost.

"But you were almost out of fuel, V-man," he said, dismissing for a moment that there was anyone else in the room. "Out of ammo, too. It was a crazy thing to do . . ."

The ghost looked up at the twin; his stare was like an acetylene torch. The hut suddenly smelled of something like burning metal.

"You think I don't know that now, General?" he replied harshly. "You think I *like* being like this?"

The other twin went to touch the ghost, in an effort of sympathy and friendship—but stopped short of actually putting his hand right through the apparition. The act caused the ghost to well up and begin to weep.

Y took another huge gulp of his drink. Crabb did the same.

"Gosh, this is going well," Crabb said dryly, under his breath.

Silence descended on the hut once more. Dead silence. The ghost was still weeping, but Y could see no tears.

Finally the ghost looked up at the twins and sadly nodded.

"How can I help you, sirs?" he asked in the best military crispness he could muster.

"These guys . . . ," one twin said with no small bitterness. "They want to know what happened to the big plane."

The ghost looked up at them—first Y, then Crabb. The living stared back.

"Why?" he asked them directly.

Y began to open his mouth—he would tell this . . . this *thing* that they were on a mission. A search and rescue mission. That finding the airplane and learning the fate of the crew was an important thing to know in the opinion of the American government. But before his words came out, he felt Crabb's elbow jab him in the ribs.

"We want to know because the men aboard that plane are our friends," Crabb said suddenly.

The ghost just stared right through them.

"Yes, they are," he said quietly. "I can see that."

"That's why it's important to know what happened to them," Crabb said. "Can you help us?"

The ghost went back to staring at his hands.

"I caught up with them," he revealed, his voice, still echoing. "They still had a swarm of Jap planes buzzing them—but they were fighting back big time. That huge airplane—what a piece of work that was! There must have been a hundred triple fifties on that thing. They were firing and dipping and diving and climbing. If your friend was flying that beast, he must be the best pilot in the world—or any other. I've never seen anything like it."

The ghost stopped talking for a moment. His eyes looked way off to the side. Y heard Zoltan start to stir on the floor near his feet. But he did not make a move to help him. Not at this point. This was too important.

"They were on fire," the ghost went on, measuring each word carefully in that eerie, cold voice. "And some Japs were pouring cannon shells into the place they were burning the worst—so that's when I stepped in. . . ."

He paused. Y thought he could see his throat get thick again.

"I just thought I'd help them out," the ghost went on. "Just helping out some Joes. That's all. And that's how I got killed. While I was firing at these two Japs as they were pouring fire into your friends, one of them poured fire into me. Took out my starboard engine, my main reaction chamber and this chunk from my head. Three seconds. Thirteen cannon shells. That's all it took. My life was over."

"You helped them," Y finally managed to croak out. "Because of you, they got away?"

The ghost just shrugged again.

"I may have."

"They were still airborne, when . . . well, when you—"

"When I was killed?" the ghost asked.

Both Y and Crabb nodded.

He paused again, staring at his hands, pulling on his fingers but not feeling a thing.

"Yeah, they were still flying," he said finally. "And the fire wasn't so bad. And most of the Japs had been shot down or had turned tail. I lost them somewhere over Formosa, I guess. At fifty-five thousand feet."

One of the twins spoke up. "With a wingspan that big, and the speed they were going," he said, "even if their engines went kaput then and there, they could have kept going for miles."

The ghost shook his head. "Their engines didn't quit then," he revealed. "Not all of them anyway. They stayed airborne for a long time after I got splashed."

Zoltan moved again on the floor, but Y kicked him and made him silent again.

"So you know w-where . . . they w-went . . ." Y had begun to stutter. "W-where they went down?"

The ghost paused for a long time and finally nodded.

"Yeah, I do," he said finally.

Y was suddenly very anxious—but he was also happily drunk again.

"Tell us where," he said to the spirit.

The ghost shook his head. "I can't," he said slowly, and barely above a whisper.

One of the twins leaned forward . "Why not V-man," he asked quietly. "Is it against the rules . . . of where you are?"

The ghost just shook his head again.

"No," he said. "I just don't know that name of the place where they finally set down. Some things. . . ." He started to rub his wound again but stopped. "Some things I can't recall. Maybe because I wasn't sure what they were in the first place."

That's when Y reached inside his pants ankle-pocket and pulled out a 2-D map of Asia. He passed it down to Crabb, who pushed it on to the twins. One opened it and placed it in front of the ghost.

The ghost stared at it for a very long time, then he finally rested his hand on a point at the very bottom of the map.

"Here," he said.

Y tried to see the spot where the ghost was pointing, but in the low light it was impossible.

"And what about the guys," the other twin asked. "Did these Joes die in the crash?"

The ghost looked up at him, and a perplexed look came across his ashen face.

"I think so," he said, but his voice was not sounding very certain. Still, Y felt his heart sink.

"All of them?" he asked.

The ghost nodded slowly. "Yes, I think so. . . ."

Crabb leaned forward. "Are you sure?"

The ghost closed his eyes, and Y imagined he was flying somewhere, looking down on some thick jungle, searching.

"I really can't say," he said finally. "But can you imagine anyone surviving the crash of a plane that size that could go that fast?"

It was a question no one else in the room could answer.

So Y pressed him again.

"Are they dead or not?" he asked, the brandy affecting his vocal cords. "Can't you tell?"

The ghost just stared up at him, mouthed the words *"Fuck you,"* and then in the next second, he was gone.

It took a few moments for everyone to realize the ghost had vanished. There was no fading away, no slow dissolve into ethereal mist. One second he was there, the next he was gone.

Y shook his head and felt like he'd been sitting in the little shack for an entire day and night. He definitely felt like he'd lost some time along the way.

He finally stood up, just to make sure he was still functioning, and felt Zoltan grabbing at his leg. The psychic was coming to. Y and Crabb helped him to his feet. The twins were now up and moving, as well.

Y walked over to the end of the table and looked at the map where the ghost had pointed. There was a small burn hole in the paper.

Y picked it up, held it closer to his eyes. He felt his head start to spin. Why was this familiar to him?

"Vietnam?" he whispered, looking at the map again.

"They made it that far?" Crabb asked.

Y did not answer. The twins walked out of the shack and he wanted to get out, too.

They collected Zoltan, dragged him down to the water and fully revived him. By the time Y looked back at the shack, it was dark again. The wind was blowing and the sound of crashing waves had returned.

He looked down at his hands and they were both shaking.

"It must be a bitch to be dead," Crabb was saying as he forced some brandy down Zoltan's throat.

Y could only nod in agreement. That was the lot of ghosts, he thought.

They knew all the secrets of the universe—and still they could not be happy.

CHAPTER 13

The seas were calm the next morning.

The aircraft carrier had spent the night anchored off the southern end of Iwo Jima, its protective ring of tugboats huddled around it as if for warmth. The huge Bro-Bird, still attached by six thick towlines, was riding the waves nearby. Utilizing the tiny squadron of easy-to-fly Bugs, the Unit 167 troopers had flown a continuous air picket around the strange collection of vessels all night, a small, mostly psychological stab at air defense.

Those on board the ships need not have worried.

The AirCats had put out the word that the carrier and its entourage should be left alone. Anyone who plied the skies around the lawless South Pacific would answer to them, should any harm come to the small American fleet. It was a warning even the toughest air thugs in the area heeded.

No one ever wanted to tangle with the AirCats.

It was now 0700 hours. Y was passed out in the carrier's captain's quarters when Zoltan and Crabb walked in.

The psychic shook the OSS man awake as Crabb pushed the button to activate the room's coffee warmer. The coffee was hot before Y finally came to. Three empty brandy bottles next to his bunk told how he'd finally managed to fall asleep after returning to the ship the night before.

But that didn't mean he'd slept peacefully.

He sat up in a start and looked at the two men. Both gave him a mock salute.

" 'Morning skipper," Zoltan said, looking around the sizable cabin. It was adorned with memorabilia from the Japanese Imperial Navy, including a large Rising Sun flag, a small incense candle altar, and a pair of suki swords crossed above the bunk. "Nice digs you have here."

Crabb began pouring coffee. "You'll be happy to know that the crew has already painted over all signs and indications that this was once a Japanese ship—on the outside anyway," he said, handing a cup of steaming coffee to Zoltan. "All of the Unit 167 guys are over here now, as well as a dozen technicians Bro culled from his crew. Between them, it shouldn't be too hard keeping all the essential stuff running on board. Electrical generators, intercoms, water-pressure systems, and so on."

But Y wasn't listening. He was holding his head in his hands.

"Did it happen?" he asked woefully, wiping the drool from his lips. "Did we really talk to a gh—"

Zoltan reached over and put his hand across Y's slimy mouth.

"Don't say it," he warned Y. "If you do, he might show up here on ship. Then we'll never get rid of him."

"And then you'll have to make the voyage unconscious," Crabb needled Zoltan as he poured out a cup of coffee for Y.

Zoltan looked pained at the comment.

"Believe me, " he said. "We'll have enough things to worry about without having a haunting onboard."

Y took the first few tentative sips of his coffee. Through the impending hangover, he tried to remember the long discussion they had had the night before, which was really just a few hours ago. What did they talk about?

Slowly it began coming back to him.

They were sailing to Vietnam. They would tow the carrier with the airplane and push it with the tugs, and if the seas were okay and the weather cooperated, they could make the Gulf of Tonkin within three or four days.

Once there, they would find the exact area indicated by Vogel the ghost, and they would probably find the bodies of Hunter and the others.

Then they could all go home.

And finally put their own ghosts to rest.

"What's the matter?" Crabb was asking Y, barging in on his thoughts. "Not enough sugar?"

Y shook himself out of his stupor.

What else happened the night before? They landed back on the carrier around midnight. They held the planning mission. They agreed to sail to Vietnam. But what about air cover?

"The AirCats will be coming aboard in about thirty minutes," Zoltan was saying, checking his watch. "Will you be watching their arrival from the deck or the bridge?"

Y just stared back up at him.

"You're asking that as if I'm the captain this tub," he said.

Zoltan and Crabb looked back at him quizzically.

"Well, you are," Crabb said finally. "Don't you remember? Last night. You told us so, yourself. And we all agreed. We drank to it, in fact."

Y put his hand to his forehead and gave it a whack, and strangely, it seemed to jog something deep inside. A second later a thought bubble percolated up from somewhere deep in his cranium.

Yes, they *had* decided that he would be the captain of the carrier, just as Bro would remain commander of the huge towing seaplane, and the Irishmen in the tugs would take orders from him. But that wasn't what Y was confused about.

What was frightening him was the nearly indescribable feeling way, *way* in the back of his head.

Like all of this had happened to him before.

Him? The captain of an aircraft carrier? One that was being moved by tugboats?

This didn't make any sense. It was like his reoccurring dream, but with much more detail. And no matter how he tried, he could not push the disturbing notion from his mind.

"So?" Crabb asked him.

Y looked up at him again. "So, what?"

"So where are you going to watch the Cats come in?" he repeated. "The bridge or the deck?"

Y shook his head again. "The AirCats?"

Zoltan got down on one knee and looked deep into Y's very bleary eyes.

"You all right?" he asked him sincerely. "Besides being hungover, I mean?"

Y just shook his head. "I . . . I don't know."

Zoltan refilled his coffee cup.

"The Cats are coming aboard, they're going to 'Nam with us, to provide air cover," he said. "You made the deal with them last night. They're working for next to nothing. It was a deal we couldn't pass up."

Y whacked his head again—and sure enough another thought bubbled up. Yes, he *did* recall the deal. The AirCats were itching for action and looking to get away from Iwo for a while. Tagging along on this bizarre expedition seemed to be just the thing for them. Plus they had a rooting interest now in finding out what happened to the B-2000's crew. After all, that's what their close friend Vogel was doing when he was killed. Now they were going to find out for him. It was like fulfilling a comrade's last request.

"Yes, I remember now," Y said. "And I guess I'll watch it from the bridge."

"The deck is better," Zoltan said.

"OK, the flight deck then," Y said, slurping his coffee with a bit of agitation.

Zoltan and Crabb took the hint.

"OK, see you in thirty?" Crabb asked him as they opened the door to leave. "Will that give you enough time to finish?"

Y looked up at them. They were both smiling at him ear to ear. But why?

"Finish?" he asked them. "Finish what? My coffee?"

He drained the cup and put it down on the table.

Both men laughed at this. "Yeah, your coffee," Zoltan said.

"Good one," Crabb said, turning out the cabin light.

Then they both left, leaving Y in the dark, sitting on the edge of his bunk, more confused than ever.

That's when he felt the hand on his shoulder . . . .

Y froze. His body turned to ice. He could not hear anything. No wind, no sea, no sounds of breath . . . .

He shot off the bed and hurled himself across the cabin. He began desperately searching for the light switch, his body shaking from head to toe.

The lights finally came on and he saw a form moving on the bunk. In his panic he shut the light off again and then struggled to turn it back on. He surely didn't want to be alone in the room with a ghost, and with the lights off.

The lights came back on, and one scary moment later, Y realized this was not a ghost he was looking at.

Rather, it was an angel . . .

An earthly one.

Beautiful hair. Beautiful face. Beautiful naked breasts.

Her name was Emma.

Y's head began spinning again.

"How? What?" he heard himself babbling.

She just smiled back at him. "You didn't forget everything, did you?" she asked him coyly.

Y couldn't take his eyes away from her. His alcohol intake was really starting to bother him.

"No," he finally blurted out. "I didn't."

Then he crawled back in bed with her.

"Not everything," he lied.

CHAPTER 14

The AirCats unit consisted of three squadrons of twelve airplanes apiece.

Thirty of the three dozen aircraft were literally F-38G2 "Lightning AirCats." The big twin-engine, twin-tail jet fighter looked both antique and futuristic. Straight-winged but incredibly agile, oversized but astonishingly fast, it carried no less than a dozen cannons on its wings and nose, and boasted the ability to lug five thousand pounds of ordnance in its small bomb bay.

The other six planes flown by the unit were known as B-6J3 "HellJets." Technically this odd airplane was a medium bomber. It was three times the size of an AirCat and in some ways resembled the famous Mitchell B-25 bomber of another place. But instead of two propellers, the HellJet had four huge double-reaction engines slung beneath its wings. Each plane carried a crew of thirteen, had no less than nine gun turrets on its body, belly, nose, and tail, and could carry many pounds of bombs within its large internal bomb bay.

The HellJet was the size of a small airliner, but oddly, one of its fortes was the long-lost art of dive-bombing. To be on the receiving end of a HellJet's dive-bombing run was indeed a hellish experience—and usually, the last for the victim. In other places a dive-bomber's objective was to get just one bomb on a target. The way to do this was simple: find the target, go into a dive, release your bomb, pull up, and let gravity do the rest. If you were good, the bomb would more or less fall straight down and nail your objective.

The HellJet followed this same tactic, but on a much larger scale. Under the right conditions the stocky bomber was capable of carrying up to thirty thousand pounds of bombs, due mostly to its solid construction and its enormous double-reaction power plants. While the airplane could carry and drop this ordnance in the standard way—arrive near target, sight it, drop the load, and cross your fingers—the plane's designers had built in an additional devilish element, which allowed the HellJet a second way to bomb something or someone into oblivion. The designers had worked a long trail of edge flaps into the HellJet's wings. When deployed, they gave the huge airplane a degree of maneuverability while in a perilous dive—a plunge that usually started somewhere above 25,000 feet and reached high supersonic speeds on the way down. After this mind-bending drop, and once the bombs were let go, these edges were lifted slightly, giving the airplane the ability to pull out of what would normally be a fatal dive, hopefully in enough time to escape the blast effects of fifteen tons of high explosives hitting in a very concentrated area.

This was heart-stopping, stomach-churning stuff, but the AirCat mercenary group had never been accused of being shy about tactics or strategies. Just the fact that the air group had six of these airplanes, and the will to use them, was usually enough to make any potential opponent think twice about running up against them.

* * *

So it was with great anticipation that those gathered on the flight deck of the aircraft carrier awaited the air merc unit to come aboard.

Zoltan and Crabb were there, as were most of the Unit 167 guys, tug crew members, and even some hookers. In fact, just about everyone connected with the mission had come out to see the unusual air unit's arrival—except Y, who had fallen back to sleep.

The scheduled time for the AirCats to come aboard was 0900 hours, and sure enough, at the stroke of nine bells, the sullen roar of an approaching aircraft could be heard.

It was the lead/scout AirCat, a slightly larger version of the fighter bomber. The plane came out of the morning clouds, dropping very fast, heading for the end of the stationary carrier. The AirCat was really a huge airplane and the carrier was actually a smallish air platform. But the Cats were known for landing and taking off in tight places. So just as this first airplane went into its final approach at high speed, there was a blinding explosion. To the astonishment of all on deck, the sky just below the falling airplane was suddenly full of yellow fire.

Those watching had to shield their eyes, so bright was this flash. But once the initial shock wore off, it became apparent that the airplane was not in trouble. This was, in fact, the standard procedure for AirCats landing in a confined area. The flash came as a result of six rocket bottles that had been lowered from underneath the AirCat scout plane's wings.

The rockets served as a massive and sudden air brake, counteracting the AirCat's forward speed and giving the big fighter bomber just enough of a kick in the ass to slow it down to a reasonable landing speed. The airplane hit the carrier deck a second later, bounced once, then came down hard again. At this point four more, small but brilliant, explosions went off—the rocket bottles were firing again, this time straight forward, serving as a ground brake for the aircraft. By the time the smoke cleared from these flashes, the bouncing aircraft had come to a stop, not far from where the deck gang had gathered. In all, the huge fighter needed but 175 yards in which to land safely. With the scream of its engines and the flash of its rocket bottles, it was made for a very impressive entrance.

Serving as the makeshift deck crew, the Unit 167 members ran out to push the expended scout plane out of the way. It was a good thing they hustled, because sure enough, another Cat was coming in right on its tail. And there was another one behind that. And another behind that.

It went on like this for the next half hour. The thirty-six airplanes touched down at forty-five-second intervals, and it was all the deck crew could do to push each one out of the way before the next one banged in. It was a hectic operation but in the end, a successful one. The huge HellJets came in last. Landing in the same manner as the smaller brothers, there was just enough room left on the deck for the last bomber to come down.

Then all was quiet again.

Per Y's previously issued order, as soon as the last AirCat was aboard and secured, word was radioed ahead to the huge Bro-Bird. Within seconds the big seaplane's engines began turning and its towlines became taut.

Then the order went out to the accompanying tugboats. Those with lines began moving forward, flanking the monstrous seaplane. Those on the ass end nuzzled their noses up against the carrier's rear. Slowly but surely, the whole conglomeration began to move.

Awake now, and somewhat coherent, Y watched this operation from the bridge. Their course was due south. In front of him was the map with the burned hole put there by Vogel the ghost. Y shivered every time he looked at it, but he knew that another map just wouldn't do. Not that he felt this map was lucky or blessed in any way. Rather, he thought it would be very *un*lucky to get rid of it.

So here it was.

* * *

They were under way only twenty minutes before there was a knock on the bridge door.

Y called out to come in, and the twin commanders of the AirCats stepped through the door.

They surprised Y by saluting him. He returned it quickly, then shook hands with both men, though a bit nervously.

After receiving a brief report stating that all of their airplanes had come aboard safely and that they were looking forward to the journey, Y told the pair to sit down. They did, taking the navigator's and engineer's chairs, respectively.

Y studied them for a moment. In the daylight it was his first chance to get a good look at their mugs. Both men were in their early fifties, and their faces were full of previously unseen character. The lines and wrinkles on their cheeks and brows told of many air battles fought and won. The wrinkles around their mouths told of many glasses of liquor drunk and laughs that resulted. Their eyes also had a slight but identical twinkle to them.

"I just realized we've never been properly introduced," Y told them. "I'm sure you know I work for the OSS, but we can dispense with formalities out here. My friends call me Yaz."

"Jones," the first pilot said, holding out his hand. "Seth Jones. This is my brother, Dave."

Once again Y shook hands with both of them, but his head was spinning so fast now, he barely knew what he was doing.

These two guys—these two brothers. Both were generals. Both were pilots. Like everything else around him lately, they seemed so damned familiar to him.

Yet Y was sure he'd never met them before.

At least, not in this lifetime.

CHAPTER 15

West Falkland Island

It was a long ride down.

The elevator door was actually behind a false panel on the other side of a cupboard in the kitchen of the small farmhouse. The lift itself was very cramped, and there was no light inside. Just a dull red glow from the elevator controls, and the slow methodical clicking as the elevator passed down through sixteen separate levels, descending slowly into the middle of the earth.

The two men did not speak on the long journey down. The man who lived in the farmhouse was still in a slight case of shock. He had come so close to losing his wife of many years that he was still shaking from head to toe. In fact, he believed now that she had actually passed away only to be brought back to life. Snatched somehow from whoever calls the living to the other side. Snatched back by the man now standing beside him in this dark lift.

Who was he?

That was the question that had been going through the

Man's mind ever since the miraculous incident in the living room the day before.

A man washes up on a beach during a titanic storm, saving the lives of dozens of children in the process—and yet he can barely remember his name? The Man's wife drops dead on their living room floor, and this same character lays hands on her and steals her back from death itself?

The Man had seen many things since coming to this world. Since dropping in himself. Strange wars. Strange potions. Strange theories proved. Fear conquered in the strangest of ways. He knew roads that no other man knew. He knew this place was just one of trillions, some almost identical to this one.

But never, not in his wildest dreams or his most fantastic waking moment, had he seen what had happened on his living room floor the day before—made even more astonishing that it was his wife who had been pulled back from the grave.

All by this man who could barely remember his name.

That's why he was taking him down to the Sixteenth Level.

There were more than one hundred people working in this vast underground facility—this holiest place of secrets. Only the most trusted, the most brilliant, were allowed to visit the Sixteenth Level.

Even fewer were allowed to work there. And no one but the Man himself was allowed to enter the chamber located at the far end of the place. This was not a self-imposed rule—it was actually an ethereal request, given to the Man by the spirit who had first showed him the hole in the sky many years ago.

What would happen if more than one person knew?

That was another question the Man had pondered ever since he and his wife suddenly found themselves flying their Piper Cub in a sky above a place that was not the same place from which they had taken off.

That's why the ghost had showed him the hole in the

sky—*that* was the big secret. Only one person could know its location, its implications, and that person was now the Man, and it was he who would carry the weight of many worlds on his shoulders until . . . well, until he died. Then it would be up to him to come back to haunt someone of his choosing and pass the mantle onto them.

Or at least that's how he'd always felt, and that's how he'd vowed it to be, in keeping with the spirit's bargain.

Until yesterday.

Now there was another voice inside his head. Heard rarely since he and his wife landed here in this other universe, but relied on many times back in his former place, this other voice was telling him that this guy Viktor, this wayward seaman with the power to raise the dead, should be made aware of the hole in the sky.

It was a big decision, and the Man supposed he would pay the penalty for making it some day.

That is, if the original ghost ever found him again.

The lift finally reached the bottom level, and the door opened very slowly.

Viktor was visibly nervous. He'd said nothing on the way down, having no idea what waited for him so deep inside the earth. When the door opened, would he see fire and the burning souls of eternity? He didn't know.

But now they were here, and the Man brought him past the mystified British guards, down a very long dark corridor to a huge metal door that looked like something from a bad horror movie.

The man punched in some kind of code and the door opened with the appropriate *whoosh!*

Beyond was a blue-hued chamber, which again looked like something from a movie set. All pipes and wires, it was a madman's dream of a laboratory—yet there seemed to be a queer sensibility to it all. In the faint light several other scientist types could be seen working in cubbyholes, or at messy desks, or within thickly glassed rooms.

A few of these people looked up, and when they saw the Man, they nodded in a reverential way. The Man simply nodded back. He directed Viktor past many electrical things, until they reached another massive door.

Another code, another twist of the lock, and now they were inside a very small vestibule and facing . . . yet another door.

They both stepped inside, and the Man locked them in.

Viktor looked around the small metal chamber and saw some strange things. There were straps fastened securely to the sides of the walls. Why would they be here? he thought. What could their purpose be? There was also an ordinary bucket filled to the brim with ordinary-looking rocks.

Rocks? Why?

But even odder, in one corner of the vault was a box containing typical military-issue parachutes.

Parachutes?

"You'll find out in a moment," the Man told Viktor, reading his mind.

Then, without another word, he strapped Viktor into one of the harnesses and then did the same to himself. With a little flourish, he punched another code into the lock of this third door. The lock spun and clicked and then sprang open.

The next thing Viktor knew, he was looking out at the clear blue sky.

He was stunned. His mouth fell open. His eyes went wide. He felt a strange jolt of something go right through him.

"How . . . how can this be?" he finally was able to mumble.

The Man did not answer. He simply pointed down. And through the clouds that were sweeping by, Viktor could clearly see the ocean about a mile beneath them. It looked deep blue yet warm and inviting. A cruise liner was passing by. Viktor could see people on the deck of this ship, swimming in the pool, sunbathing, even shooting golf balls off the stern.

He was simply astonished. It was unbelievable. This was not a hallucination, for he could feel the cold mist of the clouds wetting his face and lips. And the wind was blowing at such a clip, his harness was actually preventing him from being sucked down into the hole.

"How . . . ?" was all he was able to blurt out again.

The Man just shook his head. "We don't know," he said, staring down at the liner, which was now just passing out of their visual range.

"Is it a wormhole? A small one?" the Man asked rhetorically. "Some kind of portal created by a physics we don't know anything about? Or simply a hole in the sky? Take your pick."

He allowed a short silence to pass between them. More clouds flowed into the vault. Viktor found himself suddenly soaked from head to toe.

"All we know is what we are looking at, this place is Earth, but in a different . . . what? Dimension? Universe? Astral plane?" the Man went on. "We don't even know what to call it. It seems impossible. We are sixteen hundred feet inside a mountain on West Falkland Island, yet we are looking down on a section of the Atlantic approximately fifty miles north of Bermuda. How can you explain such a thing? How can anyone's mind even contemplate such a place exists? Yet, here it is."

Viktor simply couldn't speak. For a long moment he wished he was back on his ship—the huge liner that had been moved by thousands of rowers. The place where he took care of the children on board. The vessel that had been his home for more than a year. Things were so much simpler back then.

"Why . . . why did you bring me here?" he finally asked, his eyes glued to the absolutely impossible scene below him.

The Man just shook his head.

"I'm not really sure myself," he began haltingly. "But

I know—from what you've told me about your amnesia, about your past and also what you did . . . well, with my wife yesterday. I know from these things that you are special. You are a very special individual. And if I might say, almost *too* special for this world. As a scientist I should have to try to find an explanation for you. And as someone once said, once all the untruths are swept away, whatever remains, however ridiculous, must be the real truth. You are special, this place is special—that's why I brought you here."

Viktor felt a nudge on his elbow; the Man was handing him something. Viktor looked down and felt his eyes go even wider.

It was a parachute . . . .

"I believe you belong back there," the Man was saying. "It's the only explanation I can come up with. As a scientist, I know I should keep you here, study you, dissect you like a bug—and maybe find out just what this thing is before us."

The Man took a deep breath. "But I can't do that now," he continued. "Not after what you did yesterday. I have to pay you back for that. For bringing her back to me. The only way I can think of to do that, is to give you this opportunity. . . ."

He put the parachute into Viktor's shaking hands.

"You can put that thing on, wait for another ship to pass, and jump," the Man explained simply. "If you do, I believe you will wind up where you came from. I also believe you will be your former self—whoever that might have been. After all, you seem to recall being picked up in this part of the Atlantic last year. Obviously, with this portal looking down on that same section of ocean, that indicates you *belong* . . . back there. . . ."

Another very long pause.

"That is the only thing I can offer you for what you did for me yesterday," the Man finally concluded. "In my opinion—and maybe a few others if given the facts, I believe you are an angel. And you must be compensated. So I can give you your life back. Your old life . . ."

Viktor just stared back at him. His mouth was still open, his eyes still the size of golf balls. He was silent for a very long time.

"But . . . but," he finally began stuttering. "S-supposing I was n-not an angel . . . back there?"

The Man's brow furrowed at the comment. Even with all his knowledge, it was something that had not occurred to him before.

"It might be the chance you have to take," he finally replied.

Viktor began shaking his head slowly from side to side.

"No," he said. "No, this is not the time to do it."

He handed the parachute back to the Man.

"It isn't?" the Man asked. "When is the right time?"

Viktor stared at a big black cloud passing by the Hole.

"I seem to recall I fell into this world with two others," he began slowly. "I know one is dead. That means one remains. This person, he would know who I was Back There."

"What are you proposing?" the Man wondered.

Viktor just shook his head. "I'm not sure," he said. "But maybe . . . well, maybe I should find this guy."

Another very long pause.

"And when I do, maybe he and I should jump through this hole together. . . ."

PART TWO

CHAPTER 16

The bombardment had been going on for twenty-six days.

Every minute of every hour, twenty-four hours a day, more than a dozen high-explosive mortar shells rained down on the three-square-mile area known in another place as Khe Sanh, but in this world as Long Bat. That was more than 720 shells an hour, more than seventeen thousand explosions a day—for nearly three weeks.

No wonder the place looked like a part of the moon.

It was actually worse at night. That's when the enemy in the hills launched dozens of star flares, lighting up the battered valley even brighter than the harsh daytime.

When the siege began, the small force of surrounded mercenaries had numbered 1,202. Now less than seven hundred remained, and that was only because the earth was relatively soft in this awful place, allowing the doomed soldiers to dig their trenches, their foxholes, and eventually their graves very deep.

But they were trapped. There was no passage in and out of the valley that was not covered by the enemy in the hills. The force surrounding the mercs was estimated to be more than five thousand, and they were armed with not only high-powered mortars but also howitzer-style artillery, ultralong-range flame throwers, and more than two dozen mega-tanks.

The only mystery about the siege at Long Bat was why the enemy in the hills just didn't launch a ground attack and get it over with . . . .

"What are those guys doing there anyway?"

It was midnight. The small combat-planning room on the aircraft carrier seemed particularly cramped. There were thirteen people sitting around a huge TV monitor. Y was there, as was Zoltan, Crabb, Bro, and the Jones boys. Several of Emma's friends were also in attendance, keeping the men fresh with beer or coffee and generally sitting around, looking both beautiful and bored.

They were all watching a long-range video relay of the sad battle at Long Bat. The footage had been shot earlier in the day via a seven-aircraft linkup, which stretched for more than five hundred miles.

It was the first recon target the Jones boys had selected for examination in Vietnam. It was at that exact spot on the map that the ghost named Vogel had burned his hole.

The footage seemed unreal. This was not really a battle at all—that was soon apparent. It looked at first like the valley was actually a target range, a place for soldiers to drill in the art of lobbing antipersonnel artillery. Surely no one was on the receiving end of such a systematically overwhelming bombardment. But then, here and there, the TV cameras caught evidence of return fire. Long but scattered lines of purple and red tracer fire emanated from the center of this moonscape. This fire was symbolic, if anything—last bullets in a long ammo belt of defiance that was quickly coming to an end.

And who were those guys caught in the middle of the massive nonstop barrage?

"They might be what's left of an infantry outfit called the JF Group," Seth Jones said after studying the broadcast for a few minutes. "They were lost in Indochina about two months ago—went down there to do some jungle-fighting job. Some rinky-dink thing and never came back."

Dave Jones agreed with his brother. "I can't recall exactly," he said. "But I remember talking to some airlift guys back at the Pit who said they'd dropped supplies to a jungle-fighting unit and that they were in a hole in 'Nam getting their asses shot to pieces. Looks like JFG got caught out in the open, and that whoever controls those hills are playing with them—like a cat with a rat."

Y sipped his brandy and pushed a button that gave them a fuzzy yet close-up view of the battlefield.

"Well, they're not having a good day, that's for sure," he said. "But does this really affect us?"

The Jones boys just shrugged in unison.

"It's where the V-man made his mark on the map," Dave Jones said.

"So that's where you want to go, right?" Seth Jones added.

Y just shrugged. "Well, I don't know, I'm hardly an expert," he said. "I mean how accurate is the burning finger of a ghost?"

"*Very* accurate in this case," Zoltan suddenly piped up.

They all turned toward the psychic. There was some eye rolling in the process.

"I'm getting a very heavy vibe from this," he was saying, reaching out and actually touching the TV screen. "Something we are seeking is there . . . or may have been there."

The Jones boys joined Crabb and Y in a staring contest with the ceiling.

" '*Is*' there?" Y asked. "Or '*was*' there? It's a big difference . . . ."

"Like the difference between getting involved in that mess, or moving on," Crabb said.

Zoltan just shook his head. "I can't tell," he admitted after a few moments. "Something heavy *was* there. And might still be. The vibe remains. But what it is . . . I just can't tell."

"Well, let's look at this logically," Seth Jones said, nodding toward Zoltan. "If that's not *verboten?*"

Zoltan nodded back. "By all means. . . ."

The Jones brother set the broadcast to slow frame—essentially freezing it.

"We are looking for the biggest muthafucker of a jet bomber ever made, correct?"

Those assembled nodded. Y sipped his brandy again and wondered what Emma would be wearing once he got back to his cabin.

"Well?" Seth Jones said. "Anyone see a plane anywhere in that picture?"

The unanimous answer was no—what they were seeing was a devastated valley with thickly jungled hills surrounding it. There was not an iota of evidence that the huge bomber had been there, had crashed there, or had even flown over the place. There was a runway in the middle of the valley, and it was fairly long. But it was also horribly cratered.

However, there was another geological formation nearby. It was a huge mountain. And that's where Zoltan was now concentrating.

"Inside there . . . ," he said. "Something we want is inside that mountain."

They all turned back to the screen. Y pushed a button and now they were looking at a close-up of the mountain. It *was* big—and if there was a cave inside, there was an outside possibility that the huge bomber could have fit inside. But this seemed as unlikely as the bizarre battle that was going on nearby.

But bizarre was the name of this story. Plus those crammed into the small combat-planning center had before them two supernatural clues: the hole in the map and Zoltan's wobbling brain. Both pointed to this little bloody smudge called Long Bat.

One Jones boy just looked at the other, then they turned to Y, who was refilling his brandy glass and dreaming of Emma. Had he been more sober, he would have been dazed by the fact of how talk of going into a distant valley like Long Bat, and helping out a surrounded unit of hapless mercenaries, seemed so familiar to him.

But he was not sober.

"How close are we to Tonkin?" Seth Jones asked him.

Y scrambled to push the right buttons on his navigation screen in order to project the correct image of their progress at sea.

"If I'm reading this correctly," he said, hoping indeed that he was, "I see us in the Gulf about six and a half hours from right now. About oh-seven-hundred hours."

The twins got up, straightened out their flight suits in an identical manner, and put on their flight caps.

"OK," Dave said. "We'll leave at oh-five-hundred. . . ."

CHAPTER 17

There were so many high-explosive mortar shells landing on the valley of Long Bat this morning, the combination of the flames and fumes was being sucked up into a convex of winds that created a huge mushroom-shaped cloud.

The besieged mercenaries had dug deeper this dawn than any of the previous twenty-five; it seemed the shells being used by the unseen enemy in the hills were packing more of an explosive wallop on this nightmarish morning. Every time a shell landed lately, it seemed to shake the ground with more terror; the flame and flash from each explosion seemed brighter, and the resulting craters seemed deeper.

Forty-five of the mercs had died during the night—the highest one-day toll since the first week of the nearly month-long siege. There were only 623 mercs left now. At this rate, they would all be gone in less than two weeks.

It was strange, then, when even above the sound of shells crashing every few seconds, the embattled mercs heard yet another sound. It was a high-pitched, slightly mechanical whine that was not as distinct as the double-reaction jet engines of the day.

Those mercs who dared, crawled out of their rat holes for a few seconds, and ducking the blizzard of shrapnel, looked skyward in search of what was making the odd sound.

Then a few saw it. It was a small aircraft flying very high above the desolated cratered valley. It was gray and green and looked like a gigantic bug . . . .

There was a headquarters of sorts for the mercs' position. It was a command post made of sandbags and concrete chunks and old shattered timber, dug twenty feet into the battered bloodstained earth. Inside was the CO of the merc brigade, a Frenchman named Jean Zouvette LaFeet.

He was beside his bunk, on his knees, praying—a position he could be found in up to twenty-three hours a day—when two merc messengers toppled into the command bunker.

"Sir," one cried. "A development of which you should be aware."

LaFeet turned and smiled at them. He was quite mad by this time—and had spent the last few hours or so believing that he was the only one left at Long Bat and that the unseen enemy in the hills would soon attack, and all five thousand of them would take turns bayoneting his dying but not yet dead body.

How long would it take for him to die in such a horrible manner? One hour? Two? Ten?

It was things of this nature that LaFeet prayed constantly to avoid.

Now he looked up at the two mercs, and the smile faded from his face. If there was only three of them here, that meant it would take three times *longer* for the enemy in the hills to finally do their savage work on them.

LaFeet then planned to ask the two men to shoot each other, so he would be the last one here and then the bayoneting he was expecting would take only the three or four hours he'd prayed for.

But the looks of their faces stopped the words from coming out of LaFeet's mouth. These two men. Their eyes appeared a little less vacant. And there was, dare he say it, something more than hopelessness etched in the creases of their dirty brows.

"A development?" LaFeet asked them, rising from his knees for the first time since early the previous evening. "What kind of development?"

"There is an aircraft overflying our position," one reported. "It is hovering actually. It's been there for quite a while."

It took a few moments for this news to sink into LaFeet's addled brain. "What kind of aircraft?" he asked.

"It appears to be a jetcopter," the other merc said. "What some people call Bugs."

LaFeet stretched his creaky legs—his pants had holes right where his knees were.

"Does it belong to the enemy?" he asked.

The two mercs shrugged. "We don't know," one finally replied. "But that might be unlikely. The enemy has never displayed any sort of air assets before."

LaFeet nodded—this was true.

"It seems to be waiting for something," the other merc said. "Perhaps a signal from us that it is allowed to land."

LaFeet felt his eyes open a bit wider.

"You mean a supply drop?" he asked. "I thought that . . ."

The two mercs were shaking their heads vigorously.

"No, sir," one said forcefully. "This is not a supply plane. They might want something else."

LaFeet stared at the holes in his knees for a second. What else had he been praying for? He couldn't recall.

"Well, if that's the case . . . ," he started to mumble.

But the two soldiers didn't even wait for the end of his sentence. They were quickly scrambling out of the bunker, running along the deep trench to the remains of what was once the unit's supply bunker. Here they found the last electrical torch in the unit's possession. They turned it on and looked skyward again and were heartened to see the strange aircraft still hovering about five thousand feet above their position.

The two mercs began flashing the beacon madly. It took awhile, but then finally they saw the strange green flying machine start to descend into the nonstop mortar barrage.

Ten minutes later the Jones boys were being escorted into LaFeet's command bunker.

The AirCat commanders had seen a lot of combat sites in their time, but nothing compared to the situation at Long Bat.

The scramble-in through the trenches after their hair-raising yet successful landing was graphic enough: Destroyed equipment. Caved-in gun positions. Dozens of skeletons, some picked clean by the myriad of insects infesting the valley, still at their positions, their weapons still raised. Warriors in a ghost war, waiting for that one last charge.

If anything, LaFeet's place was even more depressing. It, too, was overflowing with insects; the walls were moving with them—patiently waiting to consume the bunker's last occupant.

The Jones boys snapped to attention and saluted LaFeet, even though they outranked him. LaFeet returned the salute as crisply as possible. Then he asked the two men to sit down.

The rain of mortar shells outside was frequent; the noise blurred into one long, loud drone. LaFeet pulled his chair close to the two men. He had to yell to be heard.

"What brings you here?" he asked them.

"We are here to save you," Seth Jones replied.

"Save us?" LaFeet asked. "From what? We are holding our position here quite well."

Both men contemplated LaFeet for a moment—they

didn't have time to go into any psychotherapy at the moment.

"OK, we are here to assist you in your current situation," Dave Jones told him. "How can we best do that?"

LaFeet's face brightened considerably.

"Well, I have a theory on how we can defeat these savages in the hills," he began.

"Let's hear it," Seth Jones said.

LaFeet looked off in the distance for a moment, collecting whatever thoughts he had left in his head.

"Well, I think what we should do is fly three hundred miles to the north," LaFeet said.

The Jones boys just stared at each other. "What?"

"And bomb the Bank of Hanoi," LaFeet replied.

The Jones boys were baffled.

"You see," LaFeet went on, "I believe that if we could just bomb the place where the money is held, from which these soldiers in the hills draw their pay, then their command structure will go bankrupt. Then it will trickle down the ranks until these bastards realize they're not getting any money and then they'll all go away and we can leave here with some dignity. . . ."

The Jones boys had no time for this.

They got up, and Dave put a heavy hand on LaFeet's shoulder.

"Look, pops," he began. "We ain't got time for this. Now we're going to run an air strike on this place. You dig? So get your men down deeper than they've ever been before and then just stay the hell out of the way until you hear from us again . . . OK?"

With that, they left.

The monsoon moved in over Long Bat early that afternoon.

The thunder seemed louder, the lightning more brilliant, and the rains more torrential.

It was a rare day when the firing from the hills stopped

just because of a rainstorm. But that's what happened this day.

Actually, the mortar barrage continued throughout most of the downpour—it was only after it appeared that the skies were clearing, that a halt came in the bombing.

Those mercs still alive peeked out of their trenches and rat holes and looked about. Why had the mortars stopped? Was this the long-anticipated ground attack they'd been dreading?

They peered into the hills and saw something very strange—there were muzzle flashes popping up here and there. But they were not pointing toward the embattled merc positions. Instead, they were pointing straight up into the air.

And then the other sound came . . . .

To the men in the trenches, it was a low droning at first—the sound of thunder, evened out and higher in pitch. It turned mechanical as quickly as the wind shifted direction. And now the last of the monsoon clouds were blown away.

And that's when they saw it. Way, way up. At around 25,000 feet at least.

But coming down very quickly.

"What was I thinking?"

That was the question going through Y's mind for at least the millionth time.

He was strapped into the reserve bombardier's seat of the aptly named HellJet dive-bomber. There were six separate belts holding him in place. The huge jet was at the moment pointing absolutely nosedown. The ground was rushing up at him in a blur of green and yellow. The green from the jungle, the yellow from the small storm of antiaircraft fire they would soon enter.

Y was smiling—it was not from happiness, though. He estimated in his extremely anxious brain that he was feeling as many as eight g's in this plunge. The airplane itself was rattling like a bucket of bolts. The pilots were grim, determined—it was obvious they had done this type of thing many times before.

In the bomb bay were no less than thirty thousand pounds of VHE/S—very high explosive/shrapnel. These killers were, as their name implied, a double whammy of high-explosive gasoline jelly in which thousands of tiny, jagged stainless-steel shards were suspended. When a VHE/S bomb exploded, the flame would wash over an area the size of a football field. Then the bits of metal were dispersed over an area ten times that size. In other words, anyone or anything within a half mile of one bomb blast was either incinerated or perforated. Ghosts who had died this way reported the preferred way to go was by flame . . . .

There were now thirty of these bombs in the belly of the diving HellJet.

They were passing through twenty-thousand feet at the moment. Their airspeed was an astounding 760 knots—way past the speed of sound and indeed, the terrain all around Long Bat was literally shuddering with repeated sonic booms.

Y knew actually their airspeed and the altitude because his eyes were fixed on the auxiliary bombardier's control panels, where the devilish numbers were clicking off in maddening precision. The faster they fell, the higher their airspeed. Y's grin only increased. He believed his bones were beginning to crack.

What was he thinking when he agreed to come on this most insane bombing run?

He wasn't sure. In fact, the only thing he was sure of at this point was that he needed a drink.

Very badly . . .

To the mercs in the trenches—those who dared to look out of their hiding spots—the sight of the huge dive-bomber coming out of the retreating monsoon clouds seemed like a nightmare.

The HellJet was five times the size of a Mitchell B-25 bomber; its four jets screamed like banshees. It was dropping so fast there was a massive vapor trail following it down. Indeed, not knowing the intricacies of heavy dive-bombing techniques, the mercs were certain that this massive bomber was crashing. The only good part of this impending disaster was that it appeared the airplane was going to impact on the hills to the east, and not on the moonlike plain of Long Bat itself.

But then, just as the airplane passed through four thousand feet, huge extra flaps were seen rising from the trailing edge of its long extended wings. At this point the airplane seemed to come to a stop in midair. In the next microsecond, its bomb-bay doors opened. A second later thirty very black needle-nose bombs began falling out of the airplane's belly. Another second passed, and the engines began screaming in an even higher pitch. The air itself began shuddering. The last sonic boom was deafening. The vapor trail caught the airplane, obscuring it for a few seconds, causing the mercs to lose sight of it for a few moments. When the fog cleared, they were amazed to see the airplane had somehow leveled off, and with a massive jolt of double-reaction power, was leaving the area at high speed toward the west.

The bombs hit three seconds later. They impacted on the side of the largest eastern hill, right on a spot that the mercs knew held a concentration of the mortar batteries. It was very strange because the witnesses thought they were imagining things. One second the hill was there. The next, it was gone. There was nothing left but a smoking hole with a crown of flames spreading out from it, like ripples caused by a rock dropped into a pond.

The storm of shrapnel came next. It was like horizontal rain. And it was only the quickness of the mercs, who fell facedown in their hiding places and let the flaming metal wave pass over them, that saved their lives.

Then there was nothing but silence. The hill looked like a volcano had suddenly broken free. The smoke from the thirty thousand pounds of bombs exploding rose like a mushroom cloud, much bigger than the one created by the nonstop mortar barrage earlier that day.

Then they heard the scream of engines again. And they looked up, this time to the north.

And they saw another HellJet begin its murderous dive from 25,000 feet.

This time the mercs stayed down in their holes.

Seeing one piece of hell this day was enough for them.

The air strike lasted just fifteen minutes. All six of the AirCat HellJets delivered massive dive-bombing loads, one each on the six hills surrounding the embattled mercenaries.

Once the big dive-bombers had departed, the smaller AirCat fighter bombers swept in. Two dozen in all, they strafed and bombed what remained of the hills in a most workmanlike fashion. It seemed almost routine.

There was no antiaircraft fire any more, of course. The concussion alone from the dive-bombing runs had iced the electronics of all weapons in the hills and many on the plain of Long Bat itself. This allowed the AirCats to go about their deadly work unopposed; indeed after ten minutes it seemed like the swarm of fighter-bombers were simply dumping bombs on places where bombs were no longer needed.

Finally the last of the attacking airplanes pulled up and out, and silence returned again to Long Bat. This time it would last for more than a few seconds.

It was strange, though. The mercs slowly crawled out of their holes. Many of them saw the sun for the first time in a month. They were all hollow-eyed, gaunt, weak. Skeletons with drooping skin, and teeth loose in the gums.

But at least they were alive. That was more than could be said for their unseen enemy in the hills, because indeed there were no more hills. Long Bat now stretched as a plain for another three miles or so in every direction until the jungle took over again.

One month of hell over in just a matter of a few minutes. The AirCats had struck again.

CHAPTER 18

Thirty minutes later the birds were singing again at Long Bat.

The runway, or crucial parts of it, had been hastily filled in by the bone-weary mercs, and nine big AirCat fighter-bombers had already set down upon it. They were lined up on the battered runway like a shiny honor guard, the only things that were not bent, twisted, or rusted in what was, just an hour before, a nonstop killing field.

Two Bugs were also on the ground. Y, Zoltan, and Crabb had arrived in one; the Jones boys had come in the other.

Y was still shaking from his gut-wrenching bombing run in the HellJet. The carrier was now anchored 150 miles off the coast of Vietnam. Returning at top speed to the ship after the air strike had taken but twenty minutes, he was met by Emma on the flight deck. Indeed it took her and a few deckhands a couple of minutes to unstrap Y and pry him out of his crash seat.

Once on deck, he had a flask containing some brandy slipped to him by Emma. Y downed it in one long, noisy slurp. Then the Bugs were brought up, he was loaded aboard and was soon on his way back to Vietnam.

And now Y was here. His hands still shaking, his breath sickly sweet, he was staring out at the hills that were no longer hills, astonished and a bit terrified at what the AirCat squadron could do.

LaFeet was there, reading a prayer to his assembled men, who were now starry-eyed at their mad commander. He was taking credit—he and God—for the positive turn of events, and when someone hands you a miracle and saves your life, you tend to accept their word for it. That's why the 623 survivors were now hanging on LaFeet's every word.

None of the AirCats or Y's gang were even listening, though. They were too busy studying a map of Long Bat.

The place that had suffered hardly any damage in the massive bombing strike was the mountain at the northern end of the valley, right at the edge of the long runway. The five men were now standing about one hundred feet away from this mysterious mountain. Even to Y's foggy eyes its formation reminded him of something.

Was it a dinosaur?

"Well, this is the place," Dave Jones said. "Now what?"

Zoltan stepped forward, closed his eyes, and indicated a need for silence. Everyone else either rolled their eyes or looked up at the deep-blue sky. But the psychic stayed focused.

"Yes!" he finally exclaimed. "In there. That's just what we've been looking for."

They all looked at the mountain.

"*In* there?" Crabb asked.

"Yes," Zoltan repeated. "There is a cavern inside. Behind a door, which we will find hidden in some shrubbery."

They did a group shrug and then approached the place the psychic had indicated. And sure enough, behind a cascade of fauna and vine they found a huge iron door.

Y felt his head start to spin again.

He was having that *feeling* again. Not so much the sensation that *he* had been here before, or that *he* had lived these events just as they were happening. But rather, everything seemed so familiar to him. Like he was reliving a piece of history—*someone*'s history—that had already gone by. It was not a pleasant feeling, this odd kind of déjà vu. Yet, he knew it couldn't be anything more than that. A feeling. It could not be a coincidence, simply because coincidences just did not happen in this world.

Bottom line, though: Thinking all this just made his head start to spin a bit faster.

Jesus, what I'd do for a drink.

The door had an enormous lock on it, of course, and a quick search of the area found no key.

"Can you think your way through that?" Dave Jones asked Zoltan snidely, indicating the lock.

The psychic, hurt again, shook his head no. But then he reached over and deftly lifted Crabb's enormous twin-barrel Magnum from its holster. In one quick motion, he fired both barrels at the lock. It was vaporized in the small fusillade, sending pieces of flaming metal in every direction except toward the group of men.

The others were shocked—Zoltan had never handled firearms before. Yet he seemed to know what he was doing with the huge Magnum.

He sensed this and smiled a bit.

"It's all in knowing where to aim," he said mysteriously.

The lock gone, it took a little effort to swing back the huge worn door. Just judging by the size of the portal, though, Y figured whatever lay beyond must indeed be vast.

This thought was confirmed when the door was finally swung free. There *was* a huge cavern beyond—it was truly enormous. Big enough to hold the B-2000 superbomber, and much more.

But there was no superbomber. Even with the lack of illumination, this was obvious.

This did not mean, however, that there wasn't an airplane within.

There was.

It was the tow plane—the Z-16 recon aircraft that the superbomber crew had taken with them.

"Son of a bitch," Zoltan whispered. "I was right . . . sort of."

CHAPTER 19

West Falkland Island

"This is insanity. You know that, right?"

Viktor looked around at the deserted beach. The waves were small this morning—the wind was coming off the land for a change, yet they were still swelling to three or four feet. Beyond, the South Atlantic looked very gray and immense and forbidding.

"I know it appears that way," he said to the Man. They were the only two on the beach. "But something is telling me that this is the way I must do it."

The Man loaded the last bag of provisions into the open boat. It was nothing more than a skiff, a rescue boat used by the British soldiers on the island for any emergency in the surf. It was fifteen feet long, built of oak and mahogany, and double-sealed all-round. A small mast of sorts had been rigged in the center, and the rudder was wired up to a very rudimentary steering wheel and to a bolted-down chair in the rear. It was a sturdy boat, but hardly an ocean-going vessel.

Yet that's where Viktor wanted to take it.

"You know, if I thought it was going to lead to this, I would never have showed you the door to Back There," the Man told him.

Viktor secured the last bag of stuff in the boat and turned back to the Man.

"Quite the contrary," he said sincerely. "I'm glad that you did. It led me to this decision. I have to find the other man who came through with me. You seem to think he is this mysterious American pilot. If it *is* him, I must find him. I won't be able to rest until I do."

The Man began pleading with him.

"But this is not the Middle Ages," he said. "This is a modern world. If you want to find someone you can use aircraft, you can hire a spy. You can make contacts. Send out feelers. There are many, *many* things you can do. I'll even send a squad of British troopers with you, if you will only agree to do it some other way than this!"

Viktor just shook his head sadly. The wind began blowing a bit harder. "There is much truth and wisdom in what you say," he said. "But there is also something deep inside me that is telling me this is the way to do it. And so I must."

The wind picked up even more now; it turned around and was suddenly coming off the water. The waves were growing in strength. And, of course, a storm was brewing off to the southwest. Blowing up from Antarctica, as always.

Viktor shook the Man's hand for a very long time.

"Thank you," he said finally. "For looking after the children. For looking after me."

The Man almost had to wipe away a tear.

"You're thanking me?" he exclaimed. He grabbed Viktor by the shoulder. "You saved the most precious thing in my life. In this world or any other. I owe my soul to you."

"You owe me nothing," Viktor said. "Except a warm bed and a hot meal, when I return."

With that, he pushed the boat out into deep water, jumped aboard, and began handling the makeshift sail.

He caught a gust right away and began moving quickly away from the shore. He turned just once and waved to the Man.

Then he did not look back again.

Long Bat, Vietnam

It took them nearly two hours to push the Z-16 tow plane out of the huge cavern.

Its brakes were locked, which was strange because it appeared as if the airplane itself had not landed here. Its wheels were as new as the day they left the ground at Bride Lake Base in California five weeks before. In fact, it appeared like the plane had landed here still attached to the superbomber, and was left this way, hidden in the cave—with its wheels locked.

"Why?" was the question on everyone's lips as they finally got the airplane out into the sunlight.

Their suspicions were confirmed when the plane's gas tanks were checked and found to be absolutely full.

"This doesn't make any sense," Y was saying. "Why would they land here, leave the tow plane, and then take off again."

He looked down the length of the runway. It was at least seven miles long. In the hands of the right pilot, maybe just enough for the massive bomber to land and take off from.

Zoltan was pressing his hand against the airplane and keening, like a rabbi at the Wailing Wall. But it was obvious that not much was coming through.

Y finally climbed inside and went up to the flight deck. Through his blurry eyes, he solved one small mystery, only to reveal a larger one.

It was weird how Y first spotted it. The plane's controls were all shut down, of course. But he noticed that there was a single red bulb blinking at the bottom and off to the far right of the flight commander's console. Y stared at the bulb. He was not a pilot but he'd flown on enough airplanes to know that this blinking light was the indicator for the auxiliary flight-control computer's D-drive. This was a kind of backup for the flight control's backup system. On an airplane when everything else was shut down—but only temporarily—the D-drive was usually left on.

This was strange. Y had no idea why the Z-16 had been placed inside this huge cavern, on this weird battered plain. But why would it have been, in effect, left on? Why hadn't *everything* been shut down?

Y yelled down to the others, and soon the Jones boys, Zoltan, and Crabb were up on the flight deck. Y pointed out the blinking D-drive light.

"Hmmm," Seth Jones said. "Maybe someone was expecting to come back here for this baby sometime soon."

"So what you're saying is that they landed here safely," Y hypothesized, "then hid this in here, took off again in the B-2000—yet left this thing with a heartbeat?"

"That doesn't make any sense at all," Crabb injected.

"No, it doesn't," Zoltan said. "Unless you just reverse that rationale."

They all looked at him, and as usual there was an orgy of eye rolling.

"Why don't you 'reverse' it for us," Dave Jones suggested.

Zoltan closed his eyes for a moment and put his fingers to his brow.

Then he came out of his minitrance, looked down at the myriad of buttons, switches and readouts on the control panel—and suddenly started pushing things.

And a few seconds later the cockpit burst to life. Everything that could be activated, was. Now there were many lights flashing, many buzzers buzzing. The airplane's ten computers snapped on, and their hard drives were now chugging themselves to life.

All from one little button . . . .

"Jeesuzzz, what the hell is this?" Crabb yelled, startled. Everything but the plane's engines was now turned on.

Zoltan was wearing a wide grin of triumph.

"I think someone was trying to leave us a message," he said.

For once, the Jones boys agreed with the psychic.

Seth Jones reached forward and pushed the plane's flight-control computer-panel main switch—and the message Zoltan had predicted appeared before their eyes.

There was a flight plan already loaded into the plane's automatic pilot. It was so intricately programmed, all it would take was a push of the activation button, and the airplane would take off and head toward its assigned destination, which, on the large TV screen, was identified as Location X.

The meaning of all this was clear to the group.

"Someone must want us to get to this Location X very badly," Dave Jones said. "Even though judging from this flight thesis, they might not have been exactly sure where Location X was."

They all looked at each other. Finally Crabb spoke the words that were on everyone's mind.

"They knew someone would come here looking for them," he said. "Just how, I can't imagine . . ."

"*How* they knew is not the question now," Dave Jones said. "The question is now, who's going to go?"

Y stood up, straightened himself out, and cleared his throat.

"We're *all* going of course," he said. "I suggest we get back to the carrier, gather some supplies—and other things—and then get a good night's sleep, and ride this thing wherever it wants to take us. . . ."

The others were only mildly surprised that Y wanted all of them to go. But there was still one big question remaining: *Where* were they going?

"Don't ask me," Zoltan said, preemptively cutting off all inquiries to him. He was staring at the alphabet soup of computer commands flashing on the control panel's main TV screen. None of them made any sense to him.

"No matter where it is, one thing is for certain," Y told them. "It's a place that the guys in the superbomber—

maybe even Hawk Hunter himself—wants us to go. So go, we must."

But again, where could that be? No one in the group had a clue—except Y.

His head was spinning again, and the weird feeling of déjà vu was now washing through him once more.

An airplane that is found in the wilds of Vietnam, with its controls already set for a predetermined point?

Yeah, he'd read that book before . . . .

CHAPTER 20

The waters of the Gulf of Tonkin were very calm this night.

A light breeze washed across the deck of the small carrier as two Bugs and two AirCats flew endless circles around the vessel on aerial picket duty.

On the deck itself, one of the massive HellJet dive-bombers was being packed with provisions: weapons, ammunition, radios, and long-range TV cameras. All this in preparation for the next day's journey. The plan was for the HellJet to carry the voyagers back to Long Bat at first light. Then once the Z-16 tow plane took off, the HellJet and four AirCat fighters would accompany the recon plane on its predetermined, mysterious journey.

The carrier itself was quiet, as well. The air strike earlier in the day had been oddly routine for the AirCats. Four fighters had provided air cover for the evacuating mercenaries as they made their way down the Dong Long road to the nearest big city and safety. Those airplanes had returned with mission accomplished at 2300 hours. After that, the ship itself shut down.

There was a huge party taking place on the Bro-Bird,

however. Anyone spared duty, whether inside the carrier or on the tug crew, was aboard the huge seaplane, drinking, dancing, and taking turns sampling the wares of the rescued hookers.

Y was not attending this bash. He was lying in his bunk, slurping a huge glass of brandy, with his eyes transfixed on the small door that led into his quarter's tiny head.

The light was on inside this small bathroom, and every few seconds Y could see a graceful shadow move about on the other side. With each of these movements, he felt his heart leap a bit.

He sipped his drink in an effort to get his heart beating normally again.

What was happening to him?

He didn't know. He'd been on dangerous missions before—he was, after all, a seasoned OSS agent. But nothing had affected his mind like this little sortie to Asia. Was he going just a bit mad? Was this constant state of déjà vu the result of a slowly creeping dementia?

No, it didn't seem to be. And it didn't seem that simple. Going insane was easy . . . or easier than this.

He felt like he was living someone else's life, with bits and pieces of his own life thrown in, too. What strange feeling was this? Since leaving Edwards, just about everything he did from the moment he woke up to the moment he passed out every night seemed *so* familiar to him.

And then there was his drinking. He'd been drunk—falling-down, blacked-out drunk—exactly twice before in his lifetime. One upon graduating high school, and again when graduating college.

But ever since this mission began, he'd craved alcohol like never before. More than food. Or sleep. Or oxygen. So he had this odd thing factored in: He was walking through this mission partially bombed. Could this be causing the strange been-here/done-this feeling? Or was the reverse true? Was he drinking so much because this ultra déjà vu was just too much to handle sober?

He slurped his glass of brandy and tried to shake all of

these weird thoughts from his mind. The answer will come soon enough, he told himself.

Or as a song once put it: "Just wait, maybe the answer's looking for you."

He leaned down to refill his brandy glass, and when he looked up again, he saw the door to the bathroom slowly opening.

Ah, yes. There was a third factor in all this . . .

And she was about to come out of the door.

Emma. She was beautiful. She was sexy. She was young. Her body was almost childlike—both to Y's shame and delight. She was so sweet, he had a hard time convincing himself that she was part of the world's oldest profession. She had such an aura about her—the perfect virgin image—that anytime he kissed her, or touched her, or did anything to her, it really seemed like it was the first time she'd ever experienced it.

Or at least that's how it seemed to him. But what would he know? He was drunk all the time and possibly losing his mind.

The door finally opened, and there she stood in the faint light of the bare bulb behind her. Hair in pigtails, just a very short T-shirt covering her, she actually put her finger to her mouth and smiled nervously.

Y gulped his drink and poured another, and then reached for her hand and guided her to the bunk.

This would be their fifth night together, yet it always seemed like the first. How strange was that? Here he was, feeling like he was doing all this before, yet when he was with Emma it always seemed like the first time.

If this is going nuts, then book me first class, he thought as she snuggled up to him.

She removed the t-shirt, and Y's heart nearly came up through his throat when he saw her erotically small breasts. More brandy, and then he kissed her. She sipped his drink and then moved her hands south of his belt.

"Do you ever dream?" he heard a voice ask.

He startled himself—he had asked the question.

"What do you mean?" Emma asked back sweetly—freezing her hands in position.

Y wasn't sure. He didn't even know why he asked the question at a time when no questions needed to be asked—never mind one so . . . philosophical?

"I guess I mean, what do you dream about . . . when you dream?"

Emma propped her head up on her hand and actually snuggled a bit closer to him. She stared off into the distance.

"Well, I dream a lot about when I was growing up," she said. "We lived all over Asia. Kong Hong, mostly. It was such fun growing up the way I did."

"You talk like it was a million years ago," Y said. "Not just two or three."

"It seems like a million," she said. "Especially after being captured by those pirates."

She was suddenly hugging him tightly.

"What would have happened if you didn't rescue me?" she asked, tears choking her words for the moment.

Y hugged her back. There was an extremely warm feeling welling up inside him.

God, he thought.

Was he . . . falling . . . in love?

"But I also have very strange dreams," she said, breaking his line of concentration.

"Strange in what way?"

She thought another moment.

"Well, I have one that keeps coming back to me every few months," she said. "What do you call that? Reinventing?"

"Reoccurring," he corrected her.

"Yes, that's it!" she said excitedly. "It keeps 'reoccurring.' Sometimes a couple times a week. It's very strange."

Y was suddenly interested in something more than a drink or getting his oil changed.

"What is it, this dream?" he asked her. "Tell me about it."

She smiled and shook her head. "No, it's too silly. Too weird."

Y sat up and took her in his arms. "Tell me," he said.

She looked up at him with her huge blue eyes and just shrugged.

"It's going to sound very strange," she began. "But I'm always sitting in a very small room. There is a man with a gun hiding behind the door. I'm wearing a negligee but it is very cold outside, and the window to this room is wide open. I can see out the window, and there are mountains that go up so high, it looks like the stars are below their peaks.

"And I'm very frightened, because the man with the gun is telling me that he'll kill me if I make a sound. But on the other hand, I'm not so frightened because someone is on the other side of the door and I'm sure he is going to save me.

"And sure enough, the door swings open and he walks in. He looks at me and I look at him, and it's as if we know each other. As if we had sailed on a ship—a ship like this one—sometime before. But he really doesn't remember. Then he spots the guy with the gun. And the guy grabs me and carries me out the window!

"Well, this hero guy chases after the bad guy—so the bad guy leaps from the window to the roof of the next building. I don't know how he didn't drop me. We just sail through the air like we were made to fly. And this is really weird—I think this has a sexual connection . . . is that the right word?"

"Connotation . . . ," Y told her.

"Yes, that's it," she said. "I see this huge bird flying over us as we are going from one building to the other. It's like a dinosaur bird. Real long beak, long weird sharp wings."

Y poured out another glass of brandy for them to share, but wound up draining it himself.

"A pterodactyl?" he said, his speech slurring badly.

"Yes, maybe," she said. "Anyway, the hero guy starts

shooting everything and everybody, and he's able to get me away from the bad guys. But then these airplane bombers come and they start dropping bombs right on top of us. And the building we are on starts to collapse. But the hero guy holds onto me—and we somehow land on the street without getting hurt. And here are these huge things blowing up all around us, and there are firemen and they are pouring milk onto the fires! Isn't *that* strange?

"Well, after that, we just go to where ever the heck I'm living in this weird town, and we are going to . . . you know . . . well, do it . . . and then some guys the hero knows come and get him. I think they are Russians. And they take him to go fly someplace. And, well, and that's it . . ."

She paused for a second.

"But you know the weirdest thing about all this?" she asked. "This hero guy. I find out what his name is. In the dream. I knew him. And his name was Hawk . . . which is really odd now because that's the name of this friend of yours that you're trying to find out here. Right?"

But Y never heard her.

The brandy had gotten to him.

He'd passed out long ago.

CHAPTER 21

The next day dawned bright and clear.

The Gulf of Tonkin was shimmering in the rising sun, the calm water reflecting the first rays like millions of diamonds stretched across the horizon.

The deck of the carrier was very busy. The HellJet bomber that had been converted to a cargo carrier was packed to the rivets with provisions, weapons, communications equipment, and ammo.

The crew had been shorn down from thirteen to four. All the onboard weapons-delivery systems had been replaced with extra fuel tanks. The ratio for the four double-reaction engines had been ratcheted down to make for better air cruising as it was not expected that this particular aircraft would be doing any high-speed, high-altitude dive-bombing anytime soon.

There was a small gathering of principals near the nose of the huge bomber. The Jones boys were there, as were Crabb, Zoltan, Bro Baulis, and the commander of the Irish tugboats.

These men had met through the night, planning the mission that lay ahead. While the preset airplane flight was going to lead to places unknown, all agreed that it was paramount that they stay in touch with the carrier. So it was determined that the carrier/tugboat/seaplane mélange would pull up anchor and head south into the Gulf of Thailand. From there, unless otherwise informed, the triad would head west, around Singapore, through the Straits of Malacca, and into the Indian Ocean, if need be.

The odd task force would find protection in the remaining AirCats on board. At various times it was agreed that the Bro-Bird would unhitch from its towing duties and take to the air as a kind of long-range recon platform. With its sophisticated radio and TV gear, it was hoped that the aerial diversion by the huge seaplane would provide those on the Z-16 with a receiver from which they could send and get secure messages.

This way the progress of the Z-16 could be monitored, no matter where it might lead.

Or at least that was the plan . . . .

It was now 0630 hours. Those taking the ride back to Long Bat were ready to go—all except one person.

No one had seen Y since earlier the previous evening. Now several crew members had gone below looking for him. Five minutes passed while those on the deck cooled their heels and waited impatiently for the wayward OSS officer. He finally appeared on deck at 0645. The mission was already fifteen minutes late in taking off.

Y had to be helped onto the deck by one crewman holding him under one arm, and Emma, looking sporty in a pair of very small, very tight combat fatigues, holding him under the other. Y was drunk, but trying his best to look sober. The Jones boys had no reaction; Zoltan and Crabb cringed at the sight of their friend. With little ceremony he was helped aboard the HellJet, his briefcase communication Boomer box stowed away with him. That's when Emma began climbing aboard—and that's when the Jones boys spoke up.

"Sorry, ma'am," Seth Jones said as politely as possible. "But under the circumstances, I don't think that—"

"She's coming," Y interrupted him.

Everyone turned back to Y slouched in his seat, already strapped in, eyes barely open.

"Do you really think that is wise?" Dave Jones asked him.

Y's eyes suddenly came to life.

"I don't give a fuck whether it's wise or not," he roared. "I'm top dog here and I say she's coming."

The Jones boys froze in place. What was going to happen here? The mission could go on without them, but it would become infinitely more dangerous without their support.

Dave Jones stepped up. "For what reason should she come?" he plainly asked Y.

Y leaned back and looked at the ceiling of the airplane. "Let's just say she'll function as a good-luck charm," he said slowly.

The Jones boys contemplated this, then Seth said: "Oh, really? Do you mind if we get an expert opinion on that?"

This comment caused Y to open his eyes a bit farther.

"Expert opinion?" he asked, slurring his words. "From who?"

They all turned to Zoltan, whose face sank a mile.

"Well, swami?" Dave Jones asked. "Is she going to be an asset or a liability if she comes along? What's your crystal ball say about that one?"

Zoltan looked a good long time at Y, then at Emma, and then at the Jones boys. It seemed like everything just stopped. The wind. The sound of the sea. Even the HellJet's whisper engines seemed to go down a notch in volume.

Zoltan closed his eyes, tranced for a few seconds, then opened them again.

He had a surprise announcement.

"Not only should Emma accompany us," he declared, "but I suggest we take along four of her companions, as well!"

* * *

There were still a few mercs left at Long Bat when the converted HellJet cargo plane landed.

These stragglers were part of the sick-bay crew left behind to heal one more day and pull double duty by guarding what was left of their former position and the cavern nearby. Sunning themselves now beside the newly tranquil runway, the handful of mercs—French Nationals all—watched as the huge dive-bomber bounced in, roared by them, and came to a halt at the end of the runway, where the large cavern now lay open, the Z-16 having been pushed back inside.

The HellJet dislodged an odd assortment of passengers—to the mercs' eyes anyway. First they saw two men in pilot's garb leap off, both were carrying full packs and several infantry weapons. Next came two men in jungle fatigues, both seemed a bit too old and too out of shape to be in any kind of military organization. They were followed by five prostituées—beautiful painted ladies—which had the mercs salivating like a squad of Pavlov's hounds.

The last to embark was a man in an air officer's uniform. He was so obviously drunk, two of the women were seen helping him just to stay vertical.

The strange group retreated into the darkness of the cavern as the HellJet cargo plane turned 180 degrees and took off with a blast of raw power. No sooner was it airborne when it was met by four of the fierce-looking AirCat fighters. Together the five airplanes began orbiting the now peaceful moonlike valley.

Five minutes passed. Then a huge roar was heard from the cavern. There was an explosion of smoke and a flash of flame, and suddenly the Z-16 airplane shot out of the cave opening like a bullet out of a gun.

It went by the mercs so quickly, the wind in its wake left a half-dozen tiny tornadoes to wreak havoc on the recovering soldiers, scattering their meager belongings, and in some cases, taking the cigarettes right from their mouths.

The Z-16 then left the ground with another roar of its double-reaction engines. There was a second burst of smoke and flame, and suddenly the airplane was hurtled upward, its long wings beginning to flap like some kind of mechanical gooney bird as it soared away.

The plane never did level off—it just kept climbing at a forty-five-degree angle, finally disappearing from the mercs' view not a minute after it had left the ground. The orbiting airplanes, seemingly startled and taken by surprise by the Z-16's sudden acceleration, all kicked in their own double-reaction engines and were soon in hot pursuit of the strange climbing aircraft.

And then, just as quickly, Long Bat was quiet again. The wind began blowing a bit, and the sun returned to its murderous intensity. The wounded mercs went back to their lounging and their cigarettes.

Only a couple kept their eyes on the sky, trying to see the last of the strange group of airplanes, which had come and gone so quickly.

"Those Americans," one soldier said at last, as all visual trace of the six aircraft finally disappeared. "Always in a hurry to go nowhere."

CHAPTER 22

By noon on the second day of his journey, Viktor's small open boat had traveled nearly five hundred miles.

He was no stranger to the currents in this part of the world—he'd sailed the very south Atlantic many times while on board the huge ship with many rowers. But even he was astonished at the speed that his boat was moving.

He had a pair of oars aboard, but he had not yet had to use them. As soon as he cleared the shallows around West Falkland Island, he'd picked up a convenient southwesterly breeze, which soon had him traveling at a rather amazing forty knots.

Somewhere around the Burrwood Banks, he picked up an even stronger wind, which added another fifteen knots to his already very rapid pace. He was going so fast at some points, he had to put his head between his legs just to get a good breath of air. Never had he imagined he would have made this much headway in so short a time.

The boat was holding together just fine. Its sturdy construction, superior wood, and double fasteners made it so solid, Viktor could hardly hear a squeak. His mast was also doing well—it was made of zylon and would resist tearing under the most violent situations. Or so he hoped.

And lastly the ocean itself was cooperating. For even though the wind was blowing at a howl, the surface of the sea itself was unusually calm, with hardly a wave or swell. And all this, while going against one of the strongest currents on the planet—it was enough to make Viktor question whether everything he was experiencing here was natural.

It was almost as if . . . and it sounded silly to even think it . . . but it seemed like a massive hand was pushing him along, massive lips blowing on his sail, giving him a speed that would be the envy of any vessel captain, big or small, wind-powered or not.

All of this conspired to keep Viktor's mind on sailing rather than where he was going. The truth was, he didn't have the faintest idea. Something deep inside him—way, way down deep in his soul—had told him, no . . . *commanded* him to get in a boat and head west, and that's what he was doing.

He was a stranger in this world. He had little knowledge of the weird events that passed as commonplace in this universe. He'd seen some odd things during his time aboard the ship with many rowers—but he knew little of what would be considered otherworldy here. Or better said, what activity would seem to his eyes *para*normal, but to anyone else simply "normal."

He was about to get a huge lesson on this topic.

The trouble started when the sun went down.

It took awhile for him to actually enter the darkness. He was moving so fast that he was almost keeping pace with the sun's descent. But finally he watched the huge red ball dip below the western horizon. After that, night fell very quickly.

The stars came out almost all at once, and suddenly he

was moving just as swiftly under a tapestry of spinning constellations and absolutely blazing galaxies.

He sailed along like this—wind in his hair, tickling his goateed face—when he detected a slight turbulence in the water in front of him. It was a wave—a big one—and he was heading right for it.

It actually came upon him so quickly, there was little he could do but ride up and over it, which he did, with much heart pounding. The swell was at least twenty feet high, frightening enough for Viktor's eyes to start searching in every direction for any similar monstrous curls.

He would soon spot another. Then another. And another.

One moment he'd been sailing smoothly along—the next he was heading for a patch of water so turbulent, the waves so high, they were blotting out half the star-filled sky.

Then just as quickly, banks of clouds moved in from all directions, blocking out any chance to navigate by starlight and making it considerably darker.

Then the rains came. Then the wind—his friend for all these hours—turned against him.

Inside of a few very anxious heartbeats, the breeze had shifted around from southwest to northeast. And just as quickly, Viktor found his small boat battling against a gale that was approaching hurricane proportions.

What watery hell was this!

He grabbed the sail's leader with one hand and his crappy little steering wheel with the other and began to ride up the sides of waves that would have dwarfed the largest skyscrapers in this world of bigger-is-better. Overhead, the clouds thickened farther, lightning was now around him. The first clap of thunder was so loud, his ears began to bleed. Even through the clouds and mist and roaring waves, Viktor could see the dim outline of land many miles to the north. Then the answer to his question somehow popped into his head.

What watery hell *was* this? It was Cape Horn, the very tip of South America. The graveyard of ships.

The waves grew even higher and the wind blew even stronger as if the Cosmos had decided to reveal its full fury now that Viktor knew his enemy's name.

His little boat was suddenly broadsided by a rogue wave from the right side. It was all Viktor could do to keep himself from being washed overboard. No sooner had this crisis passed when another wave hit him from the left; the impact dislodged half his provisions from the forward hold and washed them overboard.

Viktor could no longer see now, the salt water was stinging his eyes so badly, he had to keep them closed. The roar in his ears sounded like a thousand artillery guns firing at once. His hands were bleeding, he was holding the sail leader and the little steering wheel so tightly.

Then he began to wonder strange things. If he were to perish here, where would he go? Would he become a ghost? Would he go to another universe? Or would he simply become a few mouthfuls for the fish and then be . . . *nothing.*

He heard a voice say, "Option number one, actually. . . ."

Viktor somehow was able to remove enough salt from his eyes to open them. What he saw startled him to his core. There was a man sitting right in front of him!

Viktor began blabbering something, but coherent words would not come out.

"You will become a ghost," the man said so calmly, his words stung Viktor's ears. "Like me."

Suddenly it seemed as if the storm around Viktor's boat did not exist. Although the wind was still howling, and the waves were crashing, and the rain was coming down in long hard sheets, he could not feel them. He could only stare in astonishment and terror at the man who so suddenly appeared on his tiny boat.

"Who . . .who *are* you?"

The ghost smirked with morbid amusement.

"You mean, who *was* I?" he said. "My name, way back when, was Vogel. I was a pilot."

All around him the storm grew worse, but Viktor was no longer paying attention to Nature's fury. He was shaking too much. A ghost. He'd heard they were reality in this world—but never did he ever think he'd be talking to one. Yet here he was, a man sitting, talking, moving—just like a human. Yet when Viktor stared hard enough, he realized that he could see right through him, like a magician's tricks with mirrors, or in another place, a hologram.

"B-but why . . . ?" Viktor stuttered. "Why have you come to m-me . . . here? Like this? In *this?*"

Vogel let the wash from a huge wave pass right through him.

"I'm not really sure," he said. "But I think I'm supposed to tell you a few things and warn you about a couple others—"

"Warn me?" Viktor mumbled. "About what?"

The ghost shifted his position slightly.

"You're out looking for this guy named Hunter?" he asked. "Hawk Hunter?"

"I am," Viktor replied. "Why? Is he dead? Like you?"

The ghost became visibly agitated for a moment. "Why does everyone expect me to know that?"

Viktor just shook his head, and was soaked by yet another rogue wave. "I don't know . . . ," he sputtered. "I just . . . well, assumed that . . ."

"Assumed *what?*" the ghost snapped back. "That all ghosts know each other? That every person who has ever died and found themselves in this position, knows every other unlucky soul?"

"I'm sorry," Viktor mumbled. "I had no idea what it was like to be—"

"What? To be dead?" the ghost rankled. "Well, let me tell you, for spirits like me, it's no fun at all. I must have done something really bad while I was breathing. But damned if I know what it was. That's the worst part: You don't necessarily know what you did wrong. Oh, I mean, some souls do. But some don't. I don't. Not really, anyway."

It was to Viktor's credit that, even under the perilous circumstances, he knew enough to change the subject. Not to spare the spirit's feelings, but to retain his own. The less he knew about the dead, the better.

"You said you were here to tell me something," he asked the ghost. "About Hawk Hunter?"

"Yeah, yeah," the ghost said agitated again. "I guess I'm just supposed to tell you that you're not the only one looking for him. Dead or alive—there're some other dudes who are trying to find him, as well."

"Interesting," Viktor yelled over to him. "But how does that help me in my search?"

The ghost growled back at him. "How am I supposed to know? I'm just here to fill you in on that aspect. Maybe if you find these other people it will aid you in your search for Hunter—or more likely, his body."

Viktor began to reply snottily, but found himself holding his tongue. Instead he yelled back, "What else? What else did you come to warn me about?"

The ghost did not reply right away. Instead he looked over his left shoulder to the raging sea beyond.

"Well, this gets complicated," he said, finally turning back to Viktor. "But I guess you're a special case or something. And it ain't like I'm not trying to make my wings, you know? So, I have to tell you something that not many people know in this place."

"And what is that?" Viktor yelled back.

The ghost moved a bit closer. Even in the perilous elements, Viktor could feel an additional chill go through him.

"Well, sometimes, if the conditions are made right," the ghost began, "people in this place—people like you, though I don't know why you're so damn special—can see things that may have happened in another place. And another time. And at another point in the globe. Why this happens, or how? I don't have the slightest idea. All I know is that these things happen, and they apparently happen for a purpose—and if it happens to you, then you better damn sure make the most of it. If you don't, you'll wind up just like me, talking to schmucks just like you. . . ."

Viktor shook his head. "What the hell are you talking about?"

The ghost didn't reply. He just looked over his left shoulder again and then turned and pointed off into the raging darkness.

"I'm talking about things like that!" he said.

Viktor looked in the direction the ghost was pointing, and soon his eyes focused on the most unbelievable sight!

It was almost as if there was suddenly a very clear patch of weather in the midst of the raging gale. And what he saw first was a submarine. Not the enormous ones that he'd heard prowled the seas of this world. The sub, while large, looked like it was built by people from another place.

It was long and thin and had odd ornamentation on its snout. It looked almost Nordic in its design. It was black with some red lining here and there.

But the strange thing was, an aerial carousel of aircraft was circling the huge sub and was firing at it. There were helicopters—dozens of them—and not the crappy Beaters that were favored by the people of this place. These were sleek, powerful, smaller machines armed to the teeth—and they were sending vast streams of bullets and rocket fire into the helpless submarine.

Viktor tried wiping the salt water from his eyes over and over again as if the brine was causing this vision. But it was not. What he was seeing before him was real—and oddly familiar.

It seemed to go on forever. The battered submarine trying to get away, the swarm of aircraft pouring sheets of flame into it.

How strange was this!

Viktor was mesmerized by the vision—until the ghost turned back to him and got his attention again.

"Oh, yeah," the ghost said. "There was one other thing I was supposed to warn you about."

Viktor tore his eyes away from the surreal battle and looked back at the ghost.

"And that is?" he asked him.

The ghost just pointed behind Viktor's shoulder.

"That . . . ," was all he said.

Viktor turned and saw an enormous wave heading right for him. It was so large it blotted out everything else.

He'd just turned back in time to see the ghost slowly fading from view.

The huge wall of water engulfed his boat an instant later. . . .

CHAPTER 23

The Z-16 had been airborne for nearly twenty-four hours.

In that time the recon plane and its five-aircraft escort had covered only about fifteen hundred miles total. Not that the aircraft was going so slow—it was cruising at nearly three hundred knots. The flight computer, obeying the commands inputted by persons unknown, was *making* the airplane take a long, looping, meandering course, with many double-and triple-backs, and a dozen or more orbits that lasted an hour or more.

Luckily, the Z-16 was built for such a crazy flight path. Indeed, one thing the crew did not have to worry about was fuel.

This was because the plane's double-reaction engines needed very little fuel to operate—that was the beauty of double-reaction engine (DRE) technology. The combining of two highly-volatile chemical agents—usually xerof-2 and zerox-45—provided the catalyst for combustion in a double-reaction engine, thus its name. Because these two agents were so volatile, only minute amounts were needed to produce the combustion necessary to turn the engine blades inside a DRE.

This method of propulsion allowed the aircraft in this world a wide range of operating and design characteristics. First of all, the whole double-reaction propulsion system was small, and the chemical agents extremely lightweight. Thus, aircraft could be built larger as the weight of fuel they needed to carry was minor. Secondly, aircraft could go faster by adjusting the mixture of the two chemicals. By adding more zerox-45 to xerof-2, the aircraft would increase in speed dramatically, a kind of super-afterburner effect.

But third and most important, the relatively little need for refueling allowed aircraft with double-reaction engines to stay aloft longer. That was why some aircraft in this world were built like aerial ocean liners, while others, though smaller, were constructed with sleeping and living quarters for their crews to make long flights more comfortable. To become airborne and stay that way for days or even weeks was not unusual at all here—in fact, it was commonplace. That's why even a relatively small fighter-bomber like the AirCats drove had accommodations for their crew of three.

The Z-16 was a typical example of this aircraft-design philosophy. It had been built as an ultralong-range recon plane. The designers envisioned recon flights of up to a month or more. It was slightly reminiscent of an aircraft in another universe known as the U-2, but it was much larger, its wings were much longer, and its fuselage much thicker. It could fly extremely high—altitudes of up to 110,000 feet were not uncommon—and it could reach three times the speed of sound—more than 2,000 mph—at least for short periods of time. If necessary, it could carry as many as one hundred passengers.

That was the original idea for taking the Z-16 along as a tow plane on the B-2000 superbomber's mission to sink Japan. If the huge bomber was forced down—either by hostile action or mechanical problems after the bomb was dropped—then the Z-16 could have been used as a lifeboat of sorts. The entire bombing crew could have fit aboard her and could possibly have escaped.

Obviously, finding the Z-16 hidden in the cavern at Long Bat did not fit into this scenario.

But as it turned out, that was just *one* thing that proved unusual about the Z-16's role in the search for Hawk Hunter and the other missing members of the superbomber's crew.

The airplane had climbed to 65,000 feet upon taking off from Long Bat, but in reaching that altitude, it quickly leveled off, turned west, and started descending.

Sitting in its flight compartment, the two Jones boys were at the primary controls. They were fulfilling the wishes of the unseen person who had set the Z-16's autopilot—they were flying the plane completely hands-off. All they were doing was monitoring the aircraft's vital systems and keeping an eye on its main flight computer as it ticked off the various inputted commands.

It was a strange way to fly—as if unseen hands were doing the work for them. Watching the controls move this way and that, it had come to both their minds more than once that this is how the plane would have flown had a ghost been at the wheel.

The flight pattern was not only bizarre, but mysterious, as well. The passengers aboard the Z-16 found themselves flying in circles above huge patches of Southeast Asian jungle, mostly over Vietnam, but also Cambodia and Laos. At one point they circled the ancient ruins of Angkor Thom in Cambodia for more than three hours before the flight controls clicked again and they shot off to the south.

During most of the flight, Y slept in a bunk with Emma, and Zoltan and Crabb played cards with the four other hookers on board. Each one as beautiful and young and delectable as Emma. Their names were easy to remember. Brandee, Brandi, Brandy and Brayn-Di. All were blonde, all were abundantly friendly, and like Emma, all were striking in their very tight cutoff jungle camos.

They were also great cardplayers. After the first eighteen-hour-marathon poker session, the four girls had relieved Zoltan and Crabb of most of their monetary reserves. Once Crabb leaned over and whispered to Zoltan: "If I've got to give them money, I wish I was getting more in return than just a couple shitty straights and an occasional two pair."

The flight went on into its second day high above the ancient religious site of Angkor Wat and U-Suk-Bum.

That's when Seth Jones, who had been poring over the navigational computer trying to detect a pattern in the autopilot's maddening course, finally discovered something.

"Well, I'll be damned," he whispered.

This exclamation brought his brother, Dave, over to the huge circular computer screen. Both were now focusing on a line pattern Seth had coaxed out of the hard drive. In a small way their strange, circular, looping, repetitive flight became a bit clear.

"We are flying over old railroad beds," was Seth's conclusion.

It was true. By superimposing old maps over their current grid of Southeast Asia, it appeared that the Z-16 had actually been following the meandering route of railway lines throughout old Indochina, many of which were now in disuse, disrepair, or mostly hidden by the thick jungle canopy.

Whenever the Z-16 went into an orbit, it was usually because they were circling over an old railway exchange yard. Even near the site of Angkor Thom, there had been a large railway station at one time, complete with circular track turnarounds and serving facilities.

"That has to be it," Dave Jones said after studying what his brother had discovered. "This airplane has been set to fly over just any length of track ever laid down in this part of the world. The question is: *Why?*"

"Because the person who programmed the automatic pilot knew they would be searching for a certain railroad line," they heard Zoltan's unmistakable deep voice say.

The psychic and Crabb had joined the Jones boys at the navigational screen. Even the four "Brandys" were showing interest.

"They intended us to make the same search as they did," Zoltan continued. "At least, that's my best guess."

Seth turned toward the psychic. "Isn't everything you do simply just your 'best guess' ?"

Zoltan's brow fell a few inches. He was ultrasensitive to those who questioned his psychic abilities—but at this moment he wasn't sure if Jones was needling him or not.

"I have a perfectly acceptable success rating in these things," he told Jones. "You can peruse my service record at the push of a button."

He indicated another large computer that was located at the far end of the Z-16 flight deck. This was the Main/AC, the omnipresent computer terminal which could be found in every American military aircraft, vessel, land-fighting vehicle, and facility, from the room of the Joint Chiefs down to the lowliest supply office.

The Main/AC in the Z-16 had not been activated yet—they still considered their mission to be extremely sensitive, and turning on one's Main/AC was like lighting a beacon and letting everyone with Main/AC access know where you were and what you were doing at any given moment.

So Zoltan's challenge to Jones was a bluff of sorts. And everyone knew it.

A silence descended on the flight compartment—two worlds were close to colliding here. The military-think and hands-dirty experiences of the Jones boy against the eclectic, paranormal doings of the former Psychic Corps officer.

Oddly, it was Dave Jones who broke the spell.

"It makes sense to me," he said. "I think . . ."

They all turned their attention back to the navigational screen. The Z-16's flight path did look like it was searching for something having to do with railroad tracks. But what?

"Maybe the person who set these controls knew they would be flying over every railway in this part of the world," Dave Jones surmised. "At the moment they were inputting the autopilot commands, they didn't know what they were looking for, either. So they simply sent us on the same pattern."

"Meaning what they were looking for would be obvious to us if we overflew the same railway lines as they did?" Crabb asked.

"That's it precisely," Zoltan declared, feeling somewhat vindicated. "When we get to what they wanted us to see, we'll know it immediately—or there will be a sign left for us, to recognize the next step."

There was a group shrug.

Then the Jones boys went back to the main controls, and the cardplayers returned to the makeshift poker table. Outside, the escorting AirCats and the HellJet kept pace; their crews passed time in other ways.

Up in the Z-16's main service bunk, Y slept fitfully. His psyche was finding sweet dreams hard to come by.

Even at twenty thousand feet.

The long, winding flight continued on into a third day. They had passed up and down the length of Indochina more than two dozen times, the last twelve hours of which were spent mainly overflying Thailand and Cambodia.

It was strange—now that the Z-16 crew had a notion that the meandering flight pattern had a logic to it, they became caught up in closely examining the terrain below. The auto flight had been set with the idea that they should be *looking* for something. And so they were.

Designed as a recon plane, the Z-16 had an array of gizmos that could penetrate the thick jungle layer below them. One was called the LANTRAN. It was a combination radar-bouncing/infrared scanner that could quite effectively show a real-time map of the terrain below the jungle canopy. Once the crew was hip that railroad lines were a key to what they were seeking, the Jones boys were able to program the LANTRAN to seek out patterns that would naturally correspond to a rail line and to emit a warning buzzer whenever a new image was located.

Fairly soon into this, the LANTRAN buzzer was going off with such regularity the Jones boys finally shut the damn thing off. The lower part of Cambodia and most of the northern tier of Thailand was crisscrossed with rail lines, most of them old and little used. This part of Asia was sparsely populated—years of wars separate from the recently concluded global conflicts had made the place not very habitable.

In all their seventy-two hours of overflight, the crew of the Z-16 had been painted by antiaircraft weapons just twice, both to no consequence. Signs of civilian life below were even more rare.

But that all changed, as did the first phase of the search, when they arrived over the Thai region called Ma-What.

Through this region ran a long meandering river called the Kwai.

This area of Indochina was different from the terrain the Z-16 and its escorting airplanes had been flying over for the past three days.

Gone were the thick jungle forests, some so dense they blocked out all light from the sun. Here were rolling hills and shallow valleys, part of the River Kwai basin.

The grass here was so green, in the right angle of sunlight, it was dazzling and emeraldlike. This region actually looked out of place. It almost seemed like a slice of the African savanna.

And it was here that the Z-16 crew discovered unmistakable evidence that Hawk Hunter had gone this way not long before.

It came at midafternoon on the third day.

The Jones boys were still at the controls, the nonstop poker game was continuing.

Little had been heard from Y in the past seventy-two hours. But suddenly there was a commotion in his service bunk. Emma toppled out first, followed closely by the OSS agent.

Y looked slightly mad, slightly frightened. He quickly fell into his service fatigues and made his way up past the poker game to the flight deck.

"Where the hell are we?" he asked the Jones brothers anxiously.

Seth Jones calmly pointed to the navigational screen, which had a map grid of Thailand superimposed on it.

"Down there, the River Kwai," he told Y. "We've been following the railway ever since yesterday afternoon. This is where it led us. . . ."

Y just stared back at him. "Why . . . why are you following a railway?"

Seth looked over at brother Dave. Dave was actually two minutes older and thus as the elder sibling, it was up to him to bring the wayward OSS agent up to speed on what they'd been doing for the past several days.

Dave did just that. He briefed Y on the discovery that the Z-16's controls were actually set to follow parts of just about every rail line in Indochina. But since entering this part of Thailand, the Z-16 seemed to have been following just this one line.

Y looked like he wanted to jump out of the airplane.

"God . . . I just . . . dreamed we were actually riding on a train," he said, mumbling most of his words. "That we were still flying this airplane but we were doing it on rails. And every asshole with a gun, spear, or bow and arrow was shooting at us. . . ."

He stopped for a moment, suddenly aware of the monumental ass he was making of himself.

That's when Zoltan left the card table and climbed up onto the flight deck with them.

"Tell us more," he said simply.

Y rubbed his tired eyes. He was really not feeling himself—the last three days had been nothing but hours upon hours of nightmarish slumber—deep sleeps he had trouble waking up from. His seeming narcolepsy was cut only by occasional feeling sessions with Emma and several trips to the head.

But it was odd that he would be dreaming of railroads when, on the surface anyway, he had been unaware of the secret of the Z-16's flight pattern in the past three days.

"We came upon a hill," Y spoke again. "And on top of it, was an airplane. It was just sitting there. And there was snow around it. But wait a moment. We didn't actually see this. We were talking to a very young girl—and she was painting it! Yes, I remember now. She was shy, a bit frightened, but she had painted this strange picture of an airplane, sitting on this peak, it was red, white, and blue—and in the background, there was a city in flames and . . ."

Y stopped talking for a moment. Everyone on the flight deck was staring back at him like he was insane—Zoltan included.

But then the OSS agent pointed at the main communications console and said: "Answer that call. It's from AirCat Three . . ."

Two seconds later, the communications console lit up. One of the escorting airplanes was calling. It was AirCat #3.

"Sir," the pilot reported. "We've just spotted something pretty strange down below. . . ."

The fact that it was, ironically, one of the escorting AirCats and not the Z-16 recon plane that had spotted the object below was lost in the moment following the discovery.

What had riveted everyone's attention was that the object spotted below was an aircraft.

But it was not just any airplane. It was a vertical takeoff and landing (VTOL) Bantam. The same type that had been known to have been hanging off the wing of the

B-2000 superbomber when it went on its transpolar bombing mission.

And it was not like the airplane was just sitting on the ground—or had landed on a flat stretch of this strange region. No, it was sitting on top of the highest hill for miles around. It had not crashed there—indeed the airplane looked fairly intact. Nor had it landed there—the hill's peak was much too sharp for that. Rather, it was quite clear the airplane had been *placed* there. For someone to find.

Just like in Y's dream . . . .

CHAPTER 24

Near the River Kwai

His name was Swami Bawn Rashi Bawn Shee.

He was not a native of Thailand. Rather, he was from the country now known as Tibet.

He was a Buddhist monk, a man of God. Wrapped in orange saffron, with a crew cut, thick glasses, and leather sandals on his feet, he had sat on top of the hill with the airplane for the past month. He ate little but grass and drank only the rainwater that came down for a few minutes every afternoon at three o'clock precisely when the fast-moving monsoon passed over.

Swami had already lived a strange life—this was just another chapter. Or at least that's what he had kept telling himself in the past month or so.

He'd been born on one of the highest mountains in the Himalayas and had spent his first ten years living near its peak. He had been trained in all the ways of Buddha and believed to his last breath that the path to salvation was refusal of self and dedication to helping others.

But at just about the age of twenty, something changed

inside him. It came in a dream—one that would last more than two decades. Every night, when he fell asleep, he would dream of the most incredible female he could imagine God ever creating.

She was young, blonde, had huge eyes and white golden skin. Her mouth was small, slightly pouty, but angelic when she smiled. Her shoulders, her arms, her legs, her fingers . . . hell, every part of her was wondrous.

And in his dreams he'd seen it all. Many times. Many, many times.

Over and over . . .

Sitting on the hill now, he had to shake these impure thoughts away, at least for the time being. These dreams—these very erotic dances in the night—were the reason he was here in Thailand and not back in his home in Tibet.

These dreams had been scandalous from the first night. After ten years he knew that God or the Devil or someone was trying to tell him something. So he asked for permission from his superiors to leave his mountain home and go on a quest, to find the root of his dreams.

That quest, which began just three months before, somehow brought him here. To this hill. To sit with this airplane.

To sit, and dream.

Why here? He had no idea . . . only that it was here on this hill that he had stopped in his journey and dreamed the dream of this lovely creature and finally learned her name from it.

The name someone had called her in the dream was Chloe. That experience had been so powerful, he decided to stay here until the next domino dropped, which it did, soon afterward.

And now, watching as the six aircraft began landing on the plain below him, he knew yet another chapter in his bizarre quest was about to begin.

It took about a half hour for all the airplanes to get down and their crews to disembark.

Swami watched with great interest as the airplanes landed almost as if they were helicopters, using powerful rockets under their wings to cushion the blow and reduce the distance needed to set down on the grassy rolling plain below the hill.

Swami became fascinated with the airplane's crewmen as they alighted from their airplanes and set up a small circle of weapons posts around them. Then, leaving some behind, about a dozen men started climbing the hill where he and the airplane sat.

They arrived out of breath and sweaty ten minutes later. He greeted them with a deep bow and a blessing.

"May the green grass of earth, the blue of the sky, and the light from the stars give you peace, nature, and wisdom all of your days. . . ."

That's when one of the airmen broke to the front of the crowd. Swami could smell liquor on his breath.

"Who the fuck are you?" this man asked. He was obviously very drunk.

"I am Rashi," the swami replied. "And I can see you will need more than one blessing to see peace on this earth."

Two men came forward and yanked the drunken man back into the crowd. Swami looked at these two and felt a jolt go through him. They were twins—a very mystical sign for him.

"Excuse us . . . and our friend's behavior," one began. "We were just wondering if we could ask you a few questions. . . ."

The swami bowed deeply.

"I have been awaiting you," he said.

The Jones boys gave a wave to the rest of the group. The AirCat crewmen walked Y halfway down the hill. Zoltan and Crabb joined the two pilots in sitting at Swami's feet.

"Can you enlighten us?" Zoltan asked the monk.

"I can try," the monk replied.

One of the Jones boys gestured toward the airplane.

"How did that get up here?" he asked.

Swami laughed a bit. "Oh, you want me to start in the middle?"

"Start wherever you like," Zoltan told him.

The Swami looked over at the Bantam fighter plane.

"That air vessel was moved up here by the strength of eighty men," he began. "They came here in an airplane much much bigger than yours. They told me they were compelled to come to this place, as was I. . . ."

"But why did they bring it up here?" Crabb asked. "A lot of work—"

"They did it to bring you gentlemen here I assume," the swami said. "They left it as a sign. . . ."

Everyone started shaking their heads. "Maybe we better start at the beginning," Seth Jones said.

Swami took a deep breath.

"I was here, a full moon-cycle ago," he began, a faraway look coming over his eyes. "One moment, the night was still, calm as this day. The next, it grew darker than I have ever seen. I did not know what was happening. I thought it was the end of the world. But then I looked up and saw this enormous aircraft. It was huge! I thought it was a spaceship. An alien ship of some kind—even though I do not believe in such things.

"This airplane was so big it blotted out the stars and the moon. It took me awhile to realize that it was coming down, descending like a mad angel from the night sky. Then I realized it was trying to land here—in this valley, which until that day I called my own.

"I couldn't believe such a big thing could land here, but it did. It came in over those mountaintops and somehow it just seemed to stop in midair and then it came down. *Bam!* It shook the entire planet. I am sure of this because the birds did not sing for three whole days afterward.

"These men came from the airplane. They were so exhausted they just fell about the ground, and many slept right where they fell. They had no idea I was even here.

So, I don't know for what reason, but I stayed hidden up here and watched them for three days.

"They slept for almost twenty-four hours. I felt like they did not have a care in the world. But I also felt that they—like me—had been compelled to come to this place. Then on the second day many of them left. They went out to the railroad tracks and marched someplace off to the north.

"Another day passed. And then another. And then the most remarkable thing happened. They all returned . . . and they had a train with them. A very long, empty train."

At this point Y broke free of his handlers and crawled up the hill.

"A train?" he asked excitedly.

Swami smiled sympathetically at Y.

"Yes, a train," he replied.

Y turned to the Jones boys. "You must let me listen to this," he begged them.

"OK," Seth Jones replied. "Just be polite."

"Please continue," Zoltan urged the monk.

"I watched them for the next six days," he went on, the distant look returning to his eyes. "They did a magnificent job. They took all the weapons I could see from this massive airplane and put them on the train.

"Huge cannons and automatic guns and things that shot rockets. They had many rockets hanging from their wings. They test-fired some of them, and the birds did not sing for another three days.

"It was really amazing how quickly they worked and how efficient they were. It was as if they had been planning to do this thing for years.

"Wherever they got the train from, I don't know. Or the tools to put all their weapons onto it, I couldn't say.

"But when they were done, what they had created was awesome. Even for a man of peace like me, it was truly a magnificent sight."

Swami took a deep breath. The men before him were simply mesmerized by his story.

"Then one day as I was sleeping something woke me

up. It was one of them, he had climbed the hill and found me. He was an odd-looking person. He looked . . . *well, different,* though I don't know why.

"He asked me if I lived here and whether I'd been here for long, and I was truthful and told him that I'd seen everything they had done from the landing to the building of the armored train. And he went back down the hill after thanking me and soon came back with a lot of great food and sparkling water. I was so hungry I ate it all in front of him!

"Then he asked me to do a favor. A simple one. He asked that I stay here, and that anyone who landed and knew who he was, that I should tell them this story."

He turned and looked at the airplane.

"They dragged this up here. They said that the people looking for them would see it and know enough to land."

Y was simply astonished.

"It's just like my dream," he said over and over again.

"Sort of," Zoltan qualified.

There was a long silence. Finally Dave Jones spoke up.

"Did they say what they wanted the train for?" he asked.

The monk just shook his head no.

"Well, where did they go with this train?" he asked the monk. "Did they say that at least?"

The monk just shook his head and pointed to the west.

"All I can tell you," he said, "is that they went that way . . . into what people around here call '*Vdam Net.*' "

"And what does that mean?" Seth Jones asked.

"Loosely translated, it means 'Badlands,' " Swami said. "But that's an understatement."

"What do you mean?" Dave Jones asked.

Swami wet his lips, then looked to the west. "The territory over the next mountain has become hostile beyond belief. It is controlled by Rotkiv Khen—or Khen The Great, as I have heard he prefers to be called."

The Jones boys looked at each other. The name was not unfamiliar to them.

"Wasn't he that asshole who was going back door on

the Japanese in Manchuria while they were getting their kicks in South America?" Seth asked his brother.

"Yes, I think so," Dave replied. "They said he had the largest standing army in Asia next to the Nips. But I thought they crushed him right after they solidified South America."

Zoltan's hand was to his forehead—a sure sign a pronouncement was coming.

"The Japanese let him go," the psychic said, either tapping into the ethers or recalling some news report he'd heard or read. "They made a deal with him and he withdrew his army from Manchuria and headed south."

"Your bearded friend is correct," Swami said. "Khen's troops started arriving in this area about two months ago. When the Japanese suddenly disappeared from the map, Khen's forces were in place to fill the vacuum. He swept across Burma and the subcontinent in a matter of days—and never stopped. He is a modern-day version of Attila—I'm sure you educated men are familiar with Attila. In just a matter of a few weeks, Khen's empire stretched nearly as far as Attila's once did. They say you can travel for seven days and seven nights, either by boat, train, or airplane, and still you will always see the sun set on some part of Khen's Empire."

The Americans were all doing some quick calculations. "If that's true," Dave Jones said, "this Khen guy's influence might have stretched as far as the Middle East by now."

"He's at least that far now," Swami said. "You see, the Japanese had secretly made a pact with the Germans about one year ago. They agreed to link up when the Germans finally won World War Two, and Japan finally took over South America. Now we all know that their timing was a bit off—but the Japanese did secretly build a number of military forts stretching all the way from here to the fringe of southwest Asia, in anticipation of this great alliance. It is these forts that Khen has been able to take over and use to his great advantage. That is probably the reason he moved south after making a deal with Tokyo. He may have known the Japanese were not long for this world, and he knew that being in another part of the planet would be very advantageous. He was correct, as it turned out."

"And that's where our friends took this huge armored train?" Seth Jones asked.

Swami just nodded. "Right into the heart of the Badlands," he said. "That railway link, which the Japanese built on the backs of millions of slave laborers, stretches all the way to Europe. I don't know how far your friends went in their journey—or why. But my best guess is that you will find them dead not too far up those tracks."

Swami sighed. "It's too bad," he said sadly. "They seemed like such valiant chaps."

There was another silence and everyone involved realized that there really wasn't too much more to say.

So the Americans got up, and the Jones boys thanked the monk politely.

Then they started down the hill again.

But they got only halfway down when they stopped and had a quick animated discussion. Then Dave Jones came running back up the hill.

"One last question, sir?" he asked the monk. "If all of our friends left on the train, where is the big airplane?"

The monk just smiled and pointed to the rolling hills on the valley floor before them.

"Your big airplane," he said, "is right in front of you. . . ."

Jones spun around but could see nothing but the rolling hills of the small river valley.

But then he took a closer look and—like a puzzle that suddenly comes together before one's eyes—Jones started seeing the outline of something at the far end of the long, thin valley. What appeared to be the tallest hill was about the same size as the tail fin of the B-2000. And the rolling hills in front of, and branching out from east to west—they were in proportion to the size of the B-2000's fuselage and wingspan.

He spun around to the swami.

"Are you s-saying . . . ?" he stuttered. "Could it be?"

"The grass grows very fast here," the swami replied. "Especially when the earth wants to hide something very badly."

CHAPTER 25

Sand.

It was everywhere. In his eyes. In his mouth. In his ears. In his beard. Up his nose. This is the first thing Viktor was aware of. Sand. In his pants, between his toes, sloshing in his boots.

He opened his eyes and saw sand like he'd never seen before. It was pure white—like billions of tiny diamonds. The glare was enough to cause him to shut his eyes again, and this only caused him further discomfort. With a shaky hand, he reached up and tried to wipe the sand from his eyes. He was only partially successful—but his vision cleared enough to allow him to see his surroundings.

That's when he thought he had died and gone to Heaven.

He was lying on the beach of a tropical paradise. The sun was shining, he could feel its warmth drying out his soggy bones. The water trickling down around his feet was crystal blue. Never had he seen water like that. And up on the beach, palm trees were swaying. Bright red and yellow flowers were everywhere.

So this is what Heaven is like, he thought, still extremely groggy. Not bad. Not bad at all. . . .

It was early dawn and he was on the beach alone, and though he was conscious at the moment, he felt like he was halfway between being awake and still dreaming. His head felt like there were a million flies buzzing around inside. He picked up his hands again and realized that he was feeling pain—and this fact alone brought him back to reality and told him he was not in Heaven because he would certainly not feel pain in Heaven.

But was this Hell, then? With crystal water, diamond sand, and the brightest flowers he'd ever seen? Not likely.

So where was he?

The part of him that was still unconscious and dreaming felt something sharp against his right hand. He was able to move a bit and see that he was actually lying atop a piece of wreckage. It was metal and heavy and had very sharp edges. Even in this dreamlike state, Viktor knew something was wrong. How could this piece of whatever be able to float? It was physically impossible.

This intrigued him, so he began moving off this impossible life raft. It took some effort, but he was able to wiggle and roll and snake his way to the beach itself. Then, barely looking up, he realized this thing he'd floated in on was part of a ship's hull. It was evident by the construction and the number of rivets. In fact, it looked like it was a piece of hull torn off with a gigantic hand. But how did he come to find himself on it?

He remembered nothing since being swamped by the wave off of Cape Horn. How much time had passed since then? He felt his beard—two days of growth, maybe three. Had he really been floating unconscious on this piece of heavy metal for three days?

The thought of that was so bizarre, so impossible, he felt a jolt of panic run through him.

He crawled closer to the piece of wreckage and was amazed that he could actually read some lettering, which had been bonded into the metal. It was done in gold leaf, with very distinctive scrolling letters. It consisted of two words, two words he did not understand, yet felt were vaguely familiar to him.

"Fire Bats?" he whispered to himself, reading the words before he went unconscious again. "What the hell does that mean?"

When Viktor woke again, he convinced himself again that he was in Heaven.

This time he had more proof . . .

He was surrounded by six young females, all of them beautiful, all of them topless.

One had half a coconut filled with water and was gently caressing Viktor's head and trying to sprinkle a few drops into his very dry, salt-caked mouth.

As it turned out, Viktor's mouth was closer to this girl's naked right breast than the coconut, and even in his deteriorated state, he found a thrill run through him.

Yes, he told himself, this is Heaven.

Then he slipped back into unconsciousness.

When Viktor awoke a third time, he was lying on a straw mat, staring up at a thatched ceiling.

His head was bandaged, his wounds had been cleaned, and his body had been washed.

He turned his head and focused his bleary eyes. Nothing he saw dispelled this notion that he had died and gone on to some eternal reward. There were now two dozen topless beauties sitting nearby, watching him intently. Some were holding half coconuts filled with water, others had more bandages and clean clothes, waiting to tend him again. One was holding a huge tray of food—fruit mostly. And of all the things ailing him, hunger was paining Viktor the most.

He must have made some motion to his mouth because this girl was soon at his side, gently inserting pieces of a pearlike fruit between his lips. She smiled so sweetly as she did so, Viktor must have smiled back, because she was soon kissing his cracked and balmed lips.

Multicolored lights filled his eyes now. There were red flowers everywhere and their perfume filled the air. He could see out the front door of the grass hut for the first time and realized it was located on a cliff overlooking a glorious beach. In the distance, near the edge of this cliff, he could see a crude wooden structure that looked a bit like an airplane, covered with dead flower petals, nose pointed skyward. A half-dozen very small firepots sat smoldering around this odd sculpture, dispensing a sickly sweet cinnamon smell.

The young girl kissed him again, and in the movement, Viktor felt her tiny breasts brush against his bare shoulder. Another thrill ran through him. Then a second girl appeared at his feet and began rubbing his legs. Then a third began massaging his arms and fingers. All of the blood in Viktor's body was now rushing toward his groin.

Yep, he thought. This *is* Heaven . . . .

But then a man's voice broke the spell. The kissing stopped, as did the hand and foot massage. The sweet smells that had filled the hut suddenly disappeared, to be replaced by the acrid stench of body odor. The girls that had been surrounding Viktor a moment before simply vanished—he saw them flee to the corner of the hut and begin cowering there.

Viktor wiped his eyes again—he didn't think things like BO and cowering young girls were fixtures in Heaven. At least, he hoped they weren't.

He managed to prop himself up on one elbow and looked behind him, only to discover a man was standing there, staring down at him. It was from him that the body reek was emanating. He was very large and very dirty, his face oily, his chin covered with all sorts of unidentifiable stains, his beard containing bits and pieces of food, all of which appeared to have been harbored there for a while.

This man was gaping at Viktor, his mouth wide open, displaying a set of very rotten teeth.

"Who . . . who are you?" he began babbling in broken English.

"I have to ask you the same thing," Viktor replied. "And I must ask where I am."

"You . . . you were brought up from the beach?" the man stuttered again. "I heard there was a drowned man down there—but you . . . you've managed to come back. . . ."

Viktor's back was beginning to tighten up. He shifted from his elbow and sat up on his knees. The man jumped back at least three feet upon seeing this.

"My goodness!" he cried. "You can raise yourself back from the dead!"

"I wasn't dead," Viktor shot back at him. "At least, I don't think I was."

He checked his own pulse—a funny gesture when one thinks about it. It was beating so hard, Viktor had to believe he was still alive. So if this was not Heaven and it was not Hell, where was it?

"You are on the main island of Fiji," the man said suddenly as if he'd read Viktor's mind.

Now it was Viktor's mouth that dropped open. He stared back at the man as if the words he'd just spoken were still hanging somewhere in the suddenly putrid air.

"*Fiji?*" Viktor heard his voice roar. "That's impossible."

"Yes, it is," the man replied. "Just as a dead man can raise himself from the dead. . . ."

Viktor finally got to his feet. His entire body was aching from head to toe. The girl's work on him had been all too brief.

He turned toward the smelly man. He was short and stooped, and Viktor towered over him. But oddly, he looked somewhat familiar to Viktor.

The smelly man stepped back another few paces as he stared up at Viktor.

"You . . . I *know* you," he mumbled. "But I don't know from where."

"I feel the same way about you," Viktor confessed. "What is your name?"

The man smiled for the first time, displaying even more of his rotten teeth.

Then he bowed deeply and said: "My name is Soho. And I think I've been waiting for you for a very long time. . . ."

CHAPTER 26

Kwai River Valley, Thailand

"Is he strapped in yet?"

Zoltan checked the safety belts holding Y into his takeoff seat. Leg straps were fine. Body and shoulder straps . . . check. Neck strap, needed just a bit of tightening. His helmet strap was on and snug.

"OK, he's tight," Zoltan yelled back up to Dave Jones.

"Is he ever," was the Jones boy's reply. "OK, get in yourself, this is going to be more like a rocket launch than a normal takeoff."

These were not words that Zoltan wanted to hear. No big fan of aircraft, he'd spent way too much time away from *terra firma* lately. When the aerial search party set down on this river valley the day before, he was secretly hoping that their quest would end here—that they would find the missing American fliers, hopefully alive—and that they could all go home.

But of course, he didn't foresee that just the opposite would happen.

Their quest was just beginning, that much was clear now.

Though many unanswered questions still remained, there were some grim facts that were all too clear.

Hunter and his band of aerial adventurers had somehow made it here to the Kwai River Valley after the bombing mission on Japan, stopping first to drop off the tow plane at the battered plain at Long Bat.

Once here, and acting under God-knows-what premonitions, Hunter's gang somehow secured a train several miles long, and stripped the huge B-2000 superbomber of all of its defensive armaments. They mounted them on the train and then left, heading west, for parts unknown, but most certainly into the most dangerous territory on this very troubled earth.

Why had Hunter done this? It was a question that Zoltan had prayed over since hearing the story from the swami. The real one.

Hunter was a special case. Very few people knew that he was a man who had no past in this particular world—but a very storied one in the place from where he had come. Zoltan was one of the select few who knew Hunter's rather unnatural origins—and still, he did not know all, nor did he want to. (Only Y knew Hunter's entire story, and look where it had gotten him!)

But Zoltan knew that the Sky Ghost, which was what just about everyone in America called Hunter these days, almost always acted on instinct and pure intuition. Indeed, he had a high degree of premonition, much higher than Zoltan, though he would be the last one to admit that fact to anyone but himself.

Even examining what he *did* know was of little help. It appeared now that after dropping the bomb that sank Japan, the superbomber had continued south, and that it put down at Long Bat about six hours later. But what happened in those six hours? This was another question on everyone's mind. For it was in this period of time that Hunter had received his intuition. The airplane could certainly have made it back to friendly territory. If it had enough stability to make it to Vietnam, it could have just as easily turned east and made it to the Hawaiian islands. Why didn't it do this? What happened to Hunter in those half-dozen hours? What did he see or hear that made him want to continue south—to Vietnam and then to here, in Kwai, and then to push on into the treacherous west?

No one knew.

Least of all Zoltan.

But still, what jolt of ESP would cause Hunter and his band to land here in this desolate piece of Siam, steal a train, arm it, and take off helter-skelter into what would also be certain death? What calling had caused him to take such a mysterious action?

What voice in his ear—or in his head—would even suggest such a thing?

Again, Zoltan just did not know.

But the story did confirm a few important things: Hawk Hunter was alive, or at least he was when the big plane came down here. From the swami's story, that seemed almost a certainty now. No one else in Zoltan's opinion could rally the manpower and dedication needed to do what the American fliers had apparently done.

This did not mean of course that Hunter was *still* alive. Or even that he and the others made it more than five miles down the track.

But that was what they had to find out.

In a rare lucid moment Y had made that quite clear—their mission was to find the B-2000 and its crew. They had accomplished one half of that order. Now it was time to fulfill the second half.

No matter what.

Zoltan finally reached his seat and began strapping himself in. This takeoff was going to be rather dramatic for a few reasons. The escorting AirCat airplanes had all landed in the valley with the aid of their reverse thrusters; they would take off with these same rockets assisting their ascent and cutting down dramatically on the length of ground needed to get airborne.

The Z-16 had no such capability. Its long gooney-bird wings alone were more than double that of the AirCat fighters. But it did have powerful engines and an ability to fly almost straight up when it got airborne.

But that was the hard part: getting out of the narrow valley and getting enough running speed to actually get into the air. This time there would be no flight plan to help—no ghostly hands on the stick and controls making sure their takeoff was a safe one, as was the case back at Long Bat.

No, this takeoff would be done under the tutelage of the Jones boys, ultraqualified pilots in whom Zoltan had tons of faith and respect. But it took more than that to get a beast like the Z-16 into the air.

And try as he might, Zoltan just could not see into the future for this one. Would they survive the takeoff or not? He'd literally whacked the side of his head trying to provoke that thought bubble of foresight to come to the surface.

He looked over at Crabb now, the big guy was strapping Emma into the seat beside Y. Y was unconscious, and even though he was a good fifteen feet and a half-deck below him, the psychic could still smell the boozy odor coming from the OSS agent.

This was not from brandy, though—the drink of choice for the OSS agent for the first part of this trip—this was the after-stink of beer. Cheap beer. Zoltan had smelled its odor enough times on the Grade-C nightclub circuit to know it anywhere.

But where had Y found cheap beer in the middle of isolated Thailand?

Simple: inside the B-2000 itself.

Once the swami had told them that the superbomber was right before their eyes, the Jones boys were able to cut through the thick grass and bush canopy that had grown over the massive aircraft, and this led them to one of the many entry hatches found along the fuselage of the flying behemoth.

Once inside the airplane, they had looked for more clues as to why Hunter and his crew had set off on such an incomprehensible journey. But no leads were found. Walking around inside the darkened bomber was like walking around inside a cave. It was dark, with only flashlights to provide illumination. The fuselage was perforated with literally thousands of bullet and cannon holes, stark testament of the air battle the bomber had plowed through going in to its target over Japan and getting out once the superbomb had been dropped.

The interior had been stripped not just of the defensive arms—some 162 machine guns, cannons, and small antiaircraft guns, plus dozens of antiaircraft air-to-air missiles from the wings—but also of all its computers, navigation gear, and communications suites. Its main and secondary onboard power-generating double-reaction engines were gone, as was the small operating room, all of the medical equipment, and all of the food and provisions on board for the crew.

But what was not missing—and what Y found as soon as he entered the haunting fuselage—was a load of beer that had been carried into the air inside a cooler installed at the last minute on the B-2000 by one of its crew members, a guy named JT Toomey.

Though little was known about him—as was the case with just about everyone else in Hunter's crew—Toomey was somewhat legendary around Area 52's Bride Lake, where the B-2000 had taken off on its one-way bombing mission. While it was widely believed that each member of the handpicked crew had come to the mission with a special, if innate, talent to help fulfill the bombing run, it was well known that Toomey's main contribution was to install a beer cooler aboard the superbomber just prior to its takeoff.

In this cooler, Toomey had stocked more than two hundred bottles of cheap beer—approximately three bottles for each man on the flight. Once Y got into this cooler, he discovered all of the bottles still within—there had been no celebration after the aircraft had dropped the ultrabomb and had survived the brutal air assault by defending Japanese airplanes.

Again, why not?

There was no answer—but this didn't bother Y a bit. While the Jones boys and the other AirCats were examining the B-2000, Y had had Emma and her companions help him load the cache of beer onto the Z-16, and it was now stuffed into the bunk he'd used to sleep through the first three days of the mission.

It was the stink of this beer that Zoltan now smelled wafting through the lower deck of the Z-16's flight cabin. He sneezed once and looked over at Crabb. The big guy had just finished strapping the last "Brandy" in and was now locking himself into his jump seat.

Meanwhile the Z-16's massive engines were already screaming at full throat. The Jones boys had about 4,500 feet of rolling meadow from which to attempt the takeoff. The AirCat fighters, as well as the HellJet cargo plane, had already taken off, using their rocket assists to ascend eerily above the river plain. The Jones boys had told their pilots that should the Z-16 not be able to get off—or if it crashed shortly after the takeoff—then they should proceed with the mission. They were to follow the railroad tracks until they found any credible evidence of the B-2000 crew's whereabouts. And once this was uncovered, they were to fly home and brief the appropriate OSS authorities in the U.S.

Seth Jones called back one final warning for the Z-16's passengers. Then there was a louder screech of engines, and the next thing Zoltan knew, they were moving very quickly.

But quick did not equal smooth, and soon, due to the bumpy meadow ground, the Z-16 was bouncing all over the place. The first thing to go was about a third of Y's newly acquired beer supply. The airplane hit a large hump in the ground about ten seconds into its takeoff run that was violent enough to throw the plane about twenty feet into the air and send it crashing back down to earth again. When this happened, more than fifty of Y's beer bottles slid out of his berth and smashed to the cabin floor below.

The Jones boys did not falter. They simply laid on more speed after the huge bounce and stoically continued the desperate takeoff run. The Z-16's engines were positively screaming at this point. Zoltan couldn't believe there was any way they could generate enough power to give the plane enough speed to provide enough lift to get its big-winged ass off the ground.

Is this how it will end? That was the morbid thought flashing through Zoltan's mind as the airplane began shaking so much he thought he could see some rivets in the fuselage beginning to pop. A brilliant if shaky career cut short on a isolated river valley halfway around the world?

As it turned out, the answer to that question was no—though it came close to becoming a reality.

The Z-16 was shaking so much during its last few seconds on the ground that any thing not strapped down went flying through the cabin at very high speeds. Zoltan could barely keep his eyelids open. Somehow he managed, and this allowed him to watch the Jones boys as they calmly and coolly raced the big plane along the bumpy ground until it reached its minimum takeoff speed.

Once achieved, they both yanked back on the steering columns and kicked in the double-reaction's superflow. This felt like a foot in the stomach for Zoltan. The g forces were tremendous for an instant. But it was that kick in the ass that saved their lives as the big plane went up, faltered, and finally recovered just before it slammed into the wide railway span crossing the River Kwai.

The plane went straight up as advertised, and Zoltan was suddenly looking up at blue sky and the puffiest clouds he could ever remember seeing.

It took a long time before the plane leveled off and attained acceptable flight parameters. In those hairy seconds, whether they would stay airborne or not was still questionable, Zoltan was startled to see a vision.

He'd closed his eyes just for a moment to help relieve the g pressure in his chest. And when he opened them again, there was a person standing in front of him: pretty, middle-aged, brown haired, and sparkling eyed.

It was his late wife, Gwen! She was smiling at him in that very familiar way, where her eyes said it all: "Well, I pulled you out of another one!"

Then she blew him a kiss and disappeared.

The airplane leveled off for good a second later . . . .

CHAPTER 27

The next twenty-four hours inside the Z-16 were surreal.

Shortly after takeoff, the six aircraft formed up high above the River Kwai and, as one, turned west.

The railway ran a winding path for the next one hundred miles. It went through the heart of some very heavily forested jungle, passing little more than the occasional paddy or small lake. There was no sign of life below, no villages, no enemy guns. No hint of hostile forces anywhere.

As it turned out, this relatively peaceful first hour gave the six airplanes time to get into a solid formation and work out the best procedure by which to follow the rail bed.

After trying several different alignments, the Jones boys decided that a 1-3-2 formation was the best. This called for the HellJet cargo plane, now serving as the formation's long-range eyes and ears, flying way up at twenty thousand feet. At about 7,500 feet the three AirCat fighters flew. This position gave them the ability to climb swiftly, should the HellJet need assistance; or dive, should they be needed down below.

Flying at just five hundred feet were the Z-16 and the

remaining AirCat fighter. This heart-stopping altitude was dangerous, but the Z-16 had a type of terrain guidance/avoidance system that kept it at exactly five hundred feet, no matter what. This device also allowed them to follow the track bed itself without the Jones boys having to steer every twist and turn of the meandering railway.

The Z-16 featured a unique clear-glass belly canopy. Like a glass-bottom boat, this gave those on board an extraordinary clear view of the track bed.

Zoltan, Crabb, the five girls, and a drowsy Y were now in place around this look-down observation bubble, scanning the jungle and the track below, seeing very little.

But that changed as soon as they reached a village called U Thang.

It was located in the far western corner of Thailand, and according to their previously stored recon photos, at one time this place was a bustling train depot, a place where fuel and water could be taken on.

But the village of U Thang no longer existed. When the aerial formation arrived above the place, all they could see was devastation. The railroad yards were torn up almost beyond recognition, every building in the place was either leveled or still smoldering. Many dead bodies—and parts of bodies—could be seen scattered throughout the site.

It was clear something terrible had happened at the village—and had happened fairly recently. Just what happened was a mystery. But one clue remained.

The track beyond the destroyed city—the rail that was stretching farther west—was still intact.

They continued following the tracks. About twenty miles west of U Thang, they came upon what they would learn was a military outpost manned by Khen's soldiers.

Again, there was nothing left.

The ruins spoke of a substantial military fort, built of thick trees and cement, a five-sided heavily armored four-story structure that had featured at least thirty-six gun ports, which looked out over the valley of A Sang and boasted a wide field of fire. This was a place that must have had a garrison of at least one thousand men. Yet it was leveled and still smoldering, even though whatever went through there must have done so sometime ago.

They flew on.

The next site they reached was the ancient castle of Sing Sang, thirty-three miles down the track. This was a huge teak and stone structure that had been built twelve hundred years before and had been turned into various military outposts over the years. Sing Sang had a commanding view of two nearby valleys. One grew rice, the other boasted an ancient rubber-plant field. Both valleys were dotted with gun posts and observation towers; obviously, the people who ran Sing Sang had built these structures to maintain order over the slave laborers who worked these fields.

Nothing remained of these gun emplacements now. Every one of them had been blown up—the bodies of their gunners still remained, skeletons whose bones had been picked clean. Like in the other sites, it looked like the devil himself had cleared a pathway through the countryside, destroying anything and everything in his path.

It was at Sing Sang that the crew of the Z-16 first saw civilians. People were still working in the fields, but it was obvious they were no longer being used as slaves. It was also obvious that whatever had passed through their twin valleys had been a welcome sight.

Many civilians waved at the Z-16 as it flashed by.

It went on like this for a full day.

They passed out of Thailand and into Burma, still staying true to the westbound railway.

They flew over the city of Nsing by nightfall. It had been a major military garrison: There was evidence that many heavy weapons such as tanks and APCs had been kept here. But like in the previous sites in Siam, there was little left besides smoldering ruins and destroyed equipment.

It was obvious to those inside the Z-16 that the armored train's prime advantage was that it was arriving unannounced in these strongholds of Khen. Combining surprise and its huge parcel of weapons, Khen's men had little time to mount a defense. That's why the destruction of their strongholds was so complete.

They flew over Mandalay just as the moon was rising over the eastern mountains. This once-bustling city, and obvious major strong point for Khen, was now a ghost town. The train had apparently gone through while a major shipment of ammunition was on hand because about a third of the city had been flattened, and the pattern of the craters indicated some kind of large ammo supply had been blown up.

"One bullet in the right place might have been all they needed to get through here," Crabb remarked as they flashed over the deserted, smoldering city.

"Sometimes that's all you need," Y replied, chugging on his twelfth beer of the flight.

They passed over into Bangladesh in the early-morning hours. This rich, prosperous country had featured just four of Khen's railway military outposts, and like all those before, they had been utterly destroyed.

Using his intuition and a calculator, Zoltan determined that the train was probably moving at close to seventy miles per hour when it came upon the hapless outpost. "If every gun on that train was firing as they roared through," he offered, "and the train is several miles long as the swami said, that's an incredible amount of firepower concentrated on a small target for a very short period of time."

"They are like an army of rolling shock troops," Crabb commented, looking down on yet another devastated outpost. "A nightmare on wheels. Those guys down there never knew what hit them."

They passed through Bangladesh and into northern India. Approaching the city of Gorakhpur, they saw evidence for the first time that Khen's men had made an effort to stop the hugely armored train.

At several points along the tracks just outside the city, they saw huge logs had been cut and apparently set in place across the railway. But these logs now lay in fragments and splinters, tossed aside by the train's mighty locomotives and a battering ram Swami had spoken of as being attached to the lead engine's nose.

Farther into the city, the Z-16 observers saw several antiaircraft-gun emplacements whose barrels had been lowered to the horizontal. Apparently, they had been altered to fire directly at the train as it passed through. But again, the sheer speed and the armored plating of the train had made it difficult to get off a good shot before the guns themselves were destroyed. As it was, these gun sites were all now just smudges of black and gray against the bright green of the surrounding fauna.

In some places the jungle had already overgrown the cracked and broken gun barrels, reclaiming what it hadn't held sway over for many years.

Y crawled back up into his bunk around 0300 hours.

He was tired and drunk and getting bored at observing the path of destruction left by the armored train.

He drank three more bottles of Toomey's beer and then passed out. Emma was beside him, keeping him warm and making sure he didn't roll out of the berth. Feeling somewhat secure, Y lay back and dreamed.

He was on a huge cruise liner, a luxurious ship that always seemed to be sailing in calm weather under the hot sun. And there were two women aboard this ship, and they just would not leave him alone! For whatever reason they were always bugging him to have sex with them. Both were beautiful, but he was always too drunk to perform.

Pretty soon these two women started locking him up in chains in a small room and making him perform. It was a miserable experience and Y almost wound up peeing in his bed.

But then the ship sank, and the two women became queens or something, and he was rustled awake by Emma moving.

Then his head was filled with voices. Many voices. Then screams. Then the sound of the Z-16's engines revving very high.

The next thing he knew, Emma was shaking him awake. He slowly opened his eyes to see Zoltan pulling Emma out of the berth and jamming a crash helmet on her head. Zoltan grabbed Y and did the same thing; the OSS agent came out a lot less delicately than had Emma. He fell immediately to the floor and stumbled once the helmet was on his head.

All the while the Z-16 was bouncing all over the sky. Y caught a glance of the Jones boys up on the flight deck, and they were battling viciously with the controls.

"Jeesuzz!" Y finally cried out once his head had cleared a bit. "What the fuck is happening?"

Crabb was suddenly in his face holding a huge two-barrel machine gun.

"We are under attack," he said starkly, handing him the gun. "We must get to our battle stations. . . ."

"Battle stations?" Y said completely confused. "Who said we had battle stations on here?"

A second later, there was a huge explosion off the Z-16's right wing. The concussion sent the airplane reeling to the left. This sent Y sprawling across the flight compartment and rolling head over heels up to the flight deck itself. Just by luck, for there was no coincidence in this world, he landed—hard—on the navigation table. It was here that he was somehow able to get a firm grip, his nose pressed up against the big TV display screen.

He was able to hold on and actually read the navigational display, and that's how he knew they were now over the country of Afghanistan.

It was strange, for a moment it seemed like time stood

still. And Y's soaked brain became clear—again just for a moment.

As it turned out, he knew a lot about Afghanistan. When he was a junior OSS agent he'd studied the place and had actually done a couple drops into the wilderness country as part of the fifty-five-year war effort against Germany.

In this universe, Afghanistan was a very different place—for two reasons. Firstly, the Fifth Crusades had actually taken hold and had brought many European influences into the culture where they became firmly implanted.

Secondly, when the British empire was taking hold, the British Royal Army set up major garrisons all over the country, and stayed. They were never thrown out. This made Afghanistan a very strange place, indeed, for it was like a small part of Europe transplanted into what was actually southwest Asia. While there were plenty of mosques and marketplaces and red-tiled mud houses sprinkled throughout the rough-and-tumble countryside, the cities themselves were distinctly European. They were made up of high walls, narrow streets, stonewashed houses, Christian churches, and government buildings, which had stood for hundreds of years and resembled nothing less than medieval castles.

With his nose pressed by gravity against the navigational screen, Y was also able to see exactly where they were over Afghanistan. The Z-16 was thirty-five miles southeast of the city of Kabul Downs, not too far from the famous Khyber Pass. Y had been to Kabul Downs many times, both on duty and off.

How ironic, then, that it appeared he was about to be killed in a plane crash near there.

The Z-16 ran into another explosion, this time off its left wing, knocking the huge airplane and everyone in it to the right.

After another backbreaking tumble Y found himself pressed up against the middeck observation bubble. The g forces holding him there were so intense, it was all he could do to get a breath in and out. He felt like a gigantic hand had him by the neck and was squishing him harder and harder against the Texiglas window.

And again, it seemed like time stood still. Y could see what was going on outside, and why the Z-16 recon plane was being thrown all over the sky.

They were under attack by literally dozens of tiny airplanes, each one sporting a very large cannon in its nose.

At least, that's what the situation appeared to be at first.

What Y actually saw was a bit more complicated.

The sky was indeed filled with the tiny aircraft, which seemed to move extremely fast and were of biplane design. But in that slice of a moment Y could see that these airplanes were not all exactly alike. There appeared to be two different kinds.

One group of these tiny planes was powered by jet engines. Even though they were of biplane design—with two wings slightly askew but parallel to each other—there was a small double-reaction engine midfuselage, spewing jet exhaust and streaks of flame from the rear tailpipe.

These jets were painted in various shades of blue. They seemed to carry cannons on the wings, smaller than the other group of airplanes. To Y's eye, these odd jet-powered craft looked most like an airplane of almost ninety years before called the Spad.

The other airplanes were painted red. They were propeller driven and were lugging the huge nose cannons. They mostly resembled another ancient airplane called the Sopwith Camel. There were many more of these airplanes than the jet-powered Spads, and their pilots seemed to be firing with wild abandon.

And this is where something else became clear to Y. These airplanes weren't shooting at the Z-16 necessarily. Rather, they appeared to be shooting at *each other*.

Y tried to move his head a bit, and sure enough two red airplanes went streaking by the Z-16's bubble, clearly pouring cannon fire into the smaller, swifter, but mortally wounded jet-powered Spad. An instant later, he saw just the reverse: two jet Spads were ganged up on a lone Sopwith and were viciously pouring fire into it. Y saw the hapless pilot's head come apart in a thousand bloody pieces after taking a direct hit from the Spad's guns.

That settled it in his mind. This swarm of aircraft was not trying to shoot down the Z-16. Rather, the Z-16 had blundered into a battle.

This seemed like important information to Y—important enough for him to attempt to turn his head and yell out this news to the others aboard the Z-16.

But at that moment the Z-16 was thrown across the sky a third time, and Y was sent flying again.

He closed his eyes before impact this time, but this didn't do anything to lessen the blow of hitting the deactivated Main/AC console, shattering just about all of the critical components inside. He bounced off the Main/AC, past a vaulting Crabb, who was being thrown in the other direction, and landed again against an observation bubble.

The Z-16 was in serious trouble now. It was losing altitude, and this was bad because it wasn't flying that high to begin with. Y found himself pressed even tighter than before against an observation bubble, his bloody nose smearing the Texiglas.

Outside, the swarm of small aircraft battling each other was as fierce as ever. Y had no idea how the Jones boys were keeping the Z-16 airborne—there was so much wreckage, and so many airplanes, in the sky it was a miracle that they hadn't collided with anything. Yet . . .

At this point Y's ears cleared a bit, enough for him to hear other voices up on the flight deck.

"Why the fuck weren't these things picked up on radar?" Seth Jones was screaming at someone.

"Because they are made of wood mostly!" someone screamed back.

"Are we supposed to be shooting at these guys?" a pilot in one of the escorting AirCats was calling down to the Z-16.

"Only if they shoot at you!" Dave Jones was screaming back.

The Z-16 did another toss, and Y rolled across the floor and back up against the starboard-side observation bubble. From here, he could see that Crabb and Zoltan had stationed themselves at the next bubble down. They had opened the bubble's access hatch and were sticking two large-caliber twin-barrel machine guns out of this hole.

They went to their battle stations, Y thought, his cognitive processes now on a downturn as a result of so many whacks to the head. *Where* the hell *is mine?*

Somehow, the Jones boys were able to level off the unwieldy Z-16. Y took a deep breath—it had been less than thirty seconds since he'd been thrown from his bunk by the first aerial explosion. To him, though, it seemed like he'd been bouncing off the walls of the cabin for an hour or so.

He peered out the bubble again and was simply astonished at the number of airplanes flying all around them, guns and cannons blazing, a blizzard of red bullet streaks going every which way.

The radios were alive with calls from the escorting AirCats:

"Damn, these guys are so damn close to me!"

"Shit—if they pull that again, I'm going to shoot up a bunch of these little bastards!"

"Whoever heard of jet engines in biplanes . . . !"

It was strange. Even though these words were going into Y's ear, they were floating out the other. He was actually staring out at another scene entirely—one that sent a chill streaking through his spine and back again.

In the midst of this very crowded sky, taken up as it was by the hundreds of buzzing swift fighters, the Z-16, and the AirCats, Y's mind was seeing something else.

There were three huge aircraft about a half mile above them. Two were airplanes, but they were of a type he'd never seen before. They were both big and painted black. They both had their wing attached to the top of their fuselage, and each had four big propeller engines. High tail, snout nose, thick body—for some reason the name

"Hercules" popped into Y's addled mind, though he knew of no aircraft by that name, and he had certainly never seen any aircraft like these two before.

Another strange aircraft was attached to one of the airplanes by a long hose. It was a helicopter, a big one and it seemed to be connected to one of these Hercules airplanes by this long slender tube. Possibly this was a gas line and the airplane was refueling this huge helicopter. But then, in a wink of the eye, one of the Hercules airplanes opened fire on the one connected to the helicopter. A tremendous explosion resulted, destroying the fueling Hercules and sending the helicopter plummeting to the ground in a cloud of flaming debris.

Y's brain suddenly locked up. What the hell was he really seeing here? These strange airplanes? The helicopter? It seemed real, and then again it seemed very *un*real. In horror, he closed his eyes and gritted his teeth and took in a deep breath and opened his eyes again.

The sky was still filled with the strange, swift, battling biplanes and the AirCat fighters, but nothing else. No big airplanes, no big helicopter. Y felt a cold sweat suddenly soak him through. His mouth dropped open and words started to tumble out.

"I've got to stop drinking," he heard himself say.

Suddenly Emma was beside him. She'd retrieved the huge twin-barrel machine gun Zoltan had just given him, which he'd managed to drop during the first jolt to the airplane.

"Take this!" she commanded him. He obeyed, and somehow knew enough to cock the feed drive and slip both safeties to off. The gun was belt fed, the ammo compartment being a plain black box hanging beneath the stock. It was heavy and cold, and Y had never been within ten feet of one before.

The Z-16 was still flying somewhat straight, but this did not mean they were out of danger. If anything, the sky was even more crowded than before with the battling blue and red aircraft. Even worse, either by the jostling caused by the explosions, or possibly a stray bullet or two, the Z-16's flight computer had suddenly glitched up and wouldn't release from the LANTRAN terrain-guidance system. The last command the computer had received was to guide the Z-16 along the same direction as the westward-pointing track bed, and that's what it was doing, a mere five hundred feet above the ground. Nothing the Jones boys could do, short of firing a couple bullets into the flight computer, could get them off that automatic-course track.

The Jones boys were yelling back and forth at each other and slamming their fists on the LANTRAN console trying to unlock the hard drive, but nothing was working. They could not get control of the airplane back from the faulty computer. This was disastrous because eventually the tracks would come to an end or, even worse, split off into two directions. Then which way would the airplane go? If it lost its track reference, anything could happen, including plowing into the nearest mountain of which there were many in this part of wild Afghanistan.

In all his time with them, Y had never seen the Jones boys look nervous, ruffled, or anything but cool. At this moment, though, they seemed very nervous, very ruffled, and very, *very* uncool.

Y stole a peek forward and could see the unmistakable skyline of Kabul Downs just on the horizon.

If we have to crash, he thought, tugging Emma closer to him, *I hope we go down near the city* . . . .

The flight deck's radios were still going full blast.

"Please repeat order on defensive action?" one of the AirCat pilots was requesting urgently of the Jones boys.

A second AirCat pilot was more direct: "When can we start shooting at these bastards?"

Somehow Dave Jones was able to click in his microphone's send button.

"One last time," he shouted, slamming the LANTRAN console again to no effect. "Fire only if you've been fired upon!"

Not a second later, a ball of bright-red flames and smoke

went right by Y's bubble. It took a moment for Y to realize the flaming wreckage was one of the AirCat fighters dropping out of the sky. Frozen by shock and horror, Y saw that two airplanes—one red and one blue—had collided with the huge AirCat, and this mass of metal and wood was now plummeting to the ground.

In the next second all hell broke loose. The remaining AirCats, believing that their comrades had been attacked, opened fire on both the red and blue airplanes. Suddenly the air was filled with flaming wreckage spiraling down as the more powerful AirCat guns began blowing the strange little biplanes out of the sky.

This, in turn, caused the two swarms of biplanes to stop attacking each other and begin shooting at the suddenly very vulnerable Z-16 recon plane. The next thing Y knew he was firing his twin-barrel machine gun out the bubble access hatch at a pair of red bijets coming at him full speed from the port side.

In seconds Y's nose and throat were filled with the stink of cordite. He was firing wildly for two reasons: first, the double-MG was heavy and its kick was awesome. Second, he was very drunk and in those little slivers of time that seemed to be exaggerated by combat, he wasn't sure if he was shooting at two red bijets or four.

But somehow he was hitting targets—or at least he thought he was. The machine gun was blasting away, and there were numerous small explosions going off about fifty yards in front of him, and there were more clouds of broken wood and metal flying all over the sky.

The strange thing was that the whole air battle had commenced not a minute before. Everything was slowing down dramatically for Y. He continued firing, and things continued blowing up, and the Z-16 continued being flung all over the sky and in the midst of all this, they all passed over the next mountain and found themselves over the valley that led up to the fairy-tale, castlelike city of Kabul Downs.

One of the AirCat fighters whooshed by the observation

bubble, chasing four bijets, three blue and one red. The big plane's huge cannons were splintering the four bijets into thousands of flaming pieces. Zoltan and Crabb, firing double-MGs from the Z-16's top observation bubble, bagged two red fighters as they were trying to perforate the recon plane's flight-deck canopy. This attack caused the Jones boys—who were expert at jumping the Z-16 all over the sky—to bank the huge winged plane to the right, causing Y to be smashed up again against the observation bubble Texiglas. He almost lost the double-MG in the process.

Now he was looking straight down again, and by chance Y found himself staring at a huge railroad bed—no wonder the Z-16 was all over the sky! There were at least a hundred railway lines jutting all over the huge facility. Y couldn't imagine what havoc this was playing with the aircraft's locked-in LANTRAN terrain-tracking system. A quick glance up to the flight deck produced a blur of flashing lights and a cacophony of warning buzzers.

A moment later, there was a huge explosion up on the flight deck. Y was firing his machine gun at anything that moved, but the flash from the flight deck was enough to blind him for a few moments. The next thing he saw was a pair of missiles rising up from the ground and heading right for the nose of the airplane. Somehow the Jones boys were able to twist the big airplane away from the pair of antiaircraft missiles—but the strain on the already creaky airframe was getting to be too much. The airplane's skin was now perforated with cannon and bullet holes from the swarm of attacking fighters. The main flight console had blown up due to overloading of the LANTRAN system, and now the cry of metal against metal was telling the tale of impending double-reaction engine failure.

Y recovered somewhat, grabbed Emma closer to him, and looked down. They were right over the city of Kabul Downs itself. There were many narrow streets below them, and soldiers running through the streets, firing at each other. Y's drunken eyes told him that this war between the reds and blues was not confined to the air.

What bad luck was this? he asked himself in the beat of a heart. Busting in on someone else's war . . . .

But then Y saw one more thing that was even more disturbing: Sitting at the edge of the rail yard, not far from the center of Kabul Downs, was a train that was at least three miles long. It contained many, many flat cars, all of them holding at least several wrecked or knocked-out weapons. Machine guns, rocket launchers, triple cannons. This train was a wreck. A total wreck.

In that next blink of an eye, Y knew that they had actually accomplished the second part of their mission. Below them was undoubtedly the train Hunter and the others had armed and had taken across half of southwest Asia, just to end up here, in Kabul Downs.

But why?

Y couldn't fathom that answer—and in the next second it was gone from his mind completely. Its place was taken over by something more overwhelming.

The Z-16 was crashing . . . .

The Jones boys were fighting with the controls, but there was nothing they could do. Between the equipment fire and the numerous bee stings caused by the bijets, the huge recon plane was fast becoming unflyable. The Jones boys were trying their best to level the plane out. Their only hope was to attempt a survivable crash landing, but weight and gravity were against them on that score.

Y pulled Emma even closer to him; she was crying. Zoltan and Crabb were holding on with one hand and firing their double-MGs with the other—even now picking off bijets as their own plane was about to auger in.

And weirdly, Y's mind was suddenly at peace. *If this is where he was to die, then so be it.*

He was surprised how calm he was as the ground raced up to meet him.

Of course, he was very drunk. And in that one last time

sliver he decided this: If one has to go down in an airplane, then being drunk during the experience was the only way to go.

Wasn't it?

The Z-16 went in three seconds later . . . .

CHAPTER 28

Fiji

So, is this Heaven, or not?

It was a question that Viktor had been asking for the past twenty-four hours, and now the words themselves were taking on a comical tone.

If this was Heaven . . . would I have to ask the question?

He leaned his head back and allowed one of the bevy of bare-breasted young girls to pour another stream of sweet pineapple wine down his throat. The "pine-wine" was delicious, nutritious, and to Viktor's mind, had a slightly opiate effect to it.

He'd been drinking it almost nonstop for the past day and night, ever since he'd somehow washed up on the pearl-white beach of this paradise on earth.

He'd also been eating up a storm. Coconut soup, plum cakes, pinkfish, a hundred different types of fruit. Viktor imagined, after downing yet another long gulp of pine-wine, that he could see his previously skeletal frame taking on some bulk, though he was sure this was an illusion. In any case, in the short memory of his life, he'd never been that interested in food or drink, but now, here in Heaven, that had changed.

He looked around the guest hut, and the candles were now flickering in syncopation with the mellow electronic island music that was wafting in from nowhere. There were at least twenty-four beauties either attending him or lounging around nearby, waiting to serve. Each girl was more beautiful than the next. Each one willing to do anything his heart desired.

More pine-wine went down his throat, another piece of sweet fruit was placed on his tongue.

If that wasn't Heaven, what was?

The illusion was diluted a bit, though, when Viktor detected Soho's approach in the air.

The girls smelled it, too, and they immediately became stiffened and reserved. The stink of body odor arrived about ten seconds before the man himself did. By the time Soho actually stepped into the hut, most of the girls had fled to the far corner and had cuddled up close to a wall full of candles, hoping the heat would dissipate some of the BO.

Viktor sat up and greeted the smelly guy with a friendly nod. He didn't dislike him. After all, Soho was the reason he was having such a delightful recovery. From what Viktor had culled from their conversation the day before, just about everything—and everyone—on the island belonged in some way to Soho. He was slightly odd and slightly mysterious. His hospitality didn't seem forced, but not entirely genuine, either. He had told Viktor yesterday that he considered him his guest and that he could stay here indefinitely. Viktor had to admit that the night before he'd dreamed of staying on the island permanently.

After all, with the beautiful weather, scenery, food, wine, and girls—why leave? There were enough girls to go around for him and Soho. Viktor figured, all he had to do was best Soho in the personal hygiene department and he would get the pick of the beauty litter, so to speak.

"Are you busy?" Soho asked Viktor now. He was carrying a frying pan with him. "Am I disturbing you?"

"Not at all," Viktor lied, casting a woeful glance toward the cowering girls. "Can I do something to repay your kind hospitality?"

Soho slipped the frying pan behind his back in an amateurish attempt to hide it.

"Yes," he replied. "Walk with me. Talk with me."

So they took a long walk.

They passed the crude airplane sculpture up on the ridge, strolled along a path that led over to yet another taller cliff, and slowly meandered along the rim of an ancient volcano. The views were spectacular.

Soho did most of the talking. He spoke of how beautiful the island was, how much he cherished it, and how he had spent a lot of time arranging for the right "helpers"—the beautiful young girls—to come to this part of Fiji and stay with him.

He pointed out his favorite plants and trees. He talked about how the weather affected everything on the island, and that the weather was always perfect. Therefore, the island was perfect, too.

He spoke about how he would leave the pineapple rinds out in the sun for a week and then bury them to give the pine-wine its slight hallucinogenic affect, though Viktor did not believe this was the only reason for the wine's kick. Soho was pleasant, and in a jolly mood. Still, Viktor wanted to do nothing else but turn around and walk—no, run—back to his "recovery" hut.

Their walk went on for about a half hour before Viktor became aware that Soho was leading him around to the other side of the island, a piece of the paradise he'd yet to see.

They reached a peak that anchored the northern end of the island and provided a breathtaking view of the ocean beyond. Soho stopped and looked at the great sea beyond, the high winds blew away his cloud of body odor for the moment.

"Strange things have been happening up that way," he said, indicating a northeasterly direction. "I had a dream that someone told me most of Japan does not exist anymore."

Viktor just shrugged.

"Strange things are happening all over," Viktor said, more for lack of anything else to say. "One big war concludes, another begins. Some wars last a day, some for half a century. This is a strange world you live in."

Soho turned and looked him in the eye.

"You say that like you're from someplace else," he said.

Viktor froze for a moment. He was not going to tell this individual his life story—brief as it was to his mind. That was something the Man back on West Falkland Island had warned him about: The less people who knew his origins, the better.

"Just an expression," Viktor finally replied. "Though I have to admit, I have no idea how I made it from the bottom of South America to this paradise. One second I was being enveloped by a huge wave. The next, I'd been washed upon your shore. It's almost as if we have a link, you and I. Perhaps the cosmos wanted us to meet."

Soho just smiled and stared at him for a long moment.

"Perhaps," he said. "Perhaps . . ."

Soho started walking again and Viktor naturally followed. They went over the next hill and for the first time, Viktor realized that there was more to this island than just Soho's smelly being and a bevy of tropical angels.

Down the cliff on the beach was a long line of gigantic holding pens, each with about a hundred young men inside. The pens were all double-reinforced with thick wire, which included a roof, giving the place the look of a zoo where only the wildest and most dangerous animals might be kept.

A large black ship was anchored offshore. It was heavily armored, with a swarm of Bug copters buzzing around it.

Viktor was astonished at what he was seeing. Up until

that moment, he just assumed that Soho and the girls were alone in paradise.

"Who . . . who are those men in the cages?" he asked Soho.

"They are all the other males who live here," Soho replied, his voice getting a bit deeper, his reek getting a bit stronger. "Every able-bodied one from fifteen to fifty-five is down there. Waiting to be loaded aboard that ship you see."

Viktor could not take his eyes off the cage full of men. They all looked dejected, dopey, even sleepy.

"They are all full of pine-wine," Soho said, reading his mind. "They drank way too much of it two nights ago—and that's where it got them."

"But why?" Viktor asked.

"Because it is like you said, my friend," Soho answered. "There is a new war every minute on this planet. A new war means there must be gristle for the grinder. I'm a businessman. I sell soldiers."

"All these men are going to fight somewhere?"

Soho laughed. "Yes, they are," he said "Whether they know it or not."

"And *you* sold them into this?" Viktor asked him astounded.

"Yes," Soho replied. "Of course I did."

Viktor was feeling like this might be a dream. Either that, or he'd drunk too much pine-wine to make sense of this.

"But why?" was all he could ask as he saw men in black uniforms take about a dozen men from one pen and force them at gunpoint onto a boat, which would bring them out to the waiting ship.

"Why?" Soho laughed. "You really have to ask me why?"

Viktor just shrugged. One of the prisoners was resisting and was now being beaten mercilessly by the men in black uniforms.

"Once all these men are gone, I'll have this place plus

all the girls to myself," Soho bragged. "Who wouldn't want those circumstances?"

Viktor had to admit that Soho had a point. But at what cost?

"You understand, then?" Soho asked him. "I mean, really . . . why would I want a bunch of guys around here to ruin such a good thing? Even one other rival would be too much. With them all gone, I would be king of this paradise."

"I have to tell you, that would be a dream of mine, I guess," Viktor said.

"That's just what I thought," Soho replied.

Viktor turned just in time to see the frying pan heading right for his temple. It hit with such a force, he actually saw stars, for about two seconds. Then he slumped to the ground where Soho knelt down and whacked him on the head again. And again.

"Dream about this," he said.

CHAPTER 29

Bobby Baulis had been at the controls of the Bro-Bird for seventeen straight hours when the long-range radio message came in.

He'd just finished sharing a huge cup of coffee with one of the young hookers. She'd been on his lap for the past six hours of this long tour, keeping him company. He was looking to be relieved within the hour—in more ways than one.

The huge seaplane's position was exactly 101 miles south of the towed aircraft carrier. The carrier was about to enter the Straits of Mallaca, near what was known to some as Singapore. The seaplane was just above the northern tip of Sumatra.

This was the third long-range scouting mission Baulis had undertaken since the six-plane search party departed for inland Indochina. So far, the voyage of the seaplane-aircraft carrier tandem had been quiet. They'd met no hostile forces; they'd seen very few other ships or airplanes. In fact, things had been going remarkably smoothly considering they were traveling in rather dangerous seas.

But all that was about to change.

Bro had just readjusted his petite beauty on his lap and set in the autopilot for another hour-long, figure-eight course when his radioman climbed up to the enormous flight deck and handed him a long sheet of yellow paper. It had few words typed onto it.

"Just received and decoded, Bro," the radioman told him. "I think our friends are in some trouble."

Bro read the missive twice before the words on it really sank in. The last full message he'd received from Y and the others had reported that they had set down in the River Valley of Kwai in Thailand. That message had given their position, their fuel supply, and their general disposition, and had ended with a slightly enigmatic: "Much more later. . . ."

That had been nearly twenty-four hours ago. Now this message was sent not by Y but by the radioman inside the converted HellJet cargo plane.

It reported that the Z-16 and two AirCat fighters had been lost to hostile action, with two other AirCats damaged.

Baulis was shocked by this news—but it was the location of the plane's downing that really lit him up: Kabul Downs in the wilds of Afghanistan.

"That's the last place I would want to go," Baulis said to the radioman.

"They want to know what they should do, sir," the radioman replied. "They are awaiting further orders. Your orders . . ."

"*My* orders?" he asked. "Why me? No one has ever awaited *my* orders before."

The radioman just shrugged. "Well, Bro," he said. "I guess with that OSS guy down, and the Jones boys, as well, you're the next in line on this crazy operation."

Baulis thought about this for a long moment and finally lifted the young hooker off his lap.

It was time to get serious.

"Yell down to the carrier," he told the radioman. "Brief them on this, and tell them we're coming back. I want a meeting of all the remaining AirCat pilots at exactly sixteen hundred hours in the carrier's war planning room . . . Got it?"

"Got it," the radioman confirmed as he began to walk away.

But that's when the pretty little hooker whispered something into Bro's ear. Bro nodded once and called the radioman back.

"Make that sixteen-thirty hours," he said with a grin.

Another whispered conversation ensued.

"And tell them if I'm not there," Bro added, "they can start without me. . . ."

CHAPTER 30

Kabul Downs

Looking back on it, Y remembered almost everything with amazing clarity.

He recalled the calm that settled upon the flight deck of the Z-16 in the last few seconds before it crash-landed in the center of the city of Kabul Downs.

He remembered thousands of faces looking up at the stricken airplane as it was coming down. They were all soldiers—some in blue uniforms, some in red. They were battling each other on the wreckage-strewn streets below; the sudden appearance of the Z-16 caused an odd temporary halt in what had been a huge running battle.

Etched most clearly in his mind were the actions of the Jones boys just moments before the airplane plowed in. Somehow the pilots had kept the airplane airborne long enough to find what had to be the only flat piece of real estate inside the cluttered medieval-looking city: that was Saint Kensington Park. This was a half-square-mile area with several rolling hills and a huge lake in its exact center. It was here that the Jones boys were able to steer the broken, flaming wreckage of the big Z-16, killing the single workable engine about fifteen seconds before impact, and pulling the sharp nose up so severely, everything not tied down inside the plane wound up at the rear end of the cabin—people included.

Maybe five seconds before impact, the airplane leveled off again, and using the remaining lift caused by its ultra-long wings, the Jones boys were able to glide the plane into the large artificial lake, somehow being able to set the ass end of the aircraft down on the water first, before the nose came crashing down.

It was still a very hard impact. The Z-16 weighed thirty tons and its speed on the way down was more than two hundred knots. But the Jones boys' superb flying skills had made the best of a disastrous situation. The plane's nose hit once, bounced up, hit again, bounced again, and then finally crashed into the lake for good.

Y's next clear memory was of water—tons of it rushing into the flight cabin, sucking down everything and everyone with it.

He had a clear recollection of Crabb, with Brandee under one arm, and Brandy under the other, kicking his way up and out of the airplane through a large gash that had somehow appeared on the aircraft's roof.

He could close his eyes now and see Zoltan carrying Brayn-Di, under her shoulders, half swimming, half climbing his way out of the torn submerged fuselage.

Y's next memory was of Dave Jones pulling Emma away from him and then disappearing out of the lifesaving gash in the roof. Then, he recalled Seth Jones landing a roundhouse punch to Y's jaw, a blow that was not slowed down very much even though they were under water.

Y's next memory was of being hauled to the cement shoreline of the artificial lake and being laid out on a concrete pad that, he noticed ironically, was really a platform supporting several public-drinking fountains. He recalled soldiers running by him, all of them in red uniforms, some ignoring them, others pointing their guns threateningly before moving on.

Also clear was the sound of explosions going off all around them, and the sight of tracer streaks crisscrossing over his head making hundreds of crazy-quilt patterns against the afternoon sky. He remembered the pair of AirCat fighters—they looked so huge in flight!—buzzing the lake and the plane crash site twice before being waved off by Dave Jones.

Then he remembered turning over on his side and allowing his stomach to regurgitate several gallons of water and just about every drop of liquor he had consumed in the past week.

Then, he recalled seeing Emma lying beside him. And he remembered taking her hand and finding it very cold. Then he remembered lifting himself up and looking down into her face and seeing that she was smiling, her eyes open, her face pointing straight up but not seeing anything.

He recalled putting his mouth to hers and trying to blow breath into her lungs, but knowing that it was useless.

Then he remembered Seth Jones and Crabb pulling him away, and Dave Jones covering Emma's face with his flight jacket.

Then he remembered being surrounded by many soldiers in blue uniforms.

Then he remembered crying uncontrollably.

After that, he could remember no more . . . .

Now Y raised his head and saw nothing but black.

He was in a very dark room, carved of black stone. The floor was black with smudge and filth, the ceiling was covered with burnt-black from candles lit within for over seven centuries.

Even the bars on the tiny window were black.

He rubbed his dirty face and found it was wet again.

He'd been in this prison cell for more than twenty-four hours, and still the tears were flowing down his cheeks.

He closed his eyes and as always he saw Emma's pretty face, smiling up at him. Eyes glistening, but lifeless within. What happened to her? Had she been killed by the impact? Or had she drowned? Was there anything he could have done to save her? Could he have held her just a bit closer? Would she still be alive today if he had?

He cursed himself bitterly. He'd been drunk for ninety-nine percent of the little time he'd spent with her, and only the soggiest of memories remained. But he could still smell her sweetness on his lips, and feel her warmth in his chest. And those eyes! And that voice . . . .

He put his head in his hands again and tried to stop crying, but couldn't.

Hell was black.

He knew that now.

He stood up and stretched his chains just enough to see out the tiny prison window.

The Z-16 had come down in the middle of a huge battle in the central part of Kabul Downs. He and the others had been captured by the Blues, the soldiers who controlled the city. Apparently the Red Army soldiers had just completed a massive raid and were withdrawing back to their lines when the Z-16 plowed in. Everyone on board the recon plane was dubbed a spy for the Reds and thrown into chains.

They had all been in this cell with him at first. But the Blues had come for them one by one. First, the four "Brandy"s. Then Zoltan, then Crabb. Then Seth Jones. Then his brother, Dave.

They were being shot as spies.

Y was the last one left.

* * *

Way off in the distance, he could see a long line of trenches just outside the city's limits. Even now a huge battle was taking place out there.

To Y's bleary eyes it looked like a replay of World War One trench warfare. The trenches stretched for as far as he could see in both directions. Huge artillery pieces were firing from both sides, the sky was filled with puffs of white smoke. There were even dozens of those damn bijets flying above the battlefield, endlessly shooting at each other. The noise coming from all this was so loud, it was echoing around his cell walls.

It was strange because Y was familiar with the building in which he was being held. He had visited here many times in years past. It was known as the Lords Towers and it was a huge structure that looked like a castle and was located on the highest point within Kabul Downs.

There was a waterfall pouring out of the bottom of this castle; it flowed into the narrow Saint Yabuk river. This deep-blue waterway ran a zigzag course through the embattled city, before going under a bridge and passing beyond the lines held by the Red Army soldiers. The Yabuk was once a beautiful meandering estuary with trees and exotic plants lining both sides. Now its banks were dead, heavily littered with wreckage from a dirty little war that Y estimated had been going on for quite some time.

All this was especially ironic. He had known this city long before it had been torn apart by war. Friendly, if eccentric, people, great food, great booze, great art and music. Whenever he'd thought back on it, his eyes would see a hundred different shades of green.

Now, like his soul, it had all turned black.

He collapsed back to the floor and put his head down on his knees again. There was a rock in Y's stomach that told him he would not be a prisoner here much longer. Just as they came for the others, they would soon be coming for him.

But he didn't care. When he was shot dead, he would go to a place where Emma was—of that he was convinced. And for this moment, that's all he really wanted.

So Y was not truly terrified when the big cell door finally opened and the lone guard walked in.

He was dressed all in black, complete with a hood and cape. The guard didn't say a word. He just stood Y up and unlocked his manacles.

Y allowed him to do so willingly. Now the pit of his stomach was beginning to throb. He was just minutes away from death. Would it be painful? Would it be quick? Would the bodies of the others be there when he arrived? God, he hoped not!

Worst of all, would anyone he was close to back in America even know he was gone? His family and friends? It was so strange that his life would end here, in a city he knew so well, yet still halfway around the world from where he was born.

The guard finally got his chains unlocked and then blindfolded him. Grabbing him by the left arm, he led Y out of the cell and down a long corridor. They seemed to walk forever, Y's knees buckling slightly as they gradually turned to jelly.

Finally they stopped, and Y's blindfold was removed. They were still in a long hallway. A huge door was before them. The guard was holding a flask of some kind. He shoved it into Y's gut and whispered, "Drink it, it will make it much easier."

Y was feeling so low and hungover and sick about Emma, he simply drained the flask and handed it back to the guard. It tasted like pineapples.

The guard opened the huge door, and to Y's astonishment, he could see nothing but clear, blue sky beyond. The sun was shining. And there was a long set of steps that looked like they reached right over to that heavenly horizon.

That's when the guard took off his hood, and for the first time Y could see his face.

It was Hawk Hunter.

"Go ahead, Yaz," he was saying. "You're free."

Y woke up a second later, the sound of a key in his cell lock clanging loudly off the dark, dirty walls.

He almost smirked. How cruel was that? Having one last dream about being liberated only to have it dashed by the sound of his executioners coming to collect him?

The cell was dark now, Y had been asleep for several hours. Moonlight was flowing in the small window, the shadows cast by the bars on the wall loomed huge and ominous.

The door swung open and two hooded guards came in. Y felt his body go limp. They unlocked his chains and stood him up. Two more guards came in; they, too, were wearing hoods. One was carrying a black piece of rubber under his arm.

They marched Y out of the cell and into a long hallway. There were many more guards around. These were men in blue uniforms, their faces dirty and shallow, as if they'd been fighting a war nonstop for months—years even.

They scowled at Y as he was led by them, past many more empty jail cells and then down a long set of stone steps.

Y could hear the sound of rushing water and he knew now he was in the bottom of Lords Towers and that the water he heard was the waterfall crashing into the Saint Yabuk.

The guards led him down yet another windowless corridor, which grew darker with every step even as the sound of rushing water became louder.

They finally reached the end of the hallway—two corridors ran off of it. Y looked down the one to his right and saw five poles set up in front of a wall pockmarked with bullet holes. To the left was a small anteroom and beyond that, the waterfall.

Y felt the lump in his throat grow larger. Emma would be there after he died, right? Was he really sure of that? He whispered a silent prayer—his first in years—that this one last wish of his would come true.

But the cosmos had another surprise for him.

The guard with the piece of rubber started unfolding it. Meanwhile, another guard produced what Y believed was an air pump. As he watched in amazement, these two blew up the piece of rubber with the air pump and it soon took the shape of a large rubber inner tube.

When this was done, they put it over Y's head and pushed him toward the anteroom's window. It looked out on the waterfall.

"Can you swim?" one guard asked him as they set him up on the windowsill.

Y was totally confused.

"Can I what?" he asked.

"Can you swim?" the guard asked him again with more urgency.

But before Y could answer, the other three guards came up behind him and all four lifted him off his feet and threw him into the rush of the waterfall.

Y was suddenly tumbling head over heels. Water was going in his mouth, up his nose, through his ears.

He hit the bottom of the waterfall and kept going down. The water was black and full of debris—pieces of garbage, burned wood, shell casings, maybe even a body part or two. If it had not been for the inner tube, he surely would have drowned.

But as it was, he soon rocketed back up to the surface, breaking through with a great splash that knocked one of his bottom teeth out.

The current beyond the waterfall was very fast, and Y could not catch his breath. He grabbed onto the side of the inner tube and held on for dear life.

He was soon moving very swiftly down the filthy river,

with each second getting farther away from the castle and the place that had been his prison.

Why he had been saved, Y had no idea.

He floated downriver for what seemed to be a very long time.

The moonlight was bright, which was good as there was no other illumination in the blacked-out city.

He was totally confused; his thinking processes were not quite right. He'd hit his head several times on the way down the waterfall, and now he was drifting in and out of a hallucinogenic state.

Or at least he thought he was.

What was actually going on here? He asked himself that question over and over again, and to no good reply. Even though the guard had asked him if he could swim, he was still convinced the guards were trying to kill him, and the remark about him swimming or not was just a cruel jest. Perhaps, they had run out of bullets and had taken to drowning their prisoners.

Why, then, had they given him the inner tube?

Maybe he was dead . . . and this was Hell, just endlessly floating down a river that was far from the clear blue he recalled from years before.

The banks of the river were certainly hellish. They were jammed with all kinds of broken instruments of war. Tanks, mobile guns, airplanes. Helmets, guns.

Skeletons.

And the closer he got to the bridge, the more intense the amount of wreckage became. The sound of cannon fire began echoing through the air.

Then gunfire. Then the strange whine of the bijets and the mechanical cry of the propeller-driven biplanes. Y lifted his head above the inner tube, just enough to see that the area beyond the bridge was now lit up like it was daytime. Another battle was breaking out.

And he was heading right for it.

* * *

There were ten divisions of Red Army soldiers manning the trenchworks just outside Kabul Downs's city limits.

Many of these 100,000 men had been fighting for more than a year, nonstop, without a break except for a few hours' sleep, and if they were lucky, some time in a rear-area hospital recovering from wounds. Most were either infantry or artillery, and the constant drumbeat of combat was now so ingrained in their beings, that fighting—and killing and dying—was now somewhat routine for them.

This war had been going on for almost a year now, practically unnoticed by the rest of the world. And to a man, the soldiers of the Red Army were prepared to fight for another year, or five more, or ten. They were willing to take whatever hardship, whatever misery that the war could deliver. This was how strong they felt in their cause. This was how much they despised the hated Blue Army.

There were 150,000 Blues facing them. Though the city was surrounded by the Reds, the Blues had dug their defense in deeply, and with more men and more material, this long standoff had ensued. There were occasional breakthroughs—like the day before, when a large raiding party of Reds was able to puncture a weak point in the Blues' lines, and then pour into the city causing havoc and confusion before withdrawing again back to their lines.

These actions, while stinging for the Blues, were like the huge artillery duels both sides engaged in on a daily basis—they were brutal, but hardly crippling. Body counts increased, weaponry was expended, and another little piece of the once beautiful city was destroyed. But this was all routine. At this pace, this war *would* last for years.

There was once a time when the Reds and Blues were actually the same army. They were the Afghan National Forces (ANF)—also known as the Greens—who protected the city of Kabul Downs and acted as a kind of national police force for the country of Afghanistan.

Based along the lines of the British Royal Army, the ANF had prided itself on its professionalism, its high standards of training, and its code of initiative that had been infused in each member, from the privates to the generals. This training, which had been a tradition for decades, was actually the reason this dirty little war was taking so long to be resolved. Both sides were highly trained, highly motivated, fearless, and determined. They knew no other way to be.

But why were they fighting?

That was the question that would baffle historians in years to come. This war was a civil war, yet it had little to do with politics or internal disagreements.

In fact, this war was being fought over one thing: a woman.

Some said, the most beautiful woman in the world.

She was known by several names. The Reds knew her simply as "The Princess," and it was considered poor form to call her anything else.

The Blues knew her as *Minio-Qued,* which in local slang roughly meant "Light of the Morning."

She was the daughter of the last elected prime minister of Afghanistan. She'd grown up in the public eye, though photos of her were rare, and she'd been seen only by a few citizens before the troubles broke out. In the year of war, she hadn't been seen at all.

Like the Britain of old, the country was broken up into two factions, the Commoners and the Lords. The Lords believed their candidate should take over after the prime minister died. The Commoners wanted his daughter to rule the country. The Lords took the daughter prisoner to prevent that from happening. She was being held a prisoner somewhere in the Lords Towers, and was faced with possible execution. And therein was the conflict.

The "red bloods" against the "blue bloods" in a battle for the princess. In one year, nearly fifty thousand soldiers had died, and a large portion of the once-beautiful, if rugged country had been destroyed.

All for one woman.

Of course, Y had no idea about any of this as he floated downriver toward the growing battle.

He was about a half mile from the bridge when he saw soldiers on either bank. This was the Blues' rear area, and to his good fortune, all of the soldiers were too immersed in what they were doing—loading ammunition and rushing other troops to the front—that they did not see him slipping by in the cold, dark water.

There were explosions going off all over as he drew within one hundred feet of the bridge. Now Y could see troops on either side of the span blasting away at each other with machine guns and mobile cannons. The bridge itself appeared to be constructed of very heavy steel built on four large concrete pilings. Though battered, the span was still standing.

The river water was getting uncomfortably warm now as Y drifted close to the embattled bridge. There really was nothing else he could do but let the current take him right into the midst of the battle. It would be foolish to try to reach shore, and even if he did, he'd be right back in the hands of the Blue troops.

So Y just got down as low as he could, said his second prayer in a decade, and held onto the inner tube.

The noise from the battle was now drowning out all other sound.

The next five minutes were like a scene from Hell.

He drifted beneath the bridge, but the river was nearly clogged with wrecked military equipment, and so his progress was slowed to a watery crawl.

A large transport plane had crashed into the river just beyond the bridge some time ago. Its wing and tail fin were now blocking nearly half of its width. Y found himself bouncing off the wing more than a dozen times, not daring to use his hand to push himself along—all the while, the battle for the bridge raged right above him.

The current finally pushed him off the wing, only to get him tangled up in the twisted, rusting tail fin. This is where the watery trip became ghoulish. Soldiers killed in the fierce battle on the bridge had fallen into the water, and now their bleeding, punctured bodies were getting caught up in the same eddies as Y's inner tube.

Y found himself grappling with the freshly killed. One man's face bumped right up against his own. Eyeball to eyeball with the corpse, Y realized the man's chest had been blown away, and his stomach and internal organs were floating nearby. Y pushed himself away from this nightmarish scene only to find himself caught up in another tangle of bodies—these were wearing blue uniforms. They seemed to have been killed in the same explosion, and their bodies were fused together by the same horrific fire.

He kicked himself away from this horror and drifted past two decapitated bodies, which had been caught up on one especially jagged piece of the rotting tail fin. Then he steered the inner tube around the twisted-up left-side landing gear of the crashed airplane and found himself free again.

The current grew fast, and Y was moving very swiftly down the river. But where was he going exactly? Would he drift like this until he saw no signs of life on either side of the waterway? He didn't know.

But that question was going to be answered for him soon enough.

He drifted for another few minutes, then turned a bend and came upon a confusing, upsetting scene.

There were dozens of small boats in the water, blocking his way. These boats were crawling with red-uniformed soldiers. They were chaotically unloading large black boxes from these boats, which were obviously serving as barges. Even from his poor vantage point, Y could tell the boxes were carrying ammunition. He could tell just by the way the soldiers were handling them.

It was his bad luck to come around this bend in the river just as the major supply of ammo was being landed for the Red Army troops. There was no way he was going to make his way around this blockade.

Y had just realized this when two soldiers in a just emptied boat spotted him drifting down the river. Y felt his stomach go cold as he saw the soldiers pointing at him and yelling to others on shore.

"Here's another one!" one soldier cried from the boat.

An officer on the shoreline pulled two men from the ammo-unloading duty and directed them into the water. In thirty seconds they had waded out to Y and began dragging him in. He finally landed on a small beach in a heap.

The officer came and stood over him. He looked more perturbed than anything else.

He bent down on one knee and slapped Y a couple times lightly on the face.

"Where did you come from?" he asked in British-tinged English.

"The United States," Y replied innocently.

The officer nearly smiled.

"No," he said. "I mean just now . . . are you the last of them?"

Y pulled himself up to his knees and tried to get the water out of his ears.

"Last of who?"

The officer just shook his head. Obviously he had bigger and better things to do than deal with the waterlogged ex-prisoner.

He motioned to a pair of his aides to come forward.

"Bring him up to headquarters and put him in with the others," the officer told the men. "Make sure he gets dry, and get some hot food in him."

The officer looked down at Y and just shook his head. Y realized he must look somewhat pathetic at the moment.

"And give him a double ration of rum," the officer added to the two aides. "This bloke looks as if he needs a drink."

CHAPTER 31

Zoltan was dreaming of finding Aztec gold buried beneath an Inca plain when something startled him awake.

He rubbed his eyes and felt his right hand go immediately to his temple. His head was buzzing as if filled with a swarm of bees. He opened his eyes fully, but the glare from a nearby light was too intense. He closed them again, took a deep breath, then opened them again slowly.

"I don't believe it," he whispered, sitting halfway up on his bunk.

Crabb was sitting on the bunk next to him, drinking a cup of rum-laced coffee. Brandy, Brandi, Brandee and Brayn-Di at his side.

"Don't believe what?" he asked the psychic wearily. It had been a long twenty-four hours to say the least.

"I don't believe he actually made it," Zoltan breathed.

Two seconds later, Y came through the doors of the tent.

A cheer went up from all those gathered inside. The four girls rushed forward and smothered Y with hugs and passionate kisses—they did not know any other way to kiss.

The Jones boys, huddled in the corner talking serious business, even came forward and shook Y's hand heartily.

"We didn't think you were going to make it," Seth said to him. "You took so long in getting here."

Y began climbing into a new set of fatigues the guards had given him. He was glad to bid adieu to his old, wet combat suit.

"But where is *here* exactly?" he asked.

The Jones boys laughed. "Behind the Red Army lines," Dave answered. "Or didn't you notice when you floated in."

"Oh, I noticed," Y told them. "But why are we here?"

The Jones boys just shrugged. "The Reds saved us all from being shot," Seth told him starkly. "When we were being taken out one at a time, that's exactly where the Blue prison guards thought we were going. But the Reds had infiltrated the prison earlier in the day—lucky for us—in order to get some of their own people out. They freed us along with them."

Y just stared back at them. Freeing a bunch of prisoners—with inner tubes? Why did that sound so familiar to him?

"As to why they helped us," Dave Jones said. "Well, that's a bit more complicated."

They walked him to the corner of the tent, where they had been talking when he came in. Zoltan went back to sleep, Crabb went back to sharing coffee with the four "Brandy"s.

In the corner was a small collapsible desk and on it there was a map. Y took a quick look and realized it was a map of the city of Kabul Downs and the disposition of the opposing forces both defending and surrounding it.

Seth Jones pointed to a spot at the very edge of the map.

"We are here," he said plainly. "Mile one behind the Red Army line, at what these guys call headquarters south. As you can see, the Red lines go right around the city. These guys are stretched very thin over a twenty-two-mile front."

Seth told Y the story about the mysterious princess and how she was being held by the blue bloods and how the Reds were intent on getting her back, but had laid siege to the city for nearly a year now and had yet to come close to accomplishing that goal.

"This is being fought over a woman?" Y asked, somewhat astonished.

The Jones boys nodded gravely.

"She better be a real sweetheart," Crabb chimed in from the other side of the tent.

The Jones boys turned Y's attention back to the map.

"Inside the city, they are facing fifteen divisions of Blues. The Blues have a lot of tanks, the Reds have a lot of artillery."

He cocked his head to one side and said: "Listen . . . hear that?"

Y listened and did hear the steady *whump-whump-whump* of big guns going off in the distance.

He nodded.

"Blue tanks and Red artillery shooting at each other," Seth explained. "Whenever you don't hear that sound, you know something is up. Something big. Either we have broken through a Blue line, and they've broken through one of ours—"

Y stopped him right there.

"Wait a minute," he said. "What's with this 'we' and 'they' stuff?"

Dave and Seth just stared back at him for a moment.

"Well, look closer at that uniform you just put on," Dave told him.

To help with this, Seth shined a flashlight on Y's new combat suit. Sure enough, it was red.

"Didn't anyone mention that to you?" Dave Jones asked. "You're in the Red Army now. We all are."

Y just stared back at them, his mouth agape.

"What the fuck are you talking about?" he began. "We can't join up with these guys. Even though they did save our lives—"

Seth Jones interrupted him. "Well, listen, if that's what's bothering you, we've been assured the Reds are the good guys in this little dustup. The Blues have been committing atrocities since day one. They've been threatening to kill this princess for a year or so, and there are a lot of indications they might actually do it very soon. So, you see, we have to work like crazy to make sure that doesn't happen and—"

Y held up his hand again.

"Am I dreaming?" he asked plaintively.

"That's not a good question to ask," came Zoltan's deep intonation from across the room, even though he seemed absolutely dead asleep.

"A day ago we were in prison," Y went on. "The day before that we were flying over the longest goddamn railroad track in the world. The day before that we were in Thailand crawling all over the superbomber."

"I'm surprised you can recall all of that," Dave Jones said dryly.

Y felt his cheeks flush. He decided to ignore the comment.

"What I'm trying to say," he began again through gritted teeth, "is that we started out on a mission here. A very important mission. And nothing can prevent us from fulfilling that mission—not even these guys breaking us out of prison and saving our hides."

The Jones boys looked at each other again. It was their ritual to be performed when someone in their company had to be brought up to speed on a subject that everyone else in the room knew about.

Seth took the lead.

"That's what we're trying to tell you, dude," he said. "We've fulfilled our mission."

Y felt his head start to spin. Again.

Seth looked at Dave.

"He's confused," he said to his brother.

Dave nodded. "You want to un-confuse him, or should I?"

"I will," Seth said.

With that, he took the flashlight and then Y's arm and led him out of the tent. They walked quickly and wordlessly across the compound to another row of tents. These were bigger and more elaborate than the tent they'd been in. The security around this area was extremely tight.

They passed through one checkpoint being manned by no less than six guards. Y stared at them—they all looked familiar somehow. But in the dark and the confusion of the moment, he could not place their faces. Plus they were all wearing beards. He did however hear one guard refer to the other as "Brother Clancy."

They passed this checkpoint with a word from Jones and moved toward the large elaborate tents. There was a small, muddy field beside one of the largest, and it was here that Y saw something else that seemed very strange. There were about fifty men in this field and they seemed to be playing a game of football.

Y started to comment on this but Jones interrupted him.

"That will explain itself in good time," he said.

They finally reached the largest tent. There was a sign above it: "Red Army—Special Operations Branch."

Three men were sitting in half chairs out front, smoking cigarettes and drinking what smelled like rum. One was an Asian; another looked like a rakish college professor. The third spoke with a thick brogue.

"Now there's a man who needs a drink!" this man roared to the delight of the other two as Jones and Y passed by.

They went into the tent where they encountered a Red officer who had a distinct, slightly French accent.

"Can I help you?" he asked Jones, while eyeing Y. They both seemed to recognize each other.

"He's here to see the major," Jones said simply.

The officer nodded and indicated the next room over.

"He's in there," the officer said. "But he's real busy—as always."

"This won't take long," Jones said.

He led Y to the door of the next office and stopped.

There was a man sitting behind a desk, his back to them poring over a map.

Jones gave Y a nudge.

"You're on your own from here," he said.

Y found himself inside the room, with Jones beating a hasty retreat.

He stood there silent for a few moments. Then he cleared his throat.

"Ah . . . excuse me?" he said in a near whisper.

The man spun around and took one look at Y. Then his face lit up and he pushed his hair back and suddenly it all fell into place.

Well, sort of.

"Jeesuz, man, I never thought I'd see you again!" the officer said, coming out from behind the desk to shake his hand.

"Me neither," Y croaked.

It was Hawk Hunter.

PART THREE

CHAPTER 32

When he finally woke up, Viktor found himself in chains. He was blindfolded, cold, and hungry. But he was not alone. There were others around him. The stink of body odor was very thick in the air.

His first thought was maybe at last he really *was* dead and had gone to Hell—and Hell was a small place where he was confined with hundreds of people who smelled worse than Soho.

But in his next groggy thought, Viktor became certain this was not Hell unless Hell floated. The constant up-and-down motion was unmistakable to his bones after his experiences as a sailor. There was no doubt about it, he was on a boat—again.

Why am I always drawn back to the water?

He shook his head to clear it and now heard a cacophony of despair rise up around him. Moaning, weeping, coughing, and even some snoring.

Where the hell was he?

That's when it all came back to him.

The mercenary ship. The big black vessel he'd seen anchored in the harbor at Fiji, taking away the male islanders. That's when he had his grim answer. He was in the bottom of this mercenary boat with the rest of the exiles from Fiji.

But heading where?

He lay there for a long time, trying to block out the sounds of the unfortunates around him, and failing miserably. His chains were heavy; there would be no way of breaking free or slipping his hands out between the clasps. And even if he could, what good would that do? Other than being able to remove his blindfold, he'd still be stuck on the ship, with hostile guards and no place else to go but back into the water.

And he'd had his fill of that by now.

The sound of human misery grew around him, and now the scent of blood was thick in his nostrils. The man beside him was moaning so loudly, his voice was cracking with a sickening wheeze. This sound was going in Viktor's left ear and coming out his right. Never had he heard such a mournful cry. The man was begging to die.

Viktor stretched his chains as far as they would go. It was painful but he was able to place his fingertips on the dying man's forehead. It was burning to the touch.

Viktor wiped the sweat from the man's brow and said: "Be cool, my brother. Have peace. There is nothing to fear."

With that, the man stopped moaning. And a certain kind of peace did descend on wherever he was. All the weeping and moaning and coughing stopped. Now all he could hear were the snores.

"Very impressive," a strange voice said.

Viktor's back stiffened. Someone had been standing there the whole time, staying perfectly still, watching him.

Now a hand reached down and roughly tore his blindfold away. Viktor's eyes took a moment to focus. When they did, he saw he was indeed inside a dirty hold with greasy walls and a filthy deck. Three men were standing over him. They were all dressed in black uniforms. Viktor looked about the room. He was not surprised to find it was filled with dead and dying men.

The soldiers in black were laughing at him. They were all tall, blond, and blue-eyed. One was an officer.

"We've been watching you," the officer said. "Even the captain had a strange feeling about you, and now it looks like he was right. You seem to have a way with the dying. And the living, too."

Viktor looked over at the man he'd just comforted and saw that he had not died at all, but was now resting rather comfortably, his fever suddenly gone, a weak smile cracking his bloated lips.

"We are in the business of selling men for war," the officer said. "And in this business, every body counts. You're certainly an odd one. But we believe you might be more valuable to us alive than dead. We need a healer."

The officer pointed to Viktor.

"Take him out of chains," he snapped to the other two. "Clean him up. Put him in a uniform. We now have our medic."

CHAPTER 33

Outside Kabul Downs

Hawk Hunter—aka The Wingman, aka The Sky Ghost—hadn't slept in three days.

That was normal these days. Hunter had always viewed sleep as an annoyance. An unnecessary break in the action movie that was his life. Sleep interfered. It was lost time. Missing hours that one could never get back. He'd trained himself long before to exist on coffee and catnaps for as long as three weeks or more. In fact, at these times, he found his instincts heightened, more acute.

But there was something more to it than that. There was one indisputable fact about sleep, especially during times of intense conflict: Hunter knew that eventually his enemies would have to go to sleep. And when they did, that would give him another advantage. In combat, some times that's usually all that was needed to succeed.

Now he was downing a massive cup of coffee, no cream, eight teaspoons of sugar. It was very early in the morning. The sun would be up in thirty minutes. He was standing just outside a makeshift airplane hangar at Red Base One, a flat piece of grassy plain that served as the airfield for six squadrons of the Red Air Corps' prop-drive fighters.

Three dozen of these biplanes were warming up on the field now. This was the Red Force dawn patrol, getting ready to take off.

Hunter had been flying for the Reds for three weeks and in that time he'd fallen in love with the Red Force biplane. It looked like an ancient Sopwith Camel on steroids, but in reality it was altogether a different airplane.

It was designed like a fine classic automobile. Hunter had learned the Red Forces had built these airplanes at an old auto-assembly plant about fifty miles south of Kabul Downs, in a place called Xanana.

The biplane—officially known as the SuperCamel—had a rugged, finely tuned twelve-cylinder 3,200-horsepower engine with an unbelievable kick to it. The wings were sturdy and well wired, as was the fuselage. This gave the airplane a great degree of maneuverability.

Then there was the cannon.

One airplane from where Hunter was really from was called the A-10 Thunderbolt II. It was a ground-support aircraft, not very fast, but durable and able to withstand lots of punishment. It was built around a huge cannon called the GAU-8 Avenger.

This was in a similar style with the SuperCamel. The cannon inside the crimson biplane and it ammunition belt took up most of the fuselage. Just like the A-10, the SuperCamel was really a cannon with an airplane wrapped around it. That appealed to Hunter.

He was about halfway through his coffee now and rereading a map of this day's Blue Force disbursements. Not much had changed around the defense perimeter of the city. The Blues were just as strong as the day before, despite the huge Red Army raid, which had gotten inside the city twenty-four hours earlier.

A photo snapped of the two Blue Force airfields just a half hour earlier showed they'd be launching three squadrons, as well, this morning. Again, in the air both sides would be evenly matched.

He finished his coffee and folded the map and took a deep breath of the cool morning air.

It was time to get flying.

Hunter adjusted his leather flying cap, checked his parachute straps, and then walked out to his airplane. The rest of the squadron members were already inside their aircraft, warming the precise engines, filling the morning air with a rumbling so low, it actually shook the ground.

He reached his airplane and climbed in. Two ground-crew members helped strap him in. They handed him a last-minute weather report. The skies would remain clear and the winds would be negligible. Just the kind of atmospherics Hunter liked.

He gunned his engine and heard it growl back in fine form. He checked his cannon's diagnostic. The weapon was at full power. He checked his ammo load. It was boasting twelve hundred rounds for his disposal.

That, and a full tank of gas, was all he needed.

He saw a bright flash of red light come from the base control tower. It blinked three times, paused, then blinked twice more. This was a signal indicating that the Blue Force dawn patrol was just taking off. Once again the morning would start with a bang.

Hunter knew deep inside that in another life he had come up against a variety of aerial opponents and had bested them all. Even here in this strange world, he'd fought against German jet fighters, buzz bombs, and rocket planes, as well as the Japanese SuperZero.

But of all those opponents, he'd never come up against anything like the Blue Forces SuperSpad.

It was such an odd little airplane. Its overall appearance and design came directly from the Spad World War One fighter. This aircraft was about twice the size of the original Spad, was heavily armored and, like the SuperCamel, was made of metal and not wood. But the strangest thing about it was its power plant. It carried a double-reaction jet engine.

Now this was strange because the engine in the Super-Spad was made for an airplane at least twice its size. But the Blues, by being surrounded, had only one engine design they could make and only one airframe available, and while they did not exactly match the resulting airplane, it could fly, it could carry weapons aloft, and in the end, that's all you really want.

Just as Hunter's SuperCamel was built around its big gun, the SuperSpad was built around its big engine. It also carried four machine guns and a good supply of ammo, which made for a classic matchup. A fast, lightly armed jet airplane against a slower, heavily armed prop-driven one.

However, the Blue pilots were a tad better than the Red fliers, and so in the course of the first year of the war, the Blues had dominated the skies. That is until Hunter arrived on the scene.

But in any kind of combat, the victor always needs some kind of advantage over the eventual loser. And it took awhile before Hunter pinpointed exactly what the weakness of the SuperSpad was. But when he did, it turned the tide of the battle in the air.

Hunter knew the double-reaction engine was usually a sturdy piece of machinery, able to take some punishment and keep on working. But there was a weak link in its design. It was in the double-reaction chamber itself, where the two chemicals mixed together to provide the reaction. There was a valve that regulated the chemical mixing, called the primary-flow valve.

The first time Hunter got into an air tangle with the Blues—three weeks ago—he'd lured a SuperSpad over Red lines and then shot him down. He had the carcass of the SuperSpad hauled back to Red Base One, where he dissected it.

To no surprise, he found that the critical flow valve was located at the very bottom of the SuperSpad's fuselage on the right side. Like everything else on the SuperSpad, it was jammed tight inside the relatively narrow fuselage.

Hunter knew that a cannon shot or two in that location would be all that was needed to down a SuperSpad "super quick."

He passed this information along to Red Air Force high command, and that's when Hunter, who up to that time had just been a guy who could fly who happened to have been rescued by the pilot-strapped Red Forces on a raid inside the city, began getting noticed. He was activated as provisional major in the Red Air Corps the next day and had been flying full-time ever since.

It was important that the Reds did not give away their secret of how they could destroy the SuperSpads with minimum effort. The word went out to the Red pilots to engage the Blues in pairs. While one shot at the enemy target in the normal way—out of the sun or even head-on—the wingman would sneak underneath the Blue plane and put a string of cannon shells into its Achilles' heel. The tactic worked right away, and the air battle had turned to the Reds' advantage.

The Blues still hadn't figured it out.

Hunter's engine finally reached its proper RPMs, and everything else on his crowded but simple control panel was still green. He spoke to the tower and received his final clearance for takeoff. Another day of combat was about to begin.

He was in the process of popping his brakes when he saw an odd hunched-over figure in a long trench coat and a battle helmet stumbling toward him.

It was Y.

Hunter killed his engine and allowed the OSS agent to approach. He knew Y was going through a bad time. He'd heard about the travails he and the rest of the searchers on the rescue mission had gone through, including how

Y had taken to alcohol suddenly at the beginning of the trip, and now, just couldn't seem to shake it.

Hunter had yet to have any kind of lengthy talk with Y since the OSS man arrived in the Red camp. They had exchanged a few words the night before, but Y quickly retired to his tent, where he'd spent most of the night drinking other people's rum rations.

Hunter felt terrible about this. Y was his friend—both here and Back There. To see him in such bad shape was like a punch in the stomach. Hunter could empathize with him, though—Crabb and Zoltan had briefed him on how Y's problems only increased when he lost Emma, the brief love of his life. Crabb and Zoltan had assured him that Emma was one of the world's great beauties and a very sweet girl to boot, and there was no doubt Y was taking it very hard.

Beautiful? Sweet? But gone?

Yes, Hunter had felt that type of pain before.

Now as Y approached, he was waving his hands, indicating that Hunter should shut down his engine and that he wanted to talk. The fact that the engine was already shut down and Y didn't know it, spoke volumes about just how bad his condition was getting.

"We have to talk," Y said, finally arriving at the airplane and leaning against its side. He looked up at Hunter, and the Wingman winced. Y was a mess. His eyes were horribly bloodshot, his face was tired and drawn. He was pale and looked like he hadn't slept in a week, even though just the opposite was true.

"What do you need?" Hunter asked him. "Just name it."

"I have to . . . ask you something," Y said.

"Shoot," Hunter said, encouraging him.

"You know now the details of how we got here," Y began. "How we wound up stealing an aircraft carrier, one that needed tugboats to move it. Then we reached the place in Vietnam where you left the airplane in the cave and there was a major battle going on there. Then we found out you took a train, threw a lot of weapons on it, and drove it straight through the badlands of Asia."

Yaz paused a moment.

"Those things, and a lot of other little things," he went on, "I don't know . . . When they were happening, I felt very, very strange. Like they all seemed familiar to me—like I had either done them myself or someone else had done them and told me about it. Or, maybe like, I had read about them in some books somewhere—except they were happening to me or people that I knew. What do you make of all that?"

Hunter just stared back at his friend. He'd been fully briefed by Zoltan, Crabb, and the Jones boys on what they'd gone through trying to find him after the super-bombing. And like Y, those events *did* seem to have an eerily familiar ring to him. Even the Jones boys looked familiar to him the first time he set eyes on them, as did Kurjan, the Red Force intelligence man.

But why?

All he could theorize was that these things had in some way happened to him Back There. This was a fascinating if unsettling theory. Not only were there many parallel universes, but events in each might be similar, but not exact. Like Y, Hunter had suffered from a weird sense of déjà vu since arriving in this strange world. It was Zoltan who told him a year ago—back in Iceland during the war against Germany—that it was best he didn't think about such things too deeply. This was advice Hunter had found hard to take at first, but successful for his mental well-being in the long run.

He now told Y the same thing.

"You know I'm not from here," he said to the OSS man. "I just got to believe that back where I did come from, I did some of these things, and now, here, I'm reliving these adventures in just a slightly distorted way. Parallel events. Parallel lives. That seems to be the way it is."

Y thought about this for a moment, then his eyes brightened.

"So what you're saying, then, is that maybe, if I was to somehow get to where you originally came from, there is a chance that maybe . . ."

His voice trailed off.

"Maybe what?" Hunter asked.

"That maybe, Emma is there, too?" Y finally blurted out. "That maybe I can find her again?"

The words hit Hunter like bullets to the brain. If someone lost their love in one world, could they simply go to another world and "find" her again? Hunter felt his chest tighten, his hands balled into fists. He didn't want to address this topic; he didn't even want to think about it, because either way, in his case, the reply was too painful.

So he just shook his head.

"I don't know, Yaz," he said finally. "I just don't know."

With that, Hunter reached down to start his engine again. But Y started banging once more on the side of the airplane.

"Just one more thing, then," he asked, back to slurring his words. "How did you know to come *here*? What happened after you dropped the bomb? I have to know. That's why they sent me after you in the first place."

Again Y's words hit him like a string of bullets in the gut. Why did Hunter come here to far-off Afghanistan instead of turning for home after the superbomber survived the titanic blast?

There was no way he could explain it to anyone because he didn't quite understand it himself.

He decided to tell Y only the basics.

"A ghost told me to come here," he said truthfully. "And I think the rest should be . . . well, classified, until we get to another place that's more secure."

Y just shrugged. He was already wondering where his next drink was coming from—though the Reds had been very generous in doling out extra rum rations to him.

"A ghost, really?" he mumbled. "Now that's interesting."

Y thought a moment while Hunter inched his hand down to the engine start button again.

"Ah, just one more thing," Y said. "One last question, I promise."

Hunter nodded patiently.

"This ghost," Y began. "Was his name 'Vogel' by any chance? A real bitter guy? Used to fly with the AirCats?"

Hunter just shook his head. "His name was certainly not 'Vogel,'" he replied, again truthfully.

Y just shrugged again, and seemed to accept this answer at face value.

"Well," he said, "did he mention if he *knew* another ghost named Vogel? I mean, we communed with that guy—he's the one who led us to the god-awful place in Vietnam."

Hunter just shook his head and finally did start his engine.

"No, he didn't mention anyone named Vogel," he told Y, yelling over the noise. "And besides, from what I understand, ghosts get really pissed off if you ask them if they know other ghosts. Apparently they are very touchy about the fact that just because they are spirits, people assume they know every other spirit."

Y just shrugged again and smiled drunkenly.

"Oh, OK," he said, stumbling away. "Just thought I'd ask."

Hunter finally took off.

Once airborne, he gave the engines full throttle and was soon soaring high above the Red lines. The formerly magnificent city of Kabul Downs loomed on the horizon.

He wasn't up more than one minute when he saw the swarm of Blue planes rising into the early morning air. The noise the SuperSpad jet made was unique. Almost a whistling sound, but perversely sweet. In the key of C, Hunter believed.

The two aerial armies met head-on over the bloody bridge, which separated the lines below. As always, the

Blue planes tore through the slower Red formation. This was their first tactic every day. No firing, just flying as fast as they could through the Red formation, strictly as an intimidating tactic.

Only after the Blues went through the Red formation did they turn back, slow down, and attack in earnest. The Red Force scattered as planned, and when possible, paired off and went after single Blue Force SuperSpads. In the first thirty seconds, three Blues went down. This told Hunter it would be a good day in the sky.

He did not stick with the Red formation. He preferred to do his own thing. He dove into the thickest concentration of Blues—they tended to stick together if they had losses early on—and simply began twisting and turning and looping and diving, lining up the scattering Blues, firing one shot into the right spot on their fuselage, killing the plane and moving on.

He wove his way through the crowded skies, routinely downing the Blues' airplanes. Even though he'd been doing this for three weeks, flying the same airplane and scoring the same spectacular hits, the Blues never ran when they saw him coming. Not that they didn't want to. Obviously, it went against their orders to do so.

This had gotten Hunter to thinking . . .

Even while he was emptying the skies of the Blues' SuperSpads he was able to watch the land battle as it commenced in the trenches below him. The Blues' ground forces seemed to stick to as strict a timetable as their air corps. Every day just as the sun peaked over the mountains to the east, the Blues would launch an attack on the Red lines all around the city. The Red Forces would beat them back, and then a day of attrition and artillery duels would begin.

Hunter found this very odd. The Blue Forces were good fighters—they had ingrained in them the same legacy of bravery and toughness as the Reds, indeed they could be fierce fighters when their backs were against the wall. But they seemed too . . . *regimented.*

Why?

These were the thoughts on Hunter's mind this morning as he downed seven Blue Forces' SuperSpads with seven single bursts from his huge nose cannon.

Looking over his shoulder now, he could see dogfights beginning to take shape in the skies all around the city—all four sectors were lighting up at once. It was yet another replay of every day of battle since he'd come here. Regimented. Like the Blues were following the same script, day after day.

This morning he vowed to find out why this was so.

He downed another pair of Blue planes, watched their pilots hit the chutes and float down behind Red lines. It was now ten minutes into the dawn patrol and the skies were getting filled with airplanes and tracer streaks.

Hunter took a quick appraisal of the ongoing air battle, and decided that his Red Force comrades were making a good showing for themselves and could spare his absence for a while.

This in mind, he pushed the biplane's stick forward and increased power to his engine.

Then he pointed the nose of the airplane right toward the heart of Kabul Downs.

CHAPTER 34

Above Kabul Downs

Hunter's theory was a simple one really.

Unlike the Reds, the Blue Forces were so highly regimented because they were being controlled by a very strict central command, an entity that insisted on pulling all the strings in every aspect, of every day in this odd war.

The commanders in the field could not take the initiative ever—indeed, judging from what Hunter had seen, the Blue Force commanders had squandered countless opportunities that might have inflicted grave losses on the Reds, simply because some bozo at the other end of the phone wouldn't give them the go-ahead to do so.

This type of strict central control was not a new concept to Hunter, though it was rather out of place in this world where, more than his last place, people really tended to do their own thing, especially when it came to the military.

Back There, in his first combat against the old Soviet Empire, the American strategy was based almost entirely on the Russians' adherence to a "no-initiative" type of warfare. No attacks unless assiduously planned. No moving beyond a certain point on the map, even if the enemy was on the run. It even got to the point where Russian pilots had to ask permission to fire on an enemy airplane while in the midst of a dogfight.

It was a stupid way to run a war, worrying about staying in control and not moving onto victory. That's how the Soviet forces fought in Hunter's version of World War Three. And that's how they lost—on the battlefield anyway.

He smelled the same type of thing going on here. It really did seem like the Blues could not make a move until a certain time had clicked off the clock or a certain general somewhere—buried beneath the city in a very hardened bunker, no doubt—gave the word while ordering his lunch for the day.

Finding that invisible bunker was now foremost on Hunter's mind. The question was where to look?

If there was a central command station somewhere in the city, he knew that knocking it out would probably send chaos through the Blues' command structure.

But where would that central point be? Kabul Downs was a huge city full of skyscrapers and castles and many large block-size buildings that somehow captured an architecture halfway between Middle English and Southwest Asian. This meant lots of towers, minarets, and buildings with lots of windows that were thickly structured.

In other words, such a place could be anywhere.

But Hunter was not a babe in the woods when it came to these things. If he couldn't spot the central command station from the air, he would simply allow the Blues to tell him where it was.

So when he reached the inner city limits, he put the biplane into a steep dive, pulling up only when he reached a perilous 250 feet in altitude.

As soon as he leveled off, he realized he was right above a rear area for the Blues. It was a canteen and there were several hundred soldiers hastily eating before being rushed to the front. They were as surprised to see him as he was to see them.

He didn't want to kill anyone if he didn't have to—especially when they were eating. But that didn't mean he couldn't shake them up a bit.

So he looped around and intentionally put more gas into his engine than necessary. This created a backfiring effect that began to dull his own hearing. Then he notched down to about one hundred feet and went screaming over the mess area.

As one, the soldiers all threw up their food and went facedown on the ground. One pass and the place was a mess—literally!

"*Bon appétit,* boys!" Hunter called over his shoulder as he screamed for altitude again.

He was soon over a truck park—the Blues moved everything to the front by truck. This was a place where they kept their constant flow of supply vehicles. This was a legitimate target.

Hunter cocked his gun and set a reading for twenty shells. He flipped over, pulled back on his gas again, and went down to treetop level. The anal-retentive Blues had all their trucks parked in a neat, little row. One incendiary cannon shell perfectly placed in a fuel tank and *wham!* goodbye truck.

This happened twenty times. Actually, there were twenty-three trucks, but the resulting explosions were enough to wreck the other three. Hunter made it all happen in just two passes. A minimum of effort, and a maximum result.

He liked it that way.

He crawled back up to five hundred feet and continued on toward the center of the city. The biggest buildings were looming right ahead of him now, and he could see people in the street were turning his way. He laid on the gas again, making his plane as loud as possible, and zoomed right down the main drag of Kabul Downs, a street called Queen's Drive.

Well, this was not an everyday occurrence—a Red fighter plane roaring over the main street of the embattled capital. It was obvious even from five hundred feet that those below didn't quite know what to do.

Hunter just started weaving through the twists and turns of the canyon of buildings, following Queen's Drive for the most part but sometimes diverting off to a side street—only to scare the bejeezus out of someone walking there.

He was flying so loudly, he began hearing fire alarms going off all over the city below. This gave him a laugh.

Hunter continued his noisy run. A few soldiers on the ground took potshots at him with their rifles, but never to any harm. Oddly, he saw no antiaircraft weapons within the heart of Kabul Downs. This was interesting in that the city was actually very vulnerable to a strategic bombing attack—if only the Red Forces had some substantially sized aircraft to carry out such a campaign.

He finally reached the end of Queen's Drive, which terminated in a roundabout that in turn flowed into a short avenue leading up to the Ministers Hall. This was the seat of the blue blood's government, a queer-looking building whose architecture looked like a cross between Westminster Abbey and "1,001 Arabian Nights."

It was here that he encountered his first serious antiaircraft fire.

It started coming up about a half mile from the Ministers Hall. Three long strands of 70-mm antiaircraft artillery (AAA) shells, lighting up the early-morning sky.

Of course, Hunter knew the AAA fire was coming even before the gunners had pressed their triggers. He was already weaving and dipping before the first shell even left its barrel. The fire was directed at him from a gun emplacement on a hill about one hundred yards away from the ministry building. That, and a few guards on the ground who were firing their combat weapons at him, were the only opposing fire he drew. It was interesting that the Blues did not protect their seat of government better.

It also told Hunter that this was not where the central command station was located.

He flew on.

The next main street was called King's Walk. Before the war began, it boasted salons and fancy restaurants. It was now the location of the blue bloods rear-area hospitals. Hunter flew past this part of the city as quickly as he could.

The end of King's Walk brought him out to the huge tree-lined park located smack-dab in the middle of the city.

Here he saw for the first time the wreckage of the Z-16 recon plane. It was still there, just as Y and the others said it would be. Crumpled, wings bent, sitting with its nose down in the shallow, artificial lake.

It was very strange to see the wreck now. It brought all kinds of memories flooding into his brain—things that he'd really tried to put on hold lately. But the horror of the superbombing was a hard thing to keep locked away for too long—even for someone with above-the-ordinary psychic ability.

So even though he renewed his defenses about thinking of that horrible flight, looking at the Z-16, he couldn't help bits and pieces of it from leaking through.

The flight . . . down the coast of South America, past the battlefields of the last war . . . then under the South Pole . . . the huge B-2000 flying great . . . all systems go . . . radio silence . . . JT making sure his beer is properly iced . . . everyone else playing cards . . . music playing somewhere within the vast aircraft interior.

The trip up the other side of the world . . . over India . . . over China . . . adjusting the flight plan all the time . . . still hidden . . . still secret. . . .

Over the North Pole, turning all the time . . . beginning

the bombing run hours before drop . . . looking out at the snow . . . it's not blue like at the South Pole . . . Ben winning a big pot in cards . . . JT worrying out loud that he didn't bring enough beer for their postmission celebration . . . .

Coming south again . . . getting ready to see drop zone . . magnetic settings confirmed on bomb . . . the coded message back to Bride Lake that all was a go . . . seeing the first SuperZeros on radar coming to meet the big plane . . . Fitz saying, "They know we are coming" . . . the call to battle stations.

The swarm of Zeros rising to meet them . . . only in nightmares had he seen so many airplanes at once . . . the earsplitting sound of hundreds of cannons opening up at once . . . .

Seeing the Japanese Home Islands . . . from five miles up . . . the sound of the B-2000's engines straining as he put the big plane into a shallow dive . . . the Zeros are everywhere! . . . His cockpit window seems full of them . . .

Fitz telling him that he's received a radio report . . . the Zeros are being ordered to ram the big plane . . . the sky is filled with tracers . . . Hunter is trying to keep the big plane on its precise course . . . Twenty minutes to drop time . . . more Zeros . . . the crew is shooting them down, but more keep coming . . . ten minutes to drop . . . SAM missiles start rising toward them . . . Hunter wielding the big plane this way and that . . . avoiding the AA missiles and disrupting the airflow all around them, causing some Zeros to stall and crash . . . .

Five minutes to drop . . . some of the Zeros are getting close enough to score hits through the B-2000's very thick skin . . . two NJ-104 guys are hit and killed . . . the secondary radio antenna is blown away . . . and more Zeros are coming up.

Three minutes to drop . . . Hunter fighting the controls now, with all the weaving and dipping the plane is becoming unstable . . . "Just hold it, Hawker!" Fitz had yelled.

Two minutes to drop . . . an AAA missile grazes the right wing . . . electricity starts crackling throughout the big plane . . . short circuits are everywhere . . . two more NJ-104 guys get it . . . Hunter's hands are bleeding, he's holding the steering yoke so tight.

One minute to drop . . . the B-2000 is simply full of holes. Many critical systems are hit . . . bombing run begins . . .

Thirty seconds . . . Tokyo appears through the clouds . . . what looks like a firework display is actually AAA missiles coming up at them . . . Fitz works the bombing system . . . bomb-bay doors open . . . Hunter fights the controls to get the airplane at correct height and proper magnetic alignment . . .

Twenty seconds . . . ten seconds . . . five seconds . . . three . . . two . . . one . . . zero . . . bomb away.

Then came the horrible light . . . .

Hunter's body started vibrating, knocking him out of this painful trance.

He looked up and realized he'd flown more than a mile beyond the central park where the Z-16 lay crumpled. Now he was in what used to be the business district for Kabul Downs. He quickly shook himself back to reality.

This area was all gray/brown office buildings, sixteen blocks of them. It was a very nondescript part of the city, so why then was his body vibrating?

Hunter found out a few seconds later.

He saw the first stream of AAA fire coming from his left. It was coming from a double-triple gun, a two-tiered 70-mm antiaircraft battery containing three barrels apiece. Hunter deftly lifted the biplane up and over this fusillade, only to sense another threat off to his right. It was another barrage of triple-A, this one radar-guided. He slammed the stick down, went into a dive, and just managed to avoid this storm of lead. That's when *another* gun opened up on him. Then another. Then another.

Hunter got the biplane down so low, his wheels actually scraped the pavement of the roadway, while people below scattered thinking he was going to crash. He did a bounce and then put the biplane into a sharp climb, thousands of AAA shells rising up to meet him. Chasing him up to 500 feet . . . 750 . . . 1000 . . .

By twirling and spinning and weaving, he managed to avoid being hit—but still more guns were firing at him. He counted twenty separate AAA sites before he knew there was no need to count anymore.

He knew no matter how closely hidden, the Blues' central command station would be the most highly protected part of Kabul Downs.

And judging by the number of guns now shooting at him, he was sure he found exactly what he'd come looking for.

He spun up to five thousand feet, away from the AAA fire, and turned west toward the Red Army's lines.

There was a warm feeling in his heart, caused by his knowing that his improvised recon mission had produced results. He was certain the central command station was in the financial district of Kabul Downs, a neighborhood known as the Pennylane District. Now the question was: What should he do with this information?

As he was tumbling these factors around in his mind, he got high enough to see the trench lines clearly again. Morning battles were still raging all around the city, both in the air and on the ground.

Hunter would go back now, he decided, land at Red Base One, eat a quick breakfast, load up on gas and ammo, then do a 0900 patrol. If that went well, he could go up again at noon.

At that moment he realized he was flying right by the Lords Towers, the place where the rescue party led by Y had been kept, until the Red Army insiders broke them out.

He'd never really paid much attention to this place before—he'd never really gotten within a mile or two of it.

Yet now . . . something seemed to be calling his attention to it.

He slowed his engine and looped around the tower. It was mostly English in architecture, with very little of the Mideastern influence seen in most of Kabul's buildings. The place looked like Big Ben without the clock. It was very tall, plus it sat up on a hill, which made it appear even more imposing.

Hunter was about to turn away and head for home when his body started shaking again.

What was this all about?

He turned and realized there were no less than six SuperSpads coming right up his tail. Hunter instinctively threw his throttle forward and heard the big prop engine kick in. He was soon up to 200 knots, then 250. Then he looped back toward the Lords Towers.

It was an insane thing to do. The Spads were getting within firing range, and while he could handle a couple, or maybe three at a time, six SuperSpads were a handful.

Yet something was drawing him to the tower.

He looped around it again and stared at the top of the structure, and just as the SuperSpads started firing on him, he saw a flash of white against the dull brown brick of the top floor.

And that's when his entire body began to shake so much it was all he could do to hang onto the stick.

He saw a hand waving to him from a very small window.

Deep down in his subconscious, in a place that not even he himself could ever go, he realized the reason why he had come so far to fight in this strange war.

Then, just as quickly as it had come, the moment was gone. Hunter pulled out the throttle and twisted away from the SuperSpads dogged fire. With a huge kick of speed, he pointed the airplane's nose toward his own lines.

And though the sun was now at his back, the Light was once again shining in his eyes.

CHAPTER 35

Red Base One

Hunter bounced in ten minutes later, leaping from his airplane even before it had stopped rolling.

He ran full-out to the intelligence hut. He felt he was holding two very important pieces of information: first, he was sure he discovered where the Blues' central command station was hidden.

But more important, he was also convinced he now knew where the blue bloods were keeping the missing princess.

But when he burst into the intell hut to announce his news, he was met with a sea of stern, dejected faces.

Everyone was there: Fitz, JT, Ben, Geraci and his staff, and the JAWS boys. Y was asleep on one of the bunks, drunk again. There were several Red Army intelligence officers there, as well.

As soon as Hunter saw their faces, he knew something was wrong.

Really wrong.

He fell into the nearest chair and allowed his shoulders to slump. All of the enthusiasm quickly ran out of him.

"OK," he said finally. "Let's have it."

Major Donn Kurjan was head of the Red Army Intelligence section. Like with many other people he'd met since coming here, Hunter felt like he'd known him in his other life. Kurjan solemnly hung up a map. It showed not just Kabul Downs but the entire Southwest Asian area. This encompassed not only all of Afghanistan, but also Iran, Pakistan, India, and the vast waters of the Arabian Sea.

"We just got a very disturbing piece of news from some free-lance spies down south," Kurjan began.

He pointed to an area at the bottom of Pakistan, where that country met the waters of the Arabian Sea not far from the city of Karachi.

"Our sources say they've been watching a large dredging operation down in this area for the past three days," Kurjan went on. "Hard as it might be to believe, this appears to be an effort to link parts of the Nawa Canal to the Indus River—"

"Dredging as in making the waterway wider?" Hunter asked, his spirits continuing to plunge. He knew what this was leading up to.

"Making it both wider and deeper," Kurjan replied. "And whoever is doing the work isn't fooling around. Our people report that a DG-fifty-five bomb went off there late last night as part of this massive operation."

Hunter was stunned.

The DG-55 was the equivalent of an atomic bomb Back There. The Germans used them in their war with the U.S. Three DG-55s wiped out Paris on the eve of a peace agreement, killing more than ten million people. Next to the superbomb most recently dropped on Japan, DG-55s were the most destructive weapons on earth.

"They are using DG-fifty-fives to dredge a river?" Hunter asked somewhat astonished.

"Apparently so," Kurjan confirmed.

"Then they are linking that river and the canal for only one reason," Fitz said.

"To bring large ships up as far as they can," Hunter filled in the blank for him.

"And that can only mean one thing in this part of the world," Geraci moaned.

Everyone knew what he meant—but no one wanted to say the word.

Hunter did it for them.

"Mercenaries," he said.

The gloom in the room increased tenfold.

It was the one thing they did not want to face. The battle for Kabul Downs was already a tightrope walk. Evenly matched sides battling it out. The introduction of fresh troops on either side would tip the scales precariously. Now it appeared that the blue bloods had made an effort to do just that.

"It is the only possible explanation," Kurjan said. "This is the only conflict going on in this part of the world—the only major one anyway. This is the only possible destination for any mercenary ships. And their linking of the river and the canal tells us they're not that far away. When the dredging is over, they'll be able to bring ships up river by at least one hundred miles, probably more. That's a lot of miles to avoid walking, especially in that terrain."

"Any idea who is doing the dredging operations?" Hunter asked Kurjan.

"Nope," he replied. "But I can give you a good guess."

"Germans?" Hunter asked.

"Feet to the fire, that would be my answer," the intell man replied solemnly. "They are the only ones who know how to work with DG-fifty-fives. They lost the war, but that doesn't mean there isn't still a lot of them around. I would say there is a very good chance that we are looking at Germans doing the blasting, Germans sailing the mercenary ships. Germans as brains behind the whole operation. That means, if we don't win this war before the mercs are introduced—or even if we do—it's not going to be pretty."

Now came a very long, very gloomy silence. Every man in the room played in his head a number of ghastly scenar ios that could come to pass if the Blues introduced more troops to the current hostilities. The Americans among them had all volunteered to fight for the Reds simply because Hunter seemed to think they'd been predetermined to do so, and because, on the face of it, the Reds were in the right in this war.

But now it appeared the dangers associated with that fateful decision had just been raised significantly.

The silence went on for five full minutes.

Finally JT stood up, stretched, and yawned.

"Well, let's face it, then, we're fucked," he said graphically.

Another long silence. No one could disagree with him.

No one except Hunter.

"We're fucked only if we don't do something about it," Hunter said.

Now all eyes quickly turned to him. Those in the room could already see the wheels spinning in his head.

But Fitz had a question.

"Do something about which thing, Hawk?" he asked. "The dredging? Or winning this war before the mercs get here?"

Hunter thought about this for a very long time.

Finally he replied: "Both."

CHAPTER 36

Kabul Downs
That night

The railway yards in Kabul Downs were known officially as the Fifth Royal Delivery and Maintenance Station.

It was an expansive layout, a hub where no less than thirty-five major rail lines had once come together. Time and regional wars had cut that number in half. But still, this was a busy place—or it had been before the war began a year ago.

Any trains coming into Kabul Downs now traveled down from the north, through the mountain passes that more often than not were held by the Blue Forces. These trains mostly brought in perishable foods. The city itself had a year's supply of stored food, fuel, and medicine on hand. Fresh foodstuffs, plus ammunition and fresh water, were always at a premium.

It was for this reason, then, that "Royal Five" as it was called was usually under heavy guard. Any train making it through, was unloaded quickly, its cargo brought to the city and squirreled away with haste. The empty trains would then depart, and with only the occasional Red Army sabotage on the north track to delay them, usually left within a day or two.

There was one train, however, that had arrived at the rail yard and had not left. Indeed, it was not going anywhere anytime soon.

This was the makeshift armored train driven to Kabul Downs by "Hunter & Crew" some three weeks before.

The fact that the train had been stolen from the napping forces of Khen the Hun had had a great deal to do with its success in getting to Kabul Downs. The train had torn a path through Khen's territory on a combination of both guile and disguise. Those outposts that were caught unaware simply thought it was Khen himself rolling through. Those that had been warned that a rogue train was coming down the tracks were still reluctant to fire on it. What if some mistake had been made and this *was* Khen's personal train? It was just that small amount of hesitation that allowed Hunter's crew to get in the first shot, get the upper hand, and practically demolish anything or anyone that stood in their path. The train ride itself had lasted all of three days—but it had destroyed a substantial part of a madman's ill-gotten empire, and freed thousands of people from oppression along the way.

But that train, at once historic and proud, now lay broken and scarred on a deserted track-roundabout out of the way in the darkest corner of the Royal Five railroad yard.

Most of the weaponry had been stripped off by the blue bloods, though tellingly not one of them had been turned around to actually be used against the Reds. Many had been made unusable by Hunter and the others as they were rolling into Royal Five, unannounced. The Blues were not innovators. Though they had come into possession of several dozen large machine guns, antiaircraft guns, and various rocket launchers, their system of military doctrine didn't consider trying to make the broken work again.

They simply took the weapons off the train and threw them into storage to rust away.

All except the airplanes, of course.

Forgotten in the bold railway strike across Southwest Asia were the handful of airplanes that the gigantic B-2000 superbomber had literally lugged around the world on its apocalyptic bombing mission.

The original six had been a strange bunch: there were two Z-4 Bantams. Small, hot-rod fighters, no bigger than a small truck, they were just a bubble canopy on a pair of wings really. Yet they could pack a punch with their twin cannons and air-to-ground rocket arrays.

There was the Z-5 SuperAeroCobra, a large, bulky, over-engined, underdesigned swing-wing fighter that looked like a piece of crap but could clock in at Mach 3—and that with a heavy bomb load.

Then there were the two unnamed VTOL airplanes. They looked fairly innocuous—wings, fuselage, bubble canopy, nose, and tail. But the two engines were actually hitched to the forward fuselage, and with the push of a lever inside the canopy, were able to swing up and down. This swinging meant the airplanes could take off and land vertically—without the aid of rocket bottles. In another universe, their distant cousin was called the Harrier jumpjet.

The sixth plane had been the Z-16 recon plane, which had been left behind at Long Bat for the rescue crew to find.

Only four planes were left of this odd squad now: the two Bantam and the two VTOL planes. The Z-5 Super-Cobra had been left back in Kwai as the signal for the rescue crew to set down there. The Z-16 lay crumpled in Kabul's central park.

The four surviving airplanes were still on the rogue train. Tied down and covered by tarpaulin, the Blues had taken one look at the strange airplanes' and simply covered them back up again. They didn't have the faintest idea what to do with such exotic weaponry, which wasn't much of a surprise from a military establishment whose idea of high-tech was to place a jet engine inside the frame of a biplane.

So here these four odd, but powerful airplanes sat. Practically forgotten.

Ripe for the taking . . . .

It had been a long day in the trenches for the Blues defending Kabul Downs.

The artillery duels had been particularly long and drawn out, especially in the late afternoon around the bloody bridge to the south of the city. This was where the sides seemed to clash most often, the hot spot in the twenty-two-mile front, which practically encompassed the embattled, besieged city.

Just as soon as the sun went down, and many of the Blues began withdrawing from their forward positions for the night, the Reds launched a massive artillery barrage all along the front. This was unusual and it sent the blue-blood night commanders into a bit of a panic. They immediately began ordering weary troops out of their billets, away from their hot meals and beds, and back up to the front to face whatever the Reds were planning to do after the artillery barrage let up.

The Blues expected another raid into the city. Each and every successful raid by Red Forces into the heart of Kabul Downs had been presaged by a huge artillery barrage the likes of which was now lighting up the night sky. But this time was different. The Reds had never launched a raid on Kabul Downs during the night before.

This was enough to ratchet up the tension several notches behind the blue-blood lines.

Which was exactly the idea.

With flames from the southern front now lighting up the sky, the guards based in the Royal Five railroad yard were put on trucks and rushed forward in case a large Red Army raid was coming.

When this was done, responsibility for guarding the railroad yards was given over to a very unreliable group—the Sally-Buns. Their actual name was the "Salibun," and they had once ruled parts of Afghanistan with an iron, religious hand. Over the decades, the Buns had been assimilated into the British Empire's self-defense forces. When the war broke out between the Reds and the Blues, the Buns elected to side with the Blues. As it turned out this was a favor to the Reds.

The Buns were lousy soldiers. They were ill disciplined, poorly trained, and lazy. They were also vicious and spent much of their tenure in Kabul Downs killing each other over squabbles revolving around card games or drunken games of blood sport.

They were a force that was always held in reserve to be used only when the rest of the barrel had been scraped dry. No self-respecting commander in the Blue Forces would let any of them anywhere near the front. That's why when the rail-yard guards were rushed into duty, the Buns were dispersed throughout the Royal Five and told simply to stay out of trouble.

But even this, they would not be able to do.

The commander of the Buns rail-yard detachment was a man named Ali Bet-Assou.

He'd been drinking heavily when the call came to rush to the rail yard. Now that he was on station, nothing had changed.

He'd brought some snake wine to the rail yard with him. After lazily positioning his men in the most convenient, as opposed to the most strategic, locations, Bet-Assou took up residence in the high tower, which overlooked the rail yard, and opened his first bottle of wine.

Bet-Assou had personally killed 251 people in his adult life. Not soldiers—people. Civilians, women, elders, chil dren. In the old days he'd been paid by the number of fingernails he brought back to his Sally-Bun regional chief. Bet-Assou was known far and wide for the practice of extracting those fingernails *before* slaying his victim. Oddly enough, he had a bad habit of biting his own nails, many right down to the quick.

By 2100 hours Bet-Assou was drunk and sitting feet up on the controller's panel in the high tower watching the artillery duels on the southern front about ten miles away. He had no radio with which to talk to his men, and had made no arrangements by which they would check in with him on a regular basis.

It was not unusual, then, when Bet-Assou, taking his eyes off the battle in the distance to scan the rail yard below, saw two of his men stretched out on the ground about one hundred feet away. Arms crossed, feet propped up, they looked not so much asleep, but passed out—a common side effect of the lethal snake wine.

Bet-Assou made a mental note to pull a fingernail out of each man's right hand the next morning and went back to watching the battle and drinking his wine.

He did this for five minutes and when he looked down again on the rail yard he saw two more of his men also laying down on the job. Both atop a rail car located directly in front of the tower.

Now Bet-Assou was growing furious. He only had ten men in the rail yard and nearly half were out cold from snake wine. He took out his flashlight and directed it down into the yard looking for the other half-dozen men. He found two more—again laid out as if they were napping, again close by the train with the tarp-covered objects.

That was it for Bet-Assou. He grabbed his double-barrel machine gun, checked both clips, and then started down the ladder to the ground below. At least two of his men would have to die for this dereliction of duty. As it was, he barely made it down the long ladder alive, so drunk was he in his descent.

He cocked his rifle back and approached the first two

men. He intended on killing one man and wounding the other—but before he could pull the trigger, he noticed something first. There was already a pool of blood around each man's head.

Bet-Assou didn't believe it at first. He shined his flashlight on the twin pools of blood, and only then did it dawn on him.

He'd wanted to shoot these two for laying down on the job.

But someone had beaten him to it.

On guard now, the thought that these two had been killed by their comrades—for their bottles of snake wine—went through Bet-Assou's mind. That would not be too unusual. Still, Bet-Assou was getting very wary. The rail yard seemed very quiet all of a sudden. And very dark.

He walked slowly now, reaching the two other men laid out on the ground. Like the first pair, there was a pool of blood around each man's head. Their throats had been cut.

Bet-Assou could smell no snake wine on their persons. This sent a jolt of panic through him. He began flashing his light, a signal for his men to muster before him. But no one messaged back. Bet-Assou was suddenly very aware of two things: All his men were probably dead—and he was suddenly very alone in the rail yard.

In the next second he heard a sound that would, in fact, drive him straight to Hell.

It began as a baby's cry—the same he'd heard from some of his victims before dispatching them. This quickly transformed into a mechanical whine that was so loud, Bet-Assou found his eyeballs actually vibrating. This was quickly taken over by an earsplitting roar. This was being made by fire, fire fueled by powerful compounds. Bet-Assou's ears began to ring so loudly, he fell to his knees and clasped his hands over them. But this did no good. The sound in his head now perfectly mimicked the cries he'd heard from each one of his victims—and the din of 251 people crying in pain all at once was more than one psyche could take. Bet-Assou suddenly found himself on the ground shaking from head to toe.

In the next second, night turned into day. The two railway cars next to him were suddenly enveloped by a great flame. The brightness burned Bet-Assou' retinas. Then he felt the fire and smelled the smoke and tried to cover his eyes but couldn't.

The next thing he realized, the tarp on top of the nearby train was splitting one thread at a time, with flame and smoke erupting from beneath. Then came one more tremendous explosion and the objects on the railway cars started to move!

Before Bet-Assou's unbelieving eyes, two airplanes broke free of the tarp, and on legs of smoke and fire, rose up into the sky. Straight up! Right before his eyes.

What demon's work was this!

Even Bet-Assou knew that airplanes could not fly this way.

He watched in shock as both airplanes climbed to about five hundred feet above his head. Then he saw one come back down, a chain hanging from its belly. Now shadows were moving near him. He saw a pair of ghostly figures take the end of the chain hanging from the impossibly hovering airplane and connect it to another tarp-covered object. This done, the airplane began to lift the object, which Bet-Assou saw once the tarp fell off, was yet another airplane. This one very small, very compact.

In astonishment, he watched this combination—one plane carrying another—slowly fly off to the south. Before he could draw another breath, he saw the second hovering airplane come down, and more shadows at work, and this plane, too, lifted away another aircraft from the railroad car.

Within seconds, everything was quiet again. Suddenly there were no more airplanes. They'd all disappeared. Bet-Assou still had no idea exactly what he'd seen. All he knew was that there had been four airplanes in the rail yard when he and his men went on duty, and now there were none.

He knew his Blue Army superiors would not like that.

Bet-Assou did what he did best. He went around to the dead bodies of his squad members and rifled their corpses for money, ammunition, and flasks of snake wine.

Then he ran. Out of the rail yard, out beyond the city limits, and into the mountains north of the city.

Here he would stay for several hours, drinking what snake wine he could hold. But no amount of liquor could eliminate the awful chorus of screams that was now going around his head, nonstop, no matter how much he tried to get it to cease.

When the sun came up and the screams only got louder, Bet-Assou finally went insane. He pulled out each of his own fingernails, one by one, with nothing but his dirty and cracked teeth.

When the horrible sound still would not go away, he drank his last bottle of wine, put the barrel of his rifle into his mouth, and pulled the trigger.

Only then did the screams finally stop.

The pair of VTOL planes, being flown by Hunter and JT, flew as fast as they could back to the Red Army lines.

It was only because the VTOL planes were overpowered, and the Bantam such a lightweight aircraft, that they were able to steal the tiny fighters back from the Blues.

Still, carrying them across enemy territory and going no more than thirty-five knots in nearly full-forward hover, had been a dicey operation, but in the end a successful one.

Once back at Red Base One, they gingerly lowered the Bantam fighters dangling from their fuselages to a crowd of waiting ground personnel below. Typically anxious, JT dropped his airplane a few seconds ahead of time, resulting in a flat tire. But that was the most extensive damage incurred in the bold operation.

After dropping his own Bantam, Hunter brought his VTOL down for a bouncing landing, and was out of the cockpit before the engines had stopped turning.

The rest of the Americans now gathered around the four fighters. The VTOLs were in great shape considering what they'd been through. The Bantams were a bit banged up, had some fuel leaks and a few rough edges here and there, but were definitely flyable.

"It's strange," Fitz said, checking out the quartet of new weaponry. "We brought these along because we thought they'd protect us during the bombing run. Who could have foreseen they'd come to our aid now?"

"I could have," Zoltan interjected. "If someone had just asked me . . ."

Hunter checked the weaponry on his VTOL plane. It was filled with cannon shells and had two five-hundred-pound bombs hanging from its wings.

"It will have to do," he said, climbing back into the cockpit.

With that, he powered up his engines again and was soon lifting off, straight up once more into the night.

At an altitude of five hundred feet, he turned the jet's nose to the south and brought the engines up to horizontal. The hover jet suddenly shot ahead like it was fired out of a cannon.

Less than a minute later, all that those on the ground could see was the dull flare of Hunter's engine exhaust disappearing over the horizon.

CHAPTER 37

His name was Klaus Von Baron, though his friends long ago had bestowed on him the very unlikely nickname of "Sluggo."

For the most part, Von Baron was a proprietor of flesh. He bought and sold people—men for soldiers, girls for sex—like other people traded in cotton, wood, or oil. He was fabulously wealthy, a mover and shaker in a world that had not known more than two consecutive years of peace in nearly 325 years.

But he also fancied himself an adventurer of sorts, and that's what put him this fateful day on the porch of a prefab chalet overlooking the rather unattractive convergence of the Indus River and the Nawa Canal.

Von Baron was six foot even, with wavy blond hair, a thin, yet muscular-looking frame, and womanly hands, which he kept hidden whenever possible. His nose had been broken—by accident against a door frame—years before. Its flatness gave him an entirely undeserved tough-guy look, which he perversely relished. This chance injury also led to his nickname of Sluggo.

It was with Van Baron's money, and his verve to make

more money, that this rather despicable waterway project he was now gazing down upon from the shade of his temporary veranda had been launched.

This effort, which he had dubbed, cleverly he thought, "Little Big Dig," sought nothing less than to connect the Indus with the Nawa, and at certain points, widen and deepen both drastically.

The reason for this environmentally putrid idea was to create a huge bay leading into the upper Indus, allowing large ships to reach a point some 150 miles inland from the Arabian Sea. These ships, of course, would be carrying mercenaries. By widening and joining these two waterways—killing or displacing nearly one million people in the process—the mercenaries would cut three days off of a tough march through hilly, thickly covered lower Pakistan. For want of seventy-two extra hours, a significant part of the earth's face was being transformed without its permission.

For all this, Sluggo Von Baron would later suffer the pains of Hell.

But now, looking down on his massive project, he felt an almost sexual excitement running through him. This was money staring him back in the face. More money than he'd ever imagined—and he'd been born rich. It was a simple plan really: get as many merc ships as possible to travel up his newly opened passage, and charge them an enormous fee, which they wouldn't mind paying if it meant their men could get to the big fight up north for Kabul Downs fresh and quickly. So far, this had all worked out better than he'd dreamed.

The blue bloods had contracted for twenty divisions of forced mercs—soldiers that would be fighting against their will—as well as four professional divisions to intervene in the Kabul Downs fight. Close to a quarter of a million men would invade Afghanistan from the south, attacking the Red Army at its rear, and finally ending the fight in favor of the royals. Or so the Blues intended.

But what Sluggo knew, and very few others besides him,

was that the people who were bringing all these mercenaries to this war, had no intention of stopping once they'd rolled over the Red Army. Even though the blue bloods were paying the bill, secret plans spelled out an operation in which the oncoming "Black Army" would simply keep going after they defeated the Reds, eliminating the Blues, and taking over the strategically important Kabul Downs for themselves. At that point it would be sold—the entire city and whatever was left of the population—to the highest bidder. Sluggo Von Baron would double his already substantial wealth, just like that.

He'd just completed a briefing for some members of the Black Army high command not thirty minutes before. The secret plans for this double cross were still laid out on the table next to him, flapping gently in the breeze, as he watched the massive dredging operation continue unabated a half mile down the hill from him.

He was almost completely happy at this point. He was certainly moving and shaking—tons of dirt were dredged up every minute, widening and emptying holes left over from the five massive DG-55 bomb blasts that had started this huge project in the first place. But now, as he watched a small fleet of support boats scurrying up and around the artificial bays created by the enormous blasts, he felt something eating at his craw. What could it be? All seemed right with his world. He'd had an excellent briefing with the Black Army advance men. The double-cross plan was simple and ready to be put into effect. So what was bugging him couldn't be business-related.

Physically, his body felt good, too. He would soon retire to the small town a mile away, partake in some fine food he'd flown in and drink some great brandy. Then it would be on to the well-stocked cathouse, where he would choose from a bevy of young girls who had also been brought along on this adventure for his bodily gratification.

So what was bothering him? He really couldn't tell. But despite all this evidence that the world was spinning his way, he could not identify the slight twitch of foreboding in the pit of his stomach.

He thought about this for a few minutes until it finally hit him. It was the dream he'd had the night before causing his discomfort. It had been mildly terrifying. He was on this very porch, at this very time of day, drinking this very drink, when suddenly a huge bird had come out of the sky, swooped down, impaled him on its talons, and then flew away to a huge nest where he had been provided as a meal for the bird's equally huge, equally horrible chicks.

It was the nightmare that was making him uncomfortable, and he knew with a few deep breaths it would all go away again.

He started sucking in some of the moist, hot air and felt it sting his lungs as it went in. The air was so humid it was making him perspire. So it was strange that Von Baron felt a chill go across the back of his neck. And when there was another huge explosion about ten miles away, the rumbling under his rear end startled him in a manner that he was not very accustomed to. He was actually getting a bit of the shakes—all because of that *damn dream?*

Well, no, not exactly.

Because not a second later Von Baron felt a different sort of chill. This one was on the front of his neck, right below his rather delicate Adam's apple.

This chill was from the steel of a cold, razor-sharp knife.

"Get up," the man told him. "Slowly . . ."

Petrified, Von Baron did as told. He was convinced that the Black Army officers he'd just briefed had returned, crept up on him in an effort to double-double-cross him just as they were about to double-cross the blue bloods.

But when the man told him to slowly turn around, which Von Baron did, he was astonished to see Hawk Hunter in a Red Army uniform.

Von Baron nearly laughed. He didn't think the Reds had it in them to capture someone as important as he was.

But he was wrong . . . .

Hunter looked him over with contempt. He'd been

scouting this area since landing nearby earlier that morning. He'd watched the Black Army officers come and go, and his psychic compass had told him that the information he needed could be gotten from this man with the poster-boy looks and flattened nose.

"Get those plans, roll 'em up," Hunter ordered Sluggo. With shaking hands, Von Baron obeyed.

"Look . . . ," he began with a shaky voice. "Can we maybe make a deal here? I'm very rich. I could make you rich, too."

Hunter laughed in his face.

"You won't know what I'm talking about," he told Sluggo. "But I knew you in another world. And Back There, you were a pip-squeak. A real lowlife. And someone would have to look pretty deep into my stories just to find you. But now, here you are—you think you're rich. You think you're powerful. But you're still a pip-squeak."

Hunter took the rolled-up plans from him and then motioned with his knife.

"Start walking," he said.

Von Baron really started to worry now. This man had a very strange look about him. He just looked, well, *different.* And that scared Sluggo even more than the knife.

So he started walking, off the porch and up the road to the very top of the hill. In a clearing, Sluggo saw a very unlikely airplane hidden. On first glance he had no idea how it had fit into such a small area.

"What kind of machine is this?" he asked in his German-tinged accent. "Can I buy it from you after we have concluded our business?"

Hunter laughed at him again.

"Believe me," he said, "once we've concluded 'our business,' the last thing you will want to do is buy this or anything else from me."

Fitz, JT, and Ben were waiting for Hunter when he returned to Red Base One.

The VTOL plane roared over the airfield once, then went into a hover. He came down slowly, like a huge bird descending from the late-afternoon skies. The battle of Kabul Downs was still raging a mile away: artillery, tank fire, the occasional scream of a jet fighter passing by. These were the sounds that filled the air now.

But all of this seemed secondary as the three men ran out to Hunter's plane. The Wingman killed his engines and then leapt from his canopy. It was only then that his three friends noticed that he'd brought a strange piece of cargo back with him.

Lashed underneath the VTOL was a man. He was held in place by several pieces of simple rope. He was shivering from cold and terror, his eyes twice as wide as normal, and his face nearly powder-white.

"Well, I'll be," Fitz said. "What the hell you got there, Hunter, old boy?"

Hunter began untying Von Baron from beneath the bottom of the hover jet.

"What I've got," Hunter answered, "is a pigeon that appears ready to spill all. Isn't that right, Sluggo?"

Von Baron could hardly move, he was so frozen with fear. The hour ride up from southern Pakistan had caused him to lose control of his bodily functions several times, even though Hunter had actually kept his speed down to a mere one hundred knots, and his altitude at a reasonable one thousand feet, all to make sure Von Baron was still alive once he got to Red Base One.

And alive he was—but not yet thinking too clearly. As Fitz, Ben, and JT finally untied him from the last coil of rope, Von Baron fell hard to the runway and immediately curled up into the fetal position.

"Don't eat me," he started babbling. "Please, just don't eat me."

CHAPTER 38

The interrogation of Sluggo Von Baron lasted throughout the night, and well into the next morning.

Fitz was the lead inquisitor. Hunter, Kurjan, JT, and Ben were present, as well. They surrounded the flesh and arms trader with a tight ring of grim faces inside the Red Force intelligence hut.

Through it all, Y was laid out in a nearby corner. Sleeping off yet another drunk, he would occasionally punctuate the proceedings with a cry of "Emma . . . no!" before slipping back into his self-induced stupor. It lent an unnerving edge to the already-somber night.

The questioning lasted more than eight hours, but ironically, Von Baron could tell them only what they already suspected: The huge Black Army would be landing that morning, and if they moved swiftly, the lead elements would be close to Kabul Downs in less than two days.

Once in position, the Black Army would attack the Red Army's rear flank at first chance. By sheer numbers alone, they would most likely roll over the Reds in just a few days, especially if the Blue Forces launched an attack around the same time, still thinking that the Black Army was actually their ally.

The sun finally came up and in the cold light of dawn, those inside the Red Force intelligence hut knew they were facing an unpleasant choice of doomsday scenarios. Either be annihilated by the Blue Army or the Blacks, all as a prelude to those two fighting each other.

Even a full withdrawal was not an option. While Red Forces on the eastern and western flanks could theoretically leave their lines and move to the safety of western Afghanistan and Pakistan, those here on the southern front couldn't possibly pick up and move at the same time without inviting a breakout by the Blue Forces.

"We're caught in a vise," Fitz said at the conclusion of the interrogation. "And there ain't nothing we can do about it."

No one could argue with that logic.

Still, Hunter had a plan in mind—but the fact that the Black Army was coming on so strong made his desperate strategy even more so. Once the Blues knew their Black Army "allies" were heading north, they would have the ability to go on the offensive for the first time in the war. They would undoubtedly launch an all-out attack on the Reds, and the Reds on the southern flank would have nowhere to go with the Black Army coming right up their asses.

There was no other way of looking at it: As far as the Reds were concerned, the battle for Kabul Downs was lost. They could not win. It was a grim fact that the Red Army high command had to face. But winning the war was not the primary concern anymore: the survival of nearly one hundred thousand Red Force troops was.

Hunter felt most of that responsibility resting right on his shoulders.

"Let's all get some sleep," he suggested once Von Baron was led away to a makeshift prison cell. "Maybe one of us will dream up a way to get out of this."

JT just snorted in response.

"Good luck trying that," he said.

Hunter was only able to sleep for an hour and a half—longer than he'd rested since coming to this strange, little war, but still not as long as he'd wanted.

He knew what desperate times lay ahead, and for once he would have welcomed the onset of a dark slumber—just to get away from the inevitable calamity they were facing.

But ninety minutes into Hawk's restless sleep, Fitz ran into his billet and shook him awake.

"Hawker, you have to see this to believe it," the Irishman was telling him anxiously. "I don't quite believe it myself."

Hunter quickly slid into his red camo battle fatigues and followed Fitz out the door. They ran to the center of Red Base One, where JT and Ben had a Bug copter waiting.

"We've got to get up to the front immediately," Ben was saying.

No sooner were Hunter and Fitz on board when JT hit the power lever and off they went.

The trip to the front took two minutes. They did not talk on the way—indeed, they could not talk because JT had the noisy little chopper's engine revved so high, normal conversation was impossible.

They landed at a battered outpost close by the bloody bridge. Hunter noticed right away that the front was absolutely quiet. No artillery going off, no gunfire at all. *Eerie* . . .

They alighted from the Bug to find some of Kurjan's staff standing next to a huge trench. This was ground zero in the war between the Blues and Reds—wreckage everywhere, pools of putrid water, bones and body parts. Kabul Downs, with many sections of it still smoking, stood a silent witness in the background.

Hunter looked over the trench, only to get one of the

great shocks of his life. On the other side a table had been set up and Kurjan and three other high-ranking Red Army officers were sitting at it. Facing them were four Blue Army officers.

They were carrying a white flag.

Hunter stopped in his tracks about ten feet from them. He grabbed one of Kurjan's men, a guy named Al Nolan.

"Don't tell me they're surrendering?" he said to Nolan.

The guy nicknamed "Ironman" just shook his head no.

"They're not surrendering to us," he said. "They want us to surrender to them."

It took a few minutes for Hunter to catch Kurjan's eye. When he did, the Red Army intell man excused himself from the table and walked over to where Hunter, Fitz, JT, and Ben were waiting.

"Nice little party you got going here," Hunter told him.

Kurjan was not in the mood for jokes.

"They've got us by the balls and they know it," he said. "They're asking for a complete surrender of arms and an orderly transfer of all our troops to them as POWs—*before* the Black Army gets here."

Hunter felt his heart sink a mile in his chest. This wasn't going to be an armistice or a cease-fire. It *was* a call for an out-and-out surrender.

"Well, we can't allow all your guys to fall into their hands," Hunter told Kurjan in no uncertain terms. "Especially since we know what's *really* going to happen once the Black Army arrives."

Kurjan just nodded grimly.

"Well, that's one little secret I have yet to tell them, simply because I know they won't believe me when I do," he said.

This got Hunter thinking. Was there an advantage in letting the Blues know what Von Baron had told them?

Possibly—if they could gauge the Blues' reaction and then work around them.

Hunter turned back to Kurjan.

"Any of your superiors want another opinion on all

this?" he asked the intell man, indicating the three grim-faced Red Army generals sitting at the table with the Blues.

"At this point I think they'd love one," Kurjan replied.

Hunter turned back to JT and had a whispered conversation with him. There was an orgy of head nodding, and then the pilot sprinted back to the Bug and took off in a great whoosh.

"The problem here is," Hunter began telling Kurjan, "we've been playing by the rules. And apparently, we're the only ones who have been. We're really facing a shitty stick here, and I think we have to break a few nuts to get out of it."

Kurjan just wiped his tired brow.

"Are you suggesting that we fight on?" he said.

"Not exactly," Hunter replied with only the slightest hint of a grin.

Kurjan returned to the table while the others stood silently nearby. In less than five minutes JT returned in the Bug—with a passenger.

It was Von Baron.

They brought the prisoner up to where Hunter and the others were waiting. Kurjan once again excused himself and walked over.

"Please tell me this is just one bit of a bigger plan, Hawk?" he said to Hunter.

"That's a correct assumption," Hunter replied. "I hope . . ."

They took Von Baron's leg and hand irons off. Then Hunter grabbed him by the collar.

"OK, listen, Sluggo," he began, pronouncing the man's unlikely nickname with no little contempt. "I want you to go over there and tell those assholes in blue everything you told us—including the plans for the Blacks to bum-fuck them as soon as they arrive on the scene. *Capisce?*"

A look of terror came across Von Baron's face.

"Jeesuz, man, I-I can't do that," he stammered. "Telling you g-guys is one thing. Telling the Blues what the Blacks are going to do—they'll cut my n-nuts off right here and now!"

"Rather take another ride in my jet?" Hunter threatened him.

Von Baron just stared back at him. Hunter's grim expression left no doubt that if Von Baron went for another trip on the VTOL, it would be much longer and much higher and much colder than his initial journey.

Sluggo gulped and said: "OK, I'll tell them. But what becomes of me after that?"

Hunter looked into Sluggo's eyes and saw the lives of hundreds of innocent victims staring back at him.

"We'll let them decide that," he replied simply.

Von Baron gulped again and then was led to the table by Kurjan. A stiff wind blew across the trench line—hundreds of soldiers were standing all along the battered landscape watching these events unfold. It was like someone had pushed the pause button on the dirty, little war. No one doubted that it would continue again very soon, so the respite was not a very pleasant one.

Hunter and the others were out of earshot from the table, but they did not need to hear what was going on. Von Baron was telling his story to the astonished Blue Army officers—and it was obvious they were not taking the story well. At one point Von Baron was seen pleading with them to believe him, but it was clear that they did not—at first anyway.

Finally the Blue Army officers simply held up their hands and indicated they had had enough conversation. They packed their documents and their white flag and started walking back across the bridge toward their lines.

That's when one of them stopped, thought a moment, and then walked back to the table where the Red Army generals and Von Baron were still seated. Without a hint of warning, the Blue Army officer took out his pistol, put it against Von Baron's ear, and pulled the trigger. Sluggo went over like he'd been hit by a two-ton weight. Head blown away, he was dead before he hit the ground.

The Blue Army officer then holstered his weapon and walked back across the bridge.

"Well, I guess they finally believed him," Fitz observed dryly.

"But what has any of this bought us?" Ben asked Hunter.

Hunter scratched his own weary face.

"It's bought us the one thing we need now more than anything else," he replied.

"And that is?" Ben wanted to know.

"Time," Hunter replied quietly.

CHAPTER 39

Hunter never did get back to sleep.

He returned to his billet, with a stack of maps under his arm, and spent the rest of the daylight hours studying them.

Meanwhile, the artillery duels began anew less than thirty minutes after the abbreviated surrender talks concluded. Fighting broke out up and down the trench line once again. Fighter planes took off from both sides, and screaming dogfights were now under way just about everywhere over the front. It was business as usual in the fight for Kabul Downs. But Hunter knew these days of routine combat were quickly coming to an end.

Things were changing very rapidly, and if he couldn't cook up some logical plans, then the Red Army was going to be squeezed like a melon in a vise—and he and his friends would be squeezed right along with it.

So he tried to block out the sounds of the combat while he studied the maps, but it was not working. Maybe his head was too full of things he was trying to keep down, because if anything the sounds of the fighting seemed louder this day than any other time he could recall.

Why had he come here? It was the question that ate at him nonstop.

He'd come on the advice of a ghost. But, really, that was not an answer. Was there a *purpose* to his being here, and to his dragging just about every friend he had in this new world to this place, possibly to die like dogs in these bloody trenches?

The fighting seemed very loud as he considered the dangerous selfishness that had been running his life lately. And the questions just would not stop dogging him.

Why was he here? To help the Reds fight for their way of life? No, that wasn't it. To help them free some mysterious princess that few people had even seen? That sounded like a bad video game. What was it, then? Was he here because there were no other wars for him to fight? Was he here simply so he could play hero yet again?

Those last two questions chilled him right to his bones. Maybe the whole ghostly encounter on the superbomber had been some kind of self-induced hallucination, a way for him to rationalize his thirst to be in combat, to play the hero, to always be seen as the savior of the day. If that was the case, then his selfishness ran miles deep and miles high. To endanger his comrades, half of whom came with him on the most dangerous mission ever planned, and the other half came looking for him after he essentially went AWOL—to endanger all of them and wreak havoc on their families, just for another shot of glory, there was no more selfish act in the world, if all that was true.

But was it?

Was that really why he'd been compelled to come to this place at this time?

The simple answer: He just didn't know.

Night fell and the sounds of the war got even louder. There'd been no slacking off with the sunset today. The Blues knew they would soon have a vast advantage over the Reds—what Von Baron told them notwithstanding. If the Blues were to make their move soon, it would have to come tonight. Only an attack on the Reds could solve both their problems; in effect, only that could work to defeat both their enemies.

Hunter walked out of his tent and looked back at the city. The night sky was already afire with the ongoing artillery duel. Sirens were blaring, smoke was rising up in many places along the war-torn landscape. What secret lay for him inside that place? Would he ever know?

He walked over to the volunteer officers' billet. The first person he saw was Y. Slouched over a map table, he was drunk again. The Jones boys were there. Hunter approached them. He was sure of very few things these days, but when it came to these two, there really was no question: he'd known them both Back There. And like now, they had been valiant, heroic, brave, and loyal soldiers. It was on those attributes that Hunter now had to make a request—one that had to be fulfilled if the Red Army on the southern flank had any hope of escape.

The conversation with the Jones boys lasted but five minutes. The two pilots agreed to perform their part in Hunter's bold plan to save as many Red Army soldiers' lives as possible. They all saluted each other and then the two pilots ran out to the base auxiliary hangar, dragged out the last working Bug copter, and immediately took off. They disappeared over the southeastern horizon.

Hunter watched them go, hoping against hope that they could find exactly and quickly what he had asked them to look for.

Next he walked over to the intell hut where Kurjan and his men were still poring over maps of the battlefield.

Hunter laid out two of the maps he'd been studying all afternoon. One showed the Red Army's western flank, the other its eastern. Hunter's suggestion was that both flanks start withdrawing immediately. Under the cover of night, the western flank soldiers could move up into the mountains west of Kabul Downs, the eastern lines could move into the relative safety of Pakistan. If the timing was right and the Blues were otherwise occupied, the withdrawal could go smoothly and nearly ninety thousand men would be spared. But that still left about five thousand inside what Hunter had termed the "southern pocket." With the expected advance of the Black Army from the south, and the anticipated offensive from the Blue Army to the north, there would be little room left for these troops to maneuver once the battle began in earnest. That's where Hunter would have to become the most creative.

Kurjan agreed to send the withdrawal plans up to his high command, where he was confident they would be put into action. As to the fate of those left inside the pocket, Hunter knew that small groups of soldiers would be able to get away while the big fight to come was going on—but there would always be some leftover soldiers who would have to take the brunt of the combat while allowing these comrades to slip away.

What fate these men would face was impossible to say. At this point, only the Cosmos knew, and at the moment, no one from that place was doing any talking.

Finally Hunter walked over to the flight line. Fitz, JT, and Ben were waiting for him here, just as he had asked them to be earlier. The two VTOL jets and the pair of Bantams were also waiting, fueled up and guns chock-full of ammo. The Red Army ground personnel had just completed a tentative inspection of the four unusual jet fighters. They had pronounced them ready for combat.

"Everyone ready? " Hunter asked his three friends.

There were three solemn nods in reply.

But there was one thing they needed before they all took off: adequate head protection. There were no crash helmets in the jets. The four men finally had to settle for battle helmets of the type worn by Red Army soldiers.

They were more reminiscent of a German Army helmet from Hunter's version of World War One, a kind of oversized Fritz helmet, bright red with thick netting inside and out.

"We won't win any fashion awards with these," Hunter said, trying on several helmets before finding one that fit. "But they should do the job."

With that, they all prepared to climb into their respective airplanes—Hunter and Fitz in the VTOLs; Ben and JT in the Bantams.

Seeing this gave Hunter pause. He actually felt a lump grow in his throat.

Been awhile since we've all flown together, he thought to himself, watching as Fitz, Ben, and JT climbed into their airplanes.

What were the chances, he thought, that his three closest friends in his previous life, would also be pilots in this one, even though one was a family-man hobbyist, one a professor, and one a near-retirement reservist?

Actually, knowing a bit now about transuniverse movement, Hunter realized the chances for these stars to be so aligned were pretty good.

Hunter and Fitz waited for the two Bantams to taxi over to the runway and take off. The small fighters seemed to be going fast even while standing still. In flight they were so small and so swift, they looked more like large insects than small jet airplanes.

Once the Bantams were up, Fitz and Hunter started their own power plants. The VTOLs were noisy aircraft, but their overloaded engines made up for the racket with pure flying power. Hunter watched the critical systems run up to snuff on his control panels, an exercise resulting in five green lights popping on. A weapons check proved his systems were also in good shape. He looked over at Fitz, who was waving thumbs-up back to him.

"Time to shake things up," Hunter said to himself, applying power and allowing the VTOL to begin rising slowly into the air. "While we still have the chance."

So began a very strange night in the battle for Kabul Downs.

In the next few hours, events would suddenly begin moving more quickly than anyone could have imagined—including Hunter. Even he could not foresee what would take place before the sun rose again.

Once airborne, the four pilots discussed a rather loose strategy.

The Blue Forces would soon attack the Reds' southern flank—that was a given. The southern flank represented the piece of terrain closest to where the Black Army troops would be advancing, so clearing a path for their paid "allies" would be the most likely move by the Blues. This meant an all-out land assault by the blue bloods was inevitable.

But while Hunter and his colleagues were carrying substantial weapons stores, they knew they couldn't make a dent in the number of Blue troops that would be involved in such an assault. Four jets against one hundred thousand troops was not an even match. Bombing and strafing a few barracks would do little to alter the course of what was to come.

No, what they had to do was disrupt the Blues' lines of communications. For if a large number of Blue troops were soon to be on their way to attack the Reds' southern line, the Red Forces would be in better shape if the pilots somehow made it as difficult as possible for those troops to get to the battlefield and know what they should be doing once they got there.

But how to do this? The simplest way would have been to somehow knock out the Blues' central command station, a place Hunter suspected was hidden beneath a block of several unassuming buildings in the middle of Kabul Downs. But attacking such a hardened target would have been simply unreasonable. It simply was not an option.

Not yet anyway . . .

Another, simpler way had to be found. And in one respect, the four pilots were lucky. Kabul Downs was crisscrossed with canals. This was especially true on the outer limits of the city. Canals meant bridges to cross, and there were many of them, too.

So it really came down to basic military doctrine. The term "lines of communications" didn't mean just radio lines; it meant the lifeline of an enemy from its rear areas to its forward positions. Any way that one could make it difficult for his adversary to move men, ammo, supplies, and fuel via his lines of communications, meant one more advantage you had on him.

That's why the mission of this night was for the four jets to take out as many bridges as they could inside Kabul Downs.

They decided to split into pairs. Hunter and Ben went east; Fitz and JT went west.

After studying the maps of the city all day, Hunter knew there was a set of bridges on the east side of Kabul Downs, which ran right up to the truck park he'd attacked earlier that day.

Within two minutes, he and Ben were orbiting high above these bridges. While most of the residents of the embattled city were already awake due to the nonstop artillery battle, the sound of the two jet fighters suddenly arriving overhead only added to the substantial racket. This gave them the cover they needed.

Ben went in first. He peeled off in a classic manner, and put the first bridge in his sights. It was a forty-foot span made of wood and iron. He launched six air-to-ground missiles from his speedy little Bantam jet, directing them right into the bridge's center truss. There were six simultaneous explosions, and the bridge went down in a cloud of smoke, fire, and water.

Hunter went in next. The second bridge was all-steel, about sixty feet in length. He let go a long burst from the VTOL huge cannon and neatly sliced the center span in half.

Now it was Ben's turn again. The next target was a drawbridge, holding four lanes of traffic. He put two rockets into the control house and another two into the bridge itself. The twin explosions lifted the crucial gear works twenty feet in the air destroying them utterly.

The next target was much bigger: a 250-foot steel and girder bridge that led into the heart of the city. Hunter and Ben lined up side by side and went with cannons blazing. It took four passes, but their combined fusillade finally dropped the bridge with one big *whomp!*

The attack took about two minutes. The bridges were lined up like targets in a shooting gallery. The city defenders apparently were not yet hip to what was happening. That's why Hunter and Ben had not run into any AAA fire as of yet.

Or so it seemed.

The same was true for Fitz and JT. They had dropped no less than ten smaller canal bridges on the other side of the city in five minutes—all without receiving so much as a single AAA shot back at them.

During all this, Hunter could not get rid of the feeling that he'd done this type of thing before. Back There. The entire memory wasn't exactly clear, but the key points were.

He was fighting a battle for a city. Bridges were the key to a coming action. So he had to go out and destroy as many as he could. Where did that happen? Was it in a place called . . . Football City? *Really?*

He felt a cold chill go through him. Yes, he'd dropped some bridges at a place called Football City—just as a huge army called the Family was moving into attack it.

But what happened after that?

He felt his hands tense on his steering column. He had a very bad feeling going through him right now, so much so, he pulled the VTOL straight up and gained one thousand feet in altitude in a matter of seconds.

It was such an abrupt maneuver, Ben called over to him

"Hawk? You OK?" he asked, concerned.

Hunter just clicked his microphone twice—an indicator that he was all right.

But that wasn't the truth. Not exactly.

Because suddenly . . . everything just stood still.

The superbomb went off and he saw the bright light . . . and then he couldn't see anything else . . . even though his eyes were wide open . . . . He was the only one who looked at the blast and he was the only one who saw the light . . . and now he was the only one who was blind . . . .

It was strange . . . everyone back at Bride Lake thought that the bomb blast would be too powerful for the airplane to get out of the way . . . but it didn't happen like that at all.

The blast was widespread . . . but it only shook the plane. It did not destroy it . . . What a laugh! . . . All the worry about the biggest worry, and it never even happened. The superbomber held together . . . Mission accomplished . . . all hands on board remained safe.

But now he cannot see . . .

Ben and Fitz lead him back to the aircraft commander's stateroom . . . JT puts a cool beer against his eyes, but this does no good . . . The Japanese are still firing at them . . . but the B-2000 Colossus *is moving so fast, the Zeros can barely keep up with them . . . Fitz is saying don't worry . . . the blindness will pass . . .*

But it does not.

He was alone . . . in this small room, feeling every bump and shake of the plane . . . turbulence was a funny thing . . . it was invisible . . . you could not see . . . but it could be a killer.

The rest of the crew is busy . . . flying the plane . . . defending the plane . . . the noise of so many machine guns firing at once sounds like the drone of monks, chanting on a faraway Himalayan peak . . . How many Japanese Zeros does it take to shoot down a plane named Colossus*? . . . Only the monks would know.*

He is seeing white not black . . . but what does a blind man really see? Somewhere inside his brain, the Wingman sees faces. Women . . . smiling . . . laughing . . . crying. What is your favorite memory, one asked him . . . you know, back when you could see?

That's easy, he replied . . . He is standing in front of a huge crowd of people and the place known as Football City is burning but free in the background . . . and he is holding up a small American flag taken from the body of a patriot named Saul Wackerman and he is chanting: USA! USA! USA!

He saw the Light that day, too.

"Hawk?"

Hunter shook his head and felt the heavy battle helmet joggle just about every fluid inside his cranium.

"Hawk? You with me, buddy?"

Hunter blinked and realized he was back flying above Kabul Downs. Ben was trying to get him to answer his radio call.

"Roger, Ben . . . I'm here," he finally responded.

"I just got a weird call from base," Ben said. Hunter noted a high degree of anxiety in the normally calm pilot's voice.

"Weird as in . . . ?"

"Weird as in they have a hot read on their ADR system," Ben told him.

ADR system? As in air-defense radar? Hunter almost laughed. The Red Force had exactly two radar sets. One on the south side of their lines, the other over on the east side. They were positioned as close as possible to the main Blue Force air bases.

"What are they reading exactly?"

Ben hesitated. Hunter took the pause to get back down to the deck and blast another canal bridge with a surgical fusillade of just sixteen shells.

"Ben? Come in . . ."

"Well, this has to be wrong," he heard his friend say

"But they are getting hot reads from every Blue air base . . . full squadrons already in the air or lining up on every Blue field . . ."

Hunter needed a moment to digest this piece of disturbing information. The Blues never flew at night. But if what Ben was telling him was confirmed, they were suddenly throwing airplanes into the air at an incredible rate.

"There's more," Ben went on. "Kurjan just radioed to say that huge concentrations of Blue troops are massing near bloody bridge. At least two divisions. They appear to be ready to attack at any moment."

Hunter's head was spinning now. This was not good. The Blues were moving faster than he'd ever imagined. And while dropping the bridges had been a sound military tactic, he realized now that it might have come too late to do any good.

Way too late.

When you are blind, you see many things . . . faces, places . . . things that went before . . . Yes, the battle for Football City was a victory . . . but what went on before that?

He blinked . . . and even though he could not see, the ghostly image of one hundred airplanes became very clear in his mind . . .

It was Fitz, Ben, and JT who were in the best position to see what happened next.

There were two separate swarms of Blue Force airplanes now darkening the sky. One had arisen from the major Blue air base on the west side of the embattled city, the other was a combination of planes that had taken off from several smaller airfields in the north and east sections.

The main force, which numbered at least one hundred aircraft, was forming up directly above the center of the city at approximately 7,500 feet.

Once gaining this altitude, the SuperSpad bijets began a slow orbit around the city. As more units joined up, this bizarre carousel of airplanes became larger and larger. It seemed like such a foolish thing to do—launch so many airplanes at once, only to have them waste time and fuel by flying in one enormous circle until every last straggler was airborne.

But this was exactly what the Blues were doing—another indication that all of the orders for the city's defenders were coming from one central point of command.

After their spree of bridge busting, Fitz, Ben, and JT were all low on ammunition and fuel. As was Hunter. And the wise thing to do would be to dash back to base, do a hot fuel up, and a quick ammo resupply, and then get back into the air to meet this sudden massive air threat.

But even under that kind of rationale, all three pilots knew it was too late—by the time they landed and began their replenishment, the Blues would already be on their way to bomb and strafe whatever targets they had in their little minds this night, no doubt in coordination with the impending Blue Force ground attack.

No, time was on the side of the blue bloods now.

The three pilots were in a quandary. They had little ammo and less fuel, they were flying aircraft that were totally unfamiliar to them—especially Fitz in the other VTOL jet—and they were looking up at an enemy air force that was getting larger by the second. What could they do against such a storm of hostile aircraft?

As it turned out, all they had to do was watch.

As soon as the word came across that the Blues wer launching massive numbers of bijets, the three pilots los sight of Hunter. One moment he was there, the next h was gone. It was as if he simply disappeared.

They tried desperately to raise him on their radios, bu to no reply. They called back to the Red Force One ai base—had Hunter returned there? No, was the answe from the very panicky air controls officer. They, too, ha spotted the carousel of Blue Force airplanes circling hig above the city, as well as the enemy troops massing near the bloody bridge.

Where could Hunter be then? He was just as low on fuel as they. Just as low on ammo, too.

So where did he go?

They soon got their answer.

The three pilots had decided their best strategy was a slow withdrawal back toward Red Base One. This way, they could at least put up some kind of a fight once the blue bloods stopped their grouping-up and finally attacked.

But just as the three jets reduced speed and turned for home, they saw a streak way up in the sky, high above the carousel of Blue Force airplanes. At first Fitz thought it was a meteorite, flashing through the Earth's atmosphere, a harbinger of the doom that seemed to be awaiting the Red Forces. But then he and the others saw this streak of light make a somewhat radical parabolic turn. And from that, they knew it was no natural phenomena. This was something being steered and controlled.

They saw a small ball of flame erupt from the center of the gang of orbiting Blue Force planes. Then another and another.

Fitz turned his airplane around 180 degrees to get a closer look. These balls of flame were Blue Force bijets falling out of the sky. There went another. And another. And another.

Now the streak of light was flying a crazy pattern. It was weaving in and out of the orbiting fighters, a short burst of fire from its muzzles always followed by another ball of flame dropping out of the sky.

"My God," Fitz whispered, when he realized exactly what was happening. "It's Hunter. He's taking them on alone."

Ben and JT had also turned their airplanes around and were now slowly heading back toward the city. Between them they counted thirteen balls of flame falling from the carousel of fighters—an astounding achievement, a lifetime's worth of kills for a normal fighter pilot. Yet Hunter had accomplished it in less than two minutes.

The strange thing was the Blue Force airplanes had yet to break formation. They kept circling and circling, apparently under orders to hold their patterns and not return fire. This was lunacy of course, and more evidence that the blue bloods were so ingrained in a central command they were willing to sacrifice pilots and planes until someone high enough up the ladder gave the word to disperse and defend themselves.

That happened just a few seconds later.

If watching the bizarre merry-go-round of fighters was strange, the group's breakup was even more bizarre.

It was like someone threw a switch. One moment the Blues were flying round and round, dozens of airplanes going in a clockwise motion at several different altitude levels—the next, they all scattered like petals from an exploding flower. Where once there was order and symmetry, now there was chaos and no little panic. A third of the bijets went straight up, a third went straight down—the rest fled in all other directions.

But this made no difference.

The streak of white light, which was Hunter's VTOL jet on double-burner, never stopping firing.

When blinded, they say, all the other senses become more acute . . . and this was true. . . . Sitting in the commander's stateroom, eyes seeing nothing but white light, his sense of smell increased to a degree that he sniffed and detected the stink of cordite from all the guns firing several decks below him . . . and he stuck out his tongue and tasted blood in the air of those on board who'd been wounded in the fight . . . and he could hear the engines of the huge B-2000 straining for speed as it tried to outdistance the pursuing fighters. . . . And somewhere in the mix, the sound of several different aircraft engines . . . not just SuperZeros . . maybe three American airplanes? Was one joining the Japanese fighters in pursuit?

But it was the third eye's sense that became the most acute . . . that indefinable sixth sense that was already a gift to him . . . now it was allowing him to see things that almost made him forget that he'd been blinded by the light . . .

Because now, in the white, he could see a face . . . a familiar face . . . a crooked smile, out-of-date hairdo, massive head wound. This was a ghost, a transparency . . . here to talk to him while he was blind.

"You know me, and then you don't know me," the ghost said to him . . . but this was actually just a joke . . . a cosmic joke . . . just like the one that was responsible for Hunter being in this world in the first place. "I know you," he said back to the ghost . . . "how could I not?"

"I am here for a reason," the ghost said. "I'm here to make amends . . . to somehow make up for all the awful things I did before . . . well, before I became this."

Hunter tasted the air and laughed . . . his third eye was playing tricks on him . . . "No, it's not," the ghost replied. "I am real . . . this is real. And I'm here to pass on something to you. Something you have to do. There is someone you have to save. In the strangest place in the world."

Hunter laughed again . . . "I'm blind," he says . . . "What good can I do?" . . . But then the ghost laughed and said: "You're not blind, old friend . . . You've just seen the Light, that's all."

Twenty-three. Twenty-four. Twenty-five . . .

Hunter shook his head back into reality and squeezed his cannon trigger again. Twenty-six. The bijets were nimble, little bastards. They could spin out of the way in a split second. Twenty-seven. Twenty-eight. He found it almost harder to shoot one down in the big VTOL jet than in his old reliable SuperCamel prop plane. But a pilot's life was about innovation. Twenty-nine. Thirty. And he was innovating like hell in this dogfight.

There was a combination of factors at work. The VTOL was faster that the bijets, so this helped Hunter chase down individual airplanes or pairs of them and let just a few cannon shells do the talking for him.

That's how numbers thirty-one through forty-two went down. Just a cluster of bijets, their pilots not knowing what to do, where to go, and Hunter weaving his way through them, firing, twisting, firing, turning, firing, looping, firing, diving.

It was strange that even after the huge formation broke up, the Blue pilots tended to stick together. It made it just that much easier for Hunter to pick them off. As it was, it looked like the sky was raining downed airplanes. And not one SuperSpad had tried to fire back at him.

Fifty. Fifty-one. Fifty-two . . .

Twisting, turning, firing, diving. One hundred enemy airplanes against just him.

Yeah, he'd done this before.

Fitz, Ben, and JT were simply astonished.

They had stopped counting the number of airplanes Hunter had shot down—it was way over sixty by now.

It was almost pathetic in a way. The Blue Forces dispersed, but they did not run very far. By doing so, they simply allowed themselves to be shot down by the coolly rampaging Hunter.

About five minutes into this strange lopsided battle, there were still about thirty bijets left flying crazily above the city. Realizing they were no longer clustered together, Hunter was flying even faster, turning even sharper in order to get kills on them. The flaming bijets were coming down less frequently now, and Fitz could see some of the enemy planes were finally turning and firing at Hunter. Yet this didn't seem to have any effect on the Wingman. He was now pulling a new trick out of his bag.

As those brave Blue pilots turned to fire at him, Hunter started "viffing." This meant, he was slamming on his brakes by using the VTOL's capability to hover. This made those pursuing fighters streak right by him, allowing him to get a clean shot at their tailpipes as they roared past.

This new maneuver only scattered the remaining airplanes even further. Yet Hunter now became relentless in his pursuit. Fitz knew he must be running out of fuel.

"Hunter?" he started yelling into his microphone. "Don't you think you've done enough, old boy?"

"If there are one hundred airplanes up here, I've got to get them all," Hunter's reply came back—his voice seemed distant, eerie.

"You must be running on fumes, old buddy," Fitz warned him.

"Sometimes fumes will do just fine," Hunter replied.

Fitz checked his own gas gauge. He was way past his bingo point. He had just enough to get back to Red Base One—if he was lucky. It was the same for JT and Ben.

"Just get back to base," Hunter told them all, knocking down number eighty-nine. "I won't be long."

CHAPTER 40

Red Base One

Y was in a panic.

He'd just awoken from a very disturbing dream. He and Emma were together, on an island, somewhere near Midway in the Pacific. Their plane had crash-landed there, and their rescuers had not yet come for them. And though she was there and alive and breathing, for some reason they could not speak to each other, or touch each other, or even look at each other.

What good is this? Y remembered asking her in the dream. This is like you're still dead . . . .

The next thing he knew, he was being shaken awake by Kurjan, the Red Army intelligence officer. He was showing him the readout of the Red radar sets. A huge armada of Blue Force SuperSpads had lifted off. Many had been shot down already, but many more were heading right for Red Base One. They were only five minutes away.

He showed Y a long-range insta-film TV photo. A huge swarm of Blue Force soldiers were pouring through the

Red line at the bloody bridge. They, too, were heading right for Red Base One.

Kurjan was calling out orders to everyone he could see. There was not enough time to put any of the Red Army's airplanes into the air—therefore, they all had to be pushed back into their hangars with the desperate hope that the air barns would somehow escape the onslaught that was coming their way.

But what did Y have to do with all this?

Kurjan was desperate, he told him. Really desperate. He was ordering Y to help man a nearby antiaircraft gun. Y was shocked. He knew nothing about how to fire such a gun, but Kurjan wasn't sticking around to hear it. Already the sound of an advancing Blue Force column could be heard. The air was filled with the cry of enemy bijets on the wing.

"Just do it!" Kurjan ordered him. "*Now. . . .*"

Next thing he knew, Y was running at breakneck speed toward the gun post, joining three other "volunteers" in a rush to get the triple-barrel weapon cranked up and ready to fire.

But the sad news was, the three other men on the gun were shaking badly, too.

"Have they ever attacked the field before?" Y yelled to one of them.

"No!" one of them yelled back. "The Blues have never flown at night before. And their troops have never gotten beyond our lines—day or night!"

"Well, something woke them up at the wrong time," Y mumbled through chattering teeth.

The base was in chaos. People running every which way, the air-raid sirens blaring nonstop, the booming of the approaching guns sounding much louder now than just minutes before.

Y had never really been to war before. He'd always been safe behind the scenes doing the noodle work while others did the fighting and dying. Now, his hands shaking, looking at the firing mechanism on the long triple-A gun, he realized that here he was, on the ground, with people who wanted to kill him, coming right at him, both in the air and on the ground.

Such terror was running through his body!

He closed his eyes and whispered a silent prayer: *From this moment on, Lord, I promise I will never drink again. Just get me through this.*

He was shaking so much now, one of the young soldiers looked at him and gasped.

"You've got to calm down, guv'ner," the man said to him. "The worst that can happen is we'll all die."

With that, the man reached inside his pocket and came out with a flask.

"Drink, sir?" he asked Y. "You look like you need it."

Y looked at the silver container; he imagined he could smell the rum inside it already.

"Get your blood flowing, sir," the plucky, young soldier insisted.

Y paused, but only for a second or two. Long gone now were any thoughts that death would actually be a beautiful thing because he would join Emma in Heaven, *if* and *when* a blue-blood fusillade ran him through. That notion held no more weight than a quark for him now. For some reason, getting offed by a firing squad was a bit more romantic than being bombed or strafed out of existence.

Now, he was just plain scared of dying.

That's why he took the flask and drained it in one gulp.

"Thanks, kid," he said, handing the empty container back to him. "I owe you one."

"No problem," the kid said, checking to see if the flask was indeed empty. "No problem at all."

The rum had burned its way about halfway down Y's gullet when they heard the first signs of the approaching enemy.

Any hopes that Y had harbored that this was all one big

mistake were dashed as soon as they saw the first chevrons of the approaching enemy air armada.

It was a clear night, stars in full blaze, a full moon on the rise. But now the sky above Red Base One was covered with moving blue lights, some blinking, some not. There were so many of them, the stars were no longer visible. The moon's glow was pulsating, so many Blue SuperSpads were passing in front of it.

An eerie silence settled over the air base. Even the air-raid sirens had gone silent. Now, there was only the mild breeze ruffling through the dozens of tents at the air base—that and the frightening drone of more than one hundred enemy planes flying overhead.

"Have you got any more?" Y asked the young gunner trembling next to him.

The man never took his eyes off the sky. "You got my whole week's ration," the gunner replied. "Wish now I had it back."

Y felt his heart drop even as his stomach began burning with the previously consumed rum.

"Here, take mine."

Y heard these magic words and looked to see another flask being thrust into his hands. One of the other young gunners was offering it to him.

Y didn't think twice this time. He took the flask and drained it in another long slurp. The fire in his belly doubled.

"Thanks, my friend," Y said, giving the empty flask back to the teenage gunner's mate. "We'll make it through this . . . you'll see."

All three gunners looked at him. Their faces were dirty and lined with wrinkles, though none of them was over the age of twenty.

"No, we won't," one said solemnly.

Y, now feeling a bit looped, looked back at them. *My God, they're right,* he thought.

Now they saw a commotion off to the north. It looked

like a huge line of ants streaming over the bloody bridge and heading right for them.

Y just stared, his mouth agape, not quite believing what he was seeing. It took a moment to sink in, but then he realized that his gunmates' pessimism was indeed well placed. For at the moment it looked like the entire Blue Force Army was heading right for them.

"God, they finally did it," one of the young gunners whispered in horror. "They finally broke out. . . ."

"That they did," Y replied, the words sticking in his throat.

"How do you want to die, then?" another gunner asked over the commotion. "At the end of a bayonet? Or by some guy in an airplane?"

There was no time for anyone to reply. For the next sound they heard was the scream of many jet engines being throttled up at once.

Now the massive blanket of airplanes overhead began to break up. Like some kind of sinister ballet, the SuperSpads began peeling off one by one, engines screaming, diving down on the Red air base.

Y's fingers were frozen to the gun's firing mechanism. Why he'd been designated to do the shooting, he would never know. The young gun crew began turning the weapon on its swivel. A long belt of AAA shells was fed in, the hammers cocked and set. Y looked at his hands. They were shaking mightily now.

"Does anyone know how to fire this goddamn thing?" he yelled, trying to be heard above the increasing scream of the diving SuperSpads.

"Just pull the bloody trigger!" one of his gun mates yelled back.

Now a gaggle of SuperSpads leveled off about 2,500 feet to their north just over the Yabuk river. They went into a line across, and began heading right for Y's gun. They were no more than five hundred feet off the ground. He screamed for the gun crew to lower the weapon.

This would take a few seconds, but Y started firing anyway. In the span of a heartbeat, the night sky was suddenly filled with three lines of bright red tracers. The noise of the gunfiring shook Y right down to his bones. His premature fusillade had all the earmarks of a disaster. Not only was it making it hard for his gun mates to bring the gun down to its proper elevation, it was highlighting their position to the attacking aircraft.

But Y kept on firing anyway. The noise was simply deafening; the smoke suffocating. The line of six SuperSpads was bearing in on them. Y could see yellow flashes lighting up their wings. It took him a moment to realize this was the glare of the SuperSpads' cannons opening up on him.

The gun was now finally lowered and Y blindly sprayed the triple stream of tracers in the general direction of the oncoming enemy planes. But it was to no effect. Y kept on firing anyway. The noise was louder, the terror blowing fiercely in the wind. Other SuperSpads were roaring over their heads. Explosions were going up all over the air base. The ground beneath Y's feet felt like a giant hand was shaking the earth. One of his gun mates was crying.

The spread of six airplanes continued to bear down on them. Their muzzle flashes increased in intensity. Then suddenly red flashes began pinging up and down the gun mount. The Spads' cannon shells were hitting home!

Y kept on firing, but now it was because his fingers were simply locked in place, frozen in terror on the gun's firing mechanism. All three of his young gun mates were wailing now. It seemed like the gun post was suddenly enveloped in a bright red glow. Yet Y just kept on firing, expecting a string of red-hot cannon shells to perforate him at any moment.

Emma . . . I'm so sorry . . .

But then something very strange happened.

The line of attacking Blue fighters simply disappeared. One moment they were there—the next, there was nothing but six puffs of fire and smoke blowing in the breeze.

"Jeesuzz! Get down!" Y heard himself scream.

The next thing he knew, the gun post was swept by a

storm of flaming wreckage, cinders, and pieces of metal. This was all that remained of the six Blue Force bijets.

What happened?

Y had no idea. But the answer came a second later with the roar of two mighty engines and the gale of a small hurricane. A huge airplane swooped low over the post and then turned upward into the fiery sky.

Y couldn't believe it.

It was one of the AirCat fighter-bombers!

He looked around him now and saw that more AirCats were streaking in, firing at the Blue planes in the air, as well as the advancing enemy troops on the ground.

"Goddamn!" Y screamed, helping his young gun mates to their feet. They were burned and battered but still alive—and so was he.

"What the fuck kind of airplanes are they?" one of the gunners asked with a gasp as two of the huge fighter-bombers roared overhead.

"They're friends of mine!" Y screamed in reply. "And somehow they found us . . . just in time."

Disbelieving, Y looked straight up and saw the sky was now filled with the big AirCat fighter-bombers. They seemed to be everywhere! Many were battling the Blue Force SuperSpads, others were brutally strafing the advancing Blue troops. Y thought he heard a cry go up from those defending Red Base One.

Another horrible sound swept across the battlefield. It was a loud mechanical scream echoing from high above. Y looked up and saw a huge HellJet bomber falling out of the sky heading right for the largest concentration of Blue Army troops.

Y shook himself out of a few seconds' stupor and once again grabbed his three young gun mates and slammed them to the ground. The HellJet unleashed its huge bomb load a heartbeat later—the bombs impacted about three quarters of a mile from Y's position. The result was like a small earthquake. Y's body felt like it had turned to jelly—the ground was shaking so much Y's teeth began chat tering. A storm of dirt and debris hit them next, the second such debris cloud to sweep by them in less than two minutes.

They heard the HellJet scream for altitude—only then did Y let his gun mates up from the ground again. What they saw in front of them now was a huge crater with a mushroom cloud rising above it. There was nothing left—no more trees, no more trenches, no more advancing Blue troops. Like always after a HellJet high-altitude dive-bombing, the result looked like a piece of the cold, lifeless moon.

The silence lasted all of ten seconds. It was like someone pushed the play button again. Suddenly the sky was filled with aircraft once more—huge AirCats picking off the Blue Force SuperSpads, two more HellJets delivering their awesome bomb loads closer to the city.

Two more earthquakes shook Red Base One. In between, Y took a potshot at a couple of SuperSpads that came very low over the gun post. The stream of tracers chasing after them looked impressive, but it was obvious these two—like just about every other bijet in the sky—weren't interested in fighting anymore. They were retreating back to the relative safety of Kabul Downs.

Then it was over. Just like that.

There were clouds of smoke wafting in the air. There were numerous fires everywhere. The burning wreckage of dozens of Blue Force SuperSpads littered the landscape stretching between the Red and Blue lines. There were many bodies, too. But this battle was over for the moment. And Y and his gun mates had managed to survive.

CHAPTER 41

One hour later, the main runway at Red Base One was so crowded, there was barely enough room left over for any aircraft to land.

AirCat fighters, HellJet bombers, the two VTOL jets, the pair of Bantams, as well as the remaining Red Force SuperCamels and one lonely Bug copter were cluttering up all but the most important taxiways. Red Army ground personnel were scurrying from aircraft to aircraft, checking fuel supplies, refilling ammo loads, and patching up any hole caused by AAA fire in the quick, brutal battle that had just concluded.

It was early morning now and the sun was coming up red and bold.

The intelligence hut at the base was as crowded as the base's runways. Inside were all the principals of the fight Hunter, Fitz, JT, Ben, Geraci and his staff, the JAWS team Zoltan, Crabb, Kurjan and the Jones boys. Y was also there sucking down a huge flask of rum, just happy to be alive

The mood was very grim. The bravery of the Red Forces Hunter's astonishing one-man battle against the one hundred Blue airplanes, and the very timely arrival of the

AirCats—thanks to the successful recon mission undertaken by the Jones boys at Hunter's request—had all turned the battle in the Reds' favor.

But the Jones boys' foray to the south had brought back more than the AirCat squadron. The twins had also made a gloomy discovery down by the new convergence of the Indus River and the Nawa Canal.

This disturbing news was now posted up on the wall in the form of a very large long-range TV-recon still photograph snapped by the Jones boys from the Bug copter.

The photo showed the aircraft carrier and its fleet of ugboats resting comfortably in the lower reaches of the ndus-Nawa convergence. The carrier had detected the nan-made waterway leading up into Pakistan and had aken the opportunity to get closer to where they knew he Z-16 recon plane had gone in. The Bro-Bird was parked n the water nearby, as well.

But farther up the new waterway—clearly one hundred niles north of the carrier's present position—were six normous ships sitting at anchor. These were the vessels hat had carried the Black Army to the fight.

They were clearly unloaded and empty.

Another photo snapped by the Jones boys in their journey showed what looked like nothing less than a giant tream of insects moving north. This was the 200,000-plus nen of the Black Army on the move, heading toward Kabul owns. From the position of the merc army when the hoto was taken, and factoring in the hours that had passed nce the Jones boys first spotted the huge army, Kurjan's nen had calculated the Black Army was but a day away om reaching the fight.

"They are actually double-timing their troops to get here uickly," Seth Jones reported to the somber group. "Some lvance units are in vehicles. I'm afraid our initial estimates were only too accurate. We can expect a division nd a half to be within firing range of our position within venty-four hours. Maybe less . . ."

JT was instantly pissed.

"So what we just went through, was all for nothing?" he asked bitterly.

"Not exactly," Hunter replied. "It bought us some time, like it was supposed to."

"Time for what, though?" Ben asked.

All eyes were on Hunter now.

"The purpose here is to save as many lives as we can, is that right?" he asked the group.

This was answered by a round of somber nods.

"Then there really is only one more thing we can do," he said, picking up his flying gear and walking over to Kurjan and his men.

"If you agree that we must take the simplest way to save as many lives as possible," he said, "then you *have* to do what I'm about to ask of you, understand?"

Kurjan nodded grimly.

"You haven't steered us wrong yet, Hawk," he replied.

Hunter then looked at the rest of them. Valiant fighters all. He knew what he was about to say would stun them. But he had thought this part out very carefully and knew it was a necessary element of his plan.

"What I want you to do," Hunter said slowly, "is make contact with the Blue side at exactly noontime."

Kurjan was confused. They all were.

"What for?" the Red Army intell man asked.

Hunter took a deep breath.

"To ask for surrender terms," he said starkly.

A gasp of shock and disbelief went around the room.

"Surrender?" several of those in attendance cried at once.

Hunter just nodded.

"Yes," he said. "And whatever conditions they want give into them."

With that, Hunter shook hands with each man and then left the hut.

He walked out to one of the Bantams and checked to make sure its fuel supply was fresh. Satisfied, he climbe into the tiny jet, started the engine, rolled out to the crowded runway, and took off.

The last that the others saw of Hunter, he was streaking eastward, leaving the field of battle entirely.

CHAPTER 42

The storm of Blue Force artillery shells started raining down on Red Base One at precisely 0900 hours—exactly sixty minutes after Hunter had flown away.

The barrage became so intense so quickly, that at one point, it seemed like all the explosions melted into one huge, enduring blast. Buildings were flattened. Airplanes destroyed. The ground beneath the base shook like a nonstop earthquake.

Meanwhile, another huge Blue Force troop buildup was gathering near the bloody bridge. As many as four divisions, more than forty thousand men could be seen mustering up on the other side of the Blue line. It was obvious that the enemy was about to launch another ground assault—with twice as many men as the night before. There was little the Reds could do about it. They were low on ammo all-round. Their forward positions were little more than holes in the ground. Plus the artillery barrage on Red Base One was so intense, it was impossible for any Red Force fighters to get into the air, even if they wanted to.

Even worse, Kurjan's men had intercepted a radio message from the advancing Black Army. In breaking the code they discovered a horrifying fact: If the Black Army assault on Kabul Downs was not effective within a few hours, plans called for them to detonate a DG-55 super-blockbuster bomb just outside the city. If this was true, then everything—and everyone, both Red Force and Blue—for miles around would be turned to dust.

The only piece of good news was that during the previous night, while the southern front battled the Blue offensive, many Red soldiers on both the eastern and western flanks had managed to slip away to safe havens in Pakistan and the hills west of Kabul Downs. So at least one part of the Reds' desperate strategy—that they try to save as many lives as possible among their troops—had come true.

But this did little to relieve the sense of impending doom weighing on Red Base One. They were truly at ground zero for what was about to happen.

The fact that no one had heard from the Wingman made a bad situation only worse . . . .

The deadly artillery barrage continued unabated for the next three hours.

There was little left of Red Base One now—the central aiming point for the Blue Force shelling. Anyone still breathing was jammed into the few bomb shelters scattered about the base or huddled in the dozens of slit trenches, which ran the length of the base's main runway.

Finally the fateful hour of noon came.

Acting on the OK from his superiors, Kurjan crawled to what was left of the base's radio hut and had the communications officer inside send a message to the Blue Forces inside Kabul Downs.

"Ready to accept your previously stated surrender terms," the message read simply.

The shelling ceased completely one minute later.

Now came an interlude, which Fitz would adequately describe as a "quiet hell."

For only the second time in nearly a year, there was no

shooting along the Blue-Red line. No artillery was going off, no constant chatter of machine guns or infantry rifles. Just the wind could be heard, blowing across the blood-soaked battlefield. The city of Kabul Downs was absolutely still. It was almost as if the Blue Force, probably taken by surprise by the sudden Red Force capitulation, was pausing to catch its collective breath before designating specifics of the surrender.

It was the silence that was almost maddening.

Huddled in a particularly muddy hole near the end of the runway were Zoltan, Crabb, Fitz, JT, and Ben.

They'd spent the three hours of the murderous artillery barrage here, hands over their heads, not speaking, barely breathing. Now that the shelling had stopped, there was only nervous conversation. Dreary chitchat as they waited for the next shoe to drop.

It was an odd and uncomfortable situation. None of them really knew each other very well, plucked as they were from obscurity to follow Hunter into this strange adventure. In fact, the only thing they all had in common *was* Hunter's friendship.

And at the moment, that seemed like a very strained thing indeed.

The surreal peace finally gave Zoltan and Crabb the opportunity to ask questions. Difficult ones, to say the least. After some beating around the bush, Zoltan finally dropped a bomb of his own.

"What happened up there during that bombing run?" Zoltan asked Fitz outright. "It seems everything went screwy just after you guys dropped the big one on Tokyo."

Of the three, the Irishman seemed to Zoltan to be the most likely one to spill his guts. But Fitz wasn't biting. He was too busy with his binoculars, watching the mass of Blue troops still in position near that bloody bridge.

"I've been told that whatever happened during the superbombing mission is classified, and should remain that way," he replied coldly.

But Crabb wasn't going to let it go at that. They had the

Grim Reaper breathing down their necks. It hardly seemed the time for hiding behind military niceties, such as suddenly classified operations.

"Listen, we came halfway around the world looking for you guys," Crabb said heatedly. "And we might not get out of this hellhole alive. So don't you think we deserve to know what went down?"

Fitz just shrugged and kept looking through his spyglass. "What can I tell you then?" he finally replied. "It was rough—*very* rough. Especially on Hunter—"

"And that's all we're saying," JT interrupted with emphasis. "So just button your flaps, OK?"

Crabb took offense to that line.

"Hey, *dude*, we risked our lives to find you guys," he snapped back at JT. "Don't forget that . . ."

"Calm down!" Ben yelled, turning on Zoltan and Crabb. "What the fuck else do you want to know? Fitz is right. It was really rough on Hawk. He was a changed guy after it was over. We all wanted to go home—you think we didn't? But Hawk said something else was up. Something he *had* to pursue. He couldn't explain it. He didn't even know what it was about. But we took a vote and it was unanimous. We decided to come with him. What would you have done?"

There was another long silence.

"The same thing, I'm sure," Zoltan finally said. It was odd but he was not picking up any bad vibes from the three men. This indicated to him that whatever secrets they were holding, were buried very deeply in their psyches. Either that, or they knew very little of what happened to Hunter at all.

There was another long silence among them.

"So where do you think Hunter's gone now?" Zoltan asked Fitz.

The Irishman finally took his eyes from the binoculars and looked at the psychic.

"I have no idea," he answered gloomily.

"Think he's coming back?" Zoltan asked.

That's when JT came flying across the trench at the psychic. Punches were thrown, but none landed. Ben and Fitz stopped JT. Crabb grabbed ahold of Zoltan.

"Jeesuzz, settle down everybody!" Fitz cried. "We've got enough bloody problems without fighting amongst ourselves."

That's when Fitz got very quiet.

"Look, I really don't know Hawk that well," he said softly. "I mean, I *feel* like I know him—but I really don't. But he certainly changed that day after we dropped the bomb. He'd had a communion with a spirit, or something. After that, he was just focused on this one thing. This thing that he didn't even know fully himself. It was like he expected something to be here when we arrived. Something or someone that would make sense out of the crazy life he seemed to be leading. Whatever it was, he didn't tell me—he didn't tell anyone. But whatever it was, it was driving him hard. And it brought us here. To this hellhole. That's all we know really. . . ."

A very long silence. Nothing but the wind was crying.

"You said he changed," Crabb said at last. "Was it enough for him to just leave us here to die?"

JT had to be held down again—but Fitz was just shaking his head.

"I don't know," the Irishman said. "Once you get mixed up with ghosts . . ."

He let his voice trail off for a moment.

"It's him telling us to surrender," Fitz began again slowly. "That's what bothers me. I hate to say it, but it makes me think that maybe—"

At that point Kurjan leapt into the trench interrupting Fitz's somber speech. The Red Force intell man was holding a handful of photos—long-range recon pics.

"Ready for some more bad news?" he asked gloomily.

"No," JT replied angrily.

Fitz and Zoltan looked at the recon photos. It showed more advance Black Army troops were flooding into the area and were slowly encircling what was left of the Red southern front.

"We gave orders to everyone out on the flanks to just get out of their way," Kurjan said. "But us, the ones who are here—we got no way out. We're stuck and they're coming fast."

Fitz spit angrily.

"This quiet is driving me nuts," he said, putting the spyglass back up and zeroing in on the thousands of Blue troops just a mile or so away. "We've given up. What are they waiting for?"

He got his answer not two seconds later.

It came at first like the sound of the wind screaming. Then the air itself actually began to shake.

They all looked off to the south and were astonished to see that the sky was suddenly full with large, dark forms. They weren't airplanes—that much was certain. But they were flying machines and they were black and they were heading right for them.

"My God!" Kurjan cried. "Are those . . . *Beaters?*"

They were. More commonly known as Octocopters, Beaters were ungainly, gigantic eight-rotor flying contraptions the size of a small airliner. Once in flight, Beaters always looked like they were waging a losing war against the laws of aerodynamics. They flew, but just barely. Their engines were usually belching smoke and sometimes flames. They were noisy, slow, and always seemed to be on the verge of plowing in.

They could also carry as many as one thousand troops each. And judging by the way these Beaters were flying—under 75 mph and very close to the ground—they all seemed extremely overloaded. It was obvious they belonged to the Black Army.

"Beaters?" Fitz said over and over, not quite believing it. "That worm Sluggo never said anything to us about Beaters."

"Jeesuz, are they coming for us?" Ben wondered with no little nervousness in his voice.

They had that answer just a few seconds later when the first line of the monstrous helicopters flew over their position—and kept on going. They slowed a bit just over the bloody bridge and began setting down about a quarter mile behind the Blue Army Line.

Almost immediately the sound of gunfire could be heard.

"Son of a bitch!" JT yelled. "That asshole Sluggo was right about one thing: the Blacks are just going right over us—and putting it to the blue bloods."

It seemed strange, but it was apparently true. In seconds the air above them was filled with tracer fire from Blue Army AAA guns. It was not aimed at Red base, but at the oncoming Black Army Beaters.

"Jeesuz, how *weird* is this?" Kurjan yelled.

"They can kick ass on each other all they want," Crabb shouted back. "But what does this mean for us?"

Suddenly Fitz was standing up in the trench, his huge double-barrel machine gun up on his shoulder.

"I say, let's find out!" he cried.

With that, a second line of Beaters roared overhead. Fitz took aim on one of them and let loose a long double stream of tracer bullets. He immediately scored hits up and down the closest Beater, now just one hundred feet above them. There was a series of small explosions, followed by a much larger one.

Fitz had just enough time to yell: "Hit the deck!" The next second the huge helicopter went down and crashed at the end of the base's main runway.

There was a tremendous explosion. The ground shook beneath their feet once again. They looked up to see a big copter become engulfed in flames.

"Christ!" Crabb yelled. "This is unbelievable."

But suddenly Kurjan and Fitz were up and running toward the crash site.

"Where the hell are they going?" Zoltan yelled.

"Just watch and learn, swami!" JT shouted back at him.

Baffled, Zoltan and Crabb followed the two men as they

began crawling into the wreckage, emerging soon afterward with one of the aircraft's occupants dragging behind them.

Crabb jumped up and helped Kurjan and Fitz pull the Black Army soldier into the trench. He was badly hurt. His black uniform was stained with blood and oil from the crash. Kurjan stuck a canteen against the man's lips and began pouring. Then he sat him up and gave him the once-over.

"This guy ain't no run-of-the-mill mercenary," Kurjan declared, examining the man's uniform and equipment. "He's a Special Forces type. Part of a shock-troop unit, I'd say."

"That means they're going for something inside the city, something they need to capture before their main forces arrive," Fitz said. "But what could it be?"

"Let's ask him," Kurjan said.

He slapped the man awake. The soldier was semiconscious and in great pain. But he seemed aware that his life had been saved, at least temporarily.

"What was your target?" Kurjan asked him. "Where were you going?"

The man just laughed at him, causing a bloody gush from his mouth and nose. "Like I should tell you for nothing?" he replied in German. "Give me some morphine and I'll tell you all."

Fitz was in no mood to haggle. He drew his field knife and pressed against the man's pulsating jugular.

"Where were you going?" he asked him sternly.

The man immediately began freaking out. It took all five of them to hold him down. Finally he collapsed, took a deep breath, and started talking.

"There is a place . . . deep inside the city," he began. "A central command post . . . it is deep underground . . . impossible to bomb from the air . . . . We were to overtake it. It is the key to this battle we were told . . . . When we heard you Reds had surrendered, it forced us to make our move. We *had* to get the central command of the Blues. Those were our orders."

The man laughed again, more blood gushed from him.

"Ah, but my friends, you have simply saved me from dying later rather than sooner," he said through bloody lips. "And for this, I thank you."

With that, the man fell over, dead.

Fitz and Kurjan pushed him out of the trench and then slumped back down again.

"Well, at least we know Hawk was right about one thing," Ben said. "That central command post was the key to this whole fucking war!"

"Looking back on it," Kurjan said. "maybe we should have tried to find it and take it out ourselves."

"You mean do a ground raid?" Fitz asked.

"That would have been the only way," Kurjan replied. "Hawk himself said the place was too hard for anything we had to bomb it with. Even the HellJets—cool as they are—probably wouldn't have put a dent in it."

Fitz just nodded sadly. "Hawk said he believed the station was at least two hundred feet underground—and concrete reinforced. Though I don't know how he knew that, I'm sure he was right."

"Well, we're really fucked now then," JT said bitterly. "Whether it's the Blues or the Blacks, whoever has control of that place by the end of the day will stomp us for good. They'll be using us for target practice. What's left of us . . ."

JT's harsh words seemed to be cruelly prophetic because a moment later artillery shells began raining down on Red Base One—from two directions.

"God, how screwy is this?" Fitz yelled and they all went down for cover. "The Blacks are fighting the Blues, the Blues are fighting the Blacks, and they're *both* throwing shells at us!"

"We'll need a miracle to get out of this," Crabb said. "And I mean a *real* miracle . . ."

But just as those words were coming out of Crabb's

mouth, they were blotted out by the sound of another tremendous scream.

High above them, they saw the colossal outline of an airplane.

Kurjan nearly fainted dead away. This was the largest flying thing he could have ever imagined. It looked like a battleship with wings. It was so monstrous, it seemed to take up all of the sky.

"Holy Lazarus!" Kurjan yelled. *"What the hell is that?"*

No one in the trench could even speak. But they all knew exactly what it was.

It was the B-2000 superbomber.

"Well, at least we know where the hell Hunter went!" JT bellowed.

There was no doubt that Hunter was behind the controls of the colossal bomber. Apparently he'd rushed back to Kwai and was somehow able to lift the giant off the ground and return to the scene—all in the space of just a few hours.

But now that he was here with the flying battleship, what was he planning on doing with it?

"Just how many superbombs was that thing carrying?" Zoltan cried out.

"If he drops one here," Crabb added, "Jeesuzz, the whole country will sink!"

"Relax," Fitz told them. "There was only one bomb like that."

He turned to JT and Ben, and asked under his breath: "Right?"

They both shrugged. They had no idea.

But any notion they had that Hunter might be on a long-range bombing run was dispelled by another sudden turn of events. As streams of antiaircraft fire began rising up from the city aimed at the huge airplane, the superbomber suddenly shifted downward. They saw the bursts of flame erupt from its multitude of engines, indicating their double-burners had been lit. The additional speed was apparent right away. The huge airplane started diving at about twenty thousand feet. In seconds, it was going more than Mach 2 and heading straight down to a point somewhere in Kabul Downs.

It hit two seconds later . . . .

What happened next was so intense, those who witnessed it would have their psyches scarred for the rest of their lives.

The huge bomber hit with the speed of a meteorite zooming in from outer space. Those watching at Red Base One hit the dirt immediately—but that did no good. The ground shook mightily for two full minutes, small cracks in its surface appeared everywhere. Unlike the massive artillery barrage, this was a *real* earthquake. This impact was so intense, the dust that rose from the crash immediately became superheated. In seconds a gigantic thunderstorm broke out, with lightning so intense, it burned the retinas of anyone who dared to look at it.

Even before the ground stopped shaking, it was apparent what had happened: Hunter had slammed the big jet into the Blue Forces subterranean central command station.

The Blue artillery barrage stopped immediately.

Those in the forward trench stood up and just stared at the city and the giant lightning-packed cloud rising above it. It looked like a scene from Hell.

"Well, we wanted to take out that central command post," Kurjan said. "Looks like Hawk did it for us—and saved our asses in the process."

There was a deadly silence now. No one wanted to say what was on everyone's mind.

But combat veterans all, they knew there was no way Hunter could have survived.

Or could he?

CHAPTER 43

Above Kabul Downs

Hunter could not remember if he had ever used a parachute before.

Certainly not in this world. But how about in the other? That other life of his Back There?

He didn't think so.

It just wasn't like him to leave an airplane in flight. He was sure that Back There he'd had one special airplane—the F-16XL. He just couldn't imagine getting into so much trouble that he'd actually bail out of it.

But now, in this very different place, he was finally hitting the silk. And it looked like he was descending down into the pit of Hell itself.

The B-2000 had gone in with such an impact, it had thrown him clear of the storm cloud, clear of the lightning that was now illuminating the sky just north of him. By his own rough calculations, he estimated the giant bomber had hit the central command station at more than 2,500 mph. The result was akin to a small atomic bomb.

Now as he drifted down through the dust clouds, he

could see the huge gaping hole on the west side of the city, where the central command station had been hidden. One look and he knew nothing could have possibly survived such an impact.

The question was, would it be enough to cause both the Blues and Blacks to give up the fight long enough to allow the rest of the Red Forces to escape?

He drifted down through the next cloud layer and saw that his worst fears were being realized. The battlefield was still alit with explosions, with artillery shells falling, with machine guns spewing out streams of tracers.

So, had his plan not worked?

Or hadn't it taken effect yet?

He didn't know . . .

He drifted through the last layers of clouds, and now the stink of smoke and cordite began to inflame his nostrils.

The crashing of the big jet he'd done to perfection. But to his chagrin, he'd forgotten about the most important part: where the hell to land once he'd bailed out.

He jiggled his parachute cords now this way and that, but it was no use. He was heading for the center of a huge gun battle going on between the Blacks and the Blues.

And he had no weapon. Nothing at all with which to defend himself.

This was not good.

It took him another two minutes to reach a point about one thousand feet above the battlefield. The ground below still seemed to be shaking from the earth-shattering impact of the B-2000. There were flames all over the city, some streets were cracked wide open, and many buildings had toppled over just from the shock wave alone.

Hunter was getting pissed. Why he'd thought all fighting would stop as soon as he iced the central command station he just didn't know. Judging from what was happening beneath his boots, the fighting was raging even more furiously than before.

Had he made a huge miscalculation? Had his bold plan to stop the war actually made it worse? Had he *killed* more people than he hoped to save?

He just didn't know . . .

Suddenly he felt the air pressure around him change. His body began shaking. He twisted around in his chute ust quickly enough to see a spread of huge howitzer shells heading right for him. He moved just in time to avoid being hit, but the concussion of the shells passing by felt ike a hammer had hit him on the skull.

His head spinning, he looked back down and saw a huge explosion coming up right at his feet. Again he tried to iggle out of the way, but the huge concussive force—the econd in less than thirty seconds—hit him full force, blowing him and his parachute up about 250 feet.

He blacked out for a few seconds; when he came to, he aw that the soles of his boots were smoking. That's how lose he'd come to being consumed by the huge fireball.

He was very woozy now, praying to hit the ground even hough he wasn't sure what would be greeting him once e did. He was trying to focus his eyes on his eventual nding spot, now five hundred feet below, when another eries of huge explosions went off, one right after another, l around him. These were massive triple-A shells explodng high over the battlefield. It was like being punched as ard as possible in the head and stomach. He doubled ver in midair, never before could he remember feeling ich pain.

It was hard for him to keep his eyes open. Then his arachute collapsed. The ground was coming up at him fast, it was all just a blur of smoke and flames and rocks nd dirt.

With his last ounce of strength, he tried to brace himself r a hard landing. He tensed his muscles, took a deep eath, and gritted his teeth.

He hit—*very* hard—three seconds later. His head came own first—not the way to land from twenty thousand feet. e grazed a huge boulder that was still smoking from an explosion just seconds before. Hunter saw stars—red ones, black ones, blue ones.

Then he lost consciousness.

Hunter lay there, tangled in his parachute, head bleeding, bones cracked, for at least an hour as the battle raged around him.

His eyes were closed, his body pummeled by rocks and other flying debris. His ears bled from the sound of explosions and gunfire going on around him. He was sure he could hear tanks creaking in the distance, way off, but coming in his direction. Yet he could not move. He was stuck in place. Unable to see or cry out.

All he could do was hear—and the sounds he heard were those of brutal combat, getting closer with every passing second.

So this was how it was going to end?

How many times had he thought *that* in the past few months?

It just didn't seem right: to die here, so far away, on some unknown battlefield in a very stupid war. Yet all the evidence seemed to be stacking up that way.

He even began to see faces flash before his eyes. His parents. When was the last time he'd *really* seen them? His friends from MIT, that school from so long ago. The Thunderbirds . . . everyone, from the pilots to the ground crew. Fitz. JT. Ben. The Jones boys. How strange was his life that he'd been able to see these close friends in two lives? In two places?

Maybe it was fitting, then, that this was where he would die. What more could he ask from his life?

More faces came to him. All the beautiful women he'd known. Sarah—the pilot back home. Where was she now? Did she ever think of him? He'd left her so suddenly, he wouldn't blame her if she hated him now.

He hoped she didn't . . .

Then there was that strange woman, Elizabeth Sandlake

Beautiful but deranged—like life itself. She'd almost killed him several times Back There—and he'd seen her here in this world, posing as a crazed fortune-teller. Odd that he would be thinking of her now, at a time like this.

There was also that very pretty blonde—Chloe. He'd had an adventure to beat all with her Back There, and had fallen for her so hard, he'd heard his heart drop. He had met her here, too. Back on West Falkland Island. But he'd never made it back to her. *Damn.* And now he never would.

There were many others—all beautiful, all sexy. Just the thought of them, and their faces flashing before his eyes, filled him with a very warm feeling.

But even as it was getting warm inside, he felt himself getting cold on the outside. He tensed up. *My God,* he hought. He could feel the life draining right out of him.

Too many hits on the head? Maybe heart damage? Maybe a combination of both? Exactly *why* he was dying really lidn't make much difference to him now.

Was it all just a folly? All just a waste of time? To come o this very foreign land and fight this very foreign war? 'or what? On the advice of a ghost that he may or may ıot have even seen?

Oh, well, it didn't make much difference now. His whole ody was getting cold. He felt like going to sleep. All round him the noise got louder, and the tanks got nearer.

But *damn it!* He didn't want to be crushed by a tank. Ie tried to move, but couldn't. He felt like he was set hard ı cement.

It was strange—but there was *another* woman in his life. ıst one more. The most special. How could he have forotten?

She was so beautiful! So warm, and smart, and . . . and ıey had lived together Back There. Off and on anyway. nd when he was not with her, he'd spent the time earning for her. Dreaming about her. Fighting for her.

But she was dead . . . of that much he was sure.

And it was this thought that practically drained the last the life force out of him. Damn, wouldn't you know it, as the Wingman was drawing his last dying breath, that this woman he'd had way Back There, this beauty that had been so close to him. . .

Damned if he couldn't remember her name . . . .

Blackness now, coming in. He was going . . . slipping away. He saw a long tunnel, and there at the end of it was the Light again. The same one he'd seen that terrible day he dropped the superbomb.

Now there was a figure at the end of the tunnel beckoning to him . . . and suddenly he felt warm inside again. And he was drifting up to the Light. And all the people he'd just thought about were there, and he felt a warmth inside him that was so overwhelming, he wanted nothing more than to feel it.

Forever . . .

"Just hang on, buddy. I've got you . . . !"

What?

"I've got you, friend . . . just try to stay together . . ."

What was happening? The tunnel was fading. The warmth was going. He felt something in his arm. A hypodermic needle.

Something was shot into him. Someone was dragging him, through the muck, over jagged rocks and through putrid water.

What was happening here? He was being rescued?

Really?

Suddenly his body ached incredibly, and he was hot and he was cold and his hands were numb from the pain, and his head was pounding—and he was being dragged a few inches at a time across a very rugged landscape.

God, did he really want this?

The battle raged all around him. Hunter could feel th hot searing bullets passing so close to him they burne his skin. His ears were bleeding again with the sound o explosions going off. His whole body ached so! He wa nauseous. And this person just kept dragging him. Lik he was being yanked over a field of broken glass.

Finally they toppled into a ditch filled with water and gasoline.

Hunter fell facedown into the smelly mud.

The person rolled him over and wiped the muck from his face. Hunter finally was able to open his eyes.

But for the moment, he could only see the outline of the man who had dragged him to safety. He was wearing a black camo uniform. God, he was a mercenary . . . for the Black Army!

Hunter could not see his face.

An instant later, he felt a sting in his left arm.

"That's a shot of adrenaline," the man said. "Hang on, it's a real jolt."

Hunter was about to say something when the full force of the shot hit him. He felt like he was falling out of the sky again. His whole body suddenly felt electric.

"Jeesuzz," he murmured. "What a freaking rush . . ."

"If you think so," the man said, "then get ready for this."

He felt another needle go into his arm.

"That's fifty ccs of morphine," the man said. "To kill the pain."

Now Hunter felt another jolt go through him. Suddenly he was floating above the battlefield. He felt as strong as Superman, and he was floating, and there was no way any pain could break through his skin of steel.

He reached up and wiped the rest of the mud from his eyes, and that's when he finally saw the face of the man who had saved him.

Very thin features, sharp beard. Haunting eyes.

My God . . .

"It's you?" Hunter asked him.

"Christ!" he said. *"Hunter?"*

It was Viktor.

He was as astonished as the Wingman. His eyes went very, very wide. He jumped back. "How can this be?" he yelped.

Hunter was so stunned, he couldn't speak. Flashes of

green light went before his eyes. This man had been his mortal enemy for years—the devil on earth. But that was the *other* earth. Now, he had just risked his life to save him.

It just didn't make sense . . . or did it.

"We . . . we are not the same people that we were," Hunter was babbling now.

Viktor just looked down at him.

"I-I don't know who I was back there," he said, stammering as he covered Hunter's most apparent wounds.

A huge explosion went off nearby, covering them with rocks and shrapnel.

"Can you walk?" Viktor asked him.

Hunter was certain he could not only walk, but actually fly . . . really *fly* . . . without an airplane.

"Yes, I can," he finally replied.

They started moving. Hunter realized for the first time that they were very close to the city itself. The majority of fighting was taking place farther out toward the Red Army lines. The only wise thing to do was to seek the shelter of the city.

They began running in a low crouch, Viktor helping Hunter every step of the way, over the battlefield, onto the cracked streets, stopping only once they reached the burned-out core of a building.

There was still gunfire all around them. Explosions going off. The sky was still filled with streaks of artillery shells passing close overhead.

Viktor just stared at him and Hunter stared back. Every fiber in Hunter's being was telling him that this man, this piece of human puke, had killed millions Back There. Yet here, he was just the opposite. He was an angel of mercy. A medic, complete with a large armband with a huge Red Cross on it. And strangest of all, Viktor wasn't even aware of how much he had changed.

Hunter just shook his head. What kind of a life was he leading?

"It must be some kind of cosmic thing that we should meet again like this," Viktor was saying, taking off his field pack. "I recall hitting the water with you back then . . . and that was it. But I have met a man, down in the Falklands, he knows how we can get back to where we came from."

He put a large bandage across Hunter's forehead.

"I had a chance to go," Viktor went on. "He was going to let me. But I knew somehow that I had to wait. I was afraid of what I might be, Back There. I didn't want to go alone. So I knew I had to find you. And now I have . . . "

"The Falklands?" Hunter stammered. "You mean d-down in the middle of that mountain?"

Viktor nodded.

"There's a hole in the sky down there," he said. "There's no other way I can explain it. But it's there and if we jump through it, the Man thinks we'll go back to where we came from."

Another huge explosion went off, shattering the concrete on the street outside. Another storm of debris came down on them.

Hunter was cranked so full of drugs, he didn't feel a thing. He could hardly speak.

Viktor was shaking him. "Don't you think that's what we should do?" He was pressing him. "Go back there and jump through that hole?"

At that moment, something just clicked in Hunter's brain. It was as if the last piece of the puzzle fell into place.

Suddenly he was very coherent.

"Yes, that's *exactly* what we should do," he said. "But there is something else we have to do first."

CHAPTER 44

They started running.

Through the broken streets of the city.

Explosions were going off all around them. Gunfire was everywhere. Tracers were streaking over their heads. The roar of cannons, huge guns going off, the scream of airplane engines above it all.

But they kept running. Hunter in the lead, his veins coursing with adrenaline and morphine; Viktor trying hard to keep up with him.

The city was nearly deserted by now. They did see a few blue-uniformed soldiers running about. Though they were armed, these men did not interfere with them. They, too, were running for their lives. The city was being battered by the Black Army guns. The AirCats were strafing, and the HellJets were dive-bombing. It was total chaos. Why, then, would anyone stop two men, one in a muddy Red Army uniform, the other dressed in a black camos with a huge Red Cross on it, running like madmen into a city that was about to collapse on itself?

They soon found themselves on King's Walk, the main drag of Kabul Downs. Artillery shells were raining down on this avenue—from whose side, it was hard to tell. They raced through the explosions; Hunter running like an Olympic sprinter, Viktor doing everything he could to keep up. At the end of the street was the prime minster's house, the official seat of government. It was now in flames, one wing taken out with the crash of two Blue Force jets.

They turned north, up Queen's Lane, where two Blue Force tanks were inexplicably firing at each other. Hunter never stopped running. He dashed between the two behemoths, even as they were simultaneously launching shells at each other. It was all Viktor could do now just to keep him in sight among the explosions, the smoke, and the flames.

They reached the central park, which now looked as cratered and moonlike as the battlefield surrounding the city. Rocket fire was falling from all directions. Many of the trees were on fire. Hunter kept on running, nimbly dodging pieces of flaming debris, some before they even hit the ground.

They ran past the wreckage of the Z-16, still in place, nose crumbled, wings bent, resting like a dead seabird in the dirty waters of the lake. Viktor thought he might have seen Hunter run just a little bit slower past the wreckage—a moment's hesitation in his headlong flight to who knows where. But once beyond the wreck, the Wingman resumed his mad dash at top speed once more.

Once down the next avenue, they did come to a stop—they had to. There was an enormous hole in the earth. It was nearly a quarter mile across, and so deep, there was already water collecting in the bottom of it. It was also filled with millions of pieces of various rubble, and a few indistinguishable body parts. This was a little glimpse into Hell itself. It was where Hunter had slammed the huge B-2000 superbomber in the Blue Force central command station.

It was an eerie moment—Hunter stood, stunned, looking down into the hole. He paused long enough to allow Viktor to catch up with him. The hole was so deep, it was almost impossible to see its bottom. Hunter hesitated for a moment right on the precipice. Viktor was finally beside him—out of breath, red faced. He looked at Hunter and suddenly grabbed him, just as it appeared the Wingman was going to step off the edge and plunge into the abyss.

"No, not this hole," Viktor told Hunter, pulling him back from the edge. "This is not the right one."

Hunter didn't say a word. He pulled away from Viktor's grip and started running once again. Around the edge of the enormous crater, and beyond, he was soon back on the avenue and running just as fast as before. Viktor took a deep breath and continued his pursuit once again.

They ran for another mile or so, through cratered streets, around raging fires, over or under collapsed buildings. Finally, after a half hour of full-out sprinting, Hunter reached his destination: the Lords Towers.

It was strange. Despite all the destruction around it, the tower was still standing, still intact, though battered and smoking heavily. All of its windows had been blown out. The waterfall, which had adorned its lower floors, had stopped flowing, and the sounds of gunfire could be heard within. The place seemed fraught with danger.

Nevertheless Hunter did not hesitate a moment. He charged right through the huge front door and started bounding up the stairs.

"Wait!" Viktor screamed after him. "It's too risky to . . ."

But Hunter was not listening. He was already on the second floor—with eleven more to go.

Viktor bounded into the great open hall and raced up the stairs after the wild pilot. He caught him just as they reached the third floor.

Tackling him from behind, Viktor forced Hunter up against the wall. Suddenly everything stopped. They could hear flames crackling, glass breaking, and gunfire echoing throughout the building.

"Wait!" Viktor screamed at him, somehow finding the strength to hold Hunter still for a moment. "What are you doing here? *Why are you doing this?*"

Hunter stared back at him—a very crazed look in his eyes.

"I'm doing this because I have to," he replied with surreal calm. "I'm doing this because I was told to."

He took a deep breath and calmed down a bit.

He looked his former archenemy in the eye and said:

"I'm doing this because I believe it might be the last thing I ever do . . ."

They just stared at each other for a long time, the sound of gunfire getting louder, more intense.

"But what do you think is up there?" Viktor asked him, pointing up the staircase. "What could possibly be so important?"

Hunter looked up the tower's stairwell, he could see through the smoke all the way to the top.

"I'm . . . I'm afraid to say," Hunter replied, for the first time ever in memory using the word "afraid," and meaning it.

He took another deep breath.

"I know that whatever is left in my life, be it a minute or a millennium, I got to go up there, to the top, and find out what has been driving me since I got to this goddamn place."

They stood there, silent for a few more moments.

"It's a strange destiny," Viktor said. "But I swore I'd find you and bring you back to the hole in the sky. I guess that means I've got to stay with you."

Hunter smiled, his body began pumping again, with adrenaline and morphine.

"Then let's go," he said.

Hunter began bounding up the stairs again; Viktor had no choice but follow him close behind.

There were, appropriately enough, thirteen stories to the top of the Lords Tower. The steps were steep, and in some cases they were cracked or gone completely due to direct artillery hits.

But none of these thing impeded Hunter's wild ascent. He was quite insane now—he knew it. His brain was not working like it used to. Gone was the computerlike coolness, the precognitive edge—he had no idea what was going to happen to him at the top of the tower. Not a clue. All he could hear in his head right now were the ghost's last words to him: *"Don't stop climbing until you reach the top. The very top . . . that's where your destiny lies."*

Hunter was bounding up the stairs three at a time. Heart pounding, eyes blazing, mouth drooling, up he went, like he was going up Jacob's ladder. Above, he could hear gunfire and screams.

Now at the twelfth floor, he suddenly skidded to a stop. One last piece of precognition had somehow come to the fore, and it told him to slow down, be aware. Danger was ahead. This pause also allowed a very out-of-breath Viktor to catch up with him again.

Together they stopped moving, stopped breathing—and just listened.

Gunshots. One. Two. Three. Then silence.

Next voices. Arguing. Laughing. Drunken voices.

Then more gunshots. Then more drunken discussions.

"This is not a gun battle," Hunter said to Viktor.

Viktor nodded in agreement.

"What is it then?" Hunter asked.

They both listened again. Two more gunshots. Then a slight clanging sound—as if the person doing the shooting was firing at a piece of metal.

Viktor's face lit up.

"A prison door," he said in a desperate whisper, looking off into black space. "They are trying to shoot the lock off of a prison door. To get to whoever is inside."

Hunter's brain nearly exploded at this point. He was so close to be stopped here. What a disaster! The problem was they had no weapons with them. It was obvious the people up on the next floor did.

"What can we do?" Hunter asked Viktor helplessly. Even

in the chaotic circumstances, the irony of that question was not lost on him.

Viktor just stared off into space for a few more moments. Then he said simply: "Just follow me."

Now Viktor took the lead. Moving slowly and steadily, he went up the stairs ahead of Hunter, who crept slowly behind.

There were five soldiers in Blue Force uniforms. And indeed, they were taking turns firing at a huge lock that was holding tight a large ironclad door. This door led into a jail cell.

The five soldiers were so consumed by what they were doing, they did not see Viktor and Hunter—not at first anyway.

They were slightly crazed, these soldiers. A couple were bleeding from what appeared to be serious wounds, yet they seemed not to be at all affected. They were holding pictures—of a person Hunter could not make out—in front of them as if these photos were a talisman. And they were firing away at the mighty lock, which held this door shut. From behind the door, soft sobbing could be heard.

Viktor never stopped. He climbed right to the top of the stairs and stood before the five soldiers.

They saw him only out of the corner of their eyes. Only after one man fired off several rounds, which nearly broke through the lock, did they finally stop.

"Who the fuck are you?" one of them roared at Viktor.

"I'm here to tell you to stop what you are doing," Viktor replied calmly.

The soldiers looked at him and laughed. One indicated to the man with the gun to point it toward Viktor.

He did, and with a drunken, crazed smile, fired off two rounds at Viktor's heart. But even though the bullets came out of the rifle, they did not hit Viktor. Instead they bounced off the wall directly behind him, and just above Hunter's head, covering the Wingman in bits of stone and dust.

The soldiers were drunkenly astonished. How could their friend have missed at such a close range?

The man who seemed to be in charge took the rifle, aimed, and fired at Viktor himself.

Once again, the rifle discharged, but the bullets pinged off the wall behind Viktor, again showering Hunter with a storm of concrete debris.

He fired again. Same result.

He fired off an entire magazine. Still Viktor was unharmed.

At this point two of the men peed in their pants. A third threw up. The two others simply went pale and stared at him.

"I said, stop what you are doing and leave here now!" Viktor roared at them.

This time they listened.

The five men pushed their way past Hunter and toppled down the stairs, screaming and shrieking as they went.

Now it was Hunter's turn to be astonished. Would he lose his lunch or his bladder, too?

He picked up the rifle that had done the shooting and looked at Viktor. There wasn't a mark on him.

"W-What? How?" Hunter began stammering.

Viktor just shook his head. "I . . . I don't know," was all he could say.

Suddenly the building was rocked with a stream of artillery shells. The noise alone almost knocked Hunter on his ass. The tower began swaying. Its steel girders began moaning.

"We haven't got much time," Viktor said. "Whatever you have to do here, do it now. And quickly . . ."

But what *was* that exactly?

Hunter had obviously been drawn to this place at this time for a reason of literally cosmic proportions.

But what was it?

There was really only one answer. What he'd come all this way for was behind the locked door.

He stood before it and listened and just as another

barrage of artillery shells hit the tower, he again heard the sobbing.

He picked up one of the rifles dropped by the fleeing soldiers and aimed it at the already battered lock. He pulled the trigger once and hit the lock square on, sending a shower of sparks all over him and Viktor. The lock split in half and fell to the stone floor, still hot from where the bullet had hit it.

Hunter turned to Viktor, who took a step back.

"No, this is your dream," Viktor said to him; Hunter was quite aware of his odd choice of words. "You go in first . . ."

Hunter turned back to the door, then gave it a swift kick. It opened, slowly and with a long squeak.

It was dark inside. A single window allowed light in from the outside but it was small and the bars made the light very dim. This was a jail cell, there was no doubt about that now.

Hunter took one step inside—and at that moment everything changed. He felt his body become charged with a new electricity—not the false energy Viktor had pumped into his veins. No, this buzz was coming from an entirely different direction.

He took another step inside and felt an almost orgasmic rush swell inside his body. His eyes adjusted to the dim light, and he saw a figure standing in the shadows at the other end of the cell. He took another step—more absolutely ecstatic rushes went through his body.

What was happening?

He was about to find something he'd lost a long time ago, something he'd been looking for just as long.

Another step. The sobbing got louder. But it was no longer sad. No, these were tears of joy coming from the shadows.

Another step, and Hunter took off his battle helmet, and dropped the gun to his side. Another step and the figure in the shadows moved toward him.

Another step . . .

He saw her face . . .

Heard her call his name . . .

And that's when he went down on one knee, and lowered his head and reached out and touched her outstretched hand—and that's when he remembered the name of the woman he'd loved so deeply, and lost so long ago. And the entire Cosmos made sense to him again.

He looked up into her eyes and saw that she was smiling.

It was Dominique.

PART FOUR

CHAPTER 45

By late afternoon the territory close to Kabul Downs under Red Force control had shrunk to barely a quarter mile across.

Though nearly all of the Red Army had managed to escape the disaster in the making, the rear-action troops, close to 750 men, were now trapped, with thousands of Blue Force troops on one side and tens of thousands of Black Army mercenaries closing in on the other.

Though the destruction of the central command station had ceased all rational military activity, and had allowed many of the Red soldiers to get away, a new kind of madness had gripped the remaining Blue and Black forces. Rogue units from both sides were now pounding each other viciously—and the last of the Red Army soldiers were caught right in the middle.

Among these luckless troops were all of the JAWS team, all of NJ-104, the Jones boys, Ben, JT, Fitz, Zoltan, Crabb Geraci, the drunkenly, unconscious Y, and the entire intelligence company for the Red Army, including Major Kuran and his staff.

During the brief respite after the central command station was vaporized, Kurjan had ordered all of the remaining Red Force biplanes to withdraw. Some pilots managed to take some badly wounded troops up with them, squeezing them into their already-tight cockpits and then fighting their way to freedom. One of the AirCat fighter-bombers had landed, managed to squeeze in three wounded men along with the four "Brandy"s, then escaped by flying at treetop level right over the heads of the advancing Black Army.

The Red Army troops that were left behind gallantly fought on, but there was little doubt that very soon they would be crushed between two enormously powerful forces who, just by sheer weight alone, would eliminate the last of them and return the crazy three-sided battle to just two sides.

There was no panic as the Red Force pocket grew smaller by the minute. By Kurjan's order, all troops were to give ground only gradually, withdrawing toward the air base and the bend in the Saint Yabuk River. It was here that they would make their last stand against the two converging monsters.

There were just a few aircraft still on the ground at the air base: One was the Bug that had served the Red Force intelligence group throughout the struggle. Many of the AirCats fighter-bombers were all still in the air, launching strike after strike against the two enemy armies. Meanwhile, the HellJets were still performing their high-altitude heart-stopping dive-bombing runs on targets within Kabul Downs itself. But once their ammunition loads were gone and their presence no longer needed, the Jones boys had given the pilots orders to withdraw and save themselves.

Now as artillery shells rained down on them from two directions, Kurjan, the Jones boys, Ben, JT, Fitz, Zoltan and Crabb found themselves sharing yet another trench, this one right along the edge of the Saint Yabuk river, hard by the burning wreckage of the Beater that Fitz had brought down at the end of the base's last workable runway.

"This is a hell of a way to end this adventure," Crabb

was saying. "I'm not sure even Hawk could scrape us out of this thing."

"He can't do the impossible," Zoltan replied, ducking as a particularly brutal stream of high-explosive shells went over their heads and impacted nearby. "He did his best. He bought us some time. Just not enough, I guess."

Crabb turned and looked at his friend. They'd been through a lot together in a very short amount of time. He stuck out his hand. Zoltan took it and they shook hands for a long time.

"What do you see for our future," Crabb asked him.

It was strange because what Crabb meant was: What will our souls face on the other side.

But the moment the words left his mouth, Zoltan's eyes went up into his head.

More bombs rained down on them, the explosions were getting closer now, and the last streams of wounded and ragged Red soldiers were stumbling back toward the air base.

For some reason, Zoltan was grinning widely.

"My God," he was saying, eyes wide open, looking off into space. "My God, I just don't believe it . . ."

Crabb had to grab him and pull him back down into the trench to avoid a stream of tracer fire coming from the Black troops now only a mile away.

"What the fuck are you talking about?" he demanded of the psychic. But again Zoltan was not listening. Instead he broke free of Crabb and began crawling along the trench to where the Jones boys were huddled with Fitz, Ben, JT, and Kurjan.

Zoltan was out of breath by the time he got there. He began gasping at Kurjan: "Get everyone . . . to the river. . . . *Hurry!*"

The Red Force intelligence man looked back at Zoltan as if he'd gone insane.

"Are you crazy?" Kurjan said, stating what seemed to be the obvious. "The river is the most exposed place we could possibly go."

"We have to get there, and I mean now!" Zoltan screamed back at him—a new authority rising in his voice.

Finally Seth Jones grabbed him. He looked into his eyes, which were literally bugging out now.

"Why?" Jones asked him simply, calmly. "Why do you want us to the river?" It was probably the first time he hadn't addressed Zoltan as "swami."

"Because . . . ," he said in an absolutely eerie voice, "we are about to be saved."

Jones looked back at him. "How?"

Zoltan just smiled, pointed straight up, and said: "See for yourself . . ."

Jones looked up—they all did—and saw absolutely nothing.

But then, not two seconds later, they heard a groaning noise. It was loud. It was familiar.

"Jeesuzz!" Dave Jones screamed, nearly leaping out of the trench himself. "I don't believe it!"

A second later an immense shadow passed over the trench—the noise was incredible. They were all hit with a wind of hurricane proportions.

It was the Bro-Bird.

The huge seaplane had come to their rescue.

But as a famous military officer from another world once said, what came next was "a closely run thing."

The Bro-Bird, enormous against the smoke-filled after noon sky, began circling the entrapped pocket. At its open windows, the members of Unit 167, the valiant Sea Marines were firing all kinds of weapons at the advancing Blac and Blue troops.

This made for an intimidating sight. With Cowboy Bobb Baulis gunning his stack of engines, emitting a horribl mechanical scream, combined with the stream of fire bein sent down by the Sea Marines, many of the enemy troops—

especially the Black mercs—simply dove for the nearest hole and stayed there.

This gave Bro the time he needed. He stopped the huge bird from circling and then, with admirable precision, leveled the big plane out and started descending toward the Saint Yabuk river.

"Jeesuz!" Dave Jones cried as he saw the big seaplane start to fall out of the sky. "He's not going to . . ."

But even before the words got out of his mouth, he had his answer. Bro Baulis was going to attempt to land the flying cruiseliner on the waters of the Saint Yabuk River.

Nearly all of the remaining troops were at river's edge by this time. As one, they watched with astonishment as the enormous airplane got lower and lower. The river was only about one thousand feet at its widest here. The Bro-bird's wingspan was nearly as wide. It was most unreal to see the gigantic airplane coming down to attempt a landing in such a small area.

But somehow Bro did it. The seaplane came down fast, then at the last moment, its nose was pulled up, hitting the muddy waters of the Saint Yabuk with a mighty crash. As soon as it touched the water, Bro reversed all engines, causing the chilling scream already being emitted from the airplane to grow even louder.

Many of the soldiers down at water's edge were battered by ten-foot waves, the result of the huge plane's sudden wake. Now they were holding their ears, too, as the noise reached into the decibel levels of painful proportions.

The seaplane's bumpy if spectacular landing brought another rain of artillery shells down on the entrapment, but many were off the mark and ineffective. No sooner had the huge airplane stopped when the Red soldiers began swimming out to it. Unit 167 members opened the dozen floating ramps and were hauling Red Army troopers in as fast as they reached the big plane. As luck would have it, two AirCat fighter-bombers were still in the area. Seeing the desperate rescue attempt, they screeched in low overhead and began firing at both Black and Blue forces. All the Bro-Bird needed was a little more time—ten minutes tops, to load everyone on board.

The AirCats would help them buy that time.

In the end it took only half that long to get just about everyone on board the Bro-Bird, so hard had the Unit 167 Sea Marines worked at saving people.

In some cases they were grabbing the escaping soldiers right out of the water and literally throwing them on board the huge seaplane. Members of the JAWS team and NJ-104, along with Ben, JT, and Fitz, swam out themselves and gained entrance to the seaplane through the forward hatch. Once in, they aided the Sea Marines in getting the rest of the Red Army troopers on board. Last to leave the shoreline were Crabb, Zoltan, and Kurjan.

At about the same time this trio reached the seaplane, one of the AirCat fighter-bombers bounced in for an unexpected landing on the base's crater-filled runway. Its pilot had taken a cannon shell hit directly in the cockpit while strafing Black Army mercs nearby, shattering his arm. Two of Geraci's men swam back to shore and with great bravery, carried the wounded pilot out to the safety of the big seabird.

Now the only two people left on shore were the Jones boys. Dave was about to plunge in for the swim out to the waiting seaplane, when he sensed his brother's hesitation. A rain of artillery shells slammed down nearby, sending them both to the ground.

"What's with you, man?" he asked his twin. "We gotta go!"

Seth raised his head. "We're still missing at least one person," he said, looking toward the smoking city of Kabul Downs just two miles away.

Dave stared at his brother, and didn't like what he was seeing.

"Who?" he asked, already knowing his brother's reply.

"Hunter," Seth said. "Are we really going to leave without him?"

Another line of artillery shells came screaming down. There were many faces looking out from the seaplane's doors at them. What was the delay?

"I think Hunter's dead," Dave said. "I really do."

His words did not sound convincing.

"What if he isn't?" Seth asked. "How can we leave him here? It just isn't right. I mean, we came all this way for him . . ."

Dave Jones just shook his head in frustration. He knew his brother was right.

"But what the hell can we do?" he asked him. "We can't go back there . . ." He nodded to the burning city. "It could go up at any second."

Seth was nodding. "I know," he said. "But something . . . something inside me . . . is telling me I should at least go look for him."

Dave's next breath caught in his throat.

"God, I feel it, too," he said. He looked out at the seaplane desperately waiting for them. "You think that swami Zoltan is putting the snide on us?" he asked.

Seth just shook his head. "I don't know," he replied. "What I do know is that I have got to go look for him. The Bug is hidden in one of the hangars. If it's still in flying condition, that's what I'm taking."

Dave just looked back at him.

"Damn it," he said. "You know that I'm not going to let you go alone."

Seth just gave him a grim smile. "Well, then, I guess that means we go together."

With that, they yelled their intentions out to the seaplane, turned, and ran toward the hangar that contained the last workable Bug helicopter on the base.

The seaplane took off from the Saint Yabuk just a minute later. Flying through a hail of gunfire from both the Black and Blue Armies, it clawed its way into the air, slowly but surely climbing out of range of the enemy guns.

It soon disappeared over the southern horizon.

The Bug lifted off a minute later. Also fighting its way through a cloud of enemy gunfire, it turned north and headed for the center of Kabul Downs.

CHAPTER 46

Neither of the Jones brothers put much faith in the psychic realm.

Certainly, they had seen and conversed with ghosts. But they were also just too pragmatic, too logical, *too busy* to believe those in the afterlife could have that much effect on the real world.

Yet both were experiencing the same odd feeling as they flew the Bug toward the burning remains of Kabul Downs. Something inside was telling them they would find Hunter alive—if they just knew where to look.

It was that part of the psychic message they were missing—or so they thought.

They arrived over the city and were astonished at the amount of destruction wrought. The streets were all cracked, and smoke and flames were rising up from below. It was as if Hell itself was trying to break out. There were dozens of downed airplanes littering the urban landscape, including many of the Black Army's Beaters, which were destroyed when Hunter crashed the B-2000 into the Blues' central command station. In fact, there was not a building over three stories standing anywhere in the city—except one.

The Lords Towers.

And that's where they headed first.

Dave was piloting the small helicopter; Seth was serving as lookout. As soon as they approached the battered spiral, they could see a figure waving madly to them. It was not Hunter, though—it was a guy in the uniform of the Black Army.

"I hope we didn't come all this way just to rescue that mook," Dave Jones said.

"If that's the case, then someone up there really got their signals crossed," Seth replied.

Still, something drove them on toward the smoking tower, and as soon as they arrived over it, they saw two more people huddled atop the building. Dave brought the Bug in closer and at last they saw it was indeed Hunter, holding onto a third person. All they could see of this figure was a lot of blond hair blowing in the smoky breeze.

"Oh, I see," Dave said. "We came here to rescue Hunter, some blonde, *and* an enemy medic."

"My guess is that blonde is the princess, the woman this whole shebang has been fought over," Seth said.

Dave took a long, hard look at her, and then realized his brother was probably right.

"Man, can this get any weirder?" he breathed.

"Don't ask," Seth cautioned. "We've had enough 'weird' for a while."

They set the tiny Bug down on the edge of the Towers' roof and opened the right-side access door.

The guy in the black camos came in first. Seth took one look in his eyes and had to turn away. The guy gave him a major case of the creeps. Hunter then lifted the mysterious blonde up into the copter. Seth looked into her eyes—and never wanted to look away again. She might have been the most beautiful woman he'd ever seen. She was wrapped in a long red cloak with a white gown underneath. Her hands were so delicate they looked like they were porcelain. Her facial features were perfect. She smiled at him and he melted. He really had to force himself to look away from her.

Hunter placed her in the rear right seat, next to the creepy medic, then lifted himself aboard the Bug. He gave Dave the go sign to take off.

"I'll make all the introductions later," Hunter said.

Dave Jones wasted no time in the getaway. He wisely lifted straight up, putting as much distance as possible between them and the burning city. Once up at five thousand feet, he spun the Bug around and pointed it south.

"We all can't go very far in this thing," he yelled over his shoulder.

"There's an airplane at your base," the medic in black camos said. "We can take that."

The Jones boys looked at each other. What the guy said was true. The wounded pilot's AirCat was still at Red Base One.

But how could this creepy guy have known that?

Hunter was now jammed in the back with the blonde, holding her so tightly his hands were turning white.

"Don't ask how he knows," he simply said to the Jones boys. "You wouldn't believe it if I told you."

They flew back to Red Base One, only to find the place was completely surrounded now—Black Forces on the south, Blue to the north.

As predicted, they were pounding each other with renewed ferocity.

"What makes me think these guys are going to let us set down pretty and fly out again?" Dave Jones asked with some disgust.

"They won't see us," Viktor said from the rear seat. "We can do whatever we want . . ."

Dave turned to look back at Viktor, but Seth stopped him.

He turned toward Hunter instead.

"You're the Sky Ghost," he said. "What do you suggest we do?"

Hunter clutched Dominique even tighter to him.

"I suggest we do what he says," he said, indicating Viktor.

The Jones boys just looked at each other and shrugged. The Bug was running out of gas, and even on a full tank they could not have flown very far. Setting down and trying to get the last AirCat was really their only option.

And it did get weirder here.

Because as they zoomed into the base right over the heads of the advancing Blue Force troops, it did seem as if they were invisible. They were so close to the ground on their landing approach, they could literally see the faces of the Blue Army soldiers. Yet not one of them looked up or made any indication that the Bug was nearly right on top of them.

Dave Jones set the Bug down next to the AirCat fighter-bomber, and everyone piled out. Seth was the first one into the fighter. The cockpit was stained with the blood of the wounded pilot, but other than that, everything looked to be in order.

He immediately started the airplane's mighty double-reaction engines and felt a reassuring kick as both came to life with a great roar of flame and smoke. Dave Jones was now punching buttons and throwing levers preparing for a very hot takeoff. Hunter, meanwhile, had led Dominique into the airplane, and with Viktor's help, put her into one of the crew bunks at the rear.

He and Viktor sealed up the plane's hatches and belted themselves into the extra crew seats.

At this point, Seth Jones already had the aircraft rolling down the runway. They could see hundreds of artillery shells crisscrossing in front of them—the two huge armies were about one minute away from finally meeting each other. Seth laid on the power—the double-reaction engines were running on almost pure zerox-45 now, giving the aircraft a kick equivalent to a full afterburner takeoff. Just as the first Black and Blue troops met on the runway in front of them, Seth Jones pulled back on the airplane's column and up they went. Two solid waves of artillery and rockets were about to envelop the air base as the two sides were a heartbeat away from their final clash. Jones somehow managed to yank the AirCat all the way back to the vertical and pushed the engine to 110-percent power.

They climbed. Three hundred feet . . . four hundred . . . five hundred . . . Nearly straight up for the first one thousand feet. Only then did Jones level them off.

Everyone was breathing hard, as if they had just climbed that first one thousand feet by hands. Heart pounding, brow sweaty, Jones looped back around, and now below, they could see the two mad armies finally collide. The slaughter had begun.

"If I ever get within a thousand miles of this crazy place again," Dave Jones said. "I want someone to shoot me."

"If you come within *two* thousand miles," Seth said. "I'll shoot you myself."

They quickly climbed to five thousand feet and turned southwest.

Passing over the Indus-Nawa convergence thirty minutes later, they saw that all of the AirCat squadron had made it safely back to the carrier, as had the Bro-Bird seaplane.

Hunter cranked up the airplane's radio and contacted Fitz down on the Bro-Bird.

He told the Irishman that he had to go somewhere, to check something out, and that the Jones boys had agreed to take him there. The AirCat commanders would have a further explanation once they returned to the carrier.

It nearly killed Hunter to mislead his friend—but he had no heart to tell him the truth. He asked Fitz to say thanks to the rest of the team, and promised that he would see them all again soon.

"You can buy me a beer when you return," Fitz told him.

"I'll spring for two," Hunter lied.

It was the last time he would ever talk to Fitz—in this world anyway.

In effect he'd asked the Jones boys to fly nearly halfway around the world—to the Falkland Islands. They'd agreed only because the circumstances of their finding Hunter and the two others in Kabul Downs had been so weird, they felt compelled to take him where he wanted to go.

Still, the pilots could not look at Viktor; it was just too disturbing for them. He was sitting quietly in back of them, staring out the window at the Arabian Sea below. Hair mussed, eyes bloodshot, he looked like he hadn't slept in days, which was an accurate assessment of his condition.

Hunter was sitting right beside him, charting a course to the South Atlantic. Luckily, the AirCat fighter-bomber had a range measured in days not miles—making the Falklands wouldn't be a problem.

But what's going to happen when they got there? Hunter wondered.

"You will have the opportunity to finally go back," Hunter heard a voice answer his unspoken question for him.

Suddenly all the lights on the AirCat's control panel lit up.

"Jeesuz, *what the fuck . . . ,*" Seth Jones cursed.

That's when Hunter turned around and realized there was another presence on board with them. An ethereal one.

Viktor looked up and saw the ghost, as well.

"You?" he asked, authentically surprised.

The ghost looked at Viktor and smiled.

"Who else?"

Hunter just stared at him, jaw open slightly. The spirit had materialized on the forward flight compartment next to the small galley, about ten feet from Hunter's crash seat. He was standing there very nonchalantly, looking just as he did when he appeared to Hunter on the super-bomber.

The strange thing was, Hunter, Viktor, and the ghost all had something in common.

"Well, I did what you asked," Hunter told the ghost. His body shook a bit in its presence.

"You did what you *had* to do," the ghost replied. "And you got what you wanted . . ."

Hunter looked back to where Dominique was sleeping peacefully.

"I got what I *needed,*" Hunter mildly corrected him. "Thanks to you."

The ghost shrugged. "It's the least I could do," he said. "Especially after all the trouble I caused everyone when we first got here."

Viktor stood up and walked over to the ghost. He stared at him intently. "Yes, I know you," he said. "Don't I?"

Both Hunter and the ghost smiled.

"Our little secret," the ghost said.

Hunter took a few steps closer to the spirit.

"Did I do everything right, though?" he asked the ghost. "I mean, I was told when I got here that just by my presence, I could have . . . well, some kind of *effect* on things. But after this crazy war, I can't see how I helped anyone at all."

The ghost just smirked.

"Believe me, you did," he replied. "Look at it this way. If the Blues won the war, they would have held the rest of the region hostage for a long time. If the Blacks won, they would have sold the city to the Germans. The Germans would have linked up with Khen The Great, and their empire would have stretched from the Middle East to the Pacific Rim. But now, seeing as you wrecked the central command station, the Blacks and Blues have annihilated each other. In fact . . ."

He held his hand up—as if he was waiting for something. A second later, the whole airplane started shuddering.

"*That* was a DG-fifty-five bomb going off," the ghost said.

"That's how that big battle ended, with all those clowns in the Black Army and in the Blues wiped out. That means a couple hundred thousand more assholes coming over to my side."

"Jeesuz," Seth Jones cried from the front of the plane. "Whatever that was, it *was* big!"

The ghost just shrugged and smiled.

"So, you see, Hawk," he began again. "Whether you know it or not, you helped a lot of people in this world. You just don't realize it."

"Well, it was only with your help," Hunter said. "I guess . . ."

The ghost began to fade slightly. "But there's one more thing you have to deal with," he said.

"Name it," Hunter told him.

The spirit pointed to one of the overhead bunks next to the reserve navigator's seat. It was like a Pullman sleeper a place where a crewman could catch a nap while on a long mission.

"Open it," the ghost said.

Hunter did as he requested—and an unconscious body tumbled out and hit the floor with a thud.

Hunter was quickly on his knees, turning the person over.

It was Y.

He'd gotten drunk again and had stolen away on the airplane even while the battle for Red Base One raged around him. He still smelled of booze.

"He's been in a very bad way," Hunter said, helping to his feet.

"He's in the same position you were in," the ghost said "Just reversed. He lost someone here."

Y got his bearings, took one look at the spirit—an passed out again.

"So that's the one last favor I have to ask of you," th ghost said to Hunter. "Take him with you. He's bee through a lot—even before he met his cosmic mate. H really has to find her again."

"I'll take care of him," Hunter said. "I promise."

With that, the ghost began to fade away for good.

"Wait," Viktor interrupted. "I *know* who you are. We went into the water together, when I first got to this place. You, me, and Hunter. But I still don't know your name."

Hunter and the ghost just smiled.

"OK," the ghost said finally. "It's Elvis. Elvis Q . . . see you Hawk. Have peace wherever you go."

"I'll try," Hunter replied.

But Elvis had already vanished.

Meanwhile, the Jones boys were doing everything they could not to look back at what was going on behind them.

"Next time we 're looking for a job," Seth said to Dave, "let's make a rule: No ghosts, OK?"

Dave shook hands with his brother.

"Deal and sealed," he said.

CHAPTER 47

West Falkland Island

Colonel Neal Asten was having a dream about angels and devils getting along, having a laugh and a pint in an old English pub when he was suddenly awakened.

He'd been asleep in the commander's compartment of one of the SuperChieftain tanks protecting Skyfire Hill when an odd noise knocked him right out of his bunk.

He grabbed his rifle, crawled out of the tank, and looked up to find a strange airplane circling overhead.

His first reaction was to sound the alarm—he couldn't imagine how a plane could get this close to the island without getting picked up on his unit's extensive radar setup, and his men armed with antiaircraft weaponry. Once alert, they could bring any aircraft down in a few seconds.

But just as Asten was about to hit the alarm Klaxon, he felt a hand on his shoulder. Someone whispered in his ear. "They are friends."

Asten spun around. No one was there.

He felt a chill go through him.

What the hell was that?

By this time the airplane had circled twice more. To his astonishment, it was coming in very low, as if to land. His position was on the side of Skyfire Hill, about 150 yards of flat field and that was it. Everything else was very hilly and rugged.

Not the kind of terrain suitable for landing a plane.

The airplane's wings folded down and a bunch of rockets started firing, and the plane came in like a graceful bird. Asten thought he was still dreaming. He'd never seen anything quite like it.

He approached the aircraft as one would have approached a UFO. He was astonished again to realize that the first person to climb out from its hatch was someone he recognized. It was Hunter, the pilot who had helped them repel the brutal Japanese attack on West Falkland just a few months earlier.

Even more astounding, the second person out of the plane was Viktor, the guy who'd saved all the kids from the shipwreck only to disappear a few days later.

The third person he did not know: he was a little, wiry guy, who looked like he was recovering from a very bad hangover.

But it was the fourth person out, helped by Hunter and Viktor, who really set Asten's heart to beating. She was without a doubt the most beautiful woman he'd ever seen. She was blond, her face like a painting. She was simply radiant. She smiled at him and he felt as though a bolt of electricity had run through him. He wasn't sure why, but he went down on one knee the second he saw her.

Hunter immediately went over and helped him up.

"It's a natural reaction," he told Asten.

Hunter pointed to the farmhouse that sat atop Skyfire Hill.

"How are they?" Hunter asked, referring to the two people who lived inside.

"They are well," Asten said, still not able to take his eyes off Dominique.

"Can you tell them we're here, please?" Hunter asked him.

Asten kind of half stumbled away.

"Sure thing," he said.

Hunter turned to the Jones boys. Their airplane's engines were still turning. They would not be staying long.

"I know you guys will never understand what is going on here," Hunter said. "But I've just got to thank you for all you've done. I knew you both, in another place. You were great guys then, and you're great guys now."

They all shook hands.

"Please tell the others," Hunter began stammering. "That I-I thank them, as well. And I'll try like crazy to see them all again s-someday . . ."

But he knew that would never happen.

They shook hands again. The Jones boys walked back to their airplane, revved the engines, activated the rocket bottles, and lifted off as smoothly as they had landed. They did a 360-degree spin as soon as they were airborne.

To Hunter's mind, that was their way of saying goodbye.

Forever.

Ten minutes later, Hunter was sitting in the living room of the farmhouse.

It was strange: they were all drinking milk and eating cookies the Man's wife had just made. It seemed like such a familiar setting for Hunter. Even though it was six in the morning, the Man and his wife couldn't have been more gracious. They were very happy to see them all, especially Viktor.

Hunter did not have to say why they were here. The Man already knew.

"Are you ready to go through this?" he asked Hunter. "Have you done all you need to do here—in this place?"

Hunter contemplated both questions. His heart sank when he thought that he'd never again see the friends he'd made here. But he had no nostalgia for this odd place.

It seemed like his whole time here he'd been involved in one kind of war or another. He told this to the Man.

"I'll bet you also felt like you were reliving things that happened to you before, am I correct?" the Man asked him.

"That's for sure," Hunter replied. "It's like I lived an entire lifetime all over again in the space of one month."

The Man grinned. "Well, then, I think you're ready to go."

He looked at Dominique and smiled. She smiled back.

"She was a princess in this world," he said. "Was it worth coming to a new universe to find her?"

"Absolutely," Hunter answered right away.

The Man patted him on the shoulder in a very fatherly way.

"Well, take care of her this time, OK?"

Hunter just nodded. "I'll try," he said.

They stood up. It was time to go. Y was still stuffing cookies in his mouth. The wife came over to Hunter and looked deeply into his eyes.

"I want you to promise me that you will be careful," she said, welling up a bit. "Promise me."

Hunter stared back at her. She looked and sounded so familiar. It was as if he'd heard those exact words many, many times before.

"I promise," he said.

A few minutes later, they were all deep inside the mountain, squeezed into the small cloud chamber.

The Man pushed the button on a combination lock, and after making sure everyone was holding tight to the restraints, he opened the huge heavy metal door.

There was a loud *whoosh* and immediately the room was filled with a fine mist. The deep blue Atlantic was about a mile below them.

Y nearly passed out. A million questions started spinning in his head—but he chose not to ask any of them.

"I'm ready," he just said instead. "I know I am. I'll do anything to see her again. Even this . . ."

Hunter put his hand on Y's shoulder.

"Just remember: wherever we are going, Emma will be there too. And we will find her. OK?"

Y nodded. "Deal and sealed—that's all I want."

The Man handed them their parachutes. There were only three, but that was not a problem.

Viktor climbed into his chute, then embraced the Man warmly.

"Thank you for what you did for me," the Man told him. "Good luck always."

Viktor brushed a tear away and then without another word, stepped out into the abyss. They watched him go down, his parachute opening almost immediately.

Y went next. He closed his eyes, whispered Emma's name and then stepped out too. He fell head over heels twice before his chute opened.

Then Hunter turned back to the Man.

"Can I ask you just one more question?"

The Man nodded.

Hunter took a deep breath. His lungs filled with the fine damp mist. On the sea below, an ocean liner was passing by.

"Could you be who I think you are?" he asked him simply.

The Man began to say something but stopped himself.

"You will have to find out for yourself," he said finally. "But remember this: Wherever *you* go, *I'm* there—and so is my wife. So always look for us. OK?"

"OK . . ." Hunter replied.

With that, they shook hands and Hunter put on his parachute.

Then he took Dominique in his arms and they stepped through the hole together.

* * *

But then something went wrong.

He remembered drifting towards the water and watching Y and Viktor land safely below. He turned to Dominique and put his lips to hers. At that instant, there was a flash of blinding light. Suddenly Dominique was gone—it was as if she'd evaportated in his arms! He began falling faster, his parachute long gone. Tumbling end over end, a deep warmth began to fill him—it was a pleasant feeling, but frightfully close to what he had felt during his near-death experience just the day before.

Then the sensation of falling ceased—and suddenly, he was sitting on the floor of a rickety wooden cabin. Through the dirty and cracked windows he could see green mountains all around him. The unmistakable sound of a small airplane, flying far away, began echoing in his ears.

He turned to look over his shoulder and found himself in a dark saloon. The place was crowded with drunken pilots and beautiful bar girls. He was wearing a deep blue combat uniform. On his right shoulder was a patch with the letters "ZAP" emblazoned on it.

He felt something in his left hand and when he looked down, he found himself in the cockpit of a crashed airplane, a racy picture of Dominique trembling between his fingers. Another flash of light. He looked up to see he was in a different saloon, this one in the middle of the desert. A movie crew had all its cameras trained on him.

He took a sniff and the stink of gasoline went up his nostrils. He closed his eyes from the pungent stench and when he opened them again, he was inside the battered cockpit of his old F-16XL fighter, a jungle surrounding him. His sleek jet was mired up to its wings in what he knew was Panamanian red mud.

He wiped his eyes only to find his fingers were freezing. Another blink and he was in deep snow, the wreckage of a B-1 bomber crumpled and burning beside him.

He heard a train whistle behind him. When he turned towards it, he realized he was at the top of a steep hill, looking down into a deep river valley. A massive battleship was just barely squeezing its way through the narrow, winding waterway, heading north.

Hunter rolled down the hill and fell into the water and was immediately taken under by a huge wave. He fought his way to the surface, and when he finally came up, an island with a huge volcano appeared in front of him. He saw soldiers running up the side of the volcano, firing their guns wildly. Hunter called out to them, but they could not hear him.

Another wave overwhelmed him. When he came up this time, he was in a rice paddy. A strange pink jet was flying overhead. He suddenly had a gun in his hands but by the time he went to aim it, the pink jet had turned into a spacecraft—something that looked like a space shuttle, yet much bigger and more elaborate. It was taking off, going straight up in a cloud of smoke and flame. Hunter began firing at it. But it kept going up and up until it disappeared amongst the stars.

And then, just like that, he was flying among the stars too.